DESIRE'S AWAKENING

"Mr. Jensen?" The inquiry was tentative, almost a whisper. "Why did you touch me like that?"

Richard reached out and sketched the outline of her chin with the tip of his finger, then tipped her face up and bent toward her. A gossamer pulse rippled beneath his finger as he slowly brushed her lips with his, then moved with infinite care to the center of her mouth. He closed his eyes and let his lips rest on hers as the soft, quick rush of her breath fanned his mouth.

She opened her eyes and he saw the cloudy mists of arousal there. She blinked slowly, as if she had just stirred from a deep sleep. The flush on her cheeks deepened as Richard folded her in his arms. She felt the heat of his hand caressing her hair, then sliding down past her shoulder.

Slowly, softly, he stroked her lips with his. "Ah, Margaret, you're so sweet," he whispered. "Just as I knew you would be."

PAMELA CALDWELL
STORMSWEPT CARESS

ZEBRA BOOKS
KENSINGTON PUBLISHING CORP.

ZEBRA BOOKS

are published by

Kensington Publishing Corp.
475 Park Avenue South
New York, NY 10016

First printing: January, 1992

Printed in the United States of America

Chapter 1

Margaret Belleweather strode after the man with the captain's cap set back on his head at a rakish angle. He *must* be the captain of the *Java*.

"Mr. Jensen!"

She had waited all day in Singapore's stifling heat for a chance to talk with him, and she felt her ire rising as he continued toward the black clipper at the end of the quay.

"Mr. Jensen!"

Margaret cringed inwardly as she heard the unladylike screech in her voice. She had only an instant for regret, however, for though he must have heard her, the lean sea captain strode on toward his ship without a break.

"Perhaps he won't respond unless he's addressed as 'captain,' miss," her servant suggested.

"Yes, of course, John," Margaret said. "Captain Jensen!" Now there was a distinctly strident tone to her summons.

She urged her limbs onward to try and intercept the rapidly moving figure. Too late! In four lithe strides he had mounted the gangplank.

Richard Jensen paused and turned only when he was on deck. Even in the bright light of day there was something sinister about him. He gripped the rail and stared down at her without speaking, his loose white shirt agape nearly to

5

the waist. Several day's growth of beard coated a jaw clamped tight in irritation. When it became clear that he did not mean to speak, Margaret took the initiative.

"Captain Jensen, I wish to talk with you for a few minutes," she said.

"You may wish all you like, Miss Belleweather. Wishes are for children," he said sharply.

Margaret was shocked speechless by his rudeness. Then she realized he had addressed her by name and recovered herself. "Since you already know who I am, you will surely not object to my coming on your ship to discuss a very important matter."

"Aboard, Miss Belleweather. The word is aboard, and yes—I do object. I know what you want and I have no wish to get involved. My advice to you is to go home and not wait for any more letters from your brother."

Margaret strove for control. The man was insufferable, but in his reply was a tantalizing hint that he knew something about Christian.

"I did not come here to ask for your advice," she said. "Kindly tell your man to step aside so that I can . . ." She faltered and then, in an effort to show that she was not as rude as he, she went on. "Come aboard. I only wish to ask you a few questions."

"Questions just lead to more questions, Miss Belleweather."

"Then the sooner we start, the sooner I can leave you in peace."

Richard Jensen made a sound that might have been a cough or a laugh—she couldn't be sure which.

"Since I don't intend to start, you needn't worry about leaving me in peace," Richard Jensen replied. He lifted one hand from the rail and Margaret saw that he meant to turn away.

"If you won't let me come aboard and talk to you now, then I shall simply wait here on the dock until you come ashore again," said Margaret a shade imperiously.

Richard Jensen checked his motion. "Won't do you any good," he said. "I sail tonight." And with that, he moved

6

away from the rail.

Margaret Belleweather found herself wishing that she had the power to send Richard Jensen to the devil. Now she understood why so many people had warned her against having any dealings with the man. She stared in impotent fury at the behemoth who guarded the gangplank before turning away in frustration. As much as it might suit her mood to see Captain Richard Jensen in hell, it would not serve her purpose. The elusive captain afforded her the best, perhaps the only, chance she had of finding Christian. Margaret began a slow progress back to the bench where she had spent the whole of this wretched day.

Margaret withdrew her fan and wielded it awkwardly. John, his sallow face slicked with perspiration, made as if to take the fan but she waved him aside. "Please, I can do it."

"I beg your pardon, miss. It's only just that it's hard to watch you do for yourself when I can do it for you so much easier."

"It does not do to give in to weakness, John. I have reconciled myself to my condition and so must you."

"Yes, miss, of course."

The bench cut into Margaret's thin shanks and the small breath of air she managed to stir with the fan did little to dispel the cloying heat and humidity. She gave up on the fan and raised her parasol instead. She dismissed her bodily discomforts with a stringent effort of will, a talent sharpened by many months of practice, and turned her thoughts to what she must do next.

How infuriating to come so far and be met with such a rebuff! If not for her doggedness and an inebriated brothel owner, she would never even have heard Richard Jensen's name in connection with Christian's disappearance. She did not mean to walk away now.

From all reports, Jensen was a man who lived in the very belly of the beast, and considering that every misfit and black sheep within hundreds of miles was to be found in Singapore, such a reputation was hard come by. Or

7

perhaps, she thought, it came easily to a man like Jensen. There was a savage undercurrent to the muscular way in which he carried himself. His skin was the hue of aged oak, so darkly tanned that it made it difficult to believe he was a European, or rather an American, especially when one saw the blue-black sheen of the untidy long hair tied in a sailor's pigtail.

"An Wu asks missy come home now?"

Margaret looked up, startled from her deep reverie. The Chinese merchant's houseman dipped gracefully and gestured toward the head of Tanjong Pagar Dock. A small pony and gig stood there.

"No thank you. I have not yet spoken to Captain Jensen."

An Wu's servant bowed again and squatted down equably.

"John, would you please trouble the harbormaster for a sheet of paper and a pencil?" Margaret asked.

John cast a wary glance at his Chinese counterpart and went off with a disapproving sniff. A few minutes later he was back and Margaret slowly printed a message to the man some called Captain China. Unlike Captain Jensen, An Wu had been cordial to a fault, and in some perverse way even seemed to delight in helping Margaret flout all the conventions by which Singapore society governed itself. Christian's deserted bungalow stood cheek by jowl with An Wu's opulent compound, though not quite so close as to be considered part of the Chinese quarter. A European man living there had been remarkable enough, but for a European woman to live there was nothing short of a scandal.

Margaret carefully folded the paper and handed it to An Wu's servant. The houseman rose and cheerfully bowed his way back toward the long ramp leading to shore.

Margaret settled back and dabbed the perspiration from her upper lip as discreetly as she could. Richard Jensen. She didn't relish the prospect of another encounter with him, but after a whole year with no letters from Christian followed by three fruitless months of inquiries, she wasn't

8

about to let this chance slip away. Christian was in the islands; Christian had gone back home to England; Christian had gone off to explore Cochin China—everyone had heard a different rumor but not one had seen him get on a boat. He was simply not in S'pore any longer.

Margaret turned her attention back to the black-hulled clipper. It was as if An Wu had known the precise moment when she failed in her attempt to talk with Richard Jensen. An Wu was master of a network of spies who might already have told him the outcome of her encounter, though not its text, for An Wu was the only Chinese in the colony who spoke fluent English. It was An Wu who had suggested that she ask the master attendant to send word the instant the *Java* docked. That word had come three days ago, but despite several messages which the harbor master assured her he had given to Richard Jensen, she had received no word from the *Java*'s captain.

A stir on the dock lent weight to Jensen's declaration that he would sail tonight. A burly islander—Polynesian or Melanesian, Margaret could not tell which—supervised the unloading of the bullock carts arriving at the foot of the gangplank. Under his watchful eye, coolies with sacks over their sinewy shoulders made their way on board. Overside, in the water, were small boats, their owners making urgent representations to the beefy giant who superintended the proceedings.

Market Malay and Chinese jargon hummed incessantly on the wharf, in the rigging, across the deck, and more importunately, from the water below. The impassive giant stood by the gangway, his gaze flickering upward to the creaking hoist each time a crate passed over him. His arms were crossed stolidly, his feet wide and braced, as if the sea already tossed the *Java* beneath him. Only rarely did he speak, and then it was a loud bark which pierced even the din of the carpenter's hammer droning relentlessly in the hold below. Margaret couldn't help but reflect on the remarkable flurry of activity Richard Jensen's arrival had produced.

The water, the mightiest force of all the elements

9

present, seemed reduced to a mere stage setting, lapping sluggishly at the copper sheathing that gradually sank out of view as the loading progressed. The brackish red water yielded almost resentfully to the ship, as if annoyed by its incursion. It seemed to be biding its time, a living thing that threatened retaliation by its bigger brother, the great green sea beyond, against this mere device of man's making.

As much out of pity for the suffering of the manservant as out of real need, Margaret dispatched John to find some cold drinks. Relieved of his scrutiny, she rubbed her aching wrists and elbows. She wished she could do the same for her ankles and knees, but a lady did nothing in public that even hinted at the existence of limbs beneath her voluminous skirts. She had not dispensed with her corset as so many other ladies in Singapore did, and the remaining layers of clothing beneath her lavender dress of half-mourning were soaked with what could only be called sweat.

John returned and mercifully enough, he carried not only drinks, but drinks with ice in them.

"Where on earth did you find these?" Margaret exclaimed.

"An establishment that caters to sailors, miss," he replied.

Margaret held up the fluted glass. "It must be a rather nice sort of place," she said. "Perhaps we could go there for some refreshment later, before we start home."

John cleared his throat. "I should think not, miss."

Margaret didn't press him. John cared more for her sensibilities than she did herself, but if he counseled against the place it would be better not to go there. Too many times in these past months she had relied on him to escort her to places which he found distasteful. With a determination born of necessity, she had insisted that he either go with her or return to the bungalow and leave her to get on with her search for her brother alone. Every time, the servant had repressed a shudder and loyally gone on.

More than a year and a half ago, Christian had been sent to the East in disgrace, his only means of support a half share in Townsend and Townsend, a trading firm too short on cash to question why a handsome young baronet would suddenly exchange England's comforts for the unrelenting heat of the Straits Settlement. Always a desultory letter writer, he wrote less and less as time went by. And then nothing.

Margaret had gone on with her life, dealing with her parents' deaths in a railway accident. So much had changed in so short a time, she thought—Pensleigh left without master or mistress, drifting ponderously as Margaret, the only Belleweather still living there, fell victim to debilitating illness. Months had passed in a haze of disconnected, feverish dreams, in which she was visited by her mother, father, and brother. But when the haze cleared, she was alone again.

Her spirit had recovered even as her body resisted the pills and the nostrums, until at last she had thrown aside the doctors' restrictions and determined to get on with her life. She had enlisted the help of her father's executors to try and contact Christian while she resumed her charity work at the orphanage near Pensleigh. When their efforts came to naught, she had announced her intention of going in search of him herself.

Their horrified protests, added to those of the Reverend Childers at the orphanage, deterred her not at all. To find Christian and bring him home became paramount. The serene beauty of Pensleigh had always given her pleasure but now the house seemed gray and empty, and the grounds an uninhabited fairy-tale land waiting for a spell to be lifted. The happy rough and tumble of the children at the orphanage invigorated her during the day, but each night she returned to loneliness and solitude, until at last she could stand it no longer. Her beloved Christian must come home and marry, and fill Pensleigh with life and light again.

Margaret packed her bags and so, at the last minute, did John and his wife, finally convinced that she meant to go, with or without them. The journey was accomplished at no small expense to her comfort and well-being, but she was pleasantly surprised to discover that, contrary to what the doctors had said, the more she demanded of her body, the more it recovered.

She knew by the Townsends' quiet alarm that she had not recovered her looks by the time she arrived in Singapore, but her body was definitely more able than it had been. They welcomed her into their home and made her a part of their bustling family life, but when it came to talk of Christian, they became less voluble. No one seemed to know where he was. Even more surprisingly, no one seemed inclined to think there was any cause for concern. He would return in good time, they said. In the meantime, they would arrange her passage home, or introduce her to Singapore society, just as it pleased her.

Neither pleased her. Margaret had an uneasy sense that they knew more than they would say. Only Charles Townsend showed any inclination to help her, courteously escorting her around the city and pointing out the esplanade where Christian had played cricket, and showing her the offices of Townsend and Townsend. He endeavored to answer her questions about Christian's habits while in Singapore, but it was clear they had not been close and what he could tell her about her brother's frame of mind was limited. Finally she had struck out on her own.

Christian's trail had gone cold in the European district of Singapore, but when Margaret reached the Chinese quarter, the mention of his name had inspired flickers of recognition. Day after day, she roved the area, even the back streets—where prostitution, drug use, and worse all seemed to thrive, but it accomplished nothing to dwell on the distastefulness of it. Armed with a pen and ink sketch she had made of Christian, she could tell that he had been seen there often, but she had gained little more information.

Christian's bungalow, though long unused, was well-tended. It contained scarcely more than a few sticks of furniture—no personal items, no ornaments, no pictures on the walls—and some oil lamps with attendant matchboxes. Retreating there for relief from the heat of the day, she had resolved one afternoon to move into it in the hope that closer contact with the district where Christian had last been seen would encourage informants to come forward. Over the horrified protests of the Townsends, she had taken John, his wife, Eliza, and their baggage there that very evening. Not long afterward, she had received her first overture from An Wu.

He had initiated contact ever so delicately, sending a small flotilla of servants to her door with dainty sweets one day, a small hamper of chicken the next, flowers another, and so on. Not a word could she get out of the servants except for what she gradually understood to be a name, An Wu. One day she penned a thank-you note and pressed it into the hand of a smiling servant. That evening a pair of song birds arrived in a cage, accompanied by a thick, cream-colored card. The Chinese characters on it were executed with considerable confidence. Predictably enough, when she pointed to them, the messenger gave out the name An Wu.

Margaret set out to learn her benefactor's address, only to discover that he lived in the large, bamboo-shaded compound nearest Christian's. Well aware that the European community rigorously spurned any social contact with the Chinese, Margaret nevertheless ventured forth and, with a tremulous hand, left a calling card at An Wu's door. This simple courtesy proved to be the key to the mysterious An Wu's friendship. The next day, a servant left a similar card with John which clearly spelled out in English, "An Wu, Esquire, Exports and Imports," and an invitation to join him for tea.

"You honor my house, Miss Belleweather," the Chinese merchant said when she had been ushered into his presence. "Please forgive me for not leaving my card in person, but I did not wish to impose my humble self

13

on your household."

"But that was my purpose in leaving a card," Margaret answered.

"Yes, of course," An Wu said, "but I left some room for error, not being sure that you truly meant it as you would have in your own society."

Margaret realized that he was referring, however politely, to the fact that European women simply did not call on Chinese households in Singapore, or invite them to call in return. She covered the awkward moment by commenting on a screen nearby.

"Ah, yes, that is one of my favorites," An Wu said. He made no move to rise but seemed please by her interest. Ensconced in a veritable lava flow of brocaded cushions and attired in azure silk, the heavyset merchant discoursed briefly on the screen's history as Margaret walked to view it more closely.

The house was more nearly a roof over a raised floor, open on all sides and divided in the interior by lattice traceries and screens painted in pale porcelain colors. The few solid walls were covered with Japanese pictures and the whole impression was one of veiled perspectives. Margaret ranged slowly around their immediate surroundings, directed by her host to one treasure after another. At length, he urged her to sit and take tea. A servant brought forth a lavishly padded stool. Margaret cast a smile of gratitude in his direction, for An Wu had clearly perceived that she could not easily join him on the floor and still be sure of rising afterward.

"Tell me, Miss Belleweather, how you find the climate in Singapore," he said when they were served.

"It requires an adjustment for one accustomed to England's cooler shores," she replied.

"Ah, just so, just so," he murmured. "And do you find your brother's house comfortable?"

Margaret repressed a smile. It felt very like being interviewed by some benevolent clergyman. "Yes, thank you, although I am a trifle puzzled to know how one obtains a regular supply of water."

An Wu smiled. "Perhaps I can be of some assistance. I will direct my houseman to see that a water seller calls on you regularly. Alas, we in Singapore are at the mercy of those incompetent and lazy dogs who make their living selling what nature provides more conveniently elsewhere."

"It seems to me that those poor men work very hard for their money," Margaret said without pausing to think whether the contradiction might offend her host. "I have seen them bearing casks as large as their own persons. I can scarcely imagine what one must weigh."

An Wu gave her a brief, appraising glance and then smiled. This time the smile exceeded mere affability. "You are right, of course, Miss Belleweather. I myself did such menial jobs when I first came to Singapore. But that is of no consequence now. It is your comfort and safety that concerns me."

"Then you may set your mind at ease," Margaret replied. "I have been met with hospitality on all sides."

An Wu cleared his throat and set his cup aside. "And yet you venture to some parts of our city where no one's safety is assured. I hope you will not dismiss me as being 'old womanish,' but care must be taken."

Margaret considered this for a moment. "Am I to understand that you have been taking note of my movements?"

An Wu spread his hands in a deprecating gesture. "There is very little that happens in Singapore that does not reach my ears, Miss Belleweather. It is, after all, a small place when all is said and done."

Margaret's pulse quickened. "Then perhaps you can help me."

"It would give me great pleasure to assist you in any way I can," he replied, but Margaret detected a guarded look in his eyes.

"I wish to learn the present whereabouts of my brother, Christian," she said. "Any information at all would be most welcome."

An Wu's face lost some of its reserve. "His present

15

whereabouts? That I do not know, Miss Belleweather, though this I *can* tell you—he is not in Singapore."

Margaret knew her disappointment must be evident, for An Wu went on. "I can tell you without fear of contradiction, however, that he was not the victim of foul play."

"How can you be certain of that if you do not know where he is now?" Margaret asked.

An Wu smiled, a rueful smile that said he knew such things without even meaning to learn them. "I would have heard of it, Miss Belleweather. However, I wish you much success in finding what you seek." He clapped his hands and a servant came trotting in with a tray. "Please do me the honor of carrying my humble card with you." He handed her a thick square with the same Chinese symbols she had seen before. "It is my chop, Miss Belleweather. It will be recognized here in the Chinese quarter and elsewhere in Singapore. It may perhaps prove useful if you find yourself in difficulty."

Margaret accepted the card and An Wu arose ponderously. It was clear that the visit was at an end. What precise use she was to make of his card was not so clear. As she left, An Wu assured her that he would make some further inquiries on her behalf.

Charles Townsend evinced frank astonishment when she showed him An Wu's card.

"Well, I'll be," he remarked as he turned it over in his hand. "The old Chinaman's taken a shine to you, m'dear. It ain't often that Captain China offers this to anyone, and never a European before, from what I've heard." He handed the card back to her. "Wouldn't do to mention it to anyone else, though, 'specially not m'Mother. Not the thing to do, go calling on a Chinaman."

"I know that perfectly well, Charles, but I must do whatever it takes to find Christian. An Wu was a neighbor—I thought he might know something." Margaret paused, searching for the odd detail which had struck her. "What do you mean by calling him Captain China?"

16

Charles shook his head. "He's got a lot to say about what goes on in Singapore, your An Wu does, and not all of it fit for a lady's ears. Just have a care, m'dear." He took out his watch. "I must be running along now. Are you sure I can't persuade you to come back and spend the evening with us?"

"No, thank you anyway, Charles. Please convey my regards to your family."

"Mother and Susan are all aflutter over the theatrical next week—they assure me it will be the highlight of the season. Can I tell them you'll be there?"

"Of course. I shall be delighted," Margaret replied.

"I'll pick you up around seven then, shall I?"

"Yes. Tell them I'm looking forward to it."

Margaret watched him hurry away and step into a light carriage. A syce sprang to life and trotted ahead of the pony with a lantern to light the way down Cluny Road. Only Charles had come to visit her here, and it was Charles's gruff championship which ensured that she was still admitted to social functions in the European quarter. Beyond the fact that she found him pleasant company, she liked Charles because he would at least discuss Christian with her and did not dismiss her concern out of hand.

And so the weeks had passed into months. By day Margaret wandered the Chinese quarter, an anthill of shops with itinerant food sellers lining the streets, alongside pavement letter writers, barbers, and artisans. She repressed a shudder whenever they passed houses where the merchandise was human flesh, and not just young girls with huge doe eyes, but also boys with knowing gazes. The sweet aroma of opium hung about these places, advertising the fact that every human vice was catered to within.

When she had searched each street and alley in the Chinese quarter, she began to comb the waterfront. Although there were never fewer than a half dozen steamers in port at any one time, along with literally hundreds of smaller craft on the first reach of the Singapore River, Margaret refused to credit that Christian

17

could have boarded a ship without a soul noticing it. With John anxiously shadowing her every step, she questioned every sailor who would stop long enough to look at Christian's picture.

One day, a small, swarthy mate in a tarred cap took one look at it and gestured toward a street off Boat Quay. Unable to understand a word he said, Margaret opened her purse and held out several Spanish dollars, the most common coinage in Singapore, and gestured for him to lead them on. The mate looked her up and down and shrugged before leading off. When at last they reached a narrow house, the sailor motioned to the door and held out his hand. Without any certainty that he had brought them to a place where Christian was known, she withheld the reward and went inside.

The front room was painted dark green, and on the walls, framed pictures of ships alternated with paintings of naked women. Margaret's curiosity nearly overcame her and she had to remind herself to avert her gaze. As her eyes adjusted to the gloom, she saw that numerous girls and a few boys sprawled on low settees at the rear. A beaded curtain clicked in a dim recess of the room and John moved closer, as if to protect her virtue from whatever vice approached. Vice took the form of a stout man with a shortage of hair on the top of his head and an excess everywhere else that Margaret could see.

"Hullo, it's the carriage trade today then, is it?" he asked, wiping his hands on a towel that looked likely to leave them dirtier than before.

"That depends upon your trade," Margaret said stiffly. "I am seeking information regarding this man." She held Christian's picture out, thinking as she did so how preposterous it was to think that her brother could ever have set foot in this man's establishment.

"Nah," he said, making no move to take the picture.

Margaret breathed a sigh of relief. She wanted to find Christian, but not in a place like this.

"Ain't seen him since dry season last year."

Margaret's heart sank. "Then you do recognize him?"

18

"Sure. Always recognize a good customer."

"Do you know where he is now?"

"Don't know and don't care," the man said.

A peal of giggles wafted through the curtain and the sailor jiggled anxiously. Margaret handed him the Spanish coins and the sailor tucked them into his cap before disappearing into the back room. The proprietor eyed the transaction greedily. Margaret withdrew more money.

Margaret thought carefully for a moment and then asked, "If you were paid, might you know where my brother is?"

"Might do."

Unwilling to step nearer to him, Margaret handed money to John and watched the transfer with disdain. The place felt tainted and her spine ached with trying to keep her upright, contained and inviolate from it.

"Tell me what you know, and quickly."

"Oh, 'and quickly,' is it?" The man pocketed the money as he mimicked her. "Well, he ain't here, how's that for quick?"

"I assumed that," Margaret said frostily. Her stomach roiled as the man emitted a noxious cloud of alcohol. "I asked if you knew where he was now."

"I believe we're wasting our time, miss," John said in an undertone.

"Most likely," Margaret said briskly, "but I paid for some information and so far I have received none."

The squat man moved over to a lacquered cabinet and poured himself a drink. "Sometimes knowing where a thing ain't is just as good as knowing where it is."

"Not in this particular case," Margaret replied. Every instinct urged her to fly out the door, away from this loathsome little monkey, but she held her ground. "Tell me what you know about my brother."

"Tch, tch, tch," he said, wagging a finger at her. He lurched and Margaret realized he was quite, quite drunk. "Never tell what you know about a customer or he won't be a customer again."

19

"Then you shouldn't have taken my money!" Margaret knew it was an irrational response but she was too annoyed to care.

"Oh, yes, I'm a naughty boy, I am." He fell back into a chair chuckling.

"This is outrageous," Margaret said between clenched teeth. She turned to go and then had a sudden thought. She opened her purse again and John looked alarmed.

"I believe this may mean something to you," she said. She held An Wu's card up so that the muted daylight from the dirty window fell on it. It could do no harm to try.

The hairy little man went still. "Could do," he said cautiously.

"Precisely what does that mean?" Margaret demanded.

"It means, yeah, your brother used to come here but now he don't."

"You have told me that already. What else?"

The man gave a nervous imitation of a smile. "I heard he left Singapore."

"Oh, this is pointless! I wish to know where he is *now*."

The man licked his lips. "Well, as to that, you might try asking Richard Jensen."

Chapter 2

The tropical night fell suddenly, like a curtain being rung down. On board the *Java*, apprentices lit lanterns and hung them from the rigging as gas lights twinkled to life in the streets of Singapore. Margaret applied the last of the citronella oil to her face and hands against the onslaught of evening mosquitoes. She ached as dreadfully as she ever had at the height of her illness and her stomach clenched and gurgled in protest over missed meals. If not for the complete unseemliness of sitting alone on the dock at night, she would have sent John for food.

Blast! Her father's favorite expletive nearly burst from her lips. Richard Jensen had to come ashore sometime, if only to clear his departure with the master attendant. The last bullock carts had left an hour ago and the *Java* seemed to doze off into a fitful sleep, rising and falling softly against the lines which bound her to the dock. Her freshly greased spars and tarred rigging soared above the white deck and disappeared into the blackness beyond the lanterns' halo. A stripe of dull gold shone along the length of her gleaming black hull, and her cream-colored sails were reefed with mathematical precision. She was, Margaret thought, as sleek and well-groomed as her master was not.

Eyeing the gangplank, Margaret reached a decision. Richard Jensen had information. She wanted it. She used her parasol to push up off the bench.

"Come, John, we are going to pay a call on the rudest captain in Singapore."

John's squeak of protest was left in her wake as anger lent renewed strength to her gait. She mounted the gangplank in small steps and was confronted by a glistening mountain of flesh the instant she set foot on deck.

"I wish to see Captain Jensen," she said firmly. She tapped her parasol for emphasis.

"No. You go now."

"I will not leave until I have seen Captain Jensen." Margaret established her bulkhead more fully by sidling around the islander and taking several steps away from the head of the gangplank. The giant lumbered after her to forestall further progress.

"You go now. I give him message."

"Messages mean nothing to him. I will wait here while you inform Captain Jensen that I wish to see him in person."

The mate's jet-black eyes sparkled menacingly above his broad, flat cheekbones. "Go now!" he roared.

Margaret jumped.

John rushed forward. "Here, here—no one speaks to my mistress in that tone!" he declared. "Stand behind me, miss, for he's a dangerous fellow."

"You go now, and take the woman with you," the mate growled, "or I make you plenty damn sorry."

"I do not take my orders from you!" John retorted.

"You pretty sure will," the mate said, seizing John by the lapels.

John grunted as he was jerked off his feet and Margaret watched in horror as the huge islander shook him like a terrier would shake a rat.

"That will be enough!" she cried. Indignation overcame fear and Margaret advanced on the giant. She struck at his bare shoulders with her parasol, timidly at first, and then with more force when light blows had no effect. "Put him down or I will thrash you soundly!"

The parasol caught the big man on the ear and he

bellowed in rage. He dropped John like an empty sack and came after Margaret. She backed toward the mast as the mate bore down on her, and, when no more retreat was possible, she laid into him with all the vigor she possessed. John launched himself onto the mate's back, evoking another roar of outrage from the islander, and clung for dear life as the mountainous slab of flesh began pivoting beneath him. Margaret paused to catch her breath and then went after them.

"Don't you dare hurt him!" she cried, lashing out with her parasol, but the mate took no notice as he whirled around.

As the islander continued his violent attempts to free himself of his burden, Margaret hobbled to and fro, looking for an opening. Her stiffened joints impaired her movement so that by the time the blow landed, a different face of the lumbering mass had presented itself. Several times she struck John by accident. Margaret persisted, trying to allow for her slowness. Only because the mate accounted for a much greater surface area of the strange beast did she succeed in hitting him more often than she hit John.

Margaret interspersed her swipes with furious demands. "Stop this instant! Stop, I say!" Another whack—this time it caught John's crown and he added his howls to those of the mate's. The two-headed lump careened off with a combined chorus of wails and roars, and Margaret followed it, beating this way and that in desperation.

An alien sound interposed itself on Margaret's consciousness, an odd sound that had no relation to pain or confusion. She pulled up short just as John tumbled to the deck, leaving the islander panting and unfettered at last.

A rich peal of laughter rang out. There! That was the sound which had no place in these goings on! Who on earth found this an amusing sight? Margaret whirled. Richard Jensen! She let her trembling arm drop to her side. How dare he!

"Mr. Jensen! This is an outrage! This . . . this oversized bully attacked my manservant!"

Margaret watched in outrage as the captain doubled over in unrestrained mirth. He came up for air and took one look at her before being consumed by a fresh fit of hilarity. Margaret felt a knot of anger growing in her chest. It was obviously at her expense that he laughed. She eyed the pale circle of smiling faces beyond Richard Jensen and saw that if he did not stop, the crew's laughter would soon be added to his.

"When you have quite recovered, Mr. Jensen, I wish to speak to you," she said forcefully.

The lean captain's whoops of laughter diminished as the tight, burning fury in Margaret's chest increased. This obviously deranged man employed an uncivilized brute on his ship and then found it amusing to watch the brute rage out of control. There was no telling what he might have done to her if not for John! At last, Jensen wiped his streaming eyes with the sleeve of his shirt, and when she judged he was in no danger of going off again Margaret edged toward her servant.

"Are you all right, John?"

John, who had judged it best to remain lying on the deck until calm prevailed, stood up and dusted himself off. "That I am, miss. And you—you suffered no injury?"

"No, I am quite unharmed." Margaret glanced at the islander and saw with satisfaction that she had blackened one of his eyes. She turned back to Jensen. "I will not tolerate any violence being done to my servant, Mr. Jensen. What action do you intend to take against this man?"

Jensen chuckled. "Harkay had orders not to allow anyone on or off this ship. He was only doing his job, Miss Belleweather."

Margaret sucked in an outraged breath. "Then you condone this attack on me and my manservant?"

"What did you expect, Miss Belleweather? You forced your way on board my ship. Did you expect to be invited for tea and crumpets?"

Margaret felt two flares of heat in her cheeks. "I did not expect my man to be assaulted! He was merely defending me!"

"And then you defended *him*. Most admirable, Miss Belleweather, though if your man *had* been hurt, I think we'd have had a hard time deciding who inflicted the injury—you or Harkay. As it happens, I see it's *my* man who got the worst of it."

"And so he should have!" Margaret declared. "My John would not harm a flea."

Richard Jensen guffawed. "That's what he looked like now that you mention it—a big flea on a big dog."

"Before you lose control of yourself again, Mr. Jensen, I would like to speak to you."

"All right, Miss Belleweather—five minutes, and only because you showed such loyalty to your servant. I like that."

He made no move to go and the curious circle of onlookers stayed rooted to their spots. Margaret straightened herself.

"I would appreciate some privacy," she said.

Jensen started aft without another word, his stride loose and sure-footed. Margaret followed him, clambering awkwardly up the steep ladder to the quarterdeck and then down a companionway. For once Margaret was glad Jensen was a rude man, for a gentleman would have waited for her and witnessed her struggle to negotiate the narrow stairs.

When she descended the last step into the main saloon, Richard Jensen stood waiting. Margaret eyed him warily. In the light of the oil lantern suspended over a large table, Richard Jensen looked even more sinister than he had by day. A shock of black hair fell across his forehead, shading his eyes, and several days' growth of heavy beard darkened the lower half of his face. A thin, white scar curved along the bronzed skin of his right cheekbone, trailing off at the nostril. The only thing that kept Margaret from turning and running was the annoying fact that he still wore a faintly amused expression.

"I'm told you might know where my brother is," she said.

"I haven't heard of him recently," Jensen said. He shifted his weight and the light glittered across eyes the color of an

25

angry sea. "The last I knew he'd joined up with a Sumatran warlord with a taste for . . . well, let's just say it was a match made in heaven."

"What on earth does that mean?"

"Even you can't be so naive as not to know about your brother's . . ." Jensen paused.

"My brother's what?" Margaret asked impatiently.

Richard Jensen eyed her curiously. "What will you do once you find your brother, *if* you find your brother?"

"I intend to persuade him to return home with me. Our parents have died in his absence and he is now the Earl of Pensleigh. He will take up the responsibilities that entails."

Richard Jensen gave a sardonic laugh. "The peasants don't know what they're missing. No, I don't think that will work." His heavy, sensual mouth mirrored the contempt in his words.

Margaret clenched her hands. "I don't care for your tone, Mr. Jensen," she declared. "You seem to think my brother is some sort of reprobate, but I assure you that he is a fine man. As for any trifling misdeeds he may have committed, that is in the past."

"Oh, really?"

Jensen picked up a bottle and poured a thin dark liquid into a mug on the paper-strewn table. He didn't bother to offer Margaret any but she looked at the evil color of it and knew she would have refused it anyway. Richard Jensen tossed back the contents of the glass and wiped his mouth on his sleeve. Useful sleeve that, Margaret thought disdainfully.

"There's a taste for white slavery in this part of the world," Jensen said abruptly. "If you go in search of your brother, you may well find yourself a part of it."

Margaret decided she'd had enough. "Is that so? Surely if I went with a man like you, a man habituated to this life, I could expect to pass unmolested. I've heard you trade any commodity with any buyer who has the price."

Jensen laughed unpleasantly. "You seem to think that in meeting me you've met the lowest of the low. I assure

26

you, I represent all that is good and noble, the creme de la creme, in the hierarchy of which we speak."

Margaret stared at him. The faint, flat American accent made it hard to judge if he was being facetious or not. "I find it difficult to believe that you trade freely up and down these coasts and are welcome in ports where no other white man dares set foot and yet you haven't the power to protect someone on your ship."

"Aboard, Miss Belleweather, aboard, and anyway, I don't carry passengers," Jensen said. He poured another drink. "You don't seem to understand. I'm only evil enough to set one foot into the world your brother chose. What you need is someone even more evil than me."

"Then tell me who that is," she snapped. "I've had enough of your taunts and innuendo."

"Let's see," Jensen murmured. He sat down and put his booted feet on the table, carelessly crossing one over the other as he tipped the chair back and regarded the ceiling. "There's . . . no, he wouldn't do. He'd sell you first chance he got. Then there's . . ." Jensen stopped and looked at Margaret for a long, uncomfortable moment. "There'd be a nice price on you just for your eyes, you know. I can hear some rajah bidding up the price just so he can say he's got a girl with pansy-colored eyes. Of course, he'd call it something else, but it's all the same thing. There can't be more than a few people in the world with eyes the color of yours. What he'd expect once he bought you though— that's another thing altogether."

Margaret knew very well that her eyes were the only feature of any beauty left to her. His cruelty in pointing it out scorched the vanity she'd thought safely laid to rest. "You enjoy being a 'bad boy,' don't you? You actually *like* having a bad reputation!"

"It keeps the ladies' church auxiliary from coming to call," he said with a lazy grin. "I'd swing naked from chandeliers to avoid that."

Margaret snorted. "You've never been near a chandelier in your life!"

"Now that's where you're wrong," he said. "I may not

27

be an Englishman but they had chandeliers where I come from."

"And where is that, Mr. Jensen?" Margaret snapped. "The mouth of hell?"

Richard Jensen let out a guffaw. "That's good!"

"I didn't say it to amuse you." Margaret stared at his strong, white teeth. The man was a predator, a soulless heathen. "If you were a man of principle you would sit up and discuss how you might aid me."

Jensen's lazy smile faded. "I'm a man of very few principles, Miss Belleweather, and they're all subject to revision."

"Then I shall simply have to speak to the *Java*'s owner."

"I *am* the *Java*'s owner."

Margaret stared at him until the silence became uncomfortable. "I was afraid of that," she finally said. She embarked on a slow turn about the saloon and then stopped, feeling Richard Jensen's scrutiny of her awkwardness. "I suppose in your pantheon of values, money is a guiding principle. How much, Mr. Jensen?"

"I could use some rerigging but seeing as how I don't know where your brother is, what is it you're trying to buy?"

"Passage, Mr. Jensen. To go where you go, ask questions, learn what I can—nothing more."

His face hardened. "Oh, no. I've had all the close contact with women of your ilk that I plan to."

Margaret recoiled from the brutality in his voice. "Exactly what sort of woman do you imagine I am?"

Richard Jensen opened his mouth and then appeared to change his mind about something. "Let's just say your brother knows where Singapore is. If he wants to come back, he will. If he doesn't, he won't."

"If I could only speak to him, I know I could persuade him to come home. He wasn't welcome before but he would be his own master now."

"A loaded word, 'master.' I don't think that's what your brother aspires to."

"He always had a penchant for the lower classes,"

28

Margaret said indignantly. "Now he will have the power to do good for them."

Jensen smiled unpleasantly. "His penchant for the lower classes has become a penchant for the *much* lower classes." He mimicked her pronunciation of the word 'penchant,' drawing it out mockingly to *pon-chont*.

"Oh, please," Margaret pleaded, "can't we stop this? I must find him."

"You live in a delusional cloud of self-righteousness," Richard Jensen said, but his voice had lost some of its cutting edge. "Even if you find him, it doesn't mean he'll come home."

"Oh, I know that," Margaret said. Fatigue and despair weakened her self-control and she blinked away the moisture welling in her eyes. She was so tired. "I don't care what he's done—I love my brother and I miss him terribly. If I could only see him and talk to him, I would be satisfied."

Richard turned his back on Margaret Belleweather. The naked pain in her eyes was too genuine, and her image still burned in his mind. How could it not? Her clothing hung limp and empty on her, as if on a hanger. To call her thin would be a kindness—cadaverous was nearer the mark. Was she some aesthete who disdained such prosaic pastimes as eating? Or did she seek to glorify her soul by scouring the flesh? No, something in her eyes said not. There was none of the fanatic in them, the burning light of zealotry he'd known all too well. They were almost supernaturally large, and of a color so mesmerizing that she'd have been hung for a witch in an earlier age. They dipped toward the outer corners, a soft sloping that made them catch the light and revealed more of her thoughts and feelings than he felt sure she meant to.

Damn! Why was she not just what she appeared to be—spoiled, priggish, and narrow-minded—and why did he have to be so good at seeing through facades?

What to do? Deny her request? She'd turn elsewhere and another man would see the naivete behind the shining, violet eyes and not hesitate to exploit her drive to find

Christian Belleweather. And where was her brother? Palembang, last he'd heard, rotting, and reveling in it. What would it be like to be Christian Belleweather and be the object of such unquestioning love? Like the clasp of the sun and the wind.

Richard's heart constricted painfully. Such love might reform even the utterly debauched Englishman. What might it do for a man not nearly so far sunk in depravity?

Richard squeezed his eyes shut for an instant. When the pain of craving and never receiving that kind of love had passed, he turned back to face the birdlike creature.

"All right, Miss Belleweather, you can come along, but on my terms."

Margaret's face sagged with relief. "Oh, thank you."

There, he thought, she looked a little more human now. But first things first.

"We're not talking about some little jaunt up the Solent here. If pirates don't get you, malaria will. They still take a head or two in Borneo, and then there's the sea. There are days when it would just as soon swallow you whole as let you sail over it."

"I understand, Mr. Jensen. I'm sure you are an excellent captain, and as for my part, I am no stranger to hardship."

Who was she kidding? Hardship maybe, but all self-imposed. He looked at the hands clenching the parasol—they looked more like claws, thin and angular. Singapore's climate was the most salubrious in this part of the world and yet it was a wonder she'd survived even here. She wouldn't last the blink of an eye where he was going. Doubt assailed him.

"I want you to go home and pack a trunk, and while you're there, I want you to think carefully about whether you can stand the rigors of a trip like this. And no servants, either. I only have one spare cabin and I won't force my crew to bunk with a lubber like the one you brought with you."

"There is nothing to think about. I accept your conditions. I will send John back for some changes of clothes but I will stay aboard."

"I didn't even get done telling you all my terms. I'm trading along the coasts between here and Bali and then I'm making a run to Sydney for wool. Where I stop and for how long depends on what business I have, not on where your brother might be. If we run across him, all well and good—if we don't, that's your hard luck and nothing to do with me."

Margaret lifted her chin and returned the challenge. "I understand. I also understand that you meant to send me ashore to get a trunk and then not let me back on board."

Richard blinked. The thought *had* occurred to him. He turned away, annoyed.

"You can have the second officer's quarters," he said, brusquely gesturing to a door on the starboard side of the saloon. "I'll send Daniels down to shift his kit. Meantime you can practice making yourself inconspicuous. That's the rule, now and for all the time you're aboard. If you go on deck, stay out of my men's way, and remember, one hand for the ship at all times. If you tumble overboard, I won't come about for you."

"I came out by ship, Mr. Jensen. I will manage quite well, I assure you."

"On a damn steamship, I'll wager." He saw by her reaction that he was right. "Well, this is a clipper, Miss Belleweather, and she eats the wind for breakfast, lunch, and dinner. She'll go faster than any steamer you ever laid eyes on so you'd better be prepared to hang on."

"Yes, all right."

Richard noted the rigidity of her face and shoulders. *Oh, give me a Brit, for a stiff upper lip* . . . It was the first line of an obscene ditty he'd once heard. He was regretting this already.

"Go and give your instructions to your man," he snapped. "We sail in four hours."

He turned on one heel and was out through the companionway before Margaret could think to ask him what fare he intended to charge her. Just as well, she thought—Jensen could wait for his money until she was safely back in Singapore. Without him, the saloon

31

suddenly seemed much larger: odd since he was only an inch or two above average height. Margaret shrugged aside the observation. She had what she wanted.

John reacted with horror when she found him on deck and told him her plans. "But miss—your reputation! Not me nor Eliza to protect you, day after day at the mercy of that unshaven scoundrel . . ."

"I understand perfectly what you're trying to say, John, and I appreciate your concern, but please do as I ask. And remember, if you tell no one except Mr. Townsend, no one shall be the wiser. Simply give it out that I'm not feeling well and then no one will wonder why I'm not seen abroad."

"But, miss . . ."

"Please, John, Christian is all I have left in the world. I must do this."

When John had left, she went below again and met a curly-headed man just removing the last of his possessions from the second officer's cabin.

"You must be Mr. Daniels," she said, extending her hand.

"Aye, miss." He paused uncertainly.

There was none of the coquette left in her but Margaret tendered him a warm smile. "I'm Margaret Belleweather. Thank you very much for allowing me the use of your cabin."

"Not to worry," he said, smiling uncertainly and gingerly returning her handshake. "I'll just be taking the third mate's cabin instead," he said, inclining his head toward a door across the alleyway. "Harkay's entitled to it but he's too big to fit the berth—he sleeps in the cargo hold instead, so you're not really putting me out."

Margaret sat down on the berth when Daniels was gone. Tired, tired, tired. She must rise above it, show no weakness that would give Jensen an excuse to change his mind before they left port. She forced herself to remain upright and awake until John returned with her big leather pormanteau, portable desk, and hat box. It was far too much for the small cabin, and she selected only a few dresses before sending him away with the portmanteau still half-full. Margaret stood by the rail and tried to look confident and relaxed for his sake, but as the men began to climb into the rigging and unfurl the sail her stomach knotted with apprehension.

A full moon had risen and the wind was up when a figure came striding down the dock. Margaret's first thought was that Charles Townsend had heard of her plan and arrived to put a stop to it. John must have sent word! Relief swept through Margaret and then turned to indignation. How dare he! But when the man came in range of the oil lanterns' light, she saw that it was not Charles. Relief coursed through her again, tinged with regret. If it *had* been Charles, she would have been hard pressed to counter all the very cogent reasons he would have offered for her not going. She'd grown close to Charles and a part of her wanted him to come and talk her out of it.

Two steam tugs came alongside, the gangplank went up, and the shore lines were cast off. Short of jumping overboard, she was committed to her course now. Margaret grasped the rail and gave a small wave toward John, trying hard to mask the warring emotions inside her.

The deck was alive with noisy action—trampling feet, creaking ropes, a chantey to haul the sails by, and mates bellowing orders. To see the twenty or so men work together seemed a miracle of cooperation, and Margaret forgot her fatigue as she watched the energy pour forth around her. The yards were swung round and the sails flapped briefly before capturing the wind. It grew stronger by the minute but they achieved no great speed and Margaret could see that not even a tenth of the canvas had been set yet.

Jensen observed it all, never moving but occasionally issuing an order. The wind molded his loose white shirt to his chest as he stood the quarterdeck, wide-shouldered and heavy-biceped. He possessed such an extravagant quality of self-reliance that despite his unshaven face, not even a casual observer could have mistaken him for anything but the captain of the *Java*. Margaret did not pretend to be casual. Her success or failure was intimately linked to this man, and to see him so fearlessly in charge infused her with confidence.

The tugs were soon left behind and she felt the swell of the sea beneath her feet. Moonlight bathed the water and Singapore, too, as it receded behind them. Margaret's spirits lifted immeasurably as the breeze rippled through her clothing, making her feel something of what the *Java* must feel—not lame and stiff, but wonderfully free and strong. Watching sailing ships, she'd assumed that their motion was smooth and effortless, but now she felt the raw power of shuddering wood and billowing canvas and knew that the truth was far different.

They reached the farthest headland and she saw Jensen speak to Daniels. The second officer's strong voice carried across the deck.

"Back the main yard!"

Men hauled the main brace until the largest sail lost the wind and flapped back against the mainmast, braking the ship. A ladder was thrown overboard and Margaret saw a tug in the water, evidently sent ahead in anticipation of this moment. The man who'd come aboard last shook hands with Richard Jensen and descended from the quarterdeck. As he passed Margaret, he tipped his cap to her.

"Safe sailing, Miss Belleweather."

"Thank you," Margaret replied, startled. She watched him go over the rail and down the ladder. Who was he, in heaven's name?

She hadn't realized she'd spoken aloud until a voice at her elbow said, "That's the pilot, miss. Captain doesn't need one though, really."

She looked around to see a small boy grinning at her in the moonlight, his unruly head of hair tousled by the breeze.

"Our captain's good enough to be a pilot hisself in any waters you care to name."

"You come from London," she said in surprise, ignoring the information he so obviously desired to impart.

"St. Mary's," he declared, but that seemed to be all he wanted to say on the subject.

"Now then, cheerily men!" Daniels bellowed.

Margaret turned and saw the tug, with the pilot on board, pulling away quickly. All of S'pore would now know that Margaret Belleweather had sailed aboard the *Java*. Margaret sighed—there was nothing for it but to accept the consequences.

The clipper's main yard was hauled around again and the mainsail caught the wind with a crack like a cannon shot. The *Java* surged ahead and Margaret nearly took a tumble.

"Hang on, miss!" The little Londoner grabbed her elbow just in time.

Margaret clutched the rail and watched in fascination as more and more sails were brought into play until they dwarfed the *Java* . . . She turned to look at the 'boy' again and saw her suspicions confirmed in the odd proportion of head to body. A dwarf! First Harkay and now this—really, she thought, the *Java* was a traveling sideshow.

The clipper swept on into the night, the wind pounding her rigging. Her captain stood the quarterdeck, oblivious to the rolling and heaving as she sliced through the water, making a splendid show in the phosphorescent sea. Only Margaret's exhaustion overcame the exhilaration of riding the wind and the water so gloriously.

At last she turned to go below and would have missed Richard Jensen but for the steep roll the *Java* took at that moment. She found herself pitched up against a chest as unyielding as any wall. She felt her cheeks flame as he grabbed her waist and set her firmly away from him.

"One hand for the ship, Miss Belleweather," he snarled.

Margaret tried to stammer out some intelligible reply but the shock of having been thrown up against his full length robbed her of a ready answer. She stared at him, his black hair silvered by the moonlight, hard cheekbones in high relief above the full mouth. It was not a kind face.

"Go below and leave the sailing to sailors," he said after she'd taken several deep breaths without producing any reply. "Dogsmeat—see that she gets there in one piece."

The dwarf nodded sharply. "Best do as the captain says, miss."

Margaret staggered aft, returned to the flat-footed reality of her physical limitations. She accepted the small man's help as she lurched her way down the stairs to the saloon.

"I've put some washing-up water in the cabin for you, miss, and just generally tidied things a bit."

"Thank you," Margaret said. By the light of the lantern swinging from the gimbal over the table, she felt more normal. She groped for a name. "Dogsmeat—I can't call you that."

"Herbert's me name, but I like Dogsmeat better," the dwarf said. "I've got used to it, you see. I'm not sure as I'd even answer to the other."

"I see." Margaret let the issue drop. "Good night, then, and thank you again."

The *Java* swooped and climbed beneath Margaret as she gratefully sponged her face and loosened her hair. The cabin's smallness proved to be a godsend, for a wall to brace herself against was never far from hand. She was just congratulating herself on discovering a rhythm to the clipper's movements when a disconcerting thought struck her. How on earth would she remove her dress without help? The row of hooks and eyes down the back was far removed from her reach.

For the first time, the fact that she was the only female on board the *Java* bore in upon her. She sat down on the berth wondering what possible solution there might be to the dilemma of dressing and undressing herself. No ideas presented themselves, but before long, another, bigger problem drove that worry from her mind.

Chapter 3

A low moan and the sounds of retching from behind the second officer's cabin door put a damper on the mood of the men gathered in the saloon for breakfast. Richard Jensen pushed away from the table scowling. He wished he'd put Margaret Belleweather off with the pilot. If she'd caused the slightest bit of trouble or taken that near fall before it was too late, he would have. Now he thought of her emaciated frame with disgust. Even a short bout of seasickness and he'd be force to bury her at sea.

"I'm putting her off at Batavia," he announced suddenly.

The men exchanged furtive looks around the table. No one needed to ask who or why.

Dogsmeat spoke up hesitantly. "Captain, I'm thinking that I'll take her a bit of food when I've done here—see if that brings her round."

Richard stood up and jammed his cap on his head. "Suit yourself," he growled. "She still gets off at Batavia."

The sun was high overhead when Dogsmeat appeared on the quarterdeck wearing a triumphant grin.

"She's eaten, sir."

"What goes down can come up," Richard said curtly.

"No, sir. It's been hours and it's all staying down, right and tight. The poor thing was half-starved or she'd have never got sick. Mark my words—when you can cure seasickness with a good feed, you've got a sailor on your hands."

37

"I expect to see her at dinner then, and in the bloom of health," Richard replied tersely. His expression eloquently conveyed his disbelief in the likelihood of that happening.

Margaret tidied herself as best she could for dinner. Dogsmeat had urged her to stay below even once she felt better and now she anxiously awaited the arrival of Richard Jensen. Something in Dogsmeat's manner had told her that her place on the *Java* was in peril.

Daniels and the first officer, a fair-haired man named Dekker, welcomed her when she set foot in the saloon, but of the captain there was no sign. Margaret listened politely to their reports of the day's wind and weather but it took all her determination not to stare when Richard Jensen did appear.

This was not the Richard Jensen she had seen in Singapore! His lean, tanned face was devoid of whiskers, revealing a sharp, square jawbone, and the narrow green eyes were clear and bright beneath straight, heavy eyebrows. He wore a clean shirt and now he appeared every inch a seagoing captain and not some slovenly imitation of one. The aggressive muscularity he had evidenced on the dock was intact though—the bearing of a man who was, as the French said, 'comfortable in his own skin.' And a very masculine skin it was, too—taut over corded muscles in his neck, and liberally covered with crisp, dark hair on the strong forearms.

The men jumped to their feet as he entered and he bid them sit again. He gave a brief nod in Margaret's direction and took a drink from the tray Dogsmeat held out.

"You have the morning watch tomorrow, Mr. Dekker?" Jensen asked as he settled himself at the head of the table.

"Yes, sir."

"See that the men go to with the holystones with a will then," Jensen said. "I want a firm footing when we're windward of *Java*."

"Yes, of course, sir."

Richard Jensen fell to eating his soup without preamble, and the others followed suit. Only Margaret hesitated.

Jensen looked up between spoonfuls. "You'll hear no

sanctimonious prayers over meals here, Miss Belle-weather."

Margaret stared at him as his heavy-lidded gaze dropped back to his own plate. If he chose not to say grace at his table that was his business—she could always say one privately—but the fact that he had read her mind bothered her.

Daniels quickly asked, "Have you noted, sir, that our passenger's name means 'fair weather?'"

Margaret glanced at the second officer gratefully. His remark covered an awkward moment.

"As to that, we'll see," Richard replied dryly.

Margaret ignored him and directed a smile at Mr. Daniels. "I believe the name was affixed to one of my antecedents who safely piloted a boat bearing a royal bride across the channel."

"And for his service he got a title, eh?" Richard Jensen asked.

"I expect so," Margaret said.

"More likely a license to commit brigandage up and down the coast," Richard said, twirling the amber liquid in his glass. "You so-called aristocrats think you're better than anyone else but you're not, not by a shot."

Margaret's jaw tightened. How vulgar! "We have always been a quiet country family," she said with asperity, "and I believe we have upheld the best traditions of British society."

Jensen's lip curled but he made no reply. Dogsmeat hastily gathered the soup plates and deployed dishes around the table for the main course. Richard Jensen served himself after watching Dogsmeat serve Margaret first. Margaret didn't have to be told that the usual order of precedence on the *Java* was captain first. Jensen's narrow-eyed scrutiny made that clear.

The meal proceeded in silence but the food was surprisingly good and Margaret soon forgot Jensen's unpleasantness.

"Take seconds, miss," Dogsmeat urged her. "There's plenty more and you could use some flesh. You look like something hanging from a gibbet."

Margaret tensed and then relaxed again when she saw that the steward meant no harm. She was used to shock and pity—open raillery was new.

"I do try to eat more," she said as she helped herself to another serving. "In fact, I gained three pounds on the way out from England."

"Never say y'were even skinnier before than y'are now!" Dogsmeat exclaimed.

"I'm afraid so," Margaret answered, smiling. In a way, it was a relief to speak of it openly. "I had rheumatic fever and though my bones, or more precisely, my joints, will not recover, I expect that I will regain more weight."

Dogsmeat filled an empty spot on Margaret's plate without asking if she wanted more. "Tush," he said, "my bones are as they are, but you—you're young! Lots of good food and sea air'll see you right!"

Margaret smiled gently. Let him have his confidence— no need to go into detail over the dismal prognosis the doctors had delivered. The atmosphere around the table lightened and Margaret ate as Daniels and Dekker began a lively debate on the merits of sail versus power.

Dogsmeat never strayed far from her elbow, adding more to her plate whenever she cleared a spot. At last it was empty and she became aware that the saloon had fallen silent. She looked up and saw awestruck faces around the table and then realized that all the serving dishes were empty, too.

"Bravo, miss. Well done!" Dogsmeat declared. He fell back into a chair looking quite limp.

The embarrassment that had been about to sweep through Margaret eased when she saw the good humor on the steward's face.

Daniels eyed her with interest. "You've got a fine appetite, miss, and that's the truth." He turned to Dekker. "What wouldn't you give to see her go up against Harkay?"

Dekker's eyes gleamed. "By damn, wouldn't that be a sight!" He ducked his head. "Begging your pardon, miss."

40

The ghost of a smile lit Richard Jensen's face. He fished in his vest and flipped a gold coin onto the table. "My money's on her," he said, jerking his head in Margaret's direction.

Margaret was about to demur when Daniels jumped to his feet and emptied his pockets on the table. "Me, too!"

"I don't think it would be a very good . . ."

"I'm in, too!" Dogsmeat cried. He added several Spanish dollars to the growing pile.

Richard Jensen tipped back in his chair and aimed a lazy smile at Margaret. "I can see I'll have to make my money on you this way," he said. "It's that or double your fare to cover the cost of what you eat," he added, nodding at the empty dishes.

Margaret flushed with chagrin. "I'm sure I didn't mean to eat more than my . . ."

"Belay!" Dekker said suddenly. "If the men before the mast know what we know, they'll never bet against her!"

"Secrecy," Daniels declared, "we have to have absolute secrecy. What we've seen here tonight must stay in this room."

"Training," Dogsmeat cut in, "this'll call for training. We work up to it gradual-like. Walk her about on the deck, build up her appetite, promote the match and collect the money, and then hit them with it once we're through the straits."

"Who'll make book?" Richard Jensen asked, lighting a cheroot.

Margaret listened in amazement as the details were solidified. She might have taken offense if not for the air of good humor around the table that clearly included her. Nothing in her experience had prepared her for such a thing, and yet, where was the harm? Except for the fact that they were bound to lose their money, she thought, remembering the massive islander. Serve them right, she decided, for trying to win the crew's money away. The sense of inclusion warmed Margaret so much that this faintly censorious thought flew away the minute it formed.

41

Daniels offered her his arm for a stroll around the deck after dinner but from the pleasant conversation they shared, Margaret knew he escorted her not entirely from a sense of duty. Richard Jensen disappeared from the saloon as abruptly as he had appeared and only the glow of his cheroot on the darkened quarterdeck behind them testified to his presence on the ship.

Breakfast brought a repetition of Daniels's gallantry. He steered Margaret around the sailors hard at work scrubbing the deck and rinsing it down with sea water until it gleamed white in the sun. At lunch, Dekker's watch was down and it was he who steadied her as she made several circuits around the *Java*.

Dekker seemed less inclined to make conversation and Margaret, groping for some subject to break the silence, said, "I would surmise from your name that you share Captain Jensen's heritage?"

Dekker looked baffled.

"Swedish, Mr. Dekker, or perhaps Norwegian?"

"Oh! No, miss, I don't think so, although he speaks Swedish better than me."

Now it was Margaret's turn to be baffled. "And yet he's not Swedish?"

"I don't know, miss. He's never said and we don't ask."

"No, of course not," Margaret said dryly. She knew well enough that what Richard Jensen chose not to discuss didn't get discussed. On to something else. "How do you come to be aboard the *Java*, Mr. Dekker?"

"The *Java* was a blockade runner, miss, during the War Between the States. I was in the Navy and we bested her in a fair fight and took the crew off. I was put aboard to help bring her into port but then the Royal Navy showed up and engaged us. We didn't stand a chance with a jury rig crew. We were given our choice of going off in rowboats or staying aboard as crew, not much of a choice in the middle of the Atlantic in winter."

"But how did Richard Jensen come into it?"

"Captain Jensen was an able-bodied in the Royal Navy, then, pressed in London, I think he once said. They put

42

him on the *Angel* as third mate and some limey bastard as captain.'' Dekker blinked his ice-blue eyes. ''Begging your pardon, miss,'' he croaked.

Margaret smiled. ''For the profanity or for maligning my countrymen?'' she asked.

''Both, miss. We've got Brits on board the *Java* but they all served in the Royal Navy. They don't take offense no matter how rough you talk about their officers but I never meant to say such a thing to you.''

''I'm sure you didn't, Mr. Dekker. Go on with your story.''

''Not much else to tell,'' Dekker said. ''We worked out the war running the blockade for rebel merchants. We did get rid of the . . . Brit as master, but we got someone else just as bad. Captain Jensen worked his way up to first officer and it was him who protected us from the worst.''

''So you've been with Captain Jensen some time, then?''

''Five, six years I reckon.''

Margaret had to be satisfied with that. As she passed the afternoon in her cabin, she realized that she'd been given some glimpses of Richard Jensen oddly at variance with her assumptions. Richard Jensen in the Royal Navy was only one of the things she found hard to picture. She took out her portable desk and began sketching, idly at first, and then with purpose.

The face that emerged was Richard Jensen's. The thin scar that curved along his cheekbone was simple enough to capture, but the lean cheeks made shadowy by his heavy beard even when he was clean shaven gave her more difficulty. The full, sensuous mouth came true enough, but the eyes—what expression typified him? Margaret had to be satisfied with a few suggestive lines beneath the dominating brows. Her pen flew when it came to his hair—it blew back away from his face, exactly as it did when he stood the deck.

Margaret examined the picture critically. It was him and yet it wasn't. It captured none of his sardonic world-weariness—that was in the eyes, left hazy and indistinct— nor did it in any way suggest the controlled energy that was so elemental to the man. It was past her skill to impart that almost primitive quality.

Margaret propped the sketch on a narrow shelf and soon drifted off to sleep in the narrow berth. When she awoke, she felt sure it must be near sunset, for her stomach complained of emptiness. Smoothing down her dress, she tried to drown out the sound of her mother's voice. *A woman who hopes to be well-thought of must be utterly fastidious about her appearance, Margaret. You must never neglect your grooming.*

Sighing, Margaret pulled a comb through her hair. Was it her imagination or did the new growth show some sign of lustre? In the soft light of the gimbal lamp, Margaret couldn't be sure. When she'd first had her hair washed after the worst of the fever had passed, it had come out by the handful. Her best friend, Lucy, had commiserated with her over the loss of her looks and the honey-gold mass of hair that had been her glory.

"They're all meowing like cats in London, Margaret, and saying that your beaus are ripe for the taking now."

"I wish them well, then," Margaret had replied. "Anyone who could say such uncharitable things was never truly a friend anyway. I won't miss them one bit."

"Don't say you plan to bury yourself in the country," Lucy pleaded. "That dull old Reverend Childers will just bore you with more edifying studies. I know my mother will want you to come to London with us for the season now that your mother has passed away."

"No, I can't. I'm cowardly enough not to want to face them all looking as I do," Margaret replied. "Besides, I'm needed here at Pensleigh, and at the orphanage."

And Christian needs me most of all, Margaret thought. Her duty to him eclipsed the vain and shallow considerations that had consumed her before her illness. Tomorrow she would write to Reverend Childers and assure him that she continued to keep her focus firmly fixed on higher purposes.

Margaret looked down at her salt-stained dress. Tomorrow she *must* come up with some solution for dressing and undressing herself.

Seeing no activity in the saloon, Margaret made her way up on deck alone. The setting sun had turned the ocean into a plain of vermilion that stretched away to the west. She stopped, transfixed by the sight. Suddenly a loud curse behind her shattered the tranquility. Richard Jensen hurtled past her and vaulted over the quarterdeck rail. Faster than she could comprehend it, he had flung aside his boots and was scaling the rigging of the foremast.

High above the deck she saw a sail slatting around a small figure hanging limp in a bosun's chair. The *Java* plunged and jibed as Richard Jensen climbed upward like a coiled spring being unleashed. The man in the bosun's chair was slammed into the mast again and again as the *Java* crested the waves, and Margaret pressed her knuckles to her mouth. She did not need to see the crew standing silent below to know that the sailor was in danger of being battered to death.

Daniels manned the helm, calling out orders to the men who anchored the rope of the bosun's chair. Richard Jensen was only a speck up in the sails now. He reached the bosun's chair and pulled it firmly to the mast. The men on deck heaved away at the line but nothing happened. At least the bosun's chair no longer swayed at will, she thought, wondering how on earth they would get the man down.

A flutter of white caught her eye and then the bosun's chair hung empty. Slowly but surely, Richard Jensen began descending. As he got low enough for her to see him, Margaret drew an involuntary gasp. The crewman hung unconscious on Jensen's back, his hands bound together by the captain's shirt. Margaret's own breathing stilled in empathy as she imagined the terrible choking weight pressing against Jensen's throat.

The angle of the rigging decreased as Jensen passed the

45

joint of the topmast. Several men scrambled up to meet him but they failed in their effort to untie the shirt that bound the man's hands. The hoarse rasp of Jensen's breathing carried across the deck as he continued down, and Margaret could see his bare chest heaving. When he finally reached the rail, someone stretched up through the rigging and cut the shirt with a knife. Other hands lifted the sailor away as Jensen swung around the rigging and collapsed on the deck.

Every rib stood out against his flesh as he fought for air. He drew deep, agonized breaths, his head thrown back and his eyes shut tight. His throat was still livid from the pressure of the sailor's weight, and streaks of blood mixed with the sweat streaming off his body. Margaret's feet carried her forward. She stood to one side, breathing quickly, as if taking in more air herself would somehow help him.

"Water!" The peremptory command was out of Margaret's mouth the instant she realized there was something useful she could do. She hurried to Richard Jensen's side as Dogsmeat brought a bucket of water. Kneeling down, she watched Jensen still battling for air and waited for the moment when she could offer him water.

She wanted to reach out and smooth away the lines of pain scoring his forehead and then she remembered the blood. She ran her hand across his chest and saw with relief that his skin was whole—the blood must have come from the injured sailor. Some of the tension left her but she let her palm linger at the center of Jensen's chest, reassured by the feel of his heart hammering beneath her hand. His eyes were still squeezed shut with the force of his efforts to breathe, and Margaret began to grow dizzy with her vicarious attempts to breathe for him.

As the violent rise and fall of his chest gradually diminished, Margaret turned and dipped the cup into the bucket next to her. She slipped her arm beneath his neck and lifted his head, holding the cup to his lips. He took several swift draughts. Then he pulled away gasping for air. The salty, pungent smell of his skin rose to her nostrils and the soaking wet hair on his neck pressed into her arm as she waited for him to recover and take another draught.

How fierce his face was! It gave Margaret a curious shiver to be so close to him. The heavy brows were furrowed together over his closed eyes, and half-circles of dense, black lashes pressed against his cheeks. Sweat ran down the creases from his nose to his mouth, and Margaret stared at his lips, which were stretched in a grimace over his strong teeth. His sweat began to seep through her dress where his head pressed against her. It should have repulsed her but it didn't.

A small movement signaled his desire for more water and she lifted his head gently. He took several drinks, with long pauses for breath in between, before he finally opened his eyes. The irises were the color of a sea being beaten by the rain, a frosted green, less piercing than she remembered. Margaret averted her glance, suddenly embarrassed by the intimacy of cradling his head to her breast. His breathing quieted and she began to think about pulling away.

"Thank you." The vibration of his voice spread through her body with a queer tingling sensation.

"You're welcome," she said, keeping her eyes on the deck.

"Look at me," he said.

Margaret slowly complied. He searched her face keenly, making no move to rise.

"The eyes are the mirror of the soul. Isn't that what they say?"

Margaret nodded, pinned by his gaze.

"Then why am I seeing only a reflection of myself in your eyes?"

Margaret swallowed. Jensen's body no longer seemed heavy to her, which made no sense since he hadn't moved.

Jensen continued to study her. "You've shuttered your soul from me, haven't you? Because this isn't quite proper."

47

Margaret was acutely aware of the short hairs on his neck prickling her arm. "You needed help—I gave it," she stammered.

"And now I've thanked you and you've said I'm welcome but neither of us is moving. Why do you suppose that is?"

Labeling the paralysis broke its grip. Margaret withdrew her arm abruptly. Sounds she hadn't heard a moment ago came crashing in on her, and a hot blush crept up her cheeks. Richard Jensen braced himself on his elbows and watched her.

"Was it so terrible?" he asked.

"I don't know what you're talking about," Margaret said, wishing she didn't.

"Your hand felt so small lying over my heart, like a fairy's," he said.

Margaret nervously twitched an errant strand of hair off her face. "You're feeling fanciful."

"At the expense of your composure, I see."

A long groan sounded behind them. His glance flicked away, and Margaret took the opportunity to rise clumsily to her feet. His hand moved, and she thought he meant to reach out and stop her, but instead he sat up. She gazed at the hem of her dress without moving, but she could not avoid seeing the prominent muscles of his shoulder out of the corner of her eye.

"That's that then," Jensen said with a crooked smile. He came up off the deck in one fluid motion and picked up the bucket of water. "Stand back if you please, Miss Belleweather."

Margaret jumped back in alarm and then felt silly as she watched him lift the bucket and pour its contents over his head. For a brief instant, the silver sheeting of water melded to bronze over his deeply tanned skin. A vivid recollection of a nude Greek sculpture at the British Museum assailed her. She was still staring at the well-defined muscles of his torso as the last of the water pooled around his bare feet.

"Excuse me."

48

Margaret's face flamed afresh as Richard Jensen looked her in the eye before shouldering his way past. To be caught staring so intently at his bare flesh mortified her. She was relieved that he seemed more intent on reaching the injured sailor than on resuming the uncomfortable repartee of a moment ago. Margaret watched as he stooped over the man and probed the grotesquely swollen face with great deliberation.

Without warning, he drew his arm back and delivered a sharp blow to the man's face. Margaret cried out in horror but the sound was masked by the sailor's high-pitched scream. Margaret fumbled for the rail, made faint by Jensen's brutality. Dimly she heard him saying, "Get him below."

He rose to his feet and Margaret cringed against the rail, knowing that he was every inch the monster she had first supposed him to be. Dear God, let her live long enough to reach some port where she could disembark and never look back!

"Harkay!" Jensen yelled.

The mate stepped forward.

"Get another man aloft and see that halyard clear!" Jensen paused. "And don't ever send a man up to do a job like that unless he can handle it!"

The islander turned away, his face a dull red. He bellowed and a squat, swarthy man clothed only in a loin cloth came running. After a brief conversation of which Margaret understood not a word, the small man climbed into the rigging. Only then did Richard Jensen turn back to face Margaret. Her shock poured forth in accusation.

"You hit that man!"

Jensen's mouth tightened. He stared at her with eyes restored to their usual glittering green.

"His nose was broken, Miss Belleweather," he snapped. "I set it."

Without another word, he turned and went aft. As soon as his back was to her, Margaret sagged. It was as though his anger had been holding her upright. Her legs shook mercilessly. How could she have known? She felt as if she

49

were going to be sick at any minute.

"Miss?"

Margaret looked up to see Dogsmeat regarding her anxiously.

"Dinner's due in ten minutes. Captain'll expect it to be served prompt on the watch change. Can y'make it back under yer own power?"

Margaret stared at the bloodied remains of Richard Jensen's shirt in the steward's hands. "Yes, of course," she said, but the quaver in her voice betrayed her.

"Captain does the doctoring on this ship, miss," Dogsmeat said kindly. "Most ships, it's the cook what does it but our captain's got a sure hand for broken bones."

"But . . . but that was awful!"

"Awfuller to go round with a broken nose, miss. Leaves a man all runny-faced and short-winded if it ain't fixed proper. Besides," he said, jerking his head toward the fo'c'sle companionway, "the lad fancies himself with the ladies—wouldn't like it if he weren't pretty no more."

Margaret responded to his grin with a weak smile and began to make her way back to the saloon, still shaking.

Chapter 4

Dinner passed in silence. Jensen spoke to no one, merely glaring at Daniels and Dekker when they joined them several minutes after the watch change had been rung. Only once the dishes were cleared away did Margaret get some intimation of how angry the *Java*'s captain must be, for both officers hurriedly excused themselves and went topside without offering her the customary stroll around the deck.

Unfortunately for Margaret's peace of mind, Jensen did not seem inclined to quit the saloon. He gestured to Dogsmeat for a refill of his glass and then held it up and stared through the amber liquid reflectively. Margaret sat frozen, like a rabbit in the presence of a predator, fervently hoping that Jensen would leave soon. She studied the grain of the highly polished table in front of her, never letting her eyes stray. The unnatural stillness of her body promoted rampant activity in her mind however. Thoughts of the unfairness of her earlier words tumbled around ceaselessly. At last she could stand it no longer.

"I'm terribly sorry about what I said up on deck."

"Forget it," Jensen snapped.

"But I can't. I was wrong and you must allow me to apologize even if you don't choose to accept my apology."

"I *don't* choose to accept it," he replied irritably. He picked up a cheroot the steward had left on the table and sniffed at it before lighting up.

Margaret was nonplussed. She had seldom had to apologize in earnest for anything and never had an apology been refused.

"I will not try to talk you out of your sentiment on this," Margaret said, groping for words, "but you must believe me when I say I'm sorry."

Jensen looked at her directly for the first time. "Fine," he growled. "I believe you're sorry. Does that satisfy your painfully correct notions of propriety?"

Margaret flushed. "This is difficult enough. Must you add to it by suggesting that I'm only apologizing out of a sense of obligation?"

Jensen's mouth tightened. "Let's just drop it, all right?"

"Why will you not understand that I said what I did out of ignorance?" Margaret persisted.

Jensen leaned forward and stared at her as he blew a wreath of smoke across the table. The anger in his face subtly shifted to bored contempt.

"Because, Miss Belleweather," he said with exaggerated restraint, "if I accept your apology I'll have to act all humble, and I don't feel particularly humble at the moment. Let's just leave things the way they are. We don't like each other so let's not get all wrapped up in pretending that either of us cares what the other one thinks."

Margaret clenched her hands in her lap. "You have a way of saying the most hateful things as if they were perfectly reasonable." She stood up with all the grace she could manage. "Perhaps it would be best if I retired for the night."

"Perhaps it would be," Jensen agreed lazily. He lounged back in his chair.

Margaret tried to turn away, but the studied nonchalance in his pose argued for caution. The tight, controlled angle of his jaw said the issue between them was still very much alive, but what else could she say?

"Mr. Jensen . . ." she began again, and then corrected herself, "Captain Jensen, I do not normally propel myself into situations where I am not wanted. I'm grateful that you have allowed me to sail with you and so long as I am on your ship, I will endeavor not to trespass on your

52

generosity or good nature again."

Margaret couldn't help herself—the last words came out tinged with sarcasm. Richard Jensen looked up at her through the veil of smoke which hung motionless in the air between them while the *Java* rocked back and forth around it.

"If I accept your apology, will you bloody well go to bed?"

"I will, Captain Jensen."

"Then I accept it."

Margaret inclined her head stiffly. She had done her best. Keeping her head high, she turned and headed toward her cabin. As she reached for the handle on the door, the *Java* reared up under her and she went careening across the saloon.

Jensen sprang out of his chair and caught her even before his glass hit the deck and shattered. It took Margaret a long, dizzy moment to collect her wits. She looked up from within the circle of Jensen's arms to thank him but stopped when she saw the glittering antipathy in his eyes.

She couldn't help asking the obvious question. "Why do you dislike me so?"

Jensen flexed his jaw. "I've got plenty of reasons to dislike you. You're female, you're full of stupid, misguided notions, and you couldn't say what's really on your mind if your life depended on it."

Margaret stared at him. A trickle of fear ran through her, and something else, something stronger, but nameless.

"I beg your pardon?" she said, realizing that he'd spoken and she hadn't heard a word.

"I said, I believe in calling a spade a spade. You're like all females—you'll tie your tongue in knots telling a man everything but the truth. You aren't the least bit sorry you screamed at me in front of my men. You're only saying you're sorry because you're afraid I'll call off our deal."

Margaret flinched. The tempered steel of his words was as nothing compared to the steel of his arms.

"That's not a fair statement," she said, her voice raw with nerves. "I *am* sorry for what I said and furthermore, I have been completely truthful with you all along."

53

Jensen's lip curled. "Then why haven't you told me you think I'm a dyed-in-the-wool bastard yet?"

Margaret stared at his lips. The heat of his arms across her back softened her as they swayed to the *Java*'s rhythm.

"Perhaps it's because I don't think you *are* a . . ." Margaret faltered.

"Like hell," Jensen snorted.

"No," Margaret said, "I only use that word in the literal sense, never a pejorative one."

Jensen gave a nasty little laugh. "Then you'll be interested to know it fits me in the literal sense, too."

Margaret shrank from the humorless venom in his voice. "I wish you would not feel compelled to tell me such a thing," she said nervously.

"Why? Because you may have to jump off my ship in the middle of the ocean to preserve your maidenly modesty now that you know?"

"Of course not," Margaret retorted. Despite all the provoking things he'd said about her, this remark riled her as nothing else had. "I'm a fair-minded person. I do not hold people accountable for things they have no control over, only their own actions." Margaret bristled. "You've obviously assumed the worst about me. Do you make a habit of assuming you know what other people think without first asking them?"

"With someone like you? Sure—saves a lot of time. After all, your kind are so predictable."

Margaret rose to the bait. Predictable was she? She put her hands on his chest and pushed him away. This time he let her go.

"I'll have you know that in London I am . . . was . . . considered . . ."

Margaret stopped suddenly. She could feel the heavy beating of her heart. She had been about to tell him that she'd been proclaimed an original at the beginning of her first season, but what did that signify? Now she stood before him, a remnant of what she'd once been. Her shoulders slumped in defeat.

Richard Jensen raised an eyebrow in mute interrogation. Margaret found his scrutiny painful and tried to

54

distract him with words.

"I was going to say that I was once celebrated for my lack of predictability but that wouldn't be quite honest, and since you claim to value honesty so much, I find it impossible to maintain the fiction. It was a very calculated sort of spontaneity. I broke only the smallest of rules and only after carefully considering whether it would enhance my reputation as an original. You're right, I'm afraid—at heart, I'm very predictable."

Margaret turned away. "And now if you'll excuse me, I really believe it's time I went to bed."

Richard's brows furrowed together. What a pitiful, bedraggled creature she looked now, he thought. He had enjoyed pushing her to the limit, watching the fiery gold sparks of the lantern's reflection in the purple depths of her eyes. Now the fire was gone. He sternly resisted the remorse edging into his mind but his hand flew out in an attempt to express what he could not put into words.

She saw the flash as he reached toward her and stopped. She gazed up at him blankly, as if her thoughts were already miles away, and then she mechanically took the unmoving hand poised in the air between them and shook it. With a sad smile, she wished him good night once more and disappeared into Daniels's cabin.

Damn! A woman who could heap guilt on your platter like that was nothing but trouble. This one was even better at it than the others he'd known. He knew all too well that a subterranean current of guilt ran deep within him anyway. A woman skilled at tapping it could gut him like a fish—*had* gutted him like a fish. He'd be damned if he'd open himself up to that kind of hurt again—no, he'd keep her at arm's length, and let her know that all her mealy-mouthed politeness would get her exactly nowhere with him.

He drained the rest of his whiskey and went up on deck to clear his head. The wind was backing but it would still bring them into Demjang in good time to place an order in the morning—fruits and vegetables, some chickens, a pig, everything they'd need to satisfy their bellies on the way to

Australia and back again, and at half the prices in Singapore.

The *Java* shivvied and swooped beneath him. The *Java*—the only female he dared to love and the only one who'd ever really loved him back. Richard shoved his cold, dead cheroot between his lips and scanned the milky horizon. The stars were sharper, cleaner here than anywhere else in the world, so close you could almost touch them, not like the cold, hostile stars over the Atlantic that defied you to get a fix on them.

He braced his foot on the quarterdeck rail and inhaled deeply. Tomorrow they'd be near land and the air would be scented with frangipani but tonight it was only warm, salt tang that flowed into his lungs. A quick run to Australia would suit his mood now, to set canvas until the rigging whistled and creaked, and then set a bit more. At times like those, the *Java* didn't love him quite as much but she understood his need to drive her, and to drive himself.

The fast runs were as much a matter of pride as of money. He still savored the memory of the day they'd passed a steamer bound for Melbourne, all its passengers cheering and whistling as she overtook them under full canvas, right up to the skysails. Richard Jensen didn't like depending on anything or anybody, and that included stinking coal-burning engines. The wind was a capricious mistress but there was no malice in her, no deliberate wounding of this man or that when she chose not to blow.

"Captain Jensen?"

The soft inquiry startled him. He turned and saw Margaret Belleweather standing there, her face in deep shadow.

"I couldn't sleep," she said, pulling a shawl around her shoulders. She turned to face the bow. "I can never sleep after an argument."

Richard was puzzled by her manner. And why come to him? What more was there to be said?

"I know you don't like apologies," she went on, "and I'm not sure I even owe you one, but I wanted you to know

56

how sorry I am that you're a . . . that you were born illegitimately."

Richard stared at her profile. There was no doubting the sincerity of her words. She leaned forward and braced her thighs against the quarterdeck rail as the *Java* swept over the crest of a wave. With the shawl fluttering around her, she looked like a masthead on a ship. He had no idea how to respond to her words but she saved him by asking an unexpected question.

"Where do you come from, Mr. Jensen?"

"From a frontier town in the Midwest," he said reluctantly. "No place you'd have heard of."

"And your father and mother?"

He could detect no hint of mockery in her voice but the question still sliced into him. "I never knew my father," he said brusquely. "He was a cowboy. My mother was going west with a wagon train when she met him. When she got pregnant, he left her behind."

"So you grew up without a father?"

Richard shifted his weight. The light in the binnacle housing the compass cast a soft circle of light on the deck nearby, creating the aura of a confessional. "Gunnar Jansson," he said at last. "A man named Gunnar Jansson married her, despite . . ." He couldn't finish.

"Despite the fact that she was carrying another man's child?"

He almost didn't hear her and then her words sunk in. "It was in spite of a lot more than that. She was a foreigner, Portuguese, and a Catholic to boot. The rest of the Swedish community never forgave him. Well, at least not until after she died. But they never forgave me—I was always a foreigner, right up until the day I left town." The words ripped out of him with a bitterness he hadn't known he still felt.

Richard had felt the disapproving stares long before he was old enough to put a name to them. His mother's vibrant olive skin and achingly black hair had set her apart from anyone else in town. "Whether she tricked or bewitched Gunnar Jansson into marriage didn't much matter to the Swedes," he said. "They resented her, begrudged her every breath she drew for having snatched him away from a deserving daughter of Sweden."

"It must have been hard for you," Margaret said softly. "I suppose they loved one another very much to marry in the face of such obstacles."

"He loved *her*," Richard said sharply, "but she never loved him, not even a little. She used me like a shield, keeping me up late at night until after he fell asleep, so she wouldn't have to . . ." He stopped short, unable to spell out the intimate details. It was all so long ago and yet so fresh. Margaret Belleweather stood silent, still braced against the rail, not looking at him. It made it easier.

"I never saw Gunnar mistreat my mother, and I wondered why she turned away his affection. It was only as I got older that I realized that he adored her, hopelessly and abjectly, and I saw that it was too much for her. If Gunnar had loved her only a little, she might have managed to accept it. He didn't even mind that she carried another man's baby. Knowing she was without family or money, he went after her with the ferocity of a ship beating its way through pack ice."

"Marriages that start out with love can founder, too, I suppose, but somehow they survive," Margaret said at length.

"My mother never forgot the cowboy," Richard said abruptly. "She felt guilty all her life for marrying one man in her heart and another in law. One day a man rode through town who reminded her of him. She ran after him and even after she caught up with him and saw that it wasn't my father, she hung on to his leg and just cried and cried. Right there in the street. Everybody saw. After that it was impossible for my stepfather to pretend that theirs was a happy marriage."

"How awful for you," Margaret whispered.

More awful than he could bring himself to tell her. That night he had witnessed the first display of temper between them. Their mutual stock of English ran out quickly and then it was just grunts and slaps. The wordless fury had raged on and on, eerily quiet when so much was at stake. It made Richard realize how little they'd ever talked. He'd huddled on the stairs, blaming himself—if he hadn't been around to remind them of the cowboy, maybe she would have forgotten about him. Richard had pressed his forehead into the curved and fluted banisters until his whole head ached, and when that wasn't enough to drown the pain, he'd banged his head on them over and over, until the handrail vibrated.

Richard relit his cheroot, his hands shaking. How could it still hurt so much? He should have gone downstairs, should have translated for them and helped them make their peace with one another. He could have done it, or at least tried, but the fear that they would turn on him and see that he was to blame kept him from moving.

"What happened?" Margaret Belleweather's voice drew him back from the childhood nightmare of guilt and shame.

"My mother died less than a year later," he said tersely. "After the funeral, the Lutheran church ladies came. They filled our parlor. Me they ignored but Gunnar they welcomed back into the fold like the prodigal son. He made me go to Sunday school after that, but I never fit in. Every time the teacher made a reference to the devil, all those good little Swedish boys and girls used to look over at me. I guess I just looked like what they thought the devil would look like, dark eyes and dark hair."

Richard sighed. "After that came Hildy. She was a distant cousin of Gunnar's and I detested her from the beginning. She hated everything I stood for and found fault with everything I did. She and Gunnar got married, and after that I didn't stand a chance. I got wild, just like all boys do, only worse maybe, because of her, and she convinced Gunnar that the only answer was to beat it out of me."

"Was there nothing good in your life at all—no kind of happiness?" Margaret asked gently.

"School, I guess. That was the best thing that happened to me. Gunnar wouldn't let me go at first. He needed me at the store because I spoke English and he didn't. He taught me how to add up a bill and make change by the time I was tall enough to see over the counter. Then a traveling salesman pointed out that if I went to school, I'd be able to read and write English too—keep the books and do correspondence for him. After that Gunnar let me go half-days to school."

"Most boys wouldn't think that was very wonderful," Margaret said wryly. "You must have been different."

Richard smiled into the darkness. "I guess I was just contrary enough to want it because I'd given up hope of ever being allowed to go."

He could still remember the way the classroom had smelled, like the very stuff of freedom. He'd imbibed it like a drunk waking up to hear church bells on a Sunday morning, resolved not to waste the chance he'd been given. He'd attacked knowledge with a seriousness of purpose that stunned the school mistress at first, he was so different from the other bored and truculent boys whose families' hopes for success in America hinged on educating their offspring.

"Between working at the store and going to school, I managed to stay pretty much out of Hildy's way, too. That helped, at least for a while."

"But you still had to go home at night."

It was a simple statement of fact that demonstrated understanding. Richard felt a small swell of gratitude.

"Yes, I still had to go home at night. I guess I was fourteen by the time things came to a head. I'd found the only bar in town that would serve me and I began stealing money from the cash drawer at the store to pay for liquor." Richard took a deep draw on his cheroot. "One day I got into a barroom brawl and found out I was a natural born fighter. After that I was afraid to go home, knowing that I'd probably flatten Gunnar the next time he laid a hand on me."

"I'd have thought that by then you'd have wanted to," Margaret remarked.

"Part of me did," Richard admitted, "but I couldn't overlook the fact that Gunnar wasn't a bad father until Hildy came along. He was the only father I'd ever known. I guess it was easier just to lay all the blame on her."

"So you left town but you kept his name?"

"More or less. I passed through dozens of dry, dusty towns just like the one I'd come from. I couldn't leave them behind fast enough. It wasn't until I got to Philadelphia that I found what I was looking for."

Richard sensed her inclining her head toward him, but in the dark, confessional atmosphere of the quarterdeck, it was easy to pretend that he was talking to himself. "Clippers," he went on, "sleeker than swallows, with big clouds of canvas. I fell in love with the sea, and the clippers were its queens. I signed on one as an apprentice. That's when the spelling of my name got changed but I didn't mind. I went to Australia for wool, to China for tea, to California carrying forty-niners. No one cared who you were or where you came from, only how you did your work. It suited me fine."

"And now you're here," came the softly accented voice, "and master of your own ship."

Richard passed a hand over tired eyes. She'd brought him to the present and the spell was broken. Dawn would come soon, a brilliant violent return of the sun from the east, and she would know far more about him this day than she had known the day before, too much now that he stopped to think about it.

Richard straightened his shoulders and checked the sails.

"That jib is overtrimmed, Mr. Dekker," he said sharply. "See to it!"

"Aye, sir."

"And you, Miss Belleweather," he said to the silent figure at his side, "had better find your berth."

It came out as an order, but he was still suprised when she obeyed it.

At the last minute though, just before her head disappeared down the companionway, she turned and said, "Good night, Mr. Jensen, and thank you for everything."

It only served to increase Richard Jensen's gnawing sense of irritation.

61

Chapter 5

Margaret leaned over the rail as the wind swept them on toward land. It burst into her eyes, so green it hurt to look at, greener even than Pensleigh in spring. How tame Pensleigh seemed in her mind's eye now, dotted with cream-colored Shropshires, the deer moving like shadows through the gray mist rising from the lawns. Here everything was more alive, the sea a rich faience-blue, women the color of burnt sienna wading near shore wrapped in fabrics that glittered in the sun. It couldn't be the same sun that shone over England, Margaret thought. This one cooked clear through to one's bones, deep into aching joints that oozed with contentment even while the skin bubbled up with sweat in protest.

Margaret retired her bonnet. Amazing in how short a time it had faded and become dilapidated without Eliza's diligent care. Sad, too, the condition of her dress and person. How she longed for a proper bath! She could see the women on shore better now, and envied them the freedom of their simple wrapped sarongs, tied up through their legs so they could move through the water easily.

"Weigh anchor!"

Margaret's head flew up. She hadn't even noticed the men reefing the sails. Richard Jensen stood by as a gig was swung out over the water, evidently prepared to go ashore.

She hadn't made up her mind how she felt about him after last night. When he'd caught her in the saloon, he

62

hadn't held her brutally, quite the opposite. He'd acted to protect her, but the dark touch of his skin on hers had planted disturbing images in her mind, and given rise to a soft, slow pulsing in her veins. Ridiculous to think that he had meant to, of course.

Then she had gone on deck, and in the darkness she had met the boy he had once been. How she had longed to reach out and hold that boy, to give him the comfort and love all children craved. But that boy was long gone now, replaced by an intensely masculine man who would doubtless scoff at any hint of such tenderness.

"Miss Belleweather?"

Margaret nearly jumped out of her skin. Her startled jerk brought her face to face with Richard Jensen. She took a calming breath.

"Yes, Mr. Jensen?"

Jensen's mouth twitched. "You don't like calling me 'captain,' do you?" He went on without pausing for an answer. "I'm going ashore. I doubt you'll learn anything about your brother in Demjang, however. News that reached here would have reached Singapore, too."

Margaret didn't care for his tone. "Is that so? Well, since I have undertaken this voyage with the express purpose of making inquiries about my brother, it would be foolish to be less than thorough. I would like to accompany you."

"By all means. You wouldn't want to appear foolish."

He turned away leaving Margaret bristling. So much for the quiet understanding they had shared in the night.

"I will retrieve my sketch of Christian and join you shortly," she called out to his retreating back.

"You do that, Miss Belleweather," he said, still striding away.

He was impossible! Margaret hurried to her cabin and noticed with annoyance that her hands were shaking. Why on earth did she allow him to affect her like this? She decided it was his intentional rudeness that overset her presence of mind. He didn't play by the rules, and rules were what kept society running smoothly. Well, she wasn't going to descend to *his* level—no, she would set an example. By the time this trip was over, he would appreciate the qualities that had made the English masters of a civilized empire.

Margaret drew a comb through her hair and pinned it more tidily. She remembered with an unsettled hiccup of her stomach the scene on deck with the injured sailor. She would have to do better than that if she was to make a convert of Richard Jensen. The emotional side to her nature, about which the Reverend Childers had cautioned her so often, must be brought to heel.

On deck, Daniels stood ready to assist her down into the gig. Margaret gathered her skirts and began to descend the rope ladder. Although the green water was still as glass, the *Java* seemed to be moving about like a decoy on a stormy lake. Her hands hadn't the strength to hold her all the way down and before she reached the bottom rung, she lost her grip.

Richard Jensen caught her in a whirl of skirts. Margaret nearly shrieked as he touched her in places no man should touch, but since his grip was all that stood between her and the ocean, she stifled her protest.

"I suggest that instead of one hand for the ship, you adopt a new rule, Miss Belleweather—two hands for the ladder," he said.

She looked up into his face. The sharp green of his eyes was overlaid by a mesh of lashes as he squinted against the sun, but his look of amusement was inescapable.

"I *did* use two hands," she snapped. "I assure you, I did not mean to fall."

"You mean your mamma never told you that would be a good way to get cozy with a sailor?"

"She most certainly did not!" Margaret saw the jest in his face an instant too late to choke back the words.

Jensen grinned and put her down. The men began pulling toward shore as Margaret struggled to rearrange her dress and set her hat straight. So much for being a member of the empire-building race! Nelson as a baby would have managed better.

At the dock, Jensen lifted her out and set her on her feet

without any ceremony. He sprang from the boat with an easy grace a tiger couldn't have matched and Margaret's eyes were drawn to the long, heavy muscles in his thighs. They ran tautly into the rounded muscles of his buttocks and she followed him down the dock, absorbed in watching the way they tensed and released with each step. He stopped abruptly and Margaret nearly ran into him.

He looked down at her with keen interest. "Do I have a rip in the seat of my pants, Miss Belleweather?"

Margaret's face flamed. What could she possibly say? Overcome with embarrassment, she did the only thing she could do—she ignored the question. She lifted her chin and determinedly perused the clutter of houses and shops beyond. "Is that the town? It's a very pretty little place."

Margaret walked purposefully away down the dirt road, leaving the inane remark hanging in the air behind her. Walking away had the decided virtue of preventing Richard Jensen from further scrutinizing her face. Some situations one could not salvage.

Jensen caught up with her in a few strides. "I'll be busy all afternoon. Stay in the market area and I won't have any trouble finding you later."

He tipped his cap with a sardonic gleam in his eye and walked away, swinging his hips just a little more than was necessary. Margaret stared at his retreating backside in cold fury. She stood for a moment wishing for, of all things, a snowball. It would have given her great pleasure to hurl it at his head just then.

The idea of wishing for a snowball in the damp, steaming heat of Demjang was so ludicrous that it went some way toward restoring her sense of humor. She looked around her at the riot of color and activity in the marketplace. Bare-breasted girls sauntered along with baskets on their heads and Margaret returned their quick, shy smiles. At first she dared not look elsewhere than their faces but then she realized their shyness had nothing to do with their near nudity—that seemed as natural to them as her voluminous dress was to her. A natural gentleness pervaded their every movement, and their shyness seemed to reflect a desire not to impose.

Thatched houses with soaring roof beams resembled huge horns predominated beyond the central avenue. There were a few European-style buildings toward the end of the street, white with red-tiled roofs. Margaret started toward them, and by the time she arrived she had acquired an entourage of wickedly adorable children. She smiled and offered them some pennies but none reached out for them.

She was surprised when she emerged from the gloom of the chandler's shop to find them still waiting for her. Pulling out the sketch of Christian, she showed it to them, but just as she had in the shop, she got no reaction. Their bright, black gazes never left her face as she tucked it away again. A boy who had been cajoling a family of ducks down the road with the help of a bamboo pole stopped to join the group. Clothed in the merest nothing of a wrap around his hips, he reached out to touch her skirt shyly. Emboldened, the others did, too, and Margaret laughed, feeling like a latter-day Gulliver as they swarmed around her, fingering the small purse at her waist and even gently lifting the hem of her dress to see her shoes. They weren't so very different from the children at the orphanage, she thought, and remembered with a pang that she had made very few sketches so far to share her trip with them when she returned.

She moved off down the street and the children skipped after her like butterflies, chattering in a musical language as she went from stall to stall. Whatever business the boy with the ducks had been about evidently wasn't very urgent for he joined the parade, too, ducks and all. The fruit stalls, each one more ambitiously artistic in the arrangement of vivid red, green, and orange fruits than the one before, attracted Margaret's eye. Elsewhere, gleaming fabrics shot through with gold and silver threads dizzied her with their beauty, but when she tried to buy some the language barrier proved to be insuperable.

At last, having gotten blank stares at every stall in response to Christian's picture, Margaret admitted defeat and allowed herself to stop beneath a banyan tree. It was almost a caricature of a tree, with enormous twisting roots gnarled together into a trunk that thrust upward to end in a cool, heavenly canopy. As welcome as its shade was now, she could well imagine that by dark it assumed sinister qualities.

The heat of Demjang was stunning and the water beyond the beach glinted invitingly. The temptation to wade there was overwhelming. Well, why not? It could hardly be shark-infested or the native women wouldn't walk through it so calmly. The children followed her to the water's edge and clustered around when she bent to take off her shoes and stockings. Several little girls giggled behind their hands when she hoisted her skirts and waded in. It felt extremely bold to bare her feet and legs in public but she reminded herself that this was not Brighton or Bournemouth, but Sumatra, where girls walked bare-breasted without a trace of self-consciousness.

The little boy who had first touched her skirt followed her into the water. He rattled off a commentary as she walked along, pointing to things on the bottom. All the while his ducks scolded him from the beach. The biggest gander finally shrugged its wings and waded into the water. It rode the wavelets lapping the shore with an expression that clearly conveyed its dim opinion regarding the reliability of small boys.

The women farther out paused to look at her. Margaret concluded they must be too unfamiliar with European women to be astonished by her unusual behavior, for they soon turned back to their harvest of the sea. Starfish undulated on the bottom, and little fish too fragile and beautiful to be real darted everywhere, their flashing colors akin to the effect of turning a prism in a strong beam of sunlight.

Her self-appointed guide continued his monologue, and Margaret noted certain words recurring. She couldn't connect them to anything specific, but the delight of wading bare up to her knees made it seem unimportant. The water was not much cooler than the air around them but it soothed and relieved. She was toying with the idea of simply letting herself fall into it when a sharp pain shot up her leg.

With a startled cry, Margaret pitched face down into the water. Her small guide seized her bare ankle and held it up for inspection. Upended by his ministrations, she thrashed about, trying desperately to keep her face out of the water. The weight of her soaking wet clothing kept her from making much progress and she twisted around and gasped out a plea for mercy.

Her guardian angel looked down at her quizzically, as if surprised to recall that a body was attached to the foot he held so ruthlessly. At a word from him, the Lilliputians gathered round and hauled her toward the shore. They went straight through the gaggle of ducks, all of whom began quacking loudly. The explosive eruptions hurt her ears but her erstwhile savior rendered that discomfort inconsequential by picking up a razor sharp clamshell and incising the flesh around the reddening wound on her foot.

Margaret yelped as flames of exquisite agony replaced what had been only a dull, simmering discomfort before. Her small tormenter shot a satisfied glance in her direction. Margaret craned around and watched in horror as a stream of blood ran down toward her knee.

"Having trouble, Miss Belleweather?"

Margaret's stomach sank as she felt Richard Jensen's shadow fall over her. Speaking loudly enough to be heard above the outraged ducks, she tried to inject a note of dignity into her voice. "No, just a small mishap. I must have stepped on a shell. I would appreciate it, however, if you would get this little demon away from my foot. He aspires to be a surgeon without knowing what a proper one does."

Jensen's shadow moved away and she heard a hurried consultation between the captain and the bare, brown boy.

"Oh, hurry, do!" she exclaimed as her ankle was twisted and turned with complete disregard for her comfort.

Jensen straightened and his storm green eyes flared as he

68

looked down at her. "Your makeshift surgeon has done exactly the correct thing. You will nevertheless be a much humbler, sorrier woman before this day is out."

"By that I suppose you mean to leave me here like a piece of flotsam," Margaret shot back.

"You suppose wrong," Jensen said, "though it's exactly what you deserve." Without any warning he lifted her roughly from the sand. His jarring steps as he walked back up the beach amplified Margaret's appreciation of his anger.

He stopped in front of a house where a man sat massaging the legs of a fighting cock. An old woman with a face as wrinkled and brown as a walnut shell stopped sweeping and listened to Jensen's rapid fire Malay. She glanced at Margaret's dangling foot before disappearing. Jensen chatted casually with the old man as they waited, oblivious of the burden in his arms. Margaret stayed as still as she could, not wanting to draw any more attention to her undignified situation.

When the old woman came back, she held out a large frond with something wet and dripping wrapped in it. Jensen let Margaret down so that her feet skimmed the ground, keeping her clamped to his iron hard side with one arm while he dug in his pocket for change with his free hand. Margaret gasped as the injured foot grazed his leg.

Jensen shot her a look of pure disgust. "Exactly so," he snapped. He thrust the frond packet into her hands and swung her up into his arms once more. His hold was distinctly hostile as he strode off toward the dock and Margaret considered herself fortunate that he hadn't simply slung her over one shoulder.

"What on earth is this for?" she asked, braving his mood.

"That, Miss Belleweather, will help to keep your foot from swelling to the size of an elephant's," Jensen said tartly.

"Oh."

At the dock, Jensen fairly flung her into the waiting gig and then, because the sailor who'd rowed them ashore wasn't there, he took up the oars himself. Margaret pretended to look elsewhere even as her gaze was drawn to the sight of his heavy-biceped arms pulling strongly at the oars. The sheer mechanical perfection of his rowing action reminded her of engines she'd seen used to lay railroad track, except that Jensen, being composed of flesh, roused her admiration where a mere machine did not.

When the gig was alongside the *Java*, the thing Margaret had feared most happened. Jensen picked her up and without preamble, threw her over his shoulder. She grunted as the air was driven from her body and she found herself nearly face to face with the very posterior that had excited such interest in her before.

"Put . . . me . . . down," Margaret gasped.

"Would you care to attempt the ladder unaided, Miss Belleweather?" Jensen's muffled voice came from above and behind her.

The blood rushing to her head made a reply impossible and she knew by his tone that the question was merely rhetorical anyway. He stepped lightly onto the ladder and ascended without further comment. Margaret was thoroughly dizzy by the time they reached the deck.

"Here, here! What's gone wrong then?" she heard Dogsmeat calling out.

"She got stung by a spiny anemone," Jensen snapped, making for the quarterdeck without pausing.

"Are you all right then, miss?"

Margaret groaned inwardly as the dwarf put his face near hers and trotted alongside. Certainly not! she wanted to say—this stupid excuse for a man has me upside down! But she had a feeling Jensen might simply drop her on her head if she voiced such thoughts so she clamped her mouth shut.

Jensen bounded up the quarterdeck steps and then down through the companionway into the main saloon, making Margaret's head bounce. At last he stopped. Margaret made a preliminary wriggle with an eye to freeing herself but Jensen forestalled her by turning around abruptly. Margaret's head soared out and then slammed against his rib cage when he stopped.

Enough! Please stop, she thought, but the whirling lights inside her brain kept the words from reaching her lips.

"Dogsmeat! Rain water for the hip bath!"

"Aye, sir!"

Margaret heard Dogsmeat pattering away and her head went flying again as Jensen turned and headed aft to his own cabin. He bent forward and released his hold across her knees without warning and she slithered downward. He caught her under the armpits at the last minute so that her feet hung inches above the deck as she stared up at him through white spots of dizziness.

Her nostrils were suddenly deprived of the rich, masculine odor of sweat and soap which had emanated from his back and she watched a trickle of moisture wend its way down his cheek. She was acutely aware of his thumbs pressing against the sides of her breasts and felt the steadiness of his breathing compared with her own jerky inhalations.

"Oblige me by putting your good foot to the ground," Jensen said irritably.

It took Margaret several heartbeats to make sense of his words and then she wrested free of his grip, stumbling backward.

"Ouch!"

"Don't put your weight on the bad one, you silly woman," Jensen snapped, reaching out to steady her.

Margaret had already lifted the injured foot but the damage was done. Tears of pain sprang to her eyes. "This hurts quite enough as it is—I don't need any additional abuse from you," she said in a trembling voice.

"For God's sakes, don't get weepy," Jensen said. "If you'd listened to the boy, you'd have known not to step on that damn thing."

"I couldn't understand what he was saying," Margaret protested, fighting back more tears.

"Then you had no business going in the water." Jensen

71

planted his hands on his hips and Margaret tried hard to ignore the way it broadened his already imposing presence. His dark brows drew together in annoyance as he scanned her costume. "I think it's time you admitted you can't get out of that dress by yourself, don't you?"

Margaret lifted her chin. "Even supposing that were the case, it's hardly your business whether I can or I can't."

Jensen cracked a crooked, decidedly unfriendly smile. "That doesn't work, you know."

"What doesn't work?" Margaret asked suspiciously.

"Looking down your nose at me. You only end up looking down at my navel, don't you? Do my nether regions have some fascination for you, Miss Belleweather?"

"Oh! What arrogance! I've never met a man who possessed such an undeservedly high opinion of himself," Margaret declared indignantly.

"Your acquaintance with men being extensive, I suppose?" Jensen raised a mocking eyebrow.

"The extent of my experience is quite sufficient to allow me to make such a judgement," Margaret said haughtily.

"Fortunately for you," Jensen said, moving around her, "my experience with women is even more extensive."

Margaret felt his fingers at the nape of her neck and then the loosening of the hooks and eyes there. "Stop that!" she cried, pulling away.

Jensen gripped the neckline of her dress, immobilizing her. "Stand still," he snapped. "You're soaked to the skin with salt water and if you stay in this getup you'll develop sores."

Margaret clutched at her dress. "If I do, then I shall be the one to live with the consequences. It needn't concern you." She felt his fingers working their way down her back and gave a sideways twist to interrupt their progress.

"Would that that were true," Jensen said, following her motion without difficulty.

Margaret felt her bodice loosening further. "Oh, do stop!"

"Very well." Margaret breathed a sigh of relief as the relentless fingers stopped. "And when you've chafed

72

yourself to a fare-thee-well, let me know. By then you'll be glad to have me strip you naked and apply salve to every inch of your wretched carcass."

Margaret craned around to look at Jensen's face. He didn't seem to be joking. He also didn't seem to be taking any special pleasure in her agitation either, and that more than anything convinced her that he was merely stating a fact. She bit her lip and turned away.

Jensen took that as her answer and briskly resumed unfastening the dress. "You are to be congratulated for believing me for once," he said.

Every instinct told Margaret she should make him stop, no matter the price, but common sense won the battle. Her skin already felt raw as a result of wearing the dress for so many days, and the dunking would just make things worse. Oh, and a bath! Margaret closed her eyes in blissful contemplation and only opened them again when she felt Jensen's hands move below her waist.

"Thank you," she said, pulling away. "I can manage the rest."

"One thing you will learn about me," Jensen said as his hands doggedly pursued the fasteners down the curve of her lower back, "is that I'm thorough. In fact, most women consider it one of my charming characteristics."

Margaret hopped around on one foot to face him. "Charm! You have all the charm of a . . . of a . . . a mongoose!" she spat.

Jensen grinned, baring dazzling white teeth. "A mongoose, eh? Then that would make you the viper. How apt."

Margaret spluttered but could think of no stinging retort. She thought of Christian—only for his sake would she put up with this man's rudeness. But as she looked into Jensen's eyes, she knew that what was between them had already gone beyond mere business.

"If memory serves," Jensen said, seeming to enjoy the confusion on her face, "you have at least three more layers on beneath that dress. Why don't you turn around like a good girl and let me finish the job?"

"I'm willing to bet you pulled the wings off flies as a child and enjoyed it mightily," Margaret said with feeling.

"Still do," Jensen said. He glanced toward the door behind her. "Ah, Dogsmeat—don't forget the good soap. Our passenger hasn't bathed in a while. She'll need it."

"You're insufferable," Margaret exclaimed. "I hope you meet with someone bigger and nastier than yourself one day and find out what it's like to be tormented by someone who holds all the cards." She was seized with horror the instant she said it.

Jensen's smile disappeared and his jaw tightened. "As you undoubtedly recall, I've already had that privilege, Miss Belleweather. In fact, my stepmother was a self-righteous prude just like you."

Margaret saw the unmistakable gleam of pure hatred in the depths of Jensen's eyes and wanted fervently to dissociate herself from it. "I am *not* a self-righteous prude!"

"Then turn around and let me get on with the job," Jensen growled.

Margaret continued to stare into his eyes, feeling exactly like a viper facing a mongoose, but a small, toothless viper. Jensen's dark, heavy brows descended as he narrowed his eyes. All the well-reasoned arguments about how any woman would object to being undressed by a strange man died in her throat. Margaret slowly turned around.

Without another word, Jensen pulled her dress away from her shoulders and efficiently stripped it down to the deck. Margaret reluctantly braced her hand on Jensen's shoulder as she put her weight on her injured foot to step over it. The feel of the finely corded muscle beneath her fingers made her hand burn even more than her foot.

Margaret wished desperately that she had dispensed with wearing a corset in Singapore like many other European women had. Instead, she had to stand next to the pathetic remains of her dress and work her outer chemise over her head. Whatever Jensen was thinking as he watched her, he mercifully kept to himself.

74

When her corset was exposed, he nimbly unlaced it. His fingers were as practiced as Eliza's, Margaret thought, and his intimation that he had helped many women out of their clothes did nothing to reassure her. She had never so much as shaken a man's hand without gloves on before now. She shut her eyes to try and block out the sensation of having only one layer of thin, wet cotton left between her skin and a man's fingers. Margaret kept a stranglehold on the front of her corset as it slowly came apart in the back.

Richard felt her whole body quivering under his touch. Did she know, did she even suspect, that what she was feeling wasn't entirely indignation? He'd gentled too many women beneath his hands to mistake the signs. She'd stood surprisingly still when he pulled the sickly lavender dress down, and even now she didn't move. Had she ever known the touch of a man who could make a woman glad she had been born female? From her utter stillness he concluded that she hadn't, was only just now experiencing those first stirrings.

The fine chemise clung to skin of purest, palest marble. Only the clear outline of her backbone jutting through the fabric marred the perfection. He traced his finger lightly over the vertebrae and then up a shoulder blade as fragile as a bird's wing. The fine down of gold hair at the base of her neck drew his fingers there, and he felt a tightness in his belly as loose tendrils of her hair glanced over the back of his hand.

"Mr. Jensen?" The inquiry was tentative, almost a whisper. Richard recalled himself with an effort.

"I'm done," he said. He stepped around to face her and the rest of his words caught in his chest.

The deep purple of her eyes glowed in a wide frame of lashes tipped with gold, and her painfully thin cheeks were flushed pink. What a beauty she must have been! There was a drowsing femininity there still, a slumbering promise in the startled mouth, too soft and full for the small, pointed face. A man would have to make love to her with great care or she would surely shatter in his hands.

"Why did you touch me like that?" she asked softly.

75

Richard stared at her. She had ripened unbelievably at the merest hint of his touch and the knowledge kindled a hunger deep in his gut. He knew what he would do even as an inner voice cursed him for his stupidity.

He reached out and sketched the outline of her chin with the tip of his finger. Her eyes opened a fraction wider as he tipped her face up and bent toward her. A gossamer pulse rippled beneath his finger as he slowly brushed her lips with his. The fluttering increased as he moved with infinite care to the center of her mouth. He saw her lashes drop, and the sight of pale blue veins in the paper-thin lids aroused a tender heat in his chest.

Richard closed his eyes and let his lips rest on hers, barely touching them. There was neither art nor artifice in her response—she had not thought to close her lips and the soft, quick rush of her breath fanned his mouth. Her inexperience was like a gift, and it kept his desire in check even as he sensed the potential for passion in the volcanic stillness of her body. He shuddered and pulled back, unable to plunder the innocence.

She opened her eyes and he saw the cloudy mists of arousal there. She blinked slowly, as if she had just stirred from a deep sleep. The flush on her cheeks deepened and Richard fought the urge to fold her in his arms and tell her that what she felt was good and right. How could he pretend to understand what she felt when he had never undergone the kind of delicate awakening that had set her aglow?

Richard turned away, remembering his own first experience. He'd gotten drunk in a dockside tavern and then followed the other apprentices to a whorehouse. The women had surrounded him, stroking him as he grinned back, foolishly pleased by their assurances that they'd never seen a handsomer apprentice. His fellows had slapped him on the back and proposed auctioning him off to the highest bidder. The suggestion to reverse the usual practice produced peals of laughter from the whores but Richard never did pay for their services that night. The next day he only vaguely remembered the rest, the white limbs wrapping around him and the explosive burst of pleasure that nearly took off his liquor-heavy head. Disgust shot through him—a far cry indeed from what he saw on Margaret Belleweather's face.

He spun around again. "Get yourself cleaned up," he snapped, "and when you're done, come into the saloon."

She turned away, but not before he saw the puzzled, almost hurt look come in her eyes. Damn her! He ignored the gut-rotten feeling in his innards.

"Dogsmeat!"

"Aye, Captain?" The dwarf appeared at a run, panting.

"Get her a shirt from the slop chest!"

"Aye, Captain!"

"And see that you fetch her another dress—one she can get into and out of by herself!"

"Right away, sir!"

Jensen strode out of the cabin with Dogsmeat right behind him, and Margaret slumped to the edge of the berth. The solid lump that had formed in her throat began to dissolve, and she stifled a sob. How could she have responded to a man who was so lost to all decency, and under such circumstances?

The Reverend Childers had been right. There was a dark, unwholesome streak of sensuality in her nature. Margaret clutched her trembling hands in her lap and felt the hot, wet tears dropping on them. Now she had her proof—Richard Jensen's touch was like a flash-fire.

Chapter 6

Margaret chewed on her lip as she surveyed the results of her effort to sketch the town of Demjang. The gimballed lantern hung steady above the table, illuminating her work and reaching into the far corners of the saloon. It touched the highly polished mahogany woodwork and the oil paintings in gilded frames, all of which made Richard Jensen's lair seem more like the master's study at Pensleigh than the refuge of a seagoing scoundrel.

Margaret stared unseeing at the pen and ink sketch. He might be a scoundrel but he wasn't indiscriminate in his choice of women. Soaking in his cabin in the hip bath filled with tepid rainwater, she'd been honest enough to admit to herself that his look of disgust after he'd kissed her had had more to do with her tears than the fear that she was wanton.

She hadn't bothered to look in a mirror in many months but Richard Jensen had held up a miror of a different kind. Seeing herself through his eyes had reminded her of what she'd worked so hard to avoid thinking about. She was ugly. To be wanted, however briefly, made the truth that much harder to live with.

Margaret shifted to ease the discomfort where bones pressed flesh onto hard wood. Her foot she kept fixed in the deep bowl of water, steeping in the poultice Jensen had made from the old woman's remedy.

"Have you been taking quinine?"

Jensen's sudden question startled Margaret.

"No. Why?"

"Everyone on my ship takes it, that's why." He pushed aside the papers he'd been working on and rose. He reached into a cabinet and pulled out a multitiered box much like her sewing kit at home. He extracted a bottle and studied her critically.

"You can have it in water but I recommend wine," he said, snapping the box shut again.

Margaret flinched. "I would prefer not to take it at all."

Jensen's lips thinned. "Unless you'd like to add malaria to your list of ailments, you will. Dogsmeat!"

The dwarf arrived so quickly that Margaret knew he must have been sitting at the top of the companionway. "Yes, sir?"

"Give this to Miss Belleweather in some wine. Make sure she takes the same amount every day from now on."

Dogsmeat crossed the saloon and poured wine from a decanter not three feet from where Jensen stood. Margaret couldn't help reflecting that no matter how much Richard Jensen disdained the upper classes, he certainly expected to be waited on like an aristocrat.

Dogsmeat winked at Margaret as he handed her the wine. "Tastes awful, miss, but better than gettin' tropical fever."

Margaret shuddered as she drained the glass. It was without doubt the bitterest taste that had ever passed her lips. Dogsmeat took the glass and disappeared up the steps again, back into the night. Bursts of laughter and song came from above and Margaret wished she could walk well enough to go up on deck. The carefree sounds of the men contrasted sharply with the tense, coiled presence of their captain. Daniels and Dekker had joined them for dinner, and they had complimented Margaret on the outfit she had devised for herself by separating the skirt from another of her dresses and improvising a waistband. Dogsmeat had brought her a shirt to wear with it.

"We keep things on board for those of the men as don't come back from shore in fit condition, the apprentices

79

mainly. They take their money and spend it on drink, or gamble it away. Why, one came back aboard one time the same way his mother first saw him."

"Some of those boys are not above twelve years of age!" Margaret exclaimed. "What can Captain Jensen be thinking of to allow them to behave in such a manner?"

Dogsmeat looked at her in puzzlement. "They're old enough to do the work of a man, miss. If they can hoist a sail or tail a line, what business is it of his what they do ashore?"

His bewilderment was so genuine that Margaret didn't argue the point. Clearly, life at sea was very different from what she was used to. Let young boys drink and gamble but make sure they all stayed healthy by dosing them with quinine. It didn't make sense.

Another thing that puzzled her were the children's toys in Jensen's cabin. A faded kite hung on the wall and painted blocks filled a disintegrating string bag. Apart from those items, his cabin reflected the man, spare and blunt. She felt sure the *Java* had been fitted with the elegant hip bath before he bought her. Margaret began sketching again.

Richard watched her at her work, one brow raised as she steadily applied pen to paper, appraising her efforts. Such intensity! How could one so absorbed in her own doings be wandering around inside him, gently probing, touching the emptiness and filling it as she went?

She glanced up as if sensing his gaze. "Would you satisfy my curiosity on one point?" she asked.

A wary look came over his face. "And what is that?"

"Why did you get the old woman's folk remedy for my foot if you're so modern as to know about and use quinine?"

"That old woman's folk remedy has worked since time immemorial," he said, relaxing against the chair back. "Don't make the mistake of thinking that western man has all the answers. Besides," he added, "nature usually provides a cure for the afflictions she causes and one's not usually too far away from the other. Take a woman, for instance. The affliction is her mouth. That's at one end. The cure is at the other."

Margaret regarded him coldly. "Do you take pleasure in baiting me, Mr. Jensen?" she asked. "I've started to think so."

Richard noted an angry snap in her eyes that gave the lie to her calm response. "Yes, as a matter of fact, I do."

"Perhaps we can set a certain time each day during which you can say all the outrageous things that occur to you, and I will oblige you by huffing and puffing, or doing whatever it is that you find so entertaining in return. The rest of the time we could simply act normally."

Now that was the kind of answer he liked—not so painfully polite—but he carefully kept his expression bland. "I don't like schedules. In this part of the world, they live on 'jam karet'—rubber time. Thing's happen when they happen. That's the way I like it."

"Yes, that's all too clear."

"Don't despair, Miss Belleweather. The idea was not without merit. You'll just have to save it for some tame lap dog of a man, not me."

"No, you fancy yourself a mastiff, I imagine, or a bull terrier."

Richard felt a surge of anger and turned it into lazy indifference. "I can't be bothered to imagine myself as anything other than I am."

Instead of replying, Margaret began putting her sketching materials away in her portable desk. Richard watched the careful deliberation in her motions. He'd have bet money the routine never varied. He was distracted by the sound of the gig scraping alongside and recalled the last chiming of the ship's clock. It was after ten o'clock— that had better be the last of the crew.

He let his gaze rest on Margaret again. The sun was turning her skin a pale honey and a sprinkling of freckles had appeared across the bridge of her painfully sharp nose. They made her look younger, more vulnerable, and the newly washed hair tied back in a simple ribbon added to the impression. Despite a high color in her cheeks, she seemed more subdued tonight. Too much sun, the sting which could leave one dizzy and vague in the head for days—she was holding up remarkably well, he decided, considering.

Although the night had cooled the air, laying at anchor was always hotter than being under way. Most of the men would sleep up on deck tonight. Richard was just contemplating doing the same himself when Margaret spoke.

"My shoes!" she exclaimed. "I left them on the shore."

"They'll be there tomorrow," Richard replied mildly. "No Sumatran would dream of taking what doesn't belong to him. Europeans could learn a thing or two from them if they weren't so mired in thinking of them as backward."

Margaret lifted a shaky hand to her forehead. "I sense you're baiting me again but I'm afraid I'm not up to debating the issue."

Richard saw the weakness in her arms as she tried to push back from the table. He paused only for an instant before rising.

"Let me see your foot," he said.

She drew back her skirt ever so slightly and he saw that the fragile ankle was twice the size it should have been, and the slender foot an angry pink. She looked up at him with those extraordinary gentian eyes and he saw the tiredness there. He sternly resisted tenderness as he picked her up.

"You can sleep in my cabin tonight," he said briskly.

Instead of protesting as he'd thought she would, she let her head fall against his shoulder.

"Why your cabin?" she asked, her voice soft with fatigue.

Richard countered the answering softness in himself with pointed words. "Wits are not the prerogative of the well-to-do, Miss Belleweather. Kindly allow me the dignity of using mine."

"Yes, of course," she said.

The words died away into his shoulder.

"You'll be cooler there," he said, feeling the need to

explain after all.

In his cabin, away from the main deck, it was quiet and dark. Her body slipped pliantly onto the berth and he caught a faint whiff of violets. He was just thinking how appropriate it was when he remembered that he'd once bought some floral soaps for Emma. Dogsmeat must have given Margaret one of them to use. It took away the pleasure.

He looked down at her. The sheen of her gold hair caught the light coming through the door to the saloon. She seemed to be sleeping already—well, another night in her clothes wouldn't hurt her. He was damned if he'd undress her twice in one day. He was just about to turn and leave when she spoke up sleepily.

"To whom do the toys belong?"

Richard froze. Only Dogsmeat entered his cabin and he knew better than to bring the subject up. Margaret's eyes had fluttered open and the deep, dark, irises captured the light. The guileless look on her face wrenched at something in him.

"They were for a little boy."

"Your son?"

"No!" It came out more sharply than he'd meant it to. "Just a . . . a friend's son. I never got a chance to give them to him."

Suddenly he wanted to tell her about Jack, how he'd struck a chord that still quivered deep within. He saw her lids drop and heard a settling sigh. He walked to the porthole opposite.

"I loved him very much." He spoke so softly that the water lapping the ship below nearly effaced his voice. "I wish I knew where he was now."

The pain was as fresh as if it had happened only yesterday. Richard braced his arm against the frame of the porthole. His chest ached with wondering what Jack had thought, what Emma had told him. Gradually the hurt went away, whipped on by the brutal truth—that nothing he did now could change what had happened.

Richard straightened. He wasn't sure if he'd meant for

Margaret Belleweather to hear him or not. He heard her breathing, deep and even, and he suddenly felt foolish standing in the darkness talking to no one.

Harkay manned the helm, his smooth brown face expressionless, while Jensen scanned the horizon, his feet planted far apart and his arms crossed over his chest. They'd set sail early that morning after taking on water and supplies, and the *Java* had fairly cracked along all day. Margaret let the wind carry her spirits higher, the way it lifted the sails, snapping and shivering above. She felt wonderful after a good night's sleep, brought on with unexpected suddenness by the wine she'd drunk.

When did Richard Jensen ever sleep? When the *Java* was underway he left the quarterdeck only for meals, and then last night he'd given her his own berth, but there'd been no evidence in her cabin that he'd slept there instead. Margaret stole a covert glance in his direction. His skin was like well-cared-for leather, a sleek, rich brown, and his blue-black hair had the luster of hard coal. Except for the fact that he hadn't bothered to shave that morning, he looked as refreshed as a man who had spent a solid eight hours in bed. When it came to stamina and resilience, Jensen was clearly a man apart.

Margaret leaned on the rail, watching the breath-taking beauty of Java slip by. It was like being a spectator at a play where the stage moved past the audience. As they neared Batavia, the *Java* pulled back, slowing in deference to the thickening stream of other ships. Margaret began to discern details in the extravagant explosion of green on land—majestic loco palms, forests of bananas, sparkling streams feeding down to the sea. It was a scene so immodestly prodigal as to make Eden look barren.

When they reached Batavia, it seemed only a paltry interruption in the almost shocking opulence of Java, even though it boasted a large, imposing fortress and the waters flowing down from the mountains had been reined into canals reminiscent of Holland. The *Java* slipped into the harbor, daintily picking her way through prahus and barques, steamers and coastal tramps, an aristocrat among lesser vessels. Margaret scanned the squat warehouses surrounding the harbor as she heard the fierce chatter of the anchor chain being paid out.

"I don't much bother with the city," Jensen announced at her elbow.

Margaret glanced up. Would she ever get used to the soft-footed stealth with which he moved?

His long eyes narrowed and a moue of distaste flickered across his face.

"Customs already," he said flatly. Margaret followed his gaze and saw an official in white standing in an approaching gig. "He'll take his time and find nothing, as usual."

"Do they search every ship?"

He gave a dismissive shake of his head. "The Dutch have it in their heads that I run guns and spread sedition in their happy little colony."

"Do you?" Margaret asked.

He turned a gimlet-eyed look on her. "No, Miss Belleweather, I don't. There was a time when I first came to the East when I might have. I beggared myself to buy the *Java* and then I did what I had to do to lay my hands on money to refit her."

"So are you saying you did or you didn't?"

"Did or didn't what?" he asked with a mocking smile.

Margaret realized he didn't intend to answer her question and turned back to the gig drawing alongside.

"I started to say that I have as little to do with the city as possible," Jensen went on. "However, there's an area you should see, an area where the paternalistic Dutch haven't managed to subdue some of the more exotic variations of Javanese culture. I'll take you there if you like."

Margaret wanted to ask if it had some bearing on her search for Christian but his gaze flickered toward the activity at the top of the ladder amidships. The pinpricks of light in his eyes hardened into active dislike.

"Yes, please," she said hastily, sensing him absenting

himself from the subject at hand. "I will await your convenience."

He jerked his attention away from the white-suited figure coming on deck. "Until later," he said with a sharp nod.

The *Java*'s cargo was searched so exhaustively that they had to take a break at midday. The Dutch official made heavy conversation as Dogsmeat served them a meal on the *Java*'s signature blue-and-white china.

"You are an exception to the rule, Captain Jensen," the official said, raising a snifter of cognac and sipping appreciatively. "This meal was most excellent."

"To what rule do you refer?" Margaret asked politely.

"There is a saying that God sends the sailors but the devil sends the cook," he answered.

"The devil sends all my men, cook and sailors alike," Jensen replied curtly.

The Dutch agent looked taken aback but recovered quickly. "Ah, a joke, of course. Nevertheless, I do not think I care to ask whether the duty was paid on this brandy in case I shall not like the answer."

The Dutch official could find nothing which had not been declared in full and as he took his leave, he looked somewhat disappointed. Jensen watched him being rowed away before disappearing below deck. When he reappeared a short time later, Margaret was sure she detected a gleam of satisfaction in his eyes.

"The devil sends customs agents, too," he muttered, "but not very good ones in the case of the Dutch. Come on—let's go."

Soon afterward, she found herself riding in a small carriage with Richard Jensen through the streets of Batavia. Their progress was greatly impeded by bullock carts and throngs of Javanese as they left the old Dutch city. At last they stopped and Margaret alit stiffly with Jensen's aid.

He paid the driver as Margaret watched a rheumatic Hindu fakir busily rolling a tired little peeping chicken back into the form of an egg for the entertainment of a small group gathered on the corner. Margaret laughed as he produced a blinking toad from the beard of an astonished bystander.

"I never heard you laugh before," Jensen said.

Margaret turned to catch a curious look on his face. "I laugh quite often in the usual course of events," she said.

"Just not with me," he said with an appraising look.

"You haven't said much that was terribly amusing so far," Margaret pointed out.

"Quite right," Jensen said. "I can be terribly amusing at times, though."

"As well as thorough," Margaret replied, ensnared by the peculiar look on his face.

"Oh, yes, very thorough." Jensen smiled a secretive little smile as his lids dropped down to half shutter his eyes.

"Only just not with me," she said. Dark, impious thoughts raced through her mind. She was sorry she'd parried with his own riposte.

"Would you want me to be 'thorough' with you?" Jensen asked softly. "I wouldn't have thought so, little Margaret."

Margaret quivered. It was the first time he'd addressed her by her given name. "I should reprimand you for being familiar."

"Should you?" Jensen's tone said that he wouldn't care if she did.

The last rays of the dying sun limned his scar, touching it with gold above the black stubble on his cheeks. She stared at him, encased in his presence like a reed in winter ice. For all she knew, they might be in Kowloon or Rangoon or even, she thought with a frantic giggle at her own agitated rhymes, the far side of the moon.

"I've said something to amuse you at last?" Jensen asked, his breath whispering over her.

Cold reason asserted itself. "No." Margaret turned and slowly began walking. There was a looseness in her limbs, a melting heat that hadn't been there a minute before. She fanned herself breathlessly as Jensen fell into step beside

87

her. Talk about something else, she thought distractedly, anything else. "You said there was something I should see here. What is it?"

Jensen stopped and took both her elbows. "Tonight is in the nature of a small test. It's easy to *say* you can accept whatever your brother has become, especially if you have no idea just what kinds of things human beings do in the pursuit of . . ."

His eyes darkened as they bored into hers, searching, it seemed, for some kind of an answer. She felt the heat returning. Unable to maintain eye contact, she let her gaze wander down his cheek to the demarcation where bronze skin ended and blue-shadowed skin began.

"What human beings do in the pursuit of . . . ?" she prompted.

"You have no idea what I'm talking about, do you?" he said in a low, urgent voice.

"I'm twenty-three years old, Mr. Jensen. If there are things I don't know about, then perhaps it's time I learned."

"Very well," he said, abruptly letting go of her arms. "Let's go find out just how open-minded you really are."

He led the way down the street, past market stalls emptying after a day of business. Twilight fell as they passed narrow houses with iron-barred windows. Inside she could see the unmistakable silhouettes of naked females. Margaret tamped down an uneasy frisson as she remembered the same kinds of places in Singapore, areas where Christian's pictures had sparked glimmers of recognition.

At last Jensen stopped in front of a large, creaking pavilion.

"This is your last chance, Miss Belleweather."

"I'm quite prepared for whatever is inside," Margaret replied with asperity.

At first she could see nothing to be shocked by. It was so dim that she had to strain to see three feet in front of her and barely registered the fact that Jensen was being asked to give over any knives or pistols he might be carrying. He held out his hands, palms up, and they passed on. Clove-scented smoke drifted over a confusing jumble of tables which buzzed with the chink of dice and the ripple of cards. At one table an obese Chinaman threw slender sticks as onlookers fingered piles of money. Their glazed eyes followed the game slowly, and Margaret smelled the sweet aroma of the East, the opium which kissed all its users into a torpor.

Jensen ferried her through the crowd and she was pressed up against him by the heedless blunderings of those with too much liquor on their breath. She distinctly felt the outline of a gun at his waist and was momentarily comforted by it. Action at a gaming table caught his eye, and he propelled her toward it. Walnut-skinned men looked up as he joined them, their eyes bright with avarice.

Margaret stood by resentfully as cards were dealt out—if he thought she hadn't seen gambling before, he was sadly mistaken. Jensen lit a cheroot with elaborate care before he picked up his hand. Poker—a game of percentages and averages, Margaret thought—and she was drawn into it, remembering games played with her father. Jensen's languid manner lulled the other players and Margaret felt a cautious thrill as he played each hand with precision and daring.

Some time later, a discordant clanging impinged on her awareness. Like alarm bells disguised as music, it distracted her from the game. Turning to see the source, she realized that her knees and hips ached badly from standing still so long. When there was a break in the play at the table, she reached out and touched Jensen's shoulder.

"Oh, you!" he said. He shrugged and made some apology in Malay to the other gamblers. He gathered the money in front of him and shoved it into his pocket as he stood up.

"Let's go."

"Where?" Margaret demanded, annoyed that he had so

obviously forgotten her before.

"You'll see," Jensen replied cryptically as he took her elbow.

The Malay men in the pavilion were short but they still topped Margaret by several inches. Not until they broached the edge of the crowd did she see the dancing girls whirling and flashing on a stage at the center of the room. Silky black hair cascaded down their backs, swinging with the clanging music that had no rhythm. Jensen thrust her down on a rickety chair.

"Watch and learn," he said tauntingly in her ear.

Mouths wet and red as roses, shimmering golden skin, bright teasing eyes, slender supple limbs—Margaret had never seen such unparalleled beauty. Had Christian fallen in love with some exotic dancing girl? Was that Jensen's point in bringing her here? She turned to ask him but he was gone. She felt a stab of panic. Apart from the dancing girls, she was the only woman in the pavilion.

Margaret wove her fingers together in her lap. If Jensen had been unwilling to give up his gun, what kind of danger must there be in here? Hot sparks of fear clutched at her. Perhaps he would forget her again, simply go back to the *Java* or the gaming table and not remember where she was until tomorrow morning. Anger turned the tide. Curse Jensen's rotten soul! A gentleman *never* left a lady unaccompanied in public.

Therein lay the heart of the matter, Margaret thought— Richard Jensen was no gentleman. She forced herself to concentrate on the dancers, watching them through a haze of fury as they rolled their hips and ogled the customers. Truly, they were beautiful creatures, but why did they have to expose their flesh so shamelessly? It made her feel embarrassed for them.

"Figured it out yet?"

Richard Jensen was back at her elbow, nonchalantly sipping a drink.

"How dare you leave me alone?" she cried.

"I dare a lot," Jensen said smoothly. "Don't you like the dancers?"

He had the look of a wolf carrying a lamb in its mouth and Margaret shivered, knowing she had more to fear from this man than all the others in the room put together.

"They're very beautiful," she said stiffly.

"Christian probably liked them, too."

"And what is that supposed to mean?" Margaret demanded.

"They're sister-boys," Jensen drawled. "Men."

Margaret looked closer. Dear God! It couldn't be, but it was! Jensen's odious voice was at her ear again, insistent with its unwelcome message.

"Don't you know that some men prefer other men in their beds?" he asked. "Christian's one of them, you know."

Cold ripples of disbelief snaked through Margaret. Flashes of bright, shimmering Christian, gilt hair and crystal eyes, flew past—Christian linking arms with the stable boys, Christian home for a holiday, tangled in the sheets with a friend, laughing. The indignant roil of thoughts coalesced into one shapeless, doughy lump. She clawed her way to the surface, sticky and gasping for breath.

"No—not Christian! He's decent and kind and . . . and . . ."

"Poor Margaret," Jensen murmured, his eyes cool. "If you believed me, would your love for him lie bleeding?" He jerked his head toward the stage, and Margaret followed his gaze numbly. "I'm not saying he's like one of those, but didn't you say it didn't matter what he was?"

Margaret rose and fled into the crowd, away from the mocking voice and the awful clarity of truth cloaked until this moment. She blundered into man after man, panic and her obdurate joints making her lurch and reel as hideously as a drunk. Somehow she found the street and began running as fast as she could. The smell of strange night-blooming flowers mixed with the smells of lechery and opium in the darkened streets. Black-eyed creatures thronged the roadway, laughing and talking, their bright eyes widening with surprise as she darted past.

91

"Margaret! Wait!"

Margaret hurried on, turning a deaf ear to the black-haired devil pursuing her through the sinister streets. It was an awful dream from which she prayed she would soon wake.

A hard fist seized her arm and she spun around. "Let me go!" she cried. There was no doubt in her mind that it was Richard Jensen. Of all the unknown, unfamiliar elements in this nightmare, he was the one known.

"Stop being an idiot," he snarled. The ragged voice had that same commanding intensity he used to order his crew about. "Open your eyes! There's a carriage here."

Margaret opened her eyes. Jensen's face was up close to hers, his lips drawn back in a fierce scowl. He looked like the devil incarnate with his long narrow eyes gleaming in the moonlight. Beyond him was a trap drawn by a small Javanese horse. She pushed Jensen aside and leapt into the seat. Before he could raise his foot to step in, she seized the driver's whip and laid it across the horse's back. It leaped forward and careened off down the street.

Once at the docks, Margaret could not see the *Java*'s gig waterside. She sat on a stanchion shivering with misery. Pinpricks of light from the ships riding at anchor danced on the water like fireflies, multiplied by her tears. She could see the *Java* and she desperately wanted to be back on board where it was safe and normal. Hysteria nearly turned her tears to laughter. What a thought!

Jensen arrived, furious. "Little fool!" he hissed. "Do you want to get yourself killed?" Margaret glared at him. Why wouldn't he leave her alone?

"Did the nasty man say something you didn't want to hear?" he jeered. Without waiting for an answer he turned and let out a piercing whistle. They waited in silence, and soon Margaret heard the scrape of oarlocks and a boat shussing over the water. They returned to the *Java* without a word being spoken. Jensen turned a cold, hard profile to her, a muscle jumping in his unshaven jaw.

The glassy water around the gig created a dual world, stars above, stars below. In her mind, Margaret resisted visions of a parallel illusion—sweet, gentle Christian mirrored, not by faithful replicas, but by silky-limbed sister-boys. Her brother was not the same as other men. All the facts fit together, and she didn't want them to.

On deck, Harkay steadied the ladder as she stubbornly climbed it on her own. They were barely aboard when a sliver of moon caught in his eye, blanking out humanness in a wink. He collapsed to the deck twitching, his muscles skittering beneath the skin. Margaret forgot her own problems as she watched in horror.

"Quick! The paddle!" Jensen cried.

Someone thrust a wooden blade into his hand. He straddled the huge man's quivering chest and pushed the paddle between his teeth. Others wrestled the convulsing limbs to stillness. At last the fit subsided and Jensen gently withdrew the paddle from the now slack mouth. Another long moment passed in silence and then Harkay blinked. He stared at the sailors around him, some withdrawn to rest on their knees, the others standing.

"Again?" he asked plaintively.

Sore though her heart was with its own pain, Margaret couldn't help but feel sorry for him. Harkay looked child-like in his fright and apathy.

"Yes," said Jensen, "but it's over. Won't be another for awhile now. You can take a woman next port and not be worried."

It must have been an old joke between them. Harkay staggered to his feet, a pale smile on his big blubbery face.

"Good. Couldn't find one before."

Jensen laughed, a little hollowly Margaret thought. He gave Harkay a brotherly slap before heading aft. By the time Margaret reached the saloon, Jensen had already poured a drink.

"What happened up there? What's wrong with Harkay?" she demanded.

Jensen drained off his glass and regarded her narrowly as he refilled it. "Nothing like a little morbid curiosity," he said. "Who knows? What's wrong with any of us? It doesn't get better and it doesn't get worse."

"He should be seen by a doctor!"

"Oh, the doctors saw him all right, the island doctors. Convinced his family he's cursed by evil spirits. Said that's where he got his size and strength, too, so his people tossed him out."

"That's not fair," Margaret said indignantly. "He obviously can't help it."

"Can't he? His people would say he's got a weak character or the evil spirits couldn't have gotten in. We're all misfits here—me, Dogsmeat, Harkay—we don't fit in anywhere else but we fit in here just fine. Your brother's a misfit, too—that's why he got booted out of the old ancestral pile, isn't it?"

"*I* didn't make him leave!" Margaret declared. "I would never have made him leave."

"But now that you know the truth, you won't love him any more, will you? You'll turn tail and run for home."

"No! No, I won't! He's my brother and I'll never give up on him!"

Chapter 7

Anjer, prettiest town on the Straits of Sunda or anywhere else for that matter, thought Richard Jensen. A score of kampongs stretched away from the town where white buildings peeped from behind the coconut palms that fringed the shore. He pushed the unruly hair back out of his eyes. He'd stop and check for telegrams before threading the passage between Java and Sumatra. Not that there were likely to *be* any telegrams—it was just an excuse to go into town and escape from Miss Margaret Belleweather for a while.

Lord, but she was a proud one! They could boil her bones when she died and use the soup to starch a man's shirt collar. She'd find that rakehell of a brother and drag him back to England just to spite an American captain who'd gotten under her skin. He'd never met anyone like her. He didn't like it either, for as sure as he was that he'd gotten under *her* skin, she'd gotten under his too. It was a queer sensation—a prickling awareness that made it impossible to ever forget she was on his ship.

She was walking the deck with Daniels at that moment. Daniels was preening like a peacock, his curls ruffling in the breeze. His cheeks were flushed a brighter red than usual and his perpetually babyish face was lit up in a smile at something Margaret Belleweather had said.

What a deceptively fragile-looking creature she was. Richard turned and leaned back on the rail on his elbows in order to watch them. There was a fundamental core of honesty and loyalty in her that, despite all her other shortcomings, made him like her. And that, he conceded frankly, scared the hell out of him. Even after last night, blaming him for being the bearer of bad tidings, she hadn't turned on him the way he'd expected her to.

She'd made her declaration of loyalty to her brother and then walked slowly across the saloon. Curiously clear-eyed after her storm of weeping on the quay, she'd looked at him at last.

"Precisely why did you take me to that place tonight?" she asked.

Richard kept his face averted. Why had he? In retrospect it had been petty, a hurtful way to expose her to facts he could just as easily have explained to her.

"I shouldn't have done it," he said abruptly. "I should have just sat you down and told you." He paused. "Only maybe then you wouldn't have believed me."

Margaret stared down at the back of the bench and drew one finger along its highly polished surface. "Maybe I wouldn't have," she said. She looked up at him again, her huge eyes dark and unfathomable. "Your motives may have been questionable but you accomplished what you set out to do. You have put me in possession of facts I did not fully know or appreciate before. I suppose I should thank you for it."

Richard felt faintly nauseous. How could she be grateful to him for what had been patent cruelty on his part? "I liked it better when you were screaming at me," he said.

She regarded him solemnly. "I daresay it's easier to defend one's behavior when the other party is being completely unreasonable." A tremor passed through her and she shrugged it off. "I've been thinking about what you said—about people being unacceptable when they differ from the usual. I never understood what my brother could have done that would be so heinous as to make my father send his only son to the other side of the world. My father was a good man, a reasonable man, but he refused to

96

even talk about why he'd sent Christian away. I speculated of course—an unsuitable woman, overspending, gambling, drunkenness. Nothing I knew about Christian supported any of those conclusions. But this . . ."

She hesitated, staring sightlessly at a point somewhere just beyond him. Straightening her shoulders, she drew her gaze up to meet his again. "I never had an inkling, not until tonight anyway, but as soon as you said it, I knew it was true."

Richard clenched his hands at his sides. Had she truly come to calm acceptance so quickly? "He won't change, you know, no matter how much is at stake."

"I'll have to accept your word for that," she said with a hint of resignation. "Clearly, you know a great deal more about . . . about the ways of the world than I do. However, I love my brother. I'm prepared to accept Christian as he is."

Richard felt a faint stirring in his heart. It was a stiff, creaky feeling, like the opening of a door rusted shut from long disuse. The yearning of a man to be loved unreservedly by a woman, he thought shakily. He poured a drink with unsteady hands, aware of her unwavering gaze.

The whiskey had roared hot and raw down his throat.

"She's running better with a bit o'ballast in her, ain't she, Captain?"

Richard came back to the white glare of afternoon sun with a jolt. Dogsmeat stood beside him, watching Margaret Belleweather with a proprietary eye.

"What the devil are you talking about?"

"Miss Belleweather, sir. She's got some bottom to her now, what with all the good food she's putting away. Moves better, smootherlike."

Richard narrowed his eyes. It was true. She *did* seem to have lost some of her lameness, and with it, some of the hauteur that had set his nerves on edge. He turned his attention to the harbor. Dekker had things well in hand and Richard felt his tension draining away. He realized he'd been holding himself rigid all the time he'd been watching Margaret Belleweather. She was under his skin a great deal too much.

Fascinated by the picture-pretty town in front of her, Margaret allowed Richard Jensen to hand her ashore without the same trepidation she had felt in Demjang. The strong, brown forearms didn't seem so threatening now that she had a better acquaintance with their owner. She wandered along the dock, hoping her surroundings would divert her from the troubled thoughts that had kept her awake for much of the night.

When she found Christian, *if* she found Christian, there was no way to predict what the outcome might be. He had always been happy at Pensleigh but she knew his years away at school had been torturous. Knowing how much he loved their home had made her goal a simple one. Now she was not so sure. What changes had he been through? Could returning to Pensleigh still be the panacea it had once been?

Wrestling with such imponderables had reduced her to sleeplessness. Now she let herself release all worry and immersed herself in the glory of Java's beauty. Brilliant green foliage hung against the backdrop of a shimmering blue sky, and the cry of exotic birds lifted her spirits.

Richard Jensen caught up with her a few minutes later.

"You'll have to shift for yourself today," he said curtly as he passed her. "I've got my own plans."

Margaret gritted her teeth. He had been short-tempered all morning, but even at his best, he had a way of irritating her with the simplest of pronouncements.

"Very well," she said tartly. "I trust I can safely go about without your escort. In fact, I may be better off without it."

Jensen pivoted sharply. "Meaning?"

"Nothing," Margaret said quickly, dismayed by the hostility on his face.

"Jensen! Hoy, Jensen!"

A large, bearded man hailed them from the door of a wooden building. Richard Jensen's face lit up with pleasure.

"Bursey!" he bellowed back. "How did you know I'd be looking for you?"

"Don't you always?" The big man waited until they reached him and then thumped Jensen on the back. It was a bruising slap that would have made another man stumble but Jensen merely grinned and returned the favor.

"I heard you had a female in tow," Bursey said, turning a pair of sun-crinkled eyes in Margaret's direction. "Begging your pardon, ma'am, but it's part of my job to know who's where and what's what in this part of the world."

"Then your sources have failed you in only one regard," she replied. "I'm a 'miss,' not a 'ma'am.'"

"Hmm," Bursey said with mock severity, "so he's not done the right by you. My wife will have something to say about that."

Margaret opened her mouth to deny the implication that she had an intimate relationship with Richard Jensen but he forestalled her.

"Miss Belleweather is a passenger on the *Java*, Bursey, nothing more."

Although she herself had been about to say the same thing, Margaret felt curiously let down by the flat characterization.

"Well, I'm Ezekiel Bursey and I'm pleased to make your acquaintance anyway, Miss Belleweather, though when this pirate started taking on passengers, I'd like to know," he added with a wink.

"It's just a business arrangement," Jensen muttered.

Bursey ignored him. "Now that we've got *that* sorted out, I hope you don't mind, Miss Belleweather, but my wife made me promise that I'd bring you to her for a visit."

"I'd be happy to meet her," Margaret replied. She let herself be led off up a long, shady avenue and disregarded the two men as they fell into a hushed conversation. Towering coconut palms lined their route and a cool breeze played over her. She marveled at the plants around her, plants which would have required the tenderest of greenhouse care in England but thrived with abandon here.

"Mr. Bursey! Whatever kept you so long?"

Margaret looked up to see a sweet-faced woman regarding the bearded man with a loving smile. She stepped from the shelter of a gate and Bursey dropped a kiss on her cheek.

"I was telling this rogue about the problem in Ben Coolen and enlisting his aid to get the supplies there," Bursey said jovially, "but I have carried out my sworn duty to you, my love. Here is Miss Belleweather. She's a passenger on the *Java*," he added pointedly.

His wife advanced with a smile. "I'm Mora Bursey," she said warmly, her flat American accent more pronounced than either of the men's. "I'm so glad you didn't mind being kidnapped for the afternoon."

Margaret took Mora Bursey's hand and smiled. "I shouldn't think this meets the definition of being kidnapped," she said. She glanced around at the lush green gardens surrounding a white house. Shouts of children at play came from behind it.

Mora Bursey followed her gaze. "I'm afraid I have no special entertainment to offer you. It's just the children and me, as usual, but perhaps you'd like a cup of tea? I didn't realize you were English. When I heard that Richard had a woman on board I just naturally assumed you were . . ."

She trailed off self-consciously. What had she been about to say? His wife? An American?

"A cup of tea would be lovely, Mrs. Bursey," Margaret said.

"Please, call me Mora," the other woman said gratefully.

"Of course, and you must call me Margaret."

"Well," Jensen spoke up, "I think I'll be off to see if there are any telegrams for me."

"Me, too," Bursey added quickly.

"Shoo then—off with the both of you," Mora Bursey said. "I'm keeping Miss Belleweather for the afternoon, and I'll have no flim flam from either of you about an early tide. We'll see you both here for dinner."

100

The two men started back down the hill like boys released from servitude, and Mora Bursey laughed. "Getting telegrams indeed! I don't expect you know it, but around here that's a thinly veiled disguise to drink the afternoon away."

"What a very odd bit of cant," Margaret said as they walked up the pathway together. "How did picking up telegrams come to be synonymous with getting drunk?"

"Oh, dear," Mora laughed, "I've given you the wrong impression. It's just that the local Lloyd's agent runs a small hotel and bar and that's where the telegraph office is. It's really the hub of our social life—all the ship's captains congregate there."

"Is your husband a captain then?"

"No, he's a pilot. Anjer Loc is where all the ships stop to pick up a pilot before making their way through the straits, at least from this end." They reached the veranda and Mora Bursey gestured toward a seat. "Our tea should be here in a minute."

"I expect I should visit the hotel before the day is over," Margaret said. "There's someone I'm looking for and that would seem a likely place to find news of his whereabouts."

"That's very possible, especially if he's been a passenger on board a ship recently. We tend to hear all that sort of news—it's how I learned you were on board the *Java*."

"It seems everyone from Singapore to Australia must know. I *had* cherished the notion that I could sail on the *Java* without anyone being the wiser."

Mora Bursey smiled with a disarming candor that Margaret was powerless to resist. "There are too few Europeans in this part of the world for such an interesting bit of news to go unremarked. You mustn't take it personally though—any newcomer is bound to arouse our curiosity."

"I suppose that's natural enough," Margaret said. It was impossible to take offense when one's hostess was so full of good cheer.

Mora gestured to the panorama of the bay below, with

hundreds of white sails on fishermen's proas and other craft reflected on the water. "I love to sit and just watch the comings and goings of the boats. Then at the end of the day, Ezekiel comes and tells me what it is I've been watching all day—names, destinations, cargoes, that kind of thing. It's so different here than where I grew up."

Margaret couldn't help glancing at the white native jacket Mora wore over a sarong-style floor length skirt. Her hostess noticed and reacted with a chuckle.

"That's the least of my eccentricities," she said. "I guess I've gotten a little strange in the head living here," Mora added, but she didn't appear to be worried by it. A servant brought a tray and Mora began pouring tea. "Ezekiel is steady as a rock—he'd be the same anywhere, but I've given in to the charm of the place. You will too, if you're out here long enough. Unless, of course," she added, handing Margaret a cup of tea, "you plan to spend most of your time in Singapore."

"I must admit, the sarong looks much more comfortable for this climate. I've arrived at a sort of modified costume myself." Margaret plucked at the white shirt from the slop chest. It was soft and loose, but far too big. "I had a friend who told me that all the men in the East were so desperate for the company of a European woman that I should be careful to pack nothing but high-necked dresses."

Mora Bursey threw back her head and laughed. "Oh, yes, I've heard that one—something along the lines of them being so hard-up that they'd ogle a nun."

Margaret laughed self-consciously. It was exactly what Lucy had said. A sobering thought struck her—no man so far had seemed desperate enough to ogle *her*, and that certainly included Richard Jensen. She could still vividly recall the grimace on his face when he had pulled away from her in his cabin.

"I hope I didn't offend you," Mora Bursey said. "You've gone awfully quiet."

"Oh, no, no, not at all," Margaret said, snapping back to their conversation. "I was just . . . thinking."

"I was going to say, about your going down to the hotel

102

to inquire after . . ."

"My brother," Margaret supplied.

"Your brother, then. Does Richard know you're looking for him?"

"Yes," Margaret said. "It's the whole purpose of my trip."

"Then I'm sure he'll make inquiries for you," Mora said brightly. "He's the sort of man who'll do a kindness whenever he can."

Margaret choked on the tea she'd been about to swallow. "I'm sorry," she said when she'd recovered, "but the Richard Jensen I know doesn't fit that description."

"I know Richard gives the appearance of being uncaring," Mora replied, "and if I didn't know better, I'd probably believe he was." She set her cup aside. "He tries so hard to play the rogue that I think he's succeeded in convincing even himself that he's a hardened case."

"Everything in my experience suggest that he is," Margaret remarked.

"That's too bad," Mora replied. She seemed genuinely distressed. "He's a man with a very loving heart. You only have to watch him with the children to know that. I must admit, Ezekiel and I have always held out hope that he would eventually find a woman who saw through his pretense."

"Well, he'll have to change his manner a great deal before any woman dares to get close enough to find the heart of gold you seem to think lies within," Margaret said with feeling.

"Either that or he'll have to meet a woman who's uncommonly perceptive," Mora said with a sideways glance at Margaret. "Richard's never had a woman aboard the *Java* before and I must admit, I was hoping when I heard you were on board that you might be that woman."

"Hardly," Margaret said. "Mr. Jensen is, in general, rude beyond belief. My only wish with regard to him is that he keep a civil tongue in his head and allow me to continue my search for my brother."

Mora Bursey sighed. "He must have been on his worst

behavior with you. He really can be a stinker when he sets out to be." She settled back and put her feet on a wicker settee. "It must be wonderful to sail on the *Java* anyway. It has to be one of the most beautiful clippers I've ever seen." She directed a searching look at Margaret. "I've often envied the wives of captains, going off to sail the seas with the man they love."

Margaret controlled her amusement with an effort. Mora Bursey's oblique attempt to make sailing on the *Java* with Richard Jensen seem romantic wasn't very subtle. "I imagine that it *would* be a lovely life if one didn't value a floor which stays still under one, and a bath each morning."

"Nothing redeeming at all in the experience?" Mora asked wistfully.

"Well, not nothing precisely," Margaret admitted, "only just not Richard Jensen's company."

"I'm sorry to hear that," Mora said, "really I am. I take it you like the islands then?"

Margaret gratefully accepted her hostess's tacit opening to change the subject. They talked for some time about the sights Margaret had seen, and the special magic that seemed to pervade the islands. "Of course, once I find my brother, I'm sure I'll enjoy them even more," Margaret said at last.

"I'm sure he'll turn up," Mora assured her. "Many a young man has come out here and decided to go a bit 'native' for a while. They get it out of their systems and then they're glad to return to the fold."

"That's exactly what I've been hoping," Margaret exclaimed. "It's such a weight off my chest to hear you say so."

"Mind you, some of them calm down, get a bit more respectable again, but they decide they'd still rather live out here."

Margaret felt an inexpressible lightness. "But that would be fine with me! As long as he's healthy and happy, that's all I care about. I'd even be happy to stay myself, if he wanted me to, and keep house for him."

"That's very noble of you," Mora said a bit dubiously, "but don't you want to have your own home—get married and start a family, I mean?"

Some of Margaret's happiness evaporated. The lengthening rays of the sun cast their shadows deep into her soul. "That's something I will have to forego," she said carefully. "I was very ill before I came out and one of the results is that I can never bear children."

"Oh, dear," Mora Bursey said. "And you would have liked to have them, wouldn't you?"

"Very much," Margaret said quietly. "However, I really do think that without looks or the ability to bear children, I'd have to be regarded as a poor candidate for marriage."

"Have you allowed for the possibility of a man falling in love with you for yourself?" Mora asked with a teasing note in her voice.

"Oh, that thought has crossed my mind," Margaret replied, trying to match Mora's light tone, "but under the circumstances, I don't think I could ever be sure that a proposal wasn't motivated by love of my fortune. Rather than take that chance, I've simply set aside any thoughts of marriage."

"There is one bright spot," Mora said. "Your health must be improving for you to have made the trip out here, and to be doing so well on the *Java*. You might be surprised at how much you continue to improve."

"It would be nice if I did," Margaret murmured in response to Mora's flagrant attempt at kindness.

"No, you think I'm humoring you, but I'm not. You're really quite pretty as it is. I don't think it would take much at all for a man to fall in love with you."

"Now that is *too* blatant an attempt to salve my feelings," Margaret sputtered, laughing out loud, "but it feels good to hear it said anyway!"

"There, that's better!" Mora declared. "Enough gloom and doom. I'm going to find the girl and have her bring the evening drinks—the men should be back soon, and besides, we deserve something stronger than tea after all the work we've done this afternoon."

What a funny woman! Margaret wished she had half of Mora Bursey's optimism and vivacity. No doubt Richard Jensen found her amusing, too, and took the trouble to behave decently toward her. That was the only possible explanation for her high opinion of him, either that or the tropical climate had affected her judgment.

At that moment, the *Java*'s captain appeared quietly from out of the shadows at the end of the veranda. How long had he been there? Margaret wondered, and how much had he heard? To admit her vanity to Mora was one thing, but to have him know was another. It was altogether too personal a conversation for her to be comfortable with the idea of him hearing it.

Margaret watched warily as he stopped at the foot of the stairs, but he merely tipped his cap with a lazy grin, giving no indication that he'd heard anything he shouldn't.

"Good evening. Where's Mora?"

"She's just gone to fetch a servant," Margaret replied. She could hear the soft slap of Mora's sandals coming back.

"Evening, Mora," he said when she appeared with a small lantern for the table. "Mind if I visit with the children?"

Mora looked startled. "Goodness, you took me by surprise! Where's Ezekiel?"

"He stopped at the office to check tomorrow's schedule. He shouldn't be too far behind me."

"Oh, good. Girls! Uncle Richard is here to see you," she called.

There were shrieks and two small girls rounded the corner at top speed.

"Uncle Richard! Uncle Richard!"

Margaret watched dumbfounded as he stooped down with open arms to await them. They rushed into his arms and nearly bowled him over. He laughed, a deep, rich sound that spilled out over the garden, and caressed their fair heads with every indication that he was as glad to see them as they were to see him.

"How are you Sarah?" he chuckled, "and Emily! You're

106

nearly as tall as your sister already!"

Emily basked in his attention as the older girl gave him a kiss.

"Your face hurts my lips," Sarah declared. "You promised you'd take away your whiskers the next time you came to see us."

"And I will—next time—I swear it," he laughed. "I just forgot this time. And besides, you still haven't explained why it is that my whiskers bother you but your daddy's don't."

"Because you don't have a real beard," Emily said as she rubbed his cheek with one chubby hand. "Your whiskers feel like the pig's bristles."

Margaret had to stifle a laugh. The infamous captain of the *Java* being likened to a pig! Richard Jensen merely smiled.

"Is that so?"

"*I* think it makes you look like a pirate," Sarah said. She nuzzled his cheek unselfconsciously.

"Would you like to see our new pig?" Emily asked. "He's in a pen at the back of the garden."

"He's very nice," Sarah added hopefully, "the nicest one we've ever had."

"Then of course I want to see him." Jensen uncoiled his lean frame and offered a hand to each of the girls. "Of course, I'm counting on you to protect me from him. I'm a little afraid of pigs, you know."

"Oh, Uncle Richard!" Sarah snuggled his hand to her cheek as she smiled up at him. "You're the silliest grown-up I know."

"Ah! There's a secret about that," he said, letting himself be led off. "You see, I'm not really a grown-up. I'm just the largest child it's ever been your privilege to . . ."

Their voices faded away as the dying sun silhouetted them, the broad-shouldered man with a small child skipping at either side. Margaret turned back to see an 'I-told-you-so' look on Mora Bursey's face.

"Ahoy the house!"

"Ezekiel!" Mora turned with such a look of gladness at the sound of her husband's voice that Margaret was seized for a moment by an unreasoning jealousy. The pilot made his way to the veranda and settled in a chair as his wife pulled a foot stool nearer for him.

"The children have spirited Richard away as usual," she said, "which means we'll have a little peace and quiet for a while. Tell me all the news."

"Let's see, most of it's in there," her husband said as he set aside a copy of the *Java Bode*, "but you can read that tomorrow, my love." He withdrew a pipe from his vest and began tamping tobacco into a pipe. "As for the rest, I think the most interesting is that Richard seems to think very highly of his passenger—says she's quite a lady." He aimed a sly look in Margaret's direction.

"I'm glad he knows one when he meets one," Mora declared. "Goodness knows he's had little enough contact with real ladies since we've known him."

Bursey let out a guffaw as Mora clapped a hand over her mouth. "That's putting the fat into the fire, my love."

"I'm sorry," Mora said to Margaret, her face flushed pink. "I know you have no attachment to Richard but that was still very indiscreet of me."

"I gather there are a few things about him that you neglected to tell me," Margaret said, highly entertained.

Bursey chuckled. "If rumor is to be trusted, my friend never lacks for female company," he said. "Unfortunately, they're not the type one would marry, even supposing he were the marrying kind. I daresay my wife has told you he never takes his females aboard the *Java*, though. That's why when we heard you were on board, we just naturally thought you'd been the one to make him mend his ways."

Mora Bursey went an even brighter shade of pink. "Please, Ezekiel, I think you've said quite enough."

"Ah, mustn't stand on ceremony, my dear. Miss Belleweather is grown up enough to know that a man must be a man. The fact is," he said conspiratorially, "our Richard attracts women like honey attracts bees. Not a madam from Canton to Perth doesn't welcome him into her house."

"Ezekiel!"

"Now, now, my love—I haven't even mentioned the Balinese dancing girl," the pilot demurred.

"You've said quite enough," Mora admonished him.

"Very well," he said chuckling, "but there's no harm in a red-blooded man doing as he pleases before marriage."

"None at all," his wife agreed, "but it's not a fit subject for discussion here and now. What will Margaret think of us?"

"Actually, I find it enormously interesting," Margaret interjected. "In fact, it all fits in nicely with the fact that I first heard Richard Jensen's name in a brothel."

Mora's eyes widened. "You . . . *you* went into a . . . a . . ."

"Brothel," Margaret supplied. "I must say, it wasn't pleasant, but it did yield the information I needed."

"You see, my dear? What did I tell you?" Ezekiel Bursey chortled. "Richard said Miss Belleweather was uncommonly plucky."

"But still, a . . . a brothel?" Mora's fascination was clearly at war with her sense of propriety. "Why?"

"I was seeking information about my brother," Margaret said calmly. "I kept up my search until it yielded results." It seemed easier in retrospect and her words came out easily. "I'll stop at nothing to find him."

"You may not find it easy," said a deep, familiar voice behind her.

Margaret whirled around. "I do wish you'd stop doing that!" she snapped at Jensen. "Why? What have you heard?"

"He's apparently up in the Atjeh region now," he replied, moving around to join them at the table. He turned to Mora as if that subject was closed. "The nurse took the children in for supper."

Bursey cleared his throat. "There's been a lot of unrest up in Atjeh, Miss Belleweather. The Dutch never really have had control up there and the local warlords are making a push to throw them out entirely."

"But I needn't concern myself with that," Margaret said impatiently. "We've nothing to do with the Dutch. If that's where my brother is, then that's where I'm going."

"You'll have to do it without me," Richard Jensen remarked as he took a drink from the tray a servant had set down on the table.

"What?" Margaret couldn't believe her ears. "You know where my brother is and yet you refuse to take me to him?"

Jensen tossed back his drink before answering. "That's right. We had a deal—I go where I see fit and I don't see fit to go there. I've traded there before but it's too dangerous now."

Margaret's ire edged up a notch. "I see! The fearless, the proud, Captain Jensen can't stand the heat!"

Jensen rose, his face grim. "We have to be going now," he said smoothly to the Burseys.

"I don't believe you can be so cowardly!" Margaret cried, jumping to her feet.

Richard Jensen took her arm and forcibly turned her away from the awestruck gazes of their hosts. "I'll explain it all to you later. In the meantime, I'm sure we're boring the Burseys since this subject is well known to them." He threw a taut smile in their direction. "I'm sorry we can't stay for dinner but, as you can see, Miss Belleweather is too distressed by this piece of bad news."

Margaret tried to pull away as Jensen wrestled her down the steps. "Take your hands off me!"

"Get control of yourself or I'll do worse!" he growled under his breath. They were on the path now, moving toward the road.

"I mean it!" Margaret retorted. "I'll kick you if you don't let go of me at once!"

"What's that?" Jensen said loudly. "You had a lovely time?" He hustled her along as he yelled back over his shoulder, "Miss Belleweather enjoyed her visit and says she hopes we can call on you again on our way back to Singapore."

"See you at first light then, Richard!" Ezekiel called out.

"You're hurting me! Let go!" Margaret insisted,

struggling ineffectually against his hold as they passed through the gate.

"When we're far enough away and you stop fighting me," Jensen retorted.

"I've gone too far with you already!" Margaret snapped. She angled herself away and tried without success to direct a sharp kick at his shins.

"I'll make you sorry if you land one," Jensen muttered, propelling her along even more forcefully.

"You bastard!" she hissed.

Richard Jensen broke stride at last. "Well," he said, yanking her around to face him by the gas lights along the avenue, "I wondered how long it would take for your prim facade to crack. Not long at all, as it turns out."

His eyes glittered dangerously but Margaret didn't care. "I won't allow you to treat me like one of your strumpets," she said, glaring up at him defiantly.

For a minute she feared she had made him even angrier, but then his mouth twitched. The next thing she knew, he had thrown back his head and was roaring with laughter, the perfect arch of his white teeth exposed to her view. He dropped her arm and stumbled away, helpless with laughter.

"Really, you have the most indecent sense of humor!" Margaret cried, remembering the scene on the *Java* when Harkay had attacked John. She rubbed her aching arm as he struggled to regain control.

Wiping tears from the corner of his eyes, he finally said, "Sometimes you're almost worth all the trouble you cause."

Margaret nursed her indignation in silence.

"Come on," he said, holding out his hand, "we've got things to talk about."

Margaret marched past him, her head held high. "We have absolutely nothing to discuss," she snapped, "except how I'm going to get back to Singapore and find a ship that *will* take me to Atjeh."

"If the *Java*'s not going there, it's unlikely anyone else is," he replied, "but I might be going there."

111

Margaret stopped abruptly. "What?"

Jensen ambled past her, his hands thrust into his pockets. "I said, I may be going there. I just didn't want to tip my hand."

"What you really mean is that you wanted to infuriate me by suggesting you wouldn't go when all along you meant to!" Margaret said hotly as she rushed after him.

Jensen didn't even glance down as she rejoined him. "Hardly," he said. "Fits of pique don't interest me one way or another. No, I just didn't want to talk about it in front of Bursey."

Margaret peered up at him, trying to see his expression under the thatch of hair that had fallen forward on his forehead. "Whyever not?"

"Because, Miss Belleweather, he may be an American but he works at the pleasure of the Dutch. It wouldn't be fair to put him in the position of knowing things he'd be better off not knowing."

Margaret was now thoroughly confused. "I don't understand."

"It's very simple," he said in a patronizing voice that made her grit her teeth. "See if you can follow along. There's a war going on up there. The Dutch think I run guns. I show up there. The Dutch ask Bursey why he didn't warn them I was going there so they could stop me and he says I told him I was just taking you there on a humanitarian mission. The Dutch call him six kinds of fool and relieve him of his license to pilot in the Sunda Straits."

"But . . . I mean, what if you're *not* running guns?"

"Come, come—it's a *war*, Miss Belleweather, pure and simple, and all that matters is that the Dutch *think* I'm running guns."

Margaret had to admit it made sense but it left her anger nowhere to go. They walked along in silence.

They were almost to the docks when Jensen began chuckling again. "My strumpets," he said. "That's rich."

112

Chapter 8

Margaret Belleweather was on deck before dawn the next morning. A long night of sleeplessness had left her vulnerable to unmanageable thoughts, or perhaps it was the other way round. Did Richard Jensen mean to take her to Atjeh? And if he did, would it be for the best? Curious that after coming so far and waiting for so long she could be almost within reach of her goal and not be sure it was what she wanted.

The ambivalence had plagued her all night, that and the conviction that Richard Jensen knew more about Christian than he was saying. She prided herself on having a precise, logical mind, the result of a sound education and natural inclination. It unsettled her all the more, then, that she couldn't seem to think clearly about things now, or make a decision she didn't immediately start to question.

The East was a world apart, and while part of her felt stimulated by the new challenges, another part felt off-balance, out of touch. The freshening breeze lifted the loose shirt from her skin. Beneath the delicate pastel shades of the dawn sky, she almost felt she could fly away, never to be seen again. Only the firm reality of the *Java*'s wooden rail beneath her fingers kept her from completely giving way to the feeling.

Apprentices shuffled around on deck, coughing and muttering as they shook the sleep from their bones. The galley hummed with activity and as the men appeared, plates were handed out. The smell of food tantalized her, and she approached the door.

A small, swarthy man glanced up and grinned at her as if she came to his galley for meals every day.

"You want food?"

"Please," Margaret said hesitantly, "if it wouldn't be too much trouble."

"Trouble?" His brow creased in perplexity and he wrinkled the thick, dark mustache which dominated the lower half of his face. "You want food? No food?"

"Food," Margaret said firmly.

"Food!" He grinned again and ladled a dish high with eggs and rice, adding fruit to one side. "Fresh," he said proudly, "good for lady."

Margaret laughed. "Yes, thank you."

"Ton-ee like see lady on *Java*." He bowed low, nearly scraping the tiled floor of the galley with the long-handled ladle in his hand.

Margaret dropped a little curtsey. "Lady like Ton-ee food," she replied, feeling a shade silly.

Margaret turned to see a half-dozen apprentices grinning at her, and she smiled back sheepishly. Who would have ever pictured Miss Margaret Belleweather of Pensleigh Hall queuing for breakfast with a bunch of deckhands on a clipper anchored off Java?

A gangly boy with a neck like a chicken's caught up with her as she made her way back to the rail. "You forgot a spoon, miss."

She took it with a smile and began eating. As she chewed, the pale blue-and-pink sky whitened. In a matter of minutes the sun appeared in the east, a blurred silhouette of burnished gold that vaulted over the horizon with astonishing swiftness. The grandeur of it made her feel tiny, but not unhappily so, as if she were a small but significant piece in a larger design. She suddenly felt easier in her mind—why shouldn't she be here? She belonged as surely as any of God's creatures.

Bursey arrived on the heels of the sunrise and the men

114

weighed anchor. He and Richard Jensen stood the quarterdeck together as the *Java* began negotiating the straits. Margaret mounted the steps to the quarterdeck to enjoy the view from there, greeting the pilot when he tipped his cap to her.

"Good morning, Mr. Bursey, and how is your wife?"

"Very well, Miss Belleweather. She sends you her greetings."

"I've got something I wish you'd give her," Margaret said. She handed him a makeshift envelope.

Jensen's mouth tightened as he watched it change hands. Seeing his mistrust, Margaret said, "Open it, Mr. Bursey, please."

Ezekiel Bursey carefully pried the outer paper away, revealing a pen and ink sketch of the Bursey children tumbling with Richard Jensen in the garden. His face lit up as he studied the drawing.

"Why, that's marvelous! That's really marvelous!" he exclaimed. "That's Sarah and Emily to a tee, and *this* rascal—why, no one who hasn't seen him like this would credit it!"

Margaret smiled. During the long night hours, she'd taken refuge in sketching. It wasn't nearly as good as he made it out to be, but she'd hoped it would give the Burseys some pleasure to have and perhaps signal to Mora that her message about Richard Jensen had not fallen on deaf ears.

"I'm glad you like it," she said. "Maybe you should hang it in the pilots' office so everyone can see that the *Java*'s captain isn't without some humanity."

Richard Jensen took it from the pilot and after looking at it for a long moment, he frowned and handed it back without comment.

"Thank you," Bursey said, beaming at her, "but if you don't mind, I believe we'll give this a place of honor in our home."

"Of course," Margaret said. "It's yours to do with as you wish."

She walked a few paces away, leaving the men to keep

115

their attention on steering a safe course as they passed Thwart-the-way Island, a massive, uninhabitable rock useful only as a landmark. She let her mind wander as Sumatra slipped by on their right and Java on their left, so close at times that she could hear parrots shrieking in the jungle.

A small boat set out from shore, making its way precariously under an unwieldy load. It set a course to intercept the *Java*, and Jensen scowled as he waved it off. Margaret strained to see its cargo, curious about the cages resting atop yams, coconuts, woven mats, and shells.

"What do the cages contain?" she asked.

"Birds," Jensen answered shortly, "trapped in the inland forests."

"What do they mean to do with them?"

"Sell them to us, if we're so ill-advised as to stop," he muttered.

"Why ill-advised?" Margaret asked.

"These waters are notorious for foul play," he said, never taking his eyes off the small craft. "They may be harmless enough, but then again, they could be pirates."

"Oh," Margaret said, a little let down, "I was hoping to see the birds."

"Mora's got a soft spot for birds, too," Bursey said. "She's been after me to bring home a good singer."

Jensen turned a black look on both of them. "So you want to find out the hard way if the little thugs in this particular boat can be trusted?"

"Of course not, Richard," Bursey said. "I'm your pilot and I can't in good conscience tell you to stop, especially as it's strictly a personal matter that I would be tending to."

"Don't get all official with me," Jensen grumbled. "All right, we'll stop, but you'd better get Mora a good one because this will be the only time I stop. And no other ship's captain would be fool enough take the risk for you," he added darkly.

Margaret could hardly contain her delight when the cages were passed up on deck. She and Ezekiel Bursey carefully studied each bird before deciding they all looked healthy. Such colors, and such delicate markings! Bursey told her they were sparrows, but compared to their drab English cousins, these birds were a wonder to the eye.

The pilot chose a mating pair and dickered with the small boy who'd been sent up to conduct the negotiations while his elders stood grinning in the boat below. How appropriate, Margaret thought, that Bursey would choose a pair, a reflection of himself and Mora. And that Richard Jensen had only agreed to stop once he'd heard that Mora wanted a bird.

Margaret looked at the bright-eyed, lively sparrow she planned to buy. Was it any wonder? Mora was vivacious and feminine, thoroughly charming, while she herself was plain and uninspiring, an English sparrow. Margaret tried to feel resentful but she could not deny that any man, and most definitely Jensen, would be more drawn to Mora than herself. Made unexpectedly sad by the realization, she set aside the cage and gestured the boy away.

"No—thank you," she said, "I've changed my mind."

Richard had been watching the play of expressions on her face.

"What do you mean, you've changed your mind?" he asked. "I only stopped because you wanted one."

"No, you stopped because . . ." Margaret stopped. "I mean, it was very kind of you to stop, but I've realized that I couldn't take it back to England with me when I go."

"I see." Richard eyed her skeptically. Something else was going on here. She'd wanted the bird—he felt sure of it. "I've decided I'll buy one then," he said abruptly.

Margaret's head came up sharply. "You?" she asked. "You don't seem the type to . . ." She trailed off.

"The type to . . . ?"

She stared at him, her huge eyes smudged with shadows beneath them, the overly full mouth soft and uncertain. When had Miss Margaret Belleweather stopped being quite so certain about everything, he wondered. He felt himself unbending toward her.

"The type to . . . ?" he prompted again, more gently this time.

117

"Please, don't mind me. It's most understandable that you should want one. They're lovely."

It was back to polite banality. This time he wasn't playing.

"I have that one," he said to the boy. The boy picked up the cage Margaret had set down after staring at it for so long. Richard flipped the boy a coin after a brief exchange of lies and flattery. "Here," he said to Margaret, "it's yours."

"I'll have to leave it with you when we get back to Singapore," she said hesitantly.

He put the cage in her hands. "We'll worry about that when the time comes."

"Thank you," she said shyly. She lifted the bird to a level with her eyes, and the faraway, regretful look that had been there when she looked at it before had been replaced by something approaching happiness. It made her look almost pretty.

"Now off with you," he said to the boy, "and tell your papa and uncles and brothers not to try hailing the *Java* again just because I've been soft enough to stop today!"

The boy ducked and was gone on a puff of air.

"Well, that's a good day's work," Bursey said. "Thank you kindly, Richard."

Richard made a noncommital sound in his throat. Pictures of him playing with children, buying a tame sparrow for a woman he didn't even like—it reminded him that being soft led down dangerous paths. "I hope that medicine is ready-by when we drop you off," he said to change the subject.

"It'll be waterside, guaranteed," the pilot replied. "If it's cholera, as they're saying, I hope you'll get in and out quick."

"Faster than that boat boy disappeared," Richard retorted. "I won't stick my neck out for a passel of Englishmen living where they have no business being."

Bursey was as good as his word. When they hove to within sight of Java Head, the crate was on the steam tug that came to pick the pilot up.

"See you next time through," Bursey yelled as the tug churned away.

"It'll be a while!"

"Better not be—I make half my living just piloting *you!*"

Richard laughed and set course for Ben Coolen, cheered by the scent of sandalwood as they rounded the headland. Because he associated it with Java Head, it reminded him of the open sea, and that always lifted his spirits. Before too long, the *Java* would pass by here again, heading the opposite direction, bound for Australia. Then she'd fly!

He went below for lunch on the watch change, and found he could even be amused by the silly cooing and clucking Margaret Belleweather was making over the bird. He lingered afterward, enjoying a cheroot and leafing through the newspaper Bursey had brought for him, glancing over at his passenger every now and then as she tempted the bird with tiny bits of bread. At last he quit the saloon and went up on deck to find all was well in his absence.

A fresh wind carried them up the coast to Ben Coolen. They arrived just as the moon was reaching its zenith. No ships were moored in the small harbor, and many more lights than usual burned in the houses. It looked like a fever town.

Margaret pulled her hair back and tried to pin it off her neck more firmly. The hot, breathless air clung to her skin and glued her chemise to her body beneath the heavy layers of her skirt. She leaned over the rail, away from the heat waves rising from the dry, wooden deck, but it continued to scorch through the soles of her shoes as she peered toward the town. There was curiously little activity.

Richard Jensen had appeared on deck at first light, dressed only in a native cloth wrapped tightly around his lean, hard hips. The effect was almost diaperlike, except that the extraordinarily daunting physique in it was so far removed from that of a baby's as to be ludicrous. His hair

119

was tied back in a sailor's pigtail, and his face was set in a mask, the scimitar-shaped scar on his cheek more prominent than usual.

He looked the very figure of a noble savage as he pulled away toward shore, his skin bronze under the tropical sun and his black hair gleaming. The rest of him was as brown as his face, confirming what Margaret had previously only suspected, that he generally dressed in fewer clothes than he'd been wearing while she was on board. He'd ordered the gig lowered and shinned down the rope ladder hand over hand, disdaining the use of the crosspieces. Now the sun was high in the sky and still there was no sign of him returning. She could just make out the gig, floating forlornly off the rocky beach.

"Food?" Margaret turned quickly, startled. Tony held a plate out toward her.

"No," she said, "not just now." She rubbed her stomach and made a face. "Too hot."

"Oh, yes, Ton-ee know." He made an exaggerated fanning gesture and then pointed at the sun with a questioning look.

"Sun, yes," Margaret said. "Too hot to eat."

Tony pantomimed the sun going down. She nodded gratefully. "Yes, then food."

She turned back to the rail. The apprentices were lolling around in the shade of a makeshift shelter, extra canvas stretched from their deckhouse to the rail. Harkay sat stolidly on the capstan, puffing at a pipe that smelled as if it were filled with hemp, while Dekker and Daniels played cards on the quarterdeck. Where *was* Richard Jensen? How long could it take to drop off a crate of medicine? And hadn't Ezekiel Bursey told him not to linger in Ben Coolen? Margaret began to steam from more than the oppressive heat. He was putting himself in danger—he was putting them *all* in danger, for that matter.

Another hour passed, and, egged on by their fellows, the apprentices began diving overboard one by one. Shirts went flying as they gleefully plunged into the water. Margaret was so in sympathy with their desire to cool off that she didn't even mind when pants gave way to ratty looking bits of underwear. Harkay heaved himself to his feet and leaned over the rail, watching them with an indulgent expression. Margaret submerged her worry about Richard Jensen by bringing out her sketch pad and sitting on an overturned cask, drawing the boys.

"Say, not 'alf bad," Dogsmeat said from over her shoulder. "You've got a real gift there, miss."

Margaret smiled. "It helps to distract me from my worries," she said. "That's all it's good for, really." One of the youngest boys leaped to the rail and stood poised for a moment before arching out over the water in a spirited dive. She quickly outlined the streaking form of his descent.

"See! There! That's a far cry from nothing, I say," Dogsmeat said with delight. "Just that quick, you've got 'im!"

Margaret filled in a few details and handed the sheet of paper to him. "Here, have it then." She began making another of all the sleek heads in the water, bobbing up and floating about as easily as otters at play.

"Captain's back!"

Margaret jumped to her feet with a profound sense of relief and saw the boys racing through the water toward the gig.

"Stand off!" Richard Jensen bellowed as he stood up.

Margaret's heart began to beat double time. There *was* contagion!

"Who's had chicken pox?" Jensen yelled.

Margaret stared at him open-mouthed. Chicken pox?

The boys looked at each other in bafflement as they treaded water.

"I've had, Captain," Dogsmeat shouted, "though it were a blurry long time ago."

"Get your carcass to the ladder then. Anyone else?"

Margaret hesitantly raised her hand. "I did."

She saw Jensen's brows draw together in a frown. "I said, anyone else?"

"Dunno, Cap'n," one of the boys muttered.

121

"The lot of 'em together never had one decent mother," Dogsmeat mumbled to Margaret. "Likely as not, none of 'em can remember."

Margaret thought it an odd observation until she realized she remembered the illness clearly only because her mother and nurse had talked about it in years afterward. She saw Daniels and Dekker struggling to recall.

"I'm not sure, Captain," Dekker finally said.

"Me either," admitted Daniels.

"That's just the two of us then, Captain," Dogsmeat shouted.

"C'mon, then, Dogsmeat, and lend a hand. We've got men, women, and children, all too weak to lift a hand for themselves, and the ones that aren't sick are exhausted from tending the others. Fall back, you lads, so I can fetch him."

Dogsmeat started over the rail and down the ladder as the boys paddled away from the advancing gig. Margaret made as if to follow him and was brought up short by Jensen's voice.

"Not you, Miss Belleweather!"

"Why not me?" Margaret demanded indignantly. "If there are sick people, it's my Christian duty to help them."

"Your Christian duty," Jensen snorted. "And then I suppose it'll be *my* Christian duty to dig your grave. No, Miss Belleweather, stay here and draw your pretty pictures. This is serious business."

"Then I suggest you allow me to help," she said imperiously. "I know for a fact that I have been exposed to chicken pox and I can therefore be of some use without endangering myself or anyone else."

Seething with resentment, she angled herself over the edge of the deck and managed to find a rung to support her feet. Not caring whether her skirt rode up as she descended, she found the next rung and the next, anger lending strength to her hands and legs. She heard a scrape and saw the gig disappearing out of the corner of her eye.

"Mr. Jensen, I demand that you wait for me!"

"I give the orders around here, Miss Belleweather. Now go back up. Daniels! Lend her a hand!"

"Aye, sir!"

Margaret heard Daniels' feet thudding across the deck above. Now there was nothing but blueness below her. She contemplated simply dropping into the water and swimming to shore, but she knew her skirt would drag her down.

"Mr. Jensen," she cried, "I've known you to be stubborn before, but never stupid! This is lunacy! Now turn around and come fetch me."

The boys in the water goggled at her as she reached the bottom of the ladder and swung gently to and fro.

"Miss Belleweather, I *order* you to go back up that ladder." The words were grated out, as if between clenched teeth.

Margaret felt a wisp of amusement take hold somewhere inside. "Why, Mr. Jensen," she said coyly, "I don't believe I can. I shall be forced to dangle here until I fall into the water, at which point I will surely drown." She looked over her shoulder to see him scowling up at her, his face dark with temper. "I fear that you will then be deprived of my fare. I do hope you weren't counting on it too heavily for that rerigging you mentioned."

An extremely loud, extremely ungentlemanly oath burst from Richard Jensen. Margaret stifled a giggle and turned her face away. She heard the splash of oars in the water, oars being wielded by a very angry man by the sound of it.

"I hope you're prepared to burn that outfit you're wearing, Miss Belleweather," she heard Jensen say below her, "because everything we're wearing is going to be burned before we come back on board. That's why I risked offending your maidenly eyes with this covering of mine today."

Margaret felt the tops of her ears warming. She hadn't thought about that. It would not do to back down now, though.

"Mr. Daniels?" she called up sweetly.

123

The second officer's face appeared over her. "Yes, miss?"

"Mr. Daniels, would you be so kind as to fetch me . . ." Margaret stopped. If she asked for her only remaining dress, she would require assistance in putting it on before they returned to the *Java*.

"Throw some of the loose cloths from the slop chest into a gunnysack, Mr. Daniels," Jensen said from below, sounding almost congenial now. "Miss Belleweather is about to go native."

Margaret let Dogsmeat lend her a hand as she stepped off the ladder and into the gig. Daniels tossed a sack down and to Margaret's eyes, it contained pitifully little to cover three people. She fervently hoped that he and Jensen would mistake the bright color of her ears for sunburn.

Once they reached shore, all such considerations soon fled from her mind. Jensen had not exaggerated the pitiful condition of the townspeople. There weren't more than thirty households, but all had at least one case of the disease, with many of the rest rapidly sickening. Dogsmeat found a large kettle and began boiling water to make a plain porridge to use as a poultice for the rash.

They worked through the heat of the day without a break, going from house to house, and by midafternoon they had restored some order. The children tore the most at Margaret's heart, crying for their mothers to come to them, but the mothers who had succumbed were much more ill than their children. Margaret had just bathed and helped one such woman to rise so that she could put dry linens on the bed.

"The children," she said fretfully. "I really must go to the children."

"You're not to worry," Margaret said as she straightened the sheets. "Mr. Jensen is seeing to them, and to your husband."

"Oh, thank you," the woman said, subsiding weakly back into bed. "This has been the most dreadful experience. All the servants fled at the first sign of the disease. I shall be so glad to go back to England when our time here is over."

"I'm sure that things will look better when you're feeling stronger," Margaret assured her.

She picked up the glasses and cups left around the sickroom and made her way to the kitchen. It was a rude affair, with a hand pump to bring water into a wet sink that drained onto the ground below the raised cottage. She tidied the best she could and went in search of Richard Jensen.

She found him holding a little boy of about seven, bathing his face and neck with water. Leaning unobserved in the doorway, she marveled at the tender smile on his face as he listened to some long, drawn-out tale the boy was telling.

"And did the dragon ever come back?" he asked.

"Oh, no," the child said earnestly, "I frightened him so that he jumped into the sea. He swam as far away as he could, and he told all the other dragons not to bother coming here either."

"I guess you taught him a lesson he'll never forget," Jensen said approvingly. He glanced up and saw Margaret. "All done?"

"I think so. Would this one like some of Mr. Dogsmeat's special porridge to put on his rash to help make the itching go away?"

The child wrinkled up his nose. "I shouldn't think so," he declared. "I hate porridge!" He thought for a second and added, "Inside *or* out!"

Jensen laughed. "Nothing much wrong with you." He laid the child back on the small cot and rose. "I'll be back later."

"Good. I like you," the child said. "You look like a Sumatran warrior, only a nice one."

"That's exactly what I am," Jensen agreed, "and this woman is my prisoner. She's an English princess."

"Never!" the boy said. He stared at Margaret.

"Yes, she is," Jensen said firmly. "I sailed across the world and brought her back here just because I wanted a woman with purple eyes and yellow hair."

"Wait until I tell my mother!" the boy said. "She always says not to go far from the house or *I'll* get carried away, too."

Margaret wanted to laugh out loud but she checked the desire, not wanting to break the spell. It was hard to tell who was more caught up in the tall tales, the man or the boy.

"Quite right, too," she managed to say. "Oh, sir," she said, "your prisoner is about to faint dead away from the heat in this alien land. May I have your permission to wait outside for you?"

The boy grew even more round-eyed. "She's a good captive, isn't she?"

Jensen laughed out loud. "I'll be out in a minute," he said over his shoulder. "I'll tell you a secret about her," he was saying as she left.

Margaret wandered out and down the rough trail that led back to the beach. She really was terribly hot, and the smell of her clothes after the hours of exertion didn't bear thinking about. Another sleepless night hadn't prepared her for such toil, and fatigue was setting in.

The kettle was simmering untended and she sat down on a crude plank bench nearby and closed her eyes. Though she felt tired to the bone, it was a good feeling. She hadn't felt so useful in over a year, not since before her illness. She smiled as she thought of Richard Jensen, forever sharing secrets with small children. How readily he entered into their world!

"A watched pot isn't supposed to boil, is it?" Jensen's voice came from somewhere in front of her.

Margaret opened her eyes slowly. "I wasn't watching it," she said wearily.

"Feel like going for a swim?" he said affably as he squatted down and added a few small pieces of wood to the fire under the kettle. "You've certainly earned it." He crabbed around as he tended the fire, sitting on his heels as easily as any native.

"I'm all done in, I'm afraid," Margaret replied, "and besides, I haven't anything to . . . well, you know, bathe

126

in." She studied his back, the long, corded muscles drawn tight along his backbone, and the broader ones that bunched along his sides as he rearranged the wood. She could just make out several thin, white lines of scar tissue splayed vertically from his waist nearly to his shoulders. With a sudden shock, she realized they must be the result of a lashing.

Jensen stood up and she jerked her eyes away. "I'll row us around to a little cove I know and then it won't matter," he said. "You'll have to get out of those things sometime anyway."

Margaret eyed him. The idea of going into the water *did* sound wonderful. "What about you?"

"What about me?"

"I mean, where will you be?"

"Where would you like me to be?" he asked, his mouth twitching.

"Well, preferably not watching," Margaret answered.

"If I'm going to watch a naked female, I like it to be one of my strumpets," he said. He was grinning now, his long, narrow eyes gleaming with amusement. She had never seen him look so human. Really, the man did have charm, but she had to disabuse him of certain notions.

"Mr. Jensen," she said firmly, "I have no intention of bathing naked. I will swim in the shirt and my chemise. It should cover me well enough, but I will still expect you to absent yourself from the vicinity."

"Seeing as how the cove is only a tenth the size of this harbor, it's going to be awfully hard for me to 'absent' myself, but you can rest assured that I'm too damn tired to be much interested in looking at you."

For the first time, Margaret noticed the bluish shadows beneath his eyes. And his declaration that he had no interest in looking at her had the ring of truth about it, although she could have wished he had put it more tactfully.

Practicality won out. "Very well." Margaret stood up.

"Sensible woman," he said amiably, "and your coming along today was sensible, too. I'm sure the women appreciated a female nurse."

127

Margaret felt a satisfaction all out of proportion to his words. It was nice to earn his approval for a change, but she wasn't sure it should feel quite *this* nice.

"Captain!" Dogsmeat came trundling down the path toward them. "I have a grand meal going for them up above, and them that hasn't taken sick has undertaken to help me hand it round this evening."

"That's about as much as we can do then," Jensen said. "With a good dinner and a sound night's sleep, they'll be able to cope better tomorrow. I'm just going to row Miss Belleweather around to a cove for a swim. We'll meet you back here later."

"Right-o, Cap'n. Have a lovely swim, miss."

Margaret sighed blissfully as she floated in the water. It was so elemental, so primitive. With the sun on her face and the steady thrum of the surf to lull her, the world and all its problems seemed far away. How glad she was that she hadn't denied herself this pleasure! She let her eyes close as she relaxed into the water's embrace, her unpinned hair floating around her like a mermaid's. Every now and then she opened her eyes to ascertain that Richard Jensen was still sitting on the beach.

She could just make out his lean, brown body, stretched out on the sand. He had been as good as his word, leaving her to undress in private while he swam, making his way to the mouth of the cove and back with strong, smooth strokes. He'd flung himself on the sand afterward, hardly sparing a glance for her. It made her speech about him not looking at her seem motivated less by modesty than by conceit. He had obviously meant it when he said he had no desire to see her unclothed.

The thought robbed Margaret of her tranquility. She rolled over and began a gentle dog paddle back toward shore, feeling more supple than she had in many months. She thought of the way Jensen used *his* body, with an arrogant kind of grace that made the most masculine man in London seem stiff and spiritless by comparison. He had a beautiful body, one that she could not help but look at and admire. Coupled with his reckless air of self-sufficiency, he exercised a fascination over her—whenever he wasn't infuriating her, that is.

She waded up onto the shore and realized that he was not asleep, as she had thought.

"Had enough?"

"Yes, thank you," Margaret said. She self-consciously crossed her arms to hide her breasts.

"Come let me sluice you down with a bucket of water then," he said. She remembered the two buckets he'd filled at the settlement and put in the gig. "It'll take the salt out of your hair and off your skin," he promised. "You'll feel like a new woman."

Margaret laughed. "I believe I already do. I've never actually done anything like this."

"There! You laughed at something I said," he said with satisfaction. "Come on, then."

Margaret went and stood next to him warily.

He saw the look on her face and said, "It's only cold water, Miss Belleweather, and when I'm done with you, I'm going to do myself, and that is surely the best remedy for any unchaste thoughts either one of us might be having."

Margaret looked at him, startled. She realized she *had* been having unchaste thoughts about him for the last hour. Had *he* . . . ? But no, he was only making a joke. She turned her back and let him empty the bucket over her.

"Wrap that length of cloth around you when you've dried off a bit," he said as he stepped back.

Richard watched as she made her way to the tree where she had left the cloth. Sometime in the last weeks, painful thinness had begun to give way to slim delicacy. Moreover, seeing her drenched to the skin, he had been made forcibly aware of certain aspects of her body that her too-large, shapeless clothes had hidden until now.

In full health, she must have been extraordinarily beautiful. As he thought about it, it occurred to him that their lives up until now had been the reverse of one

129

another. He had grown up by hook and by crook, and only as an adult had he managed to make of his life what he wanted it to be. She, on the other hand, had grown up privileged, the beautiful and undoubtedly cherished daughter of fond parents.

And now she had nothing, except for the money—no mother, no father, no brother, no dazzling parties, no ardent suitors. Worst of all, she could not have children. Her disembodied declaration of that fact had come clearly through the night to him as he stood in the Burseys' garden. The ineffable sadness in her voice had saddened him, too. Of all women—she who would be strict but always kind and full of love for her children. He didn't know what made him so sure of it, but he had no question that she would have been a wonderful mother.

"Mr. Jensen?" Margaret Belleweather's hesitant voice broke into his reverie.

"Yes?"

"How does one fasten this . . . this garment?"

Richard felt a bubble of mirth rising in him but he repressed the urge to tease her. She'd done nothing but good today, and he wanted to be decent in return. "Arrange the wrapping so that the leading edge of the cloth is in front of you. Then all you need to do is tuck it inside to secure it."

"Oh." There was a long pause. "That's what I'm doing, but it doesn't seem to be working."

"If modesty allows, Miss Belleweather, perhaps I can help."

There was another long pause. He waited, braced for a rebuff. Instead, he got another answer, one that tickled him with its combination of candor and naivete.

"Well, I don't see any other recourse, Mr. Jensen, only you must promise me that you won't be quite so thorough as is your custom."

The bubble of mirth could be contained no longer. Richard laughed out loud. "Oh, Miss Belleweather," he said when he could speak again, "you do have a way of putting things."

"But what is your answer?" she said uncertainly from behind the tree.

"My dear Miss Belleweather, I solemnly swear to reserve all my thoroughness for my strumpets. How's that for an answer?"

"I suppose it will have to do," she said, stepping out from behind the tree. Richard saw that she was smiling a little sheepishly.

He returned the smile. "You haven't done too badly," he said, surveying the cloth wrapped snugly from her breasts to her knees. "In fact, if I didn't think it would offend you, I'd tell you that you look quite nice in that."

"I wouldn't be offended at all," she said quietly.

Richard went taut. She was gazing at him with the same frankness that she had the day he'd kissed her in his cabin. Her innocent sexuality was as devastating now as it had been then. My God, did she have any idea what a look like that could do to a man?

Think! What had she said? He cleared his throat and tried to find someplace to look that would interrupt his body's response. He settled for turning and studying the gig. It had the advantage of being neither her body nor her face, and the position kept his lower body out of her sight.

"Just a moment, Miss Belleweather," he said, seized by inspiration. "I think the boat may have started to drift. I'll be right back."

The water wasn't quite cold enough to do the trick, but by the time he'd heaved himself over the side and deliberately let all his weight hang over the gunwale for several minutes, he felt ready to return to the beach. He retrieved the food he'd taken from the *Java* that morning and waded back to shore, trying to cover the livid red mark across his ribs with the bag.

He set down the bottle of wine he'd had Dogsmeat uncork, along with the parcel of food. He saw her questioning look. "In case it wasn't safe to come back to the *Java*, I decided I deserved one last decent meal from aboard . . ."

"There was that risk, wasn't there?"

131

He shrugged. "Life's full of risks."

"Oh, look, you've hurt yourself," she said. She reached out and touched his side with the hand that was not holding the loose edge of the sarong.

"Don't!"

She jumped back. He hadn't meant to be so abrupt, but the naked look of concern on her face coupled with her touch threatened to undo the effects of his trip to the gig.

"I'm terribly sorry," she said. She lowered her head and he could see tears sparkling on her lashes.

"I didn't mean to scare you. It's just that it's sore and I'd rather you didn't touch it." It wasn't entirely untrue.

She blinked several times before looking up again, the dark violet eyes still glistening but in no danger of spilling her tears. "Of course. I understand."

"Look, let's get you squared away and then have something to eat, all right?" he said briskly. Her vulnerability had exactly the same effect on him as her innocence. He'd be back and forth to the gig until sunset at this rate.

She seemed glad of the diversion. "I'm sure this is perfectly simple but I just cannot manage it."

Richard took hold of the cloth and realized with an inward groan that he would have to tuck his fingers in against her skin, along with the cloth. Gritting his teeth, he made quick work of the job, trying not to dwell on how soft her skin was, and how indecently lush her breasts were for one so slender.

She suffered his ministrations with closed eyes, holding her breath until he was done. He secured the last of the cloth and as she exhaled, he turned away and made for the other bucket of water. He splashed it over himself, wishing it were colder, and then said over his shoulder, "Get out the food, why don't you?"

They shared the bread and meat, wiping their hands afterward on a shared napkin. They were forced to pass the bottle of wine back and forth, since he hadn't thought he'd need a glass. They sat without speaking for a long time, watching the colors of the setting sun beyond the cove.

Then the wine seemed to loosen her tongue. "You don't think Christian will want to come back with me, do you?" she said quietly.

It was a subject that made him uncomfortable. He didn't give a damn what Christian Belleweather did with his life, but he hated the fact that she cared so much for someone who wasn't, in all likelihood, going to reciprocate.

"I don't know. Why don't you wait and see?"

"Then we are going to Atjeh?" she asked.

Richard sighed. "Why not? I haven't traded up there for a while but I know the rajah he's visiting."

"Thank you." It seemed to close that subject. "Would you mind if I asked you a personal question?"

Richard tensed. "So long as you don't mind if I don't answer it."

"What are the marks on your back from, the scars?"

"Oh, those. They were a gift from a countryman of yours. He didn't like my attitude."

"Whatever do you mean?"

"I was pressed by the Royal Navy. The first officer took it amiss that I didn't look on it as a privilege."

"Surely there must have been more to it than that," Margaret protested. He could hear the mingled disbelief and horror in her voice.

"Well, since you're not satisfied with the sanitized version, I'll tell you the real story. He liked the look of me, kept trying to waylay me in isolated corners of the ship. One night I woke up with a broken bottle at my neck and his stinking hand in my . . . well, where it had no business being. I grabbed the bottle and made him sorry he hadn't kept his hands to himself." He ran a finger along the scar on his cheek unconsciously and then quickly withdrew his hand when he realized what he was doing.

Margaret Belleweather didn't miss the gesture. She gazed at him unswervingly, her purple eyes luminous in the late afternoon sun. "And so he beat you for it?"

"I wish it had been that easy." Richard locked his arms around his knees and stared out to sea. It wasn't his favorite memory. "The ruckus woke up the rest of the crew

133

berthed in the fo'c'sle. The first officer hadn't endeared himself to any of them. They finished what I'd started and flung the body overboard."

"Dear God," Margaret whispered. "And you took the blame for it?"

"There wasn't any blame, just a missing officer. Of course, the captain was pretty sure what had happened. You don't share close quarters at sea without having a good idea of what goes on beneath the surface. None of the crew would speak against me—I was a bit of a hero for having stood up to the bastard—so the captain had to be satisfied with flogging me on a trumped up charge of insolence."

"No wonder you don't have much sympathy for Christian," she said softly.

Richard looked at her in surprise. "What a man's preferences are don't bother me one way or the other, as long as he respects mine. The first officer wouldn't take no for an answer. That's why I beat the hell out of him, not the other."

"I'm still surprised that you can keep an open mind after . . . well, under the circumstances."

"Maybe I'm not making myself clear," Richard said. "I just don't like anybody pushing me around, telling me what to do."

The corner of Margaret's mouth quivered. "The philosophy of Richard Jensen, in a nutshell."

Richard lay back on his elbows. "I never thought about it in so many words, but, yes, I guess that about sums me up."

Several minutes went by.

"Why did you choose to come to this part of the world?" she asked.

He held out his hand for the bottle of wine and took a long swig.

"Mainly by accident," he finally said.

"By accident? That doesn't sound like you. You strike me as someone who knows exactly what he wants and goes after it in no uncertain terms."

"Do I? Well, let's just say that some things don't work out the way I intend them to. I got drunk one night in Charleston and set sail the next morning. I just decided to go as far east as I could. It shouldn't have worked out as well as it has. The last time I'd gotten drunk ashore before that, I ended up in the bosom of the Royal Navy instead of the . . ."

"The bosom of a strumpet?" Margaret finished the comparison he'd thought better of finishing.

He rewarded her with a grin. "I like it when you say what you're really thinking." He passed her the bottle of wine. "Have some more."

She smiled and took another swallow. "I'm quite sure I shouldn't have had any more," she said as she handed the bottle back.

"Now there—that's a perfect example. Do you really think you shouldn't or do you just think you should *say* that you really shouldn't?"

"I'm not sure." The perplexed look on her face was so comical that Richard nearly laughed.

"It doesn't matter," he managed to say. "The point is, there's no reason not to loosen your laces sometimes."

Margaret giggled. "I don't have any laces to loosen at the moment."

"And has the world come crashing down around your ears?" he asked. "Is the future of civilized man in jeopardy?"

She screwed her face up earnestly. "I think I see what you're driving at," she said, "but oughtn't we to maintain *some* standards?"

"You're asking *me?*" Richard couldn't help but laugh at that.

"*You* do," she said indignantly.

"I do?" He could see her forming one of those thoughts that to a drunk man seem perfectly logical. He waited in amused anticipation.

"Yes," she said firmly, the 's' a little sloppy, "you have set yourself up as an *enfant terrible,* but you're more like a mother bear, really."

Richard choked back the laugh. It was even better than he'd thought it would be. She looked so very appealing at that moment, like a wayward child, with her hair tumbling in untidy waves around her small face and over her shoulders, and a half-defiant, half-uncertain look on her face.

"Maybe you'd like to explain that one," he said indulgently, "how it is that I'm like a mother bear, I mean."

"It's perfectly true," she said, thrusting out her chin for emphasis. "You growl at everyone but in the end, you look out for them. Those boys, the apprentices—they're all runaways and strays, aren't they?"

Richard straightened up, frowning. "Who says?"

"Dogsmeat—he said none of them had a decent mother. And Harkay—he's a reject, and I'll bet Dogsmeat and Daniels and all the rest are too," she concluded with satisfaction. She hiccuped. "Except Dekker. He told me how he came to be on the *Java*, and it sounded a perfectly reasonable story."

"You're tired," Richard said abruptly. "I'll take you back to the ship."

"I'm right, aren't I?" she demanded. "You feed them and clothe them, and make sure they take medicine, and eat well, and doctor them when something goes wrong, and . . . and . . ."

"And in return, I expect a damn good day's work out every one of them," Richard said sharply. She was too close to something he hadn't let himself see before.

"I'll bet other ship's captains aren't so nice," she declared.

"Nice, is it?" he growled. "That's it. You've had too much wine."

He picked her up and swung her over his shoulder. She was as limp as an empty sack.

"You're right," she sighed from somewhere down near his hip. "I *am* tired."

Richard merely grunted. He waded out to the gig and put her in it. It didn't help his mood when he arrived at the

Java to be greeted by cries of, "What's the matter?" and "What's happened to her?" He walked past the crew and down the companionway without answering.

Margaret Belleweather smiled at him sleepily as he put her in her berth. "Hmm, this is nice," she murmured as she curled up under the cover he threw over her. "And you're nice, too, even if you don't like to hear me say it."

"You'll feel differently in the morning," he growled. "Take my word for it."

"No, I won't," she said, "and thank you for buying the sparrow for me," she added, her voice growing faint.

A tapping at the door distracted him.

"Sir?" It was Tony. "Lady, she leave this . . ." He handed Margaret's sketching materials to Richard and jerked his head toward the deck overhead. "I afraid the . . ." He puffed out his cheeks and made a whistling sound, fluttering his fingers vigorously. ". . . you know."

"Thanks, Tony."

The little cook peered anxiously at Margaret, who appeared to be soundly asleep now. "Lady okay?"

"Yes, the lady's fine," Richard grumbled. "Go tell them all so they can stop yammering about it. She's just tired."

"Good," Tony declared. "Is nice to have lady on boat."

"In a pig's eye," Richard snapped. Tony left, throwing a puzzled look back at the captain.

Richard put the sketch book on the small bureau built into the forward bulkhead. By the last of the daylight coming through the porthole, he could see numerous other sketches. He glanced at Margaret again to be sure she was asleep and then lit the small, gimbal-mounted lantern next to the berth. He trimmed the flame to a soft glow and began leafing through the sketches.

The passion in them rocked him. She captured the joyous freedom of life in the islands with no hint of censure. There were pictures of bare-breasted girls in Demjang, a duck boy ambling along with his flock, even the streets of Old Town in Batavia, with the fakir on the corner. The faces were alive, each individual and as distinct from the other as if she knew them personally. And then there were his deckhands and apprentices in varying states of nudity, sporting about in the water and lolling on deck.

He looked again at Margaret Belleweather, her lashes casting wispy shadows on the pale, faintly freckled cheeks, her hair awry, abandoned in sleep. The contrast between who she seemed to be and the person who'd drawn these pictures bewildered him.

Chapter 9

The sun was high in a sky dotted with clouds when Margaret Belleweather emerged on deck the next morning. She wore yet another shirt from the slop chest, one which she supposed Dogsmeat had thought to leave on her bureau, on top of all the sketching materials he had tidied and secured there for her. She had spent the morning painstakingly transforming her last dress into another skirt, bracing herself firmly in the berth against the unruly motion of the *Java*.

The wind was especially lively today, and the *Java* bucked and kicked from one tack to the next over a fast-running sea. Every hand manned a rope, and the apprentices climbed into the rigging at regular intervals to reset canvas. Richard Jensen gave the orders himself instead of relaying them through Daniels. The smooth, effortless quality of his voice had always impressed Margaret, and now it carried cleanly out over the deck, above the screech of the rigging and the pounding of wind on canvas.

He wore a loose shirt bleached to bare-bones whiteness by the sun and age, and an old pair of black pants so tattered and worn that more of his long, brown legs showed than was covered. It still covered more than the sarong of yesterday, but, as she reflected on it, she felt strangely unembarrassed about that.

Despite her state of undress, and his, he'd taken no

advantage of the situation, even when she'd had too much wine and might not have resisted an advance by him. The bare, bronzed shoulders—how would they feel to the touch? And the heavy, bow-curved mouth—what would it be like to feel it pressed against the bareness of her throat and breast? She felt a distinct heat in her belly as she remembered the one, slow kiss he had given her in his cabin weeks ago. The temptation to find out more assailed her, but he clearly had not been tempted to touch *her*.

She clung for dear life to the quarterdeck rail as she watched him laugh at something Daniels had said. The wind whipped her skirt around her and tore at her hair, loosening it from its pins. She stood for perhaps an hour, lost in her thoughts, enjoying the wind and the waves under the brilliant sun, and even the pitching of the deck beneath her feet.

Jensen made his way forward and down the steps opposite where she stood. He moved across the main deck, barefooted and utterly at ease. Stopping next to Dekker, he rode the deck, never seeming to shift his weight and yet always in balance with the ship. His dark head contrasted sharply with Dekker's fair one, the sunlight striking it with blue lights.

He yelled an order to Daniels, who was manning the helm on the quarterdeck, and stared upward, his lean, dark cheeks stretched hollow by the angle of his head. Dekker said something and a grin split his face. They took up positions on each side of the mainmast rigging as the other hands craned to see them. Something was afoot.

At a signal from Harkay, they each started upward on the underside of the rigging, rolling over to the outer edge when they reached the first platform. They raced on, toward the next, hand over hand, as the crew cheered them on. Tendrils of hair lashed Margaret's cheeks as she squinted upwards, afraid to let go of the rail with even one hand to shield her eyes from the sun.

For sheer power, Dekker was no match for Jensen. The captain pulled away steadily, every iron spring and steel coil in his body working perfectly. He was perhaps sixty or seventy feet above the deck now, still climbing rapidly, and Margaret's breath caught in her throat as she strained her head back to follow his ascent. He reached the final platform and she watched in horror as he curled like a beetle over the last yardarm and continued up the bare mast. At last he stopped, nearly riding the sky it seemed, like a cowboy on a bucking bronc as he wrapped himself around the top of the reeling pole and waved a triumphant arm.

The crew let out a yell and Jensen began a leisurely descent, letting his legs swing loose from the rigging as he came down the underside of it. Margaret watched the play of muscles across his back and shoulders and wondered what it must be like to live in a body of such strength and grace.

He was so unafraid! And not just of physical challenge, she thought, but of life. What hardships he had been through, and yet he had survived and grown stronger, throwing out old ways and adopting new ones. For a boy from a small frontier town to grow into a man who so confidently captained his own clipper was no small achievement. And what was more, he had made room for other, less fortunate men, to share the life that had resulted from his hard work.

She felt so timid by comparison, and ashamed of herself for fearing what might lay ahead. It would not do, she told herself, to succumb to the unspoken dread she felt whenever she thought about the imminent meeting with Christian. She was determined to be strong, for his sake and for her sake. She turned her attention back to the deck, her resolve strengthened by Richard Jensen's example.

The man himself was now shaking his first officer's hand, smiling broadly. He made his way aft as Margaret covertly admired him. Once one got past the unconventional clothes and the often unshaven cheeks, he was undeniably handsome, in an elemental, charismatic way.

The straight brows were perhaps too thick, the nose a little too long and thin to be strictly proportional to the bold cheekbones, but her artist's eye found the flaws more appealing than perfection. The eyes, the narrow green cat's eyes fringed with dense black lashes—those had yet to come right in any of her sketches of him. Her hand simply could not capture their intensity, or the emotions that lurked behind them.

Margaret set her sights on the sea ahead as Jensen called another course change. The high clouds were thickening and merging, closing off all but a patch of sun here and a patch of sun there. The effect over the broad expanse of sea was breathtaking, a tapestry of light and shadow, and she moved to the center of the railing to observe it better.

The ship shivered and swayed once more, kicking her stern high and about across the wind. As she did, the heavy spanker boom began to swing, slowly at first, and then, gathering momentum, it began its flight across the quarterdeck.

It was fortunate, thought Richard, that he spared some thought for what went on near him as well as above and beyond, for Margaret Belleweather stood directly in the boom's path. Checking his seaman's instinct to duck, he hurtled in her direction, just an arm's span ahead of the boom. He launched himself at Margaret's frail shape, feeling the whisper of wood across his neck as he seized her on the fly. They hit the deck with a force that drove the breath from him and made stars jangle in his head.

They rolled together, ending in a heap against the frame of the skylight to the saloon below. She stared at him in shock, her lips bloodless and her eyes wide with fright.

"Why did you do that?" she gasped.

He shook his head to clear it and rose to his feet. Without answering, he pointed grimly to the spanker boom, now steady to port.

"But it would have passed over me," Margaret said as she struggled to her feet. "I've stood beneath it and it misses my height by inches."

Richard growled, a low sound in his throat that was all but lost in the high wind and the thundering sea. "It doesn't do to tempt fate," he said. "Wood gives, rope gives—in these conditions, it could sweep those few inches lower." Without consciously deciding to do it, he reached out and took her by the shoulders to steady her against the *Java*'s tossing.

She swallowed and he stared into those wide eyes so close to his own. Washed by the overcast light, they were the color of lavender silk, and he saw the pupils widen as she absorbed what he had said. A shudder passed through her and he checked his impulse to elaborate on what might have happened—the sharp sound of crunching bone, a strangled cry, and then a fierce tumbling through space and over the rail. He had seen it happen. But the look on her face told him that her imagination had put her in possession of the logical consequences.

"I'm sorry," she whispered. The wind snatched the words from her lips but he saw the words that formed there.

A chill ran through Richard. In that instant, he realized that she was not half as sorry as *he* would have been if the boom had caught her. He gripped her harder, to counter the image of an insubstantial daub of lavender cloth and golden hair floating on the sea and slowly disappearing beneath the surface. The thought tore at something deep inside him.

"Mr. Jensen?" This time he heard as well as saw the whisper. "You're hurting me."

Richard shook himself. "Am I, Miss Belleweather?" He softened his grip. "Why don't I take you below? This wind is only going to get stronger." He nodded toward a mare's tail on the horizon. "That's a big blow heading this way."

"If you think it wise."

"Keep the course, Mr. Daniels," he yelled, "and set more canvas if you dare. I'll be below."

He guided Margaret to the top of the companionway. Reluctant to let her go, he took her waist and angled his way down with her at his side. If he touched her, she must exist, and could not be slowly sinking to the bottom of the sea.

The saloon seemed unearthly quiet after the wind on deck.

"Are you all right, Mr. Jensen? You look rather pale," she said as he seated her at the table.

"Yes, I'm fine," he said, nearly undone by the concern in her face. He poured a drink with unsteady hands. What in God's name was the matter with him?

"You have a bruise just coming up on your left temple," she insisted.

He had nearly forgotten the blow to his head. That would account for the shakiness he was experiencing. "It's not the first knock I've taken and it won't be the last," he assured her.

"Still, I wish we had some ice to put on it," she said.

He let out a low chuckle. "There's not enough sawdust in the Orient to keep ice on board in this climate."

She smiled, a sweet, wistful smile. "I'm rather fond of ice. What an irony it is that the more one wants it, the less likely one is to find it."

"Miss Belleweather," he said suddenly. He stopped. What he was about to ask felt odd in the extreme.

"Yes?" she said, looking at him expectantly.

He felt stupid, foolish, worse than a boy trying for his first kiss. If he didn't say it right away, he'd lose his nerve.

"Miss Belleweather," he said quickly, "would it strike you as a good idea if you called me Richard and I called you Margaret?"

She looked thoughtful for a moment. "I think it would be very appropriate, especially as you have undoubtedly just saved my life."

So it had to have some justification. Richard drained his glass. It had been a bad idea.

"I just wondered," he said abruptly. "I didn't mean I wanted us to."

She looked down at her hands curled together in her lap. "No, of course not."

He stood up. "I'd better get back on deck. If we don't beat that storm to the north tip of Sumatra, we'll have no choice but to turn and run in front of it, maybe all the way south to Bali." He started for the steps and then turned. "Perhaps you'd like to pass the afternoon by drawing here

144

at the table. Shall I bring you your sketching supplies, Miss Belleweather?''

She looked up at him solemnly, her purple eyes fathomless. "Yes, please, Mr. Jensen. It's very kind of you to suggest it.''

Margaret swam up toward wakefulness. After five days and nights of swift sailing, she could feel that the *Java* was barely moving. She got on her knees to look out the porthole above her berth. Dark, indigo-green plains sloped down from jungle-clad hills to end at a vaporous shore. Low islands wavered like floating mirages in the misty heat between the *Java* and the shore.

Anxious to see it all better, Margaret pushed back the bedclothes and jumped out of her berth. She washed her face vigorously and cleaned her teeth before working the brush through her hair. It took some time until she was satisfied with it, for the damp heat made it curl and frizz. Smooth, perfectly straight hair had been the order of the day at her finishing school, but here that was impossible. It was there, too, that she had learned to tolerate the ever-tighter lacing of her corset, another inch smaller each month, until she reached the ideal waist size. Corsets, also, were a thing of the past.

Margaret felt an air of well-being, a vigor and freedom of movement that had not been hers since she was a young girl, before she'd been sent away to prepare for womanhood. Even the sense of accomplishment she'd felt when she was presented, knowing she met society's expectations in every particular, could not compare to this.

For a brief moment, she thought about looking at herself in the small, hazy mirror mounted inside the cupboard in the corner. But no—why spoil the illusion? If she felt well, was that not enough? Why ask for the stars when the moon, at least, was within her grasp? To feel healthy again was enough and more than she had dared hope for when she lay aching and wretched for so many months at Pensleigh.

Margaret dressed, happy at the thought of seeing Christian again, and relieved that she felt that way now that the moment was at hand. She heard the anchor chain rattling out and hurried to put on her shoes. She passed through the saloon and smelled the lingering odor of breakfast. Sleeping through breakfast had become routine, but Tony always put something to one side for her in the cookhouse. As long as she arrived before he'd finished cleaning up and the stove lost all its heat, she'd have a warm breakfast.

Richard Jensen stood by the mizzenmast, deep in conversation with Daniels, Dekker, and Harkay. Not one of them so much as glanced up as she passed. She watched them as she ate, and saw Dogsmeat join the group. They all looked so serious that she wondered what they could be talking about. At last they dispersed and Jensen went to the far rail, lighting a cheroot and smoking it as he looked out toward land.

The mist gradually lifted and Margaret heard a rhythmic chanting in the distance, accompanied by the splash of oars. She handed her plate back to Tony and went to see what was happening. She joined Jensen on the foredeck and saw a large settlement of wooden houses that the mists had cloaked before.

"What is that sound, Mr. Jensen?"

Jensen turned to her with a frown, his eyes hard. "That, Miss Belleweather, is trouble. The rajah apparently intends to come on board."

"Why is that a bad thing? Do we not want to meet him and ask about Christian?"

Jensen glanced worriedly over his shoulder. "They're coming on fast. Look, you must do exactly as I say, now and when he comes on board. There's real danger here, for all of us." He began to drag her back toward the quarterdeck. "Above all, don't open your mouth!"

Margaret bristled. It was the return of the old, dictatorial Richard Jensen. This one was clean-shaven, but that was the only difference. It was doubly disappointing because she had grown used to, and very much liked, the other

Richard Jensen she had been seeing of late, the one who sat and talked with her after dinner.

"Have you taken leave of your senses?" Margaret snapped as he jolted her along. She tried to wrest her arm away but failed. "Mr. Jensen, I am not a sack of yams!"

"No, you're much more valuable than that," he growled. "About ninety pigs is my guess."

He propelled her up the steps to the quarterdeck and down into the saloon in record time. Margaret was breathless by the time he thrust her into his cabin. He released her arm and she spun around.

"What on earth is this about?" she demanded.

"Strip and get into bed!" He began rummaging in a low drawer.

"What?" Margaret stared at his back, stunned.

"I said, strip and get into bed." He straightened up and threw a diaphanous silk wrapper in her direction. "You can cover yourself with that." Margaret caught it without thinking. It weighed exactly nothing.

"You must be mad!" she cried.

The chanting had been coming closer all the while and suddenly it stopped. There was a solid thud as a boat came alongside. Jensen's face was thunderous.

"*Now*, Miss Belleweather, unless you want to spend the rest of your days in the rajah's harem, or see me with a dagger stuck between my shoulder blades."

There was no doubt that he believed what he was saying. Margaret's mouth went dry with fear—either Jensen was mad or he was telling the truth. Either way, she judged it best to do as he said. She quickly threw the wrapper over her clothes and crawled into the oversized berth. She turned to see him flinging his shirt into the corner. He shot a quick look in her direction and stopped cold.

"If this wasn't a matter of life and death, I might find that comical. *Strip*, Miss Belleweather—our lives may depend on it."

"I won't," she gasped. "I can't possibly . . ."

He hurriedly began unbuttoning his trousers. "You can and you will, or I'll do it for you." His eyes never left hers, and in their green depths, she read a hint of fear.

She turned her back and with controlled panic, unfastened her blouse.

"Hurry, for God's sake!"

She heard the soft whoosh of his pants flying through the air and then she felt his fingers at the back of her skirt. He roughly undid the fastening and pulled it to the floor, leaving her in only her chemise.

She whirled to face him. His bare chest rose and fell rapidly just inches from her eyes. "Surely this is good enough," she said.

Heavy footsteps on the deck above gave way to raised voices, Daniels's among them. "I estimate you have no more than one minute, Miss Belleweather." She kept her eyes fixed straight ahead, not wanting to look down by accident. "What's it to be? Do you want to keep the chemise on and just have me take the best deal I can for you? I assure you though—you won't enjoy being a member of a harem."

"Don't!" Margaret cried, her voice sharp-edged with fear. "Turn your back. I'll do it."

She pulled the chemise over her head and felt the air on her bare breasts. Flushed with embarrassment, she swiftly pulled the wrapper on and climbed into the berth, pulling the covers over her. Jensen moved rapidly around the cabin, stowing their clothing out of sight. She stared at the wall to avoid seeing his nakedness, but from the corner of her eye she saw flashes of white from the paler skin around his hips.

A booming male voice filled the saloon, and Jensen slid under the covers next to her, his weight drawing her down toward his body. There was a banging on the door.

"Remember, Miss Belleweather, let me do all the talking," he said in an undertone.

But it wasn't talking he did. He took her in his arms and without preamble, began kissing her, ignoring the commotion outside the door. The feel of his heavy, sensual mouth against hers shocked Margaret into immobility. She felt his hand caressing her hair and sliding down past

148

her shoulder as the hammering on the door increased.

He pressed her back against the pillows and half lay over her, slowly stroking her lips with his. "Ah, Margaret, you're so sweet," he whispered, "just as I knew you would be."

Incredibly, Margaret felt a flush of pleasure. The hard maleness of his body coupled with the tender words combined to do what fear and threats had not. Hesitantly, she lifted her arms and put them around his neck. She gasped as his slowly wandering hand found her breast. She shrank back.

"Don't, Margaret," Richard said softly in her ear. "Let me make love to you, just for this moment."

His voice flowed through her like wine and she relaxed. She could still hear the voices outside the door, but more faintly now, her senses tuned to the touch of his hand as he cupped her breast. She felt the flush of her arousal deepen even as another part of her detached itself, wondering how she could possibly respond to him in this bizarre circumstance.

The assault on her senses won out over the purely intellectual. The heady scent of his clean male skin, mingled with his cheroot, drove her closer into his arms. She touched his cheek and felt it joined to hers as he kissed her again. Nothing in its appearance had prepared her for the rough thrill of it beneath her fingertips.

The door to the cabin burst open and slammed against the bulkhead. Margaret jerked convulsively but Richard stilled her with the length of his body. He captured her hand and held it against his face.

"Steady," he whispered against her lips. He ground his mouth down onto hers so that even if she had wanted to speak, she couldn't have.

But she didn't want to. She moved against him, returning the heavy, sweet kiss. She slid her hand to the back of his neck, threading her fingers through hair damp with sweat. Something wet and warm probed softly at her mouth and at first she didn't know what it was. With a shock, she realized it was his tongue, and the shock only added to the forbidden thrill. A groan rose in her throat as it touched her own, sending currents of heat down into her belly.

"Jen-sen." A deep voice rumbled from beyond the bed, barely penetrating the rush of blood drumming in her ears.

In the same leisurely way he had been kissing her, Jensen slowly withdrew his mouth from hers. He lifted himself on one elbow and looked casually over his shoulder at the square-bodied Sumatran who'd planted himself just inside the door.

"Ah, Atam Datu," he drawled, "nice to see you again. Welcome aboard."

The rajah grinned slyly and said something in Dutch, his shining black eyes focused on Margaret.

Jensen grinned back, leaning nonchalantly against the bulkhead. He glanced at Margaret with a predatory smile.

"No, Prince, this one is mine. No sale."

The rajah stared at her, a look of undisguised lust on his face. Margaret trembled, all too aware that the silk wrapper barely covered her. Jensen casually slipped his hand under it and massaged her breast, not as tenderly as before. Margaret understood that it was a gesture of ownership and managed to keep her body quiescent. The golden-skinned warlord licked his lips. He spoke again, his eyes avidly following the motion of Jensen's hand.

"Not even for ten times that amount of pepper, Prince," Jensen answered. "However, I do have some other things you might be interested in."

The rajah dragged his gaze back to Richard with a palpable effort. His expression shifted. He nodded toward Margaret and she distinctly heard him say Christian's name. She struggled to sit up but Jensen held her in place, firmly pressing his elbow down on her shoulder.

Margaret felt the warning in it. She glanced at him but he only nodded at the rajah, never taking his eyes off him.

"Yes, she's his sister." Jensen's chest and shoulders were coated with perspiration. She tried to curb her answering fear—it was warm in the cabin but not that warm. The rajah spoke again and Jensen let out a rich chuckle that Margaret would have thought was genuine if she hadn't felt the tension in his body where it pressed up against hers.

He turned to Margaret. "He says I've done well for myself." His expression was as cunning as the prince's, but behind his eyes she read an urgent plea for her to remain silent. "He says that if you're Christian's sister, then you must be a fine bed partner."

Margaret felt a rosy flush spreading across her cheeks and the rajah roared with laughter. He asked another question, nodding toward her.

"The rajah asked me if you understand Dutch," Jensen said.

Margaret shook her head. The rajah clucked.

"You want a cheroot, Prince? Some brandy maybe?" Jensen angled himself to a sitting position, letting the sheet fall across his lap.

No! Margaret wanted to shout. Don't encourage him to stay—get him out of here!

"Dogsmeat! Some brandy and a couple of stogies!"

The little Cockney came in with a tray, acting as if seeing his captain in bed with Margaret were nothing out of the ordinary. He deftly handed glasses around. The rajah sniffed at his, a calculating look on his face.

"Oh, it's the good stuff, all right," Jensen said. "You want some? I'll bring a cask ashore."

The prince grunted and swallowed the contents of the glass. He said something and then jerked his head toward the saloon.

"The prince wants to do a little business now, honey," Jensen said. He leaned over and gave her a lingering kiss.

Margaret received the kiss without any of the accompanying pleasure his others had given her, too aware of the rajah's speculative, deep-hooded eyes on them.

"Now don't you go anywhere—I'll be back as soon as I can," Jensen said.

She giggled, a silly, high-pitched giggle that hinted at the hysteria just below the surface. He slapped her hip with what an onlooker would have taken for fondness, but Margaret felt the sting in it and knew he was trying to steady her nerves.

Jensen stood up, seemingly indifferent to his nudity, and offhandedly took the pants Dogsmeat handed him. The rajah looked over his finely formed body almost greedily and then his eyes darted back to Margaret. Margaret's skin crawled—it seemed as if the rajah couldn't decide who he liked the look of better. She took a sip of brandy, striving to emulate Jensen's relaxed air.

They left the cabin and she pulled the sheet up over herself with a shudder. Dear God in heaven—she couldn't have stayed calm another minute! Whatever Jensen had had to do to keep the rajah away from her now seemed perfectly reasonable. If he'd rolled on top of her and taken her right in front of the warlord, she knew it would still have been preferable to the alternative.

"Are you all right, miss?"

Margaret's hand jerked and brandy slopped onto the sheet, soaking through to her stomach. "Dogsmeat! You frightened me!"

"Sorry, miss," the dwarf whispered. "Captain wanted me to tell you to stay put, says he'll get rid of that nasty bugger as fast as ever he can but you're not to show your face until he does."

"Believe me, I have no desire to cross his path again," Margaret said.

"Captain'll see you fine and dandy-o," Dogsmeat assured her. He took the nearly empty glass from her and refilled it. "We was all set to bring your brother aboard to see you, and keep you under wraps—had it all planned out—until that jumped-up monkey had hisself rowed out here. That's his way though—what he wants, he gets."

"Well, he didn't get me," Margaret declared.

Dosgmeat chuckled. "Captain did some quick thinking there—Atam Datu won't be thinkin' you're for sale after how the captain handled it."

Margaret felt her cheeks pinking up. "Couldn't he have just told him we were married?"

Dogsmeat's eyes widened in disbelief. "Marriage don't mean nothin' to that monkey! He would've thought the captain was just holding out for more money and had his guts for breakfast. What he saw—now *that* he understands, and he knew better than to mess with the captain's woman if he wants him to come trade here again."

The inexorable logic began to sink in but she persisted. "I could have just hidden until he was gone," she suggested weakly.

Dogsmeat snorted. "Too chancy—he'd've sliced the captain up for trying' to keep 'im out of anywhere he wanted to go on board. You see," he explained patiently, "he owns the whole bleedin' lot round here—animals, crops, people, the lot—and he don't take kindly to bein' said no to. No, miss, you take my word for it—the captain done the only thing what he could, and you was right game goin' along with it like you did."

But Margaret didn't feel game. As soon as Dogsmeat left, she began to shiver uncontrollably despite the heat. She took another sip of the brandy. It warmed her mouth—nothing like the way Richard Jensen had, but it still tasted good. It seemed like hours before she finally heard the chant of the rajah's oarsmen pulling away. She thought of the almost mystically beautiful green shore she'd seen earlier—amazing how venal a presence it could shelter.

The door swung open and Richard Jensen walked in with a grim look on his face. He made straight for the brandy he hadn't touched before and tossed off the contents of the glass.

"By God, that was a close thing," he muttered. He looked at Margaret. "That's the second time I've nearly lost you."

Margaret went still. It sounded as if he might actually care whether or not he lost her.

"Are you all right?" he asked.

Margaret nodded, studying his face. He had an ashy look about him. "Are *you* all right?" she asked.

He sat down on the edge of the bed. "I'll be better when we get the hell out of here."

"What made you so sure the rajah would want me? I mean, it's not as if I'm any prize to look at."

"You haven't looked in a mirror recently, have you?"

Margaret started—how did he know? A sudden thought struck her. "My eyes! It was my eyes, wasn't it? You warned me about that before but I didn't believe you."

Jensen laughed and some of the color returned to his face. "Oh, Margaret—sometimes you can be so perceptive and sometimes . . ." He didn't finish.

"And sometimes I'm thick as a plank," she said.

He smiled. "That's not what I was going to say." He reached and pushed a piece of hair back off her face. "I really think that you *must* call me Richard from now on." He inclined his head toward the bed. "Too much water has gone under the bridge for you to go on calling me Mr. Jensen."

Margaret smiled tremulously. The humor was inescapable. "Then I expect you had better call me Margaret."

"I was planning on it," he said. His expression grew serious. Margaret felt her breath coming more rapidly as he studied her, the green of his eyes flecked with darker lights.

"You were very brave, Margaret," he said softly, "and very sweet."

He leaned forward and gently kissed her forehead. Margaret lay utterly still. How did she confess that it had been the pleasure of his touch that had gotten her through it and not bravery?

He moved down, pressing his lips to her temple. "Not one woman in a thousand could have carried that off like you did," he said.

The heat of his mouth warmed her, kindling a ravenous warmth in all the pulse points in her body. "Oh, Richard," was all she could say. It came out as a sigh. His cheek drew her hand like a magnet and she laid her palm on it.

She felt him hesitate and then draw a ragged breath next to her ear. He put his arm across her and leaned his weight on it as he kissed his way down to her cheekbone. Margaret

154

trembled and reached out to enclose his face with her other hand.

His breath fanned her cheek and her pulse thickened as she deliberately guided his face downward. She let her eyes close as his mouth settled over hers, hot and sweet. Fiery threads of pleasure raced through her as she kissed him back. He pulled away after a long moment.

"It was you," she murmured, to keep him close. Her breath came sharp and short.

"Me?" he said thickly as he showered small, urgent kisses along her jawbone.

Margaret clutched at his head, running her fingers through the unruly black hair. "I couldn't have done it if you hadn't made me want you so." She tipped her head back, inviting him to do whatever he would with her.

He stopped breathing for an instant and then resumed in a rush, the air coming harsh and fast. "Oh, God," he whispered, slipping his hand around her waist. He kissed her again, feverishly, and she rose to the passion in him like the tide to the moon. At last he pushed her away, slowly, reluctantly, his bronzed chest heaving. "Margaret, you can't tell me that."

"Why not?" she countered. His roughened hand, sliding over the silk of the wrapper and then across her bare skin, made her reckless with desire.

"Because," he said hoarsely, "I want you, and hearing you say that only makes me want you more."

Margaret had never felt so wonderful. "Good." His green eyes were almost black with intensity, and it excited her.

Richard drew back slowly, looking at her in puzzlement. "You don't really mean that," he said.

"Don't I?" Margaret felt the first stirrings of doubt.

He withdrew his hand from her waist and cupped her chin with it, his breathing still irregular. "This is only happening because of what went on here with Atam Datu, and the brandy. You're not yourself."

Her arousal began to wane in the face of his earnestness. *I didn't have that much brandy*, she wanted to say—*it's you that's got my blood racing.* But she had already told him how he affected her, and he had stopped anyway. She could only embarrass herself further by admitting again how much his touch aroused her.

"Perhaps you're right," she said softly, unable to meet his eyes.

"Margaret," he said quietly. He lifted her chin so that she was forced to look into those storm-sea eyes. "Some day, when you're back in England, you'll look back and see that I was right. Nothing good could come of this."

Margaret lowered her lashes so that he wouldn't see the humiliation in her eyes. He had let her down gently but it didn't help. It was still painful, horribly painful. She focused on the strong, cupid's bow of his upper lip, and the full curving line of the lower. "I'll get dressed, then," she said, when she could trust herself to speak, "as soon as you've finished whatever it is you came here to do."

He let his hand drop away from her chin. "I'll just get a shirt and then I'll be out of your way."

Margaret stifled a bubble of humorless mirth. Just a minute ago she had wanted to give this man everything, and now all he wanted was to put his clothes back on and get away. The last joy of feeling his strong, fearless body next to hers ebbed swiftly.

"We need to talk about your brother, and about Atam Datu," she heard Richard say. She looked up to see him standing in the doorway. "Come up on deck when you're dressed."

Richard lingered in the saloon after he'd closed the cabin door behind him. What in the name of God had happened in there? He'd never known a woman to become so thoroughly aroused so quickly. Before, when Atam Datu was watching them, she'd groaned and gone on kissing him. He'd been astonished by her ability to set aside her prim ways and her animosity toward him.

But this! This hadn't been feigned, and neither, he realized now, had the other. The ache between his legs reminded him that he hadn't been acting either. To be responded to like that was intoxicating—it had fueled an answering lust in himself like nothing he'd ever experienced. Richard shook his head. Who could have guessed that she would let that passion in her sketching out into the light of day, and with him of all people?

He went up on deck and got a cup of coffee from Tony as he passed the cookhouse. He needed something to clear his head—the brandy certainly hadn't done the trick. It would be insanity to let himself slide over the brink he'd been teetering on these past few days. Margaret Belleweather. For God's sake, he'd be a fool to let himself feel anything for her. When they got back to Singapore, she'd walk away from him without another thought. What was happening between them was the purest manifestation of a shipboard romance.

No, it ended here. He was still drumming that message into his head when she appeared on the quarterdeck. She came down the steps—almost gracefully now, he noticed—and across the deck, her lavender skirt sweeping the deck. She faltered when she saw him watching her. The mouth he'd kissed just a short time ago was trembling, and her extraordinary gentian eyes looked even larger than usual, wide with uncertainty under the delicate golden brows.

He wanted to go to her and put his arms around her—tell her that he'd wanted her every bit as much as she'd wanted him. Kiss her thoroughly and feel her rise to meet him again. Above all, he wanted to chase that haunted look from her face.

Before he could let himself act on that impulse, she took a deep breath and rearranged her features. She drew herself up so that she no longer appeared so painfully small and vulnerable, and resumed walking toward him. The moment had passed. He turned away and leaned on the rail.

"Mr. Jensen?" she said behind him, and then, more softly, "Richard."

His heart twisted. It was going to be difficult to deny the pull he felt toward her. "I'm going to get some more coffee," he said abruptly. "Would you like a cup?"

157

"No, thank you just the same."

She was standing motionless at the rail when he returned, in that utterly still way of hers that conveyed a sense of myriad emotions boiling just below the surface. She made the news he had to break easier for him by keeping her gaze on the shore while he spoke.

"Atam Datu wants us to join him for dinner tonight," he said carefully. "He's got it in his head that you and Christian are a matched set. Either of you by yourself would be a rarity in this part of the world, with your hair and eyes, but two of you side by side strikes him as a trophy of sorts that he'd like to see at his table."

He felt rather than saw her shudder.

"I'd prefer not to," she said. "Perhaps you could oblige me by bringing Christian back here with you after dinner."

He cleared his throat. "I guess I'll have to be plainer," he said. "If you want to see Christian, it'll have to be on the rajah's terms. I even had to promise the rajah I'd bring him some guns the next time through to get him to let you come ashore."

"Guns!" He caught her startled glance. "But you told me yourself how dangerous that could be. You mustn't!"

"Don't worry" he said, "I'm not going to—I just told him I would. He went over the ship with a fine tooth comb and didn't find any. Otherwise he'd have taken them now."

"But what about the next time?" she asked with a frown.

"There's not going to be a next time," he said grimly. "Old Atam Datu's getting too big for his britches. He's always been a tricky son of a bitch, but now, with the war against the Dutch, he's even less pleasant than before."

"I appreciate you at least telling him that you'd bring him guns," she said. "But this other, about Christian—is he some kind of prisoner? Why do I need Atam Datu's permission to see him?"

Richard sighed. "Look, just come and see Christian tonight. I don't know what Atam Datu's game is. I do know that other people have come and gone from here as his guests. I get the feeling that Christian's just another guest."

"Then Christian could leave tomorrow if he wanted to, or even tonight after dinner?"

"I have no reason to think it's not his choice," Richard said.

He gazed at the sparkling beach and lush forests above the village. Along the shore, there was rampant activity— small fishing boats being paddled to and fro, nets being laid out on the sand to be mended, and children running and splashing. It was a happy scene that contrasted darkly with a thought that had occurred to him as Margaret spoke.

Suppose it was in Atam Datu's head to keep Margaret here as his 'guest' until Richard returned with the promised guns? Richard narrowed his eyes. There was no doubt that the rajah was taken with her, and so his grounds for keeping her might be twofold. Whether such a scheme had occurred to the rajah would hinge on how much he thought Richard himself valued her. After the scene in his cabin that morning, the rajah would be justified in thinking she meant everything to him. Tonight he'd be careful to correct that impression.

Chapter 10

Margaret glanced uneasily about her. Frangipani scented the air as they made their way along a path of crushed shells that shimmered in the moonlight. Atam Datu's compound was unexpectedly luxurious, but a knot of dread in her stomach made it hard to take in all the details as they walked through the elaborate gardens leading to the eating pavilion. The semicircular structure was open on the sides, fronting a pond that caught the light of the smoky orange-yellow torches inside.

She mounted the stairs with Richard's arm at her elbow, searching with eager eyes for Christian among the throng inside. To her intense disappointment, he wasn't there. A breathtakingly beautiful girl greeted them at the entrance, her bee-stung lips curved in greeting. She salaamed and waved in the direction of a low teakwood table surrounded by hassocks and mounds of pillows.

Richard sat down and sipped at a drink she handed him, flirting outrageously, but Margaret felt only a fleeting stab of jealousy, too anxious for a glimpse of Christian after all this time to worry about another potential source of heartache. Across the floor of hard, shining wood, beyond squared and polished poles, she searched for the fair hair that would be so unmistakable in this dark-skinned, dark-eyed crowd. Animated chatter filled the air as more people arrived, but still there was no sign of Christian.

The buzz of talk filled her head, dizzying her as she

160

clenched and unclenched her hands. She withdrew her handkerchief and twisted it around her fingers. Had Atam Datu changed his mind? The wait was unbearable. Without warning, the crowd stilled, and all heads turned in one direction. Almost sick with nerves, Margaret wavered unsteadily on the hassock, straining to see beyond them.

The rajah appeared, wearing a white sarong of silk, a brocaded jacket, and a white turban with an emerald. The diamond-studded hilt of a kris protruded from his wide sash, catching the torches' light and making his already spectacular progress more dazzling. Richard rose lazily to his feet and Margaret jumped up, her heart pounding as she glimpsed a fair head behind Atam Datu's shoulder.

"Christian!" she cried. Richard shot her a look of warning but she couldn't heed it. Filled with longing to get a good look at her brother, she edged forward, twisting her handkerchief in damp hands.

The rajah came to a halt. He grinned and made a sweeping gesture, flushing Christian out from behind his splendid bulk. Her brother looked thinner than she remembered him, but it suited his fine bones and only made him handsomer. He smiled at her, the same lopsided grin she had loved in him as a boy. Margaret could stand it no longer. She raced across the open floor and threw herself into his arms.

"Here, here," he laughed. "What's all this? Have you lamed my horse? Broken my toy soldiers? You always run at me like this when you've done something awful and want to get the apology over with."

Margaret was torn between laughter and tears. Just to hear his voice filled her with joy. "I've done absolutely nothing wrong," she said shakily. "It's you who owes *me* an apology."

"I suppose it's about all the dratted letters I haven't written," he said, tweaking her nose and smiling down at her.

A loud throat clearing nearby interrupted them. The rajah held out his arms, framing the two of them, and

161

made an announcement that was met with applause. Hundreds of bright eyes studied them curiously.

"We're a better display than those alligators in the pond outside," Christian said casually. "Prepare yourself for celebrity, my dear sister."

"I haven't come to be seen," she retorted. "Why on earth did you leave Singapore, and why *didn't* you write?"

"Oh, come, come," he laughed, "a scold after all this time?"

His enormous charm had the same effect on her it had always had. She smiled tearfully up at him. Just to see him was a relief beyond measuring. "You can't blame me for at least asking," she said, unable to take him to task for the past when the future was all that mattered.

She let him lead her back to the table where he reclined with careless grace on the pillows next to her seat. The sapphire eyes twinkled with amusement as he regarded her. "Lost a bit of weight, haven't you?"

"Just a bit," she said, unwilling to discuss her illness, "but I'll soon be in the pink again."

"Some people don't take to this climate," he said. "I, on the other hand, was born for it."

"You certainly look as if it agrees with you," she said. He wore an outfit identical to the rajah's, save for the turban and kris—white silk draped around his narrow hips, and a brocaded jacket of turquoise and ochre.

"And the bare feet, too," he said, waving his browned toes. "I never could abide shoes."

Margaret laughed. She had a sudden memory of him down by the stables at Pensleigh, chucking a new pair of school shoes into the dungheap. "Do you remember the time you . . . ?"

Christian chuckled. "In spades. I couldn't sit down for a week when father got done with me."

Margaret sobered. She would have to tell him about their parents, but not now. Perhaps later she could arrange to speak with him privately.

"So," Christian said, glancing toward Richard Jensen, "I see you've taken up with the notorious captain of the *Java*."

"Oh, hardly notorious," Margaret demurred, "though perhaps a little more colorful than the captain of my steamer coming out." She flushed at the realization that she had failed to deny the most important assertion first— that she had taken up with Richard Jensen.

"I must say, he's got the insouciance to go with his reputation," Christian commented before she could correct herself. Margaret followed his gaze.

Richard was leaning back, perfectly at ease as the girl stood behind him, massaging his heavy biceps with languid strokes. She whispered in his ear as they watched. He kept his eyes on Atam Datu, who was speaking, and reached up to cover one of her hands. He made a quick, whispered remark out of the corner of his mouth and the girl giggled.

Margaret was stabbed to her core by the sight of the girl's exquisitely tapered hands moving across Richard's shoulders. The girl leaned forward, rubbing her firm, high breasts against his back. Margaret's dismay gave way to raw anger as Richard angled back into the caress, his green eyes narrow with pleasure.

"She'll give you more than a little competition," Christian remarked, idly reaching for a piece of fruit, "but then I hear he's very popular with all the ladies."

Margaret fumed, unable to answer him as she glared in Richard's direction. The fact that it made her angry made her angrier still—how dare he have that effect on her!

Food began to arrive and Christian named things for her, and made recommendations which Margaret scarcely heard through her unvarnished rage.

Christian flicked her arm. "Come on, old girl," he said, "he's not the only fish in the sea. Look here, try the pisang goreng—Atam Datu's cooks really do have the most marvelous way with it."

Margaret forced her attention onto the food. It was obviously useless to deny she had *some* feeling for Richard Jensen. Christian handed her a plate and she ate mechanically, never quite managing not to look at Richard as the girl fed him sweet pieces of mangosteen and small bits of fish by hand. When he was done, he sucked her slender rose-brown fingers clean one by one, all the while looking up at her seductively.

"Christian, could we go for a stroll?" Margaret said hastily.

"Not quite the thing to do, sister dear, getting up and walking away from Atam Datu's table."

"I don't give a fig for Atam Datu!" she snapped.

The rajah, hearing his name, looked over at her, a broad smile on his crafty face.

"Whatever's happened to our quiet little Margaret?" Christian said wonderingly. "If it's the American who's got you so fired up, I heartily suggest you let this one get away and cast your net elsewhere."

"I haven't cast my net anywhere," Margaret replied tartly.

"Ah, here we go," Christian said urbanely, "just the thing." A lacquered bowl filled with rolled cigarettes had appeared on the table. He picked one up and a small boy darted forward to light it. "Thank you, Jolibo," he said as he puffed the thing to life, "most kind." He held it out to Margaret. "Care for some? Amir makes strong magic."

"No, thank you," Margaret said distractedly. Musicians began to play bamboo xylophones and gongs that kissed the night air with a soft, mysterious melody.

"Liang's going to dance for us," Christian remarked between puffs. "There's a rare treat."

Margaret watched coldly as the girl left Richard's side and began to weave a dance through the notes of music. Her bare feet stroked the ground as she glided around to face the table, all alone on the shining floor. She moved from the hips, slowly, softly, tenderly, and her huge brown eyes smoldered in Richard Jensen's direction. Atam Datu seemed to find it amusing, even as a lascivious glow lit his face.

Liang's hips were bound tightly in a sarong flecked with gold, and as she moved, she radiated an unmistakably feline aura, sensual and erotic. Each gesture and move defied gravity and anatomy, her breathing invisible to the eye. Her tapered fingers fluttered as she moved, almost seeming to be in a trance now. Margaret was awestruck. The girl was superb, like liquid gold in motion.

This was the kind of beauty Richard Jensen would appreciate, and Liang had already made it clear that she was his for the asking. Margaret swallowed the bile that rose in her throat. What shred of pride would be left to her when Richard disappeared into the night with this girl, as he surely would? She turned away quickly, unable to gaze on the brilliant beauty that lured Richard Jensen into the kind of net which she could not cast.

"Christian," she whispered, "do let's go outside."

His eyes focused slowly on her. "We can talk here," he said. "Liang won't mind—she's got the only audience *she* wants." He tipped his chin toward Richard. "If she was raw meat and he was a tiger, he couldn't be more interested."

Margaret refused to look. She knew well enough what Richard's face must look like. She had seen naked passion on his face only that day, for that scantest of moments before he had come to his senses and pushed her away. She let the urgency of what she had to say carry her past the dismal memory.

"I came all this way to find you for a purpose," she said in an undertone. "I want you to come home with me. Mother and father are dead—they were killed in an accident last spring. Father took mother to see the blasting on the last section of the Birmingham line. I was supposed to go, too, but I wasn't feeling well. A rock wall collapsed and heavy equipment rolled down the slope and over the area where they stood. Three others were killed also."

"So his damned railroads killed him," Christian murmured. *"Quel apropos.* A shame he had to take mummy along with him."

A quick chill passed through Margaret. Christian's eyes seemed glazed over. Constrained by her surroundings, Margaret couldn't question him, ask for an explanation of his callousness. Had Christian really hated their father so much? She reached out and took his hand, the one that wasn't holding the slowly burning cigarette, in an effort to

165

assure herself that he wasn't cold in fact as well as in manner.

"Poor lamb," he said, gazing up at her. "It must have been horrendous for little you."

"It has been." His reactions seemed so skewed, so out of keeping with his tender-hearted nature, that she forewent any description of events afterward, of how the creeping sense of unwellness she'd felt the day of the gala track-laying had grown. She'd barely kept on her feet until the funeral was over, and then fever had ripped through her, leaving her broken and mindless for weeks. Hot, tender, swollen joints assailed her relentlessly, the pain migrating from one to the next until she longed for death.

She'd drifted in a haze of pain for months after the fever abated, sailing leadenly along in the damask-draped bed in her corner bedroom at Pensleigh. Often she had imagined she was the lady of Shallot, being inexorably carried downstream, her life bleeding away as the last notes of her song drifted up to Camelot. The illusion passed as she recovered. In the afternoons she was read to by Reverend Childers, and she was forced from bed each morning by a resolute Eliza, to sit for the prescribed half hour in the chaise by the window. The monolithic bed always beckoned her back—the windows were too high and wide, the sun too bright, the lemon yellow drapes too overwhelming for eyes weakened by months of gloom.

Her father's solicitor had come when the phalanx of physicians had at last given their approval. Reclining on the chaise, a rose-colored mohair shawl across her legs, she'd waited for him, lifting one after another of the silver-framed miniatures from the cherry table at her side. Looking at pictures of her mother and father and Christian, she had thought how pointless it all seemed without them. Sure she was too numb to care what the disposition of the estate might be, she nevertheless reacted with shock when she learned that Pensleigh had been left to her.

The damning evidence of their father's having changed his will within a year of banishing Christian to Singapore had galvanized Margaret's recovery. To find her brother and bring him home had become her single purpose in life. She would not be a party to perpetuating Christian's exile.

Looking at her brother now, she felt a surge of protective love. He was too sweet and gentle, and yes, perhaps frivolous; but together they made a whole. With her steadfastness, they could live together at Pensleigh and be happy.

Liang sank gracefully to the floor and wild stamping filled the air. Richard Jensen leaned forward, applauding heartily. He grinned at the Sumatran beauty around the cheroot clenched in his mouth, his eyes narrowed against the smoke. Atam Datu slapped his thighs and spoke to Richard. With a nod, Richard rose.

"Come," he said to Margaret, "I'll take you back to the *Java*."

"But I've hardly had a chance to talk to Christian," she protested.

"I'm not asking you," he snapped. He held out a hand peremptorily.

"Christian, tell him I'm staying," Margaret said to her brother.

"Atam?" he asked of Richard. Richard nodded tensely. Christian turned back to her. "Sorry, Margaret—you'll have to go."

"But . . . but we haven't even had a chance to discuss you returning home with me, and what we'll do with Pensleigh."

"You can have the old pile for all I care," he said lazily. He smiled up at her, the sapphire eyes abrim with a disarming candor that made the unthinkable nearly thinkable. "I haven't the ambition to lug my carcass to bed, never mind back to England."

"Oh, Christian," she cried, "you can't mean it!" Next to her, she could feel Richard fairly vibrating with annoyance.

"I'll prove it to you," Christian said cheerfully. "Aloud! Ali! To bed, lads!"

Two lithe boys came running, their faces alight with smiles and their golden bodies glistening with the taut musculature of adolescence. With practiced motions, they lifted Christian and prepared to bear him away, recumbent on their shoulders. He smiled down at Margaret with heavy-lidded eyes.

"You see? Mummy had fabulous servants but nothing to compare with this."

"Christian!" Margaret seized his dangling hand. "Don't go!"

"Calm yourself, pet," he said. "This isn't *au revoir*, only *à demain*, or possibly *après du midi*. Who knows? The spirit will be willing, but the flesh is oh-so weak."

He clucked and the boys stepped out in unison, bearing him away smoothly. Margaret clutched at his outstretched hand for one last frantic second, dimly noting yellow-green discolorations on his wrist where the jacket sleeve had ridden up.

"If you don't come with me, I'm going to sling you over my shoulder," Richard grated next to her ear.

She whirled. "How dare you!"

"I haven't *begun* to 'dare,'" he snarled. She recoiled from the fury in his face. His eyes were slits of green ice. "I said you'd see your brother and you have. Now you're going to get out of here before anyone decides they've got more interesting uses for you."

Margaret fled from the hateful look on his face. She rushed around the array of pillows on the floor and down the steps. Christian couldn't wait to get away from her and Richard Jensen was in a lather to be done with her so he could return to Liang. Feeling furious, hurt, and utterly alone, she walked rapidly back down the path to the shore. When she reached the edge of the sand, she heard the crunching of shells behind her and knew that Richard had followed her to enforce his orders. Be damned to him!

"Dogsmeat!" he called out from behind her.

"Aye, Cap'n! Just here." The gig rocked gently in a shadowy patch of moonlight, the dwarf standing smartly to attention next to it.

"Is everything secure aboard?"

"Aye. Daniels, Dekker, and Harkay are all on the sharp, just like you ordered."

"Good. Take Miss Belleweather back. I'll whistle you up later." He turned and was gone almost before they knew it.

Margaret sat silent in the bow of the gig as Dogsmeat rowed. At some point in the evening, she had become convinced that something was very wrong. Christian danced to Atam Datu's tune, content to be a showpiece, and then he smoked amir, whatever that was. And the bruises! *Was* he some sort of prisoner? Had he been induced to take some other sort of drug *before* he arrived at the eating pavilion in order to make him behave as if nothing was wrong?

She *had* to go back, talk to him in private.

"Dogsmeat," she said suddenly.

"Yes, miss?"

"I've just remembered—my brother gave me a very important letter and I've left it behind. Turn back please."

Dogsmeat paused, the oars dripping molten silver into the sea. "I don't know as how I should, miss. We'd best leave it to the captain—he'll find it for you tomorrow."

"But that will be too late," she exclaimed. "My brother told me he's going inland on a . . . a tiger hunt tomorrow. Please—it will only take a minute. I know exactly where to find him." Amazing how easy it was to lie when the stakes were high enough.

"You'll be as quick as ever you can?" he asked doubtfully.

"Truly, just a few minutes," she said.

"And you're sure you know right where to find him?"

"Quite sure," she said.

Dogsmeat turned back. She alit at the shore and made her way quickly up and into Atam Datu's gardens before the steward could change his mind. She walked to one side of the path so that she could pass soundlessly. Nearing the pavilion, she skirted the pond, mindful of Christian's remark about the alligators. A brief glance told her that

169

Atam Datu, Richard, and Liang were no longer within the open eating area.

She kept to the shadows as she struck off in the direction where the boys had carried Christian. Numerous raised houses glowed yellow inside with torchlight as she made her way up the hill. Soft laughter and conversation pierced the night, and she lingered near each house to see if she could pick out her brother's voice. At long last, nearly breathless with exertion and tension, she heard him.

She crept through the heavy, flower-scented darkness, stumbling occasionally as she pinpointed the house, more Western-style than the rest. Mindful of the potential for embarrassment if she blundered into the wrong place, she mounted the stairs and paused in the shadows of the veranda. Somewhere nearby, she thought, Liang and Richard were undoubtedly absorbed in one another. Painful thoughts of his lean, brown body draped over and around the rose-brown one assailed Margaret.

She squeezed her eyes shut. It made the darkness only a little darker, and helped to push the image aside. Christian's voice drifted to her again, speaking some few words of Dutch as far as she could make out. It sounded oddly muffled, mingled with grunts almost. She was about to knock on the door when she heard another voice. Atam Datu!

Paralyzed with fear, Margaret stilled her breathing so that she could hear better. She had no wish to see the rajah again. The odor of fear rose to her nostrils and she realized as the minutes dragged by that the smell came from her own person. The volume of sound increased inside, throaty laughter—Atam's—coupled with groans—Christian's. Alarmed, she inched toward a window. Her brother sounded as if he were in pain—it seemed to confirm her fear that he was somehow being kept here against his will.

The next moment provided her with a scene that would remain forever burned in her memory. Atam Datu stood over Christian's prone body, a triumphant leer on his face as he slashed at the Englishman's naked stomach and thighs with a bundle of palm leaves bound together in a flexible whip. Christian moaned and fought against the

170

restraints which bound his wrists to the wall above his head.

Sheer horror retarded Margaret's instinct to burst in and put a stop to it. One faltering step was as far as she got before Christian cried out and the rajah paused, breathing heavily. Another figure leaped forward, one of the youths who'd carried Christian from the dining pavilion. He held a lit cigarette to Christian's lips. Christian inhaled deeply and grinned dazedly up at the rajah, a sickening lassitude on his face.

Margaret felt every limb begin to shake as she comprehended that her brother was in no way being coerced to participate in the spectacle before her. Incapacitated with shock, she stood there trembling as Atam Datu partook of the cigarette too, and then resumed the awful whipping. How long she stood there, Margaret did not know, but it was long enough for all the details to be seared into her memory—how Christian likewise became aroused and at length was freed, only to perform other acts that she would have given all she owned not to witness.

She prayed for release from the bondage of revulsion, but not until all the occupants of the room lay spent and panting could she force herself to turn and stagger away. Visions of Christian's beautiful face, soaked with sweat and distorted by compulsions of an unspeakable nature, followed her as she hurtled into the night. She stumbled and slid blindly down the hill, tumbling over rocks and lurching into trees and bushes.

A burly shadow moved to the window as she fled. Atam Datu smiled out into the night. Oh, it had been good tonight—impossibly good! He'd meant to swap with the American tonight—his woman for Liang—so that he could have first the brother and then the sister, but how infinitely better this had been! He'd been angry with Jensen for sending his woman back to the ship at first. Now that he knew what the crafty captain had had planned, his anger evaporated. What pleasure he'd had, and all of it trebled by the knowledge that his golden-haired lover's sister was watching in disgust!

Chapter 11

Richard heard Atam Datu's raucous laughter spilling into the night and pushed Liang aside abruptly. Anything that so vastly pleased the rajah could only bode ill for someone else. He tuned his ears to the darkness beyond and heard something crashing through the undergrowth not far away. Liang pulled gently at his face, offering up her lips with a smile of pure arousal. Rigid with the effort to hear, Richard didn't respond. The sounds came closer. He heard labored breathing and then a sharp thud.

The cry which followed brought him up off the sleeping pallet in one swift motion. Margaret was supposed to be safely back on the *Java!* Liang twined around his leg as he reached for his pants, but he shook her off. Not even bothering to retrieve his shoes and shirt, he punched his way through the curtain draped across the entrance and raced down the hill.

He caught up with Margaret near the beach after what seemed like an eternity of forcing his way through the jungle, pausing every so often to listen for the sound of her movements. When he was still a few steps away, he called out.

"Margaret!"

She whirled and stared at him, her eyes huge with shock. Moonlight silvered the tears on her cheeks as she gasped for air.

"What's wrong?" he panted.

172

"Christian . . . I went back and . . ."

He reached for her, needing no more details. She reeled into his arms and he crushed her to his bare chest. Wracking sobs tore loose from her and he stroked her hair, shaking nearly as hard as she was. Damn Christian, and damn Atam Datu! He whistled, one long, high urgent sound that streaked out across the water. And damn Dogsmeat! He'd had his orders. How in God's name had Margaret managed to get back ashore?

"Richard . . ." The odd note in her voice caught his attention immediately. He held her away from him and saw that her face was stark white. "Richard, I think I'm going to . . ."

With an efficient twist of his body, he turned her so that she could be sick. Shudders racked her again and again until it seemed as if she must have brought up everything she'd ever eaten. He supported her head with one hand under her forehead, and, when the worst of it was over, he felt the trembling weakness in her. The gig scraped on the sand, and he waited as several more dry heaves gusted through her before hoisting her into his arms. Richard scrambled into the gig with his burden and Dogsmeat stared at them in alarm. He opened his mouth to speak.

"Shut up!" Richard snarled.

The dwarf jumped to the oars and pulled toward the *Java*, which rode at anchor far enough out to be beyond easy reach of a raiding party. It would have been faster for Richard to row the gig himself but not for anything would he set Margaret aside. She lay unnaturally still in his arms, her breathing faint and rapid.

For once, he regretted that the only way to carry her up the ladder was over his shoulder, afraid that it would set off another bout of retching, but he decided against waiting for the bosun's chair to be rigged. Dogsmeat followed him hastily up on deck and Richard rounded on him, shifting Margaret to his arms again.

"Get the hell out of my sight and stay out of it, you bastard! I should have left you on the docks of London!"

The dwarf flinched but offered no challenge.

173

"Tony!" Richard bellowed. The swarthy cook jumped up off the coil of rope where he'd been sitting. "Tea—my cabin—right away!"

"But I got no fire in . . ."

"Now!" Richard roared. "Daniels!"

"Sir!" The answer came aft.

"Cast off!"

The sheets on his berth were fresh since the morning, he noted, the lantern lit and trimmed low, and fresh water in the sink. None of it mattered—he'd still kick that little Cockney rodent from bow to stern if he saw him anytime soon. He hipped the door shut behind him and lowered Margaret to the berth. She clutched at him and he shushed her gently, disengaging her hands so that he could bring a wet cloth to wipe her face. She grabbed at him desperately when he returned, her nails digging deep into his bare arms.

He ignored the pain and wiped her face clean. Her cheeks were pinched and her lips colorless. But it was her eyes, liquid with pain and shock, that wrenched at him. He removed the few remaining pins from her hair and combed it back from her face with his fingers as she sat there unresisting.

A hesitant knock on the door made her jerk. "Come in," Richard said. Because Margaret wouldn't let him go, he nodded to the chest of drawers by the berth. "Leave it here, Tony."

When the door closed again, she burrowed into his chest like a small animal seeking shelter. She whimpered, and he sat back against the bulkhead, drawing her up to lay alongside him. Oh, Margaret, he thought—*you weren't ready for any of this. You were just a little innocent despite all your brave words*.

As if sensing the direction of his thoughts, she whispered brokenly, "You were right about everything, about Christian . . ."

"Hush," he said. He reached out for the steaming mug. "Here, have some tea. It will help your stomach." He angled her up so that she could drink it, but her hands

174

were shaking so badly that he had to put his hand over hers to steady the cup.

"I saw . . ." She looked up at him over the rim of the cup. "Did you know that he and Atam Datu . . . ?"

"I suspected," he said shortly. He nudged the cup and she took another swallow.

"And those boys," she said, withdrawing her mouth from the cup. "They were all . . ."

"Yes, I can imagine the rest," Richard said, cutting her off. But she told him everything anyway, halting at times, but very literal and painstaking nonetheless. When she was done, Richard took the empty cup from her. He hoped the telling had been cathartic, because the listening had been hell. He folded her in his arms and gave her the only comfort he could, the warmth of his body and the steady beat of his heart beneath her cheek.

At last she fell into an exhausted sleep, somewhere near dawn. He left her just long enough to go up on deck and tell Daniels to set a course for Java Head. She'd want to go back home now. She'd go, and he would keep to himself the realization that had come to him in the night as he held her and listened to her breathing.

Lightening flickered along the horizon as the day darkened early. To hold the course for Java Head meant sailing right into the storm, but that was what he meant to do. He'd sailed into the teeth of a gale before, and never with better cause. Margaret Belleweather had slept through the morning, and each time he checked on her, the sight of her slim, small body in his berth had reminded him that it was better to tackle the hardest issues head-on.

The sea let the *Java* pass easily enough for now, still docile at this distance, but he estimated it would be no more than another hour or two before they'd hit the squall in earnest. The smell of the sea change conveyed that to him more accurately than any barometer.

A flash of lavender caught his eye and he turned in surprise. He hadn't expected to see Margaret Belleweather on deck at all this day. She made her way down to the main deck and leaned on the port rail, staring at the storm up ahead. On the pretext of warning her about the heavy weather, he went forward. Even to himself the excuse felt thin. She was no fool—she could see it as well as he could, but the compulsion to be near her was too strong.

Dogsmeat scuttled away at his approach. Richard stood next to Margaret, emptied of the message he'd been going to deliver by the fresh scent of violets drifting from her. The steward had undoubtedly seen to her need to wash and dress in fresh clothes. The idiot was good for some things—too bad he had failed her so abysmally last night by not following orders.

Margaret stared out to sea. Richard wasn't even sure she knew he was standing there until she spoke without warning, as if continuing out loud a conversation that had been running through her head.

"I've decided I can't afford to be so blind anymore."

"So blind?"

"So naive. I must open my eyes and see the world and the people in it for what they are." Her eyes narrowed. "To have been so unable to understand what I was looking at with my eyes wide open—it's unforgivable."

There was a hardness in her, not the brittle, peremptory manner of before, but true steel.

"You're being pretty hard on yourself, aren't you?" he said. "It's a rare person who would have guessed about your brother based on what you knew."

"*You* knew." It had an accusatory ring.

He shrugged. "I've seen too much of the world to be ignorant of such things."

"Ignorance!" she spat. "I've always despised ignorance." In the distance, lightning flicked, and in the gathering gloom, the reflection painted her eyes with pain. "Knowledge is what separates us from the animals, but now I see that in what's important, I'm as ignorant as any animal." Waves of self-disgust rolled off her.

"You *are* an animal," he countered, trying to temper the heat of her words. "We're *all* animals. To be ignorant of

176

that is to be ignorant of everything. We all share the same needs—to be warm, to eat, to have shelter, to feel pleasure."

"There!" she said, still in that ragged tone of self-accusal. "That's the kind of thing I mean. That's a matter of simple logic and I completely overlooked it. You're right, of course."

The way she was whipping herself disturbed him. "Margaret," he said gently, "you've led too sheltered a life to blame yourself for not having known about Christian."

"And it's left me desperately, dangerously naive," she snapped. "Everyone always told me what a fine mind I had, and I believed them. Now I see that all the education in the world serves no purpose unless there's wisdom to go with it, common sense."

Richard had no answer for that. Still, he wanted to gentle her. "Common sense comes through mistakes and learning from them. It's never too late for that."

"Since I'm so new at this, perhaps you'd better help me," she said bitterly.

Richard wondered what in the world he could tell her that would bring her any comfort. Her violet eyes shimmered with self-contempt and her shoulders were hunched up, as if braced for a blow. He had to say something, help her to find a reasonable middle ground. "Common sense will tell you that everyone has to run his own life. We all make bad decisions at times." He laughed self-deprecatingly. "God knows, *I* have. But in the end, they were *my* decisions, and no one else's. It's the same for Christian. What he does with his life is his own business."

She exhaled sharply. *"That* I can't accept."

"You must," he said calmly, "and you assured me in Batavia that you could and would, or I'd have never taken you to Atjeh."

"But . . . but . . ." She faltered for the first time. "He can't decide freely. He's in thrall to the amir. How else could he allow the rajah to . . . to beat him." She stopped, staring sightlessly out over the lead-colored sea. "And the other . . ." she said with a tremor in her voice that hinted at what it cost her to go on, "to let that man touch him and to . . ."

"Margaret." He took her by the shoulders and pulled her around to face him. "The way you're tormenting yourself is hardly any less awful than what Christian allows Atam Datu to do to *him*."

Her eyes widened with shock and her mouth dropped. "I'm only trying to face the truth clearly, so I can see how best to help my brother."

"No, you're not. You're letting yourself be torn apart, Margaret, and you can't do that. You're berating yourself over *Christian's* choices." He shook her impatiently and fixed his eyes on hers. "Maybe the drug *does* play a part. Maybe he wouldn't have slipped so far over the edge if he didn't use amir, but don't you see? It was his choice to smoke it."

"No!" A dawning horror on her face revealed that she saw where he was leading.

"Yes, Margaret," he said equally forcefully. He gripped her tighter so that she couldn't evade his gaze. "Christian *knows* what the amir does. Maybe he even smokes it purposely, because it frees him to follow his uglier inclinations."

"No!" It was less sharp this time but no less haunted.

"Yes!" His eyes bored into hers. "The amir doesn't make him forget what happens while he's under its influence. When he woke up this morning, he remembered everything he did last night, everything you saw, and tonight, he'll smoke it again."

"No . . ." This time it was barely more than a whisper and he felt her sag against him.

"I wish it weren't so, for your sake, but it is. He came here of his own free will and he smokes the amir of his own free will." A sudden thought struck him. "He started using opium in Singapore—he found places where he could indulge himself in some of the kinds of things you saw last night. Why do you think he left? Because it still wasn't enough. Men do peculiar things, Margaret, men *and* women, to satisfy their urges, but it was Christian who embarked on this course, and Christian who'll go on down

178

this road until *he* changes his mind. Don't you think he knows we'd have taken him away with us if he asked? Did he ask, Margaret? Did he?''

She moaned and he felt her slipping out of his grasp. He quickly let go of her shoulders and took her by the waist. Her face was a mask of pain.

"It was the only thing he *didn't* say," she admitted raggedly. "I waited and I hoped, but he didn't. That's why I went back, to ask him again. I thought Atam Datu was keeping him prisoner, that he couldn't speak freely in front of him. I saw the marks on his wrist and I thought . . .''

She finally crumpled and Richard caught her up against him. He held her fiercely, bending his head to bury his cheek in the golden hair. "I wasn't positive myself, not until last night," he said quietly. "That's another reason I offered Atam Datu guns, so that he'd be disposed to let Christian leave if he wanted to go."

"Oh, Richard—it's no use, is it?" Her muffled voice came up from between them, weak with misery. "He's not ever coming back."

"No, I don't think so," he said. It was gut-wrenching to say it but he couldn't let her go on deluding herself. If he hadn't held out some small hope that the rumors were wrong, he never would have brought her to Atjeh. It had been a mistake, *his* choice, and a wrong one, as it turned out.

They stood for a long time without speaking. He held her and stroked her hair, oblivious to the occasional sidelong glance from a crewman.

"I don't want to go back home now," she mumbled at long last. "There's no reason to without him."

Richard's heart constricted painfully. Was this a chance for him? But he couldn't trade on her misery. "You'll feel different once this is behind you. Give yourself time."

She pulled back, a little surer on her feet now, and gazed at him clear-eyed. "I intend to. Richard . . .'' She paused, measuring him with her eyes. "I want to stay here, on the *Java*, for a little while longer. I can't face going back to

England just yet, being all alone at Pensleigh. If you'll let me stay, I'll find a way to be useful."

The erratic rhythm of his heart increased and his mouth went dry as he felt the fervor in her words and saw it in the gentian eyes. Even so, he found a gentle humor in her proclamation, and wanted to give her a graceful way out. "And how do you intend to be useful here?"

"I've thought about that," she said solemnly, "and it seems to me that there are a lot of things I could do—mend clothing, especially for the apprentices, or teach them how to do it—and perhaps help Tony with the cooking."

An impossibly frail, delicate happiness pounded at his heart, begging entry. He wanted to laugh out loud. Margaret Belleweather mending clothes, cooking? Didn't she know where her true value lay—just in letting him be near her?

Getting no response, she went on. "I don't know what else, but surely there are other things, too. I won't stay forever, I promise, and I know enough not to get in anyone's way, or be a bother."

"Oh, Margaret, never that," he said gently. He smiled, forbidding himself to feel the ache of the words: *I won't stay forever.*

"You needn't be kind," she said. "I know that I *have* been a bother in the past." Her lashes swept downward and she continued speaking softly, her gaze fixed on his chest. "You really have been kind though, right from the beginning, by treating me as an adult and trying to tell me the truth about Christian. I see that now." She looked up again suddenly, her eyes unusually bright. "That's one of the reasons I want to stay. I feel . . . I feel as if you're the only person left in the world who cares about me, and I . . . Richard . . ." She reached out and touched his cheek, her eyes imploring him for understanding. He felt his pulse beating heavily. "Richard, I care about you, care *for* you, I should say. I won't be a nuisance about it, but I need someone just now and . . ."

He put a finger to her lips, wanting to stop her at just that point. The fullness in his chest swelled until it threatened to burst. Did he dare tell her? Her lips trembled under his finger. What had she really said? That she wanted to stay with him, for at least right now—that that would be enough.

He lifted his finger from her mouth, softly drawing it across her cheek. "That will be fine, Margaret. I'd like that," he said quietly.

She smiled, a full, radiant smile that made his blood quicken. "What do we do now?" she asked. There was an expectancy, a lightness in her voice that told of how much she had feared the wrong answer, and how happy the right one had made her. Out of all this awfulness, she had already learned the first and most important lesson—to be happy for whatever happiness came her way. It had taken him much longer to learn.

"We go to Australia, my little Margaret," he said, exhilarated by the thought of her sailing on with him.

She laughed in response to his unspoken joy. "Through that storm?"

He glanced over his shoulder. He'd almost forgotten it. "Regrettably, yes, through that storm. Once we make it to Java Head, I can set a course."

"Why not from here?" she asked, her face still alight.

"Because, dearest one," he said, "with this overcast sky, I'm forced to rely on a charted heading, and the chart only gives course headings from common points. This," he said with a sweeping gesture, "is the middle of nowhere."

"I understand that," she said, still smiling, "but if you know approximately where 'here' is, and where 'there' is, can't you strike out to sea now in roughly the right direction and wait for a clear sky to shoot a sight later? You could make the necessary course correction then."

He smiled at her naive assumption. "I *do* know, close enough without shooting a sight, where 'here' is, and I double damn sure know where Darwin is, but a sextant reading isn't going to give me a reliable enough position out in the middle of the ocean."

"Perhaps I'm not following you," Margaret said, frowning. "Do you mean to say that your sextant isn't very accurate?"

Richard smiled. She looked so dear, her face screwed up

earnestly. "No, what I mean is that the reading will be reliable but calculating a position from its results in only a very imprecise location."

"Even using the line of position formula?"

Now it was his turn to frown. "Line of position? What do you mean, line of position?"

"Oh, Richard," she said with a happy smile, "I'm going to start being useful even sooner than I'd hoped. Come," she said, taking his hand, "I'll show you what I mean."

He let himself be pulled across the deck, astonished. "You don't mean to tell me that you know something about . . . ?"

"I certainly do," she said as she towed him up the quarterdeck. "My father, although he was the fifth earl of Pensleigh, studied engineering so that he could invest more intelligently in the railroad boom." She paused at the top of the companionway to the saloon. "Quite simply, he taught me all the higher mathematics he knew, including how to reckon line of position, which he thought one of the most brilliant advances to have been made in his lifetime."

"Incredible," he said.

She laughed. "Not incredible at all."

They were in the saloon now. Dogsmeat was just lighting the gimballed lantern over the table against the premature darkness. He sidled away as they entered but Richard was in the mood to forgive him, indeed, to forgive anyone who'd ever done him a wrong.

"Stay, you gutter rat, and see that you figure out everything I want the instant before I even know that I want it," he said gruffly.

A grin split the dwarf's face. "Aye, Cap'n!"

"We're going to do some navigational ciphering," Margaret said happily.

"Ah." Dogsmeat said knowingly. "Then you'd be wanting the charts and such."

Once the charts and maps were laid out, Margaret rapidly grasped the fundamentals. "Give me the sextant reading of a location for which you know the coordinates," she said. "Then I'll show you how the formula is applied."

Feeling incredibly lighthearted, Richard took the cheroot Dogsmeat held out. "You're quite sure about this?" he asked.

Margaret glanced up and smiled at him. "Quite sure. Besides, you needn't take my word for it—you can check my result to satisfy yourself that it's the location you know it to be."

"Really incredible," he said. He puffed the cheroot to life as he searched through the papers. "Boxing a compass and using the standard charts is all anyone does most of the time. If this line of position business is as accurate as you seem to think it is, I'll be hell on the high seas from now on."

Margaret laughed. "I was under the impression that you already were."

He leaned forward eagerly. "Lies," he said impatiently, "everything you've heard." He waved aside her riposte. "You'll teach me what you know?" Just the prospect of sitting at the table, shoulder to shoulder with her, gave him joy.

"If you'll teach me what *you* know," she said.

He reached across the charts and took her hand. "Whatever it is you want to know, Margaret, whatever it is you want to know."

She blushed, almost imperceptibly, and he was intrigued. "Let me think about what that might be," she said, before pulling her hand away and returning her attention to the charts.

He sat back and watched her working busily over the reading he'd given her, loving the play of the lantern's light across the gold of her hair, and the graceful curve of her slender neck. No doubt she'd tell him, in the fullness of time, just what thought had inspired that faint pink tinge. For the moment though, he felt no urgency to know, content with what was, on the face of it, a remarkable development.

Chapter 12

They stood on deck and inhaled the air of the open ocean. Countless stars pulsed in the blackness overhead. It was that rare time of month when no moon played over the water—last night had been its last in the cycle. Richard longed to put his arms around Margaret, to hold her to the swaying rhythm of the *Java*, but she hadn't asked for that, only to be here.

He had never known greater happiness than in the past week, setting a fast pace to Darwin over a sea that welcomed them, and spending hours at Margaret's side, watching her slender, competent hands reduce the mysteries of survey mathematics to child's play. She'd even tried her hand at making duff, the simplest of sailor's desserts, under Tony's guidance. What resulted hadn't been exactly what any of them remembered as duff, but her desire to be a part of the *Java*'s daily routine pleased him beyond measure.

He wanted more, much more. Sometimes he awoke with cramps in his legs and belly from wanting her, and lay in the darkness for hours, damp with the sweat of frustrated need. He had come to realize that his desire for Liang had been fueled in great measure by his hidden ache to make love to Margaret—an ache which he had thought an aberration at first, the result of a situation and not deep feelings for her.

To be tentative was utterly alien to his nature, but the

pragmatist in him said to watch and wait for an opportune time only made sense. Margaret seemed curiously shy with him just now, and rather than risk frightening her away altogether, he bided his time, fervently hoping that there would come a moment when he could be sure she would welcome his embrace.

"It's late."

Margaret's voice failed to startle him even after the long silence; his awareness of her was constant. His skin tingled with the sensation of being less that a handspan from her in the darkness. Seeing her go below to close Daniels' door behind her each night was a kind of torture. Tonight he couldn't bear to part so easily.

"Would you like some sherry before you go to sleep?" he asked. It sounded idiotic, like some parlor dandy's gambit, but it was all he could think of.

"Yes, please," she said softly.

Dogsmeat had trimmed the lantern in the saloon back after dinner, but Richard didn't bother to turn the flame up. The pale saffron glow still seemed too bright after the pitch of the night. He handed Margaret a glass of Spanish sherry. The amber liquid glistened in the light. She sipped at it slowly, and he was mesmerized by the sight of her soft, full lips on the edge of the glass.

She seemed unusually still tonight. Only the faint flaring of her nostrils in the otherwise motionless face betrayed her, giving mute testimony to some turbulent emotion within.

"What are you thinking about?" he asked.

She glanced up, her eyes luminous in the soft light. "I was thinking how very beautiful Liang was."

He snorted. "Is that all?"

She hesitated. "Was Liang very . . . I mean, did you have a good . . ." She stopped.

Incredulous, he said, "Just what is it you're asking me?"

She flushed and lowered her eyes. "Nothing. I just meant that you must have enjoyed . . ."

He couldn't help it. He laughed. "You're jealous!" The thought filled him with happiness.

185

She looked up and he was sorry he'd been so cavalier, for it was obviously a serious matter to her. He set his glass down and knelt by her seat. "Yes, she's very beautiful, and no, I didn't."

Relief swept across her face like a cloud scudding across the sky. "I know I have no right to concern myself with your affairs, but . . ." She blinked. "That was a poor choice of words," she said, quickly recovering herself, "only . . ."

"Only you were jealous?" He could barely keep the tender triumph out of his voice. He took her face in his hands. "Oh, Margaret, I never thought you would be or I'd have explained. I didn't want Atam Datu to think you mattered *too* much to me, so I was prepared to play along with Liang—not that it would have been a great hardship, at least before I met you."

"Do you mean that Richard—that knowing me made it different somehow?"

"After the performance we did for the rajah?" he asked, rubbing his thumbs softly across her cheekbones. "I wanted to make love to you like no woman I've ever known."

"You've known a lot of women, haven't you?" she asked quietly, her eyes never leaving his.

It was an odd question, not one he'd expected. He studied her and felt her charged stillness beneath his hands. It didn't seem the moment to hedge. "I have," he said.

"Teach me, Richard," she said simply. "Teach me about pleasure."

Desire roared up in him, white hot. It was devastating in its intensity, all from those few, unadorned words. The thought of her inexperience was the only thing which checked his impulse to seize her and have her then and there, in the saloon, to devour her in one cataclysmic burst.

He took the glass of sherry from her with shaking hands and pulled her to her feet. "Gladly."

Exerting rigorous control, he steadied his hands and took her face again, tenderly and slowly, and brought his mouth down on hers with infinite patience.

For just an instant, he tasted the sweetness of the sherry, and then he was past it, to the infinitely sweeter taste of her. She trembled as he moved his lips over hers, and he was afraid that just the thoughts he was thinking were scaring her. But she brought her hands up over his and he realized with a surge of gladness that she welcomed his touch.

Incredibly, it was she who broached the gentle kiss first. She softly opened her mouth and ever so lightly touched his lower lip with her tongue. Fire raced through him as he savored the intimate plundering. Who was seducing who?

With a heady feeling of triumph, he pulled away and smiled, deep and shining, into her eyes. "Oh, Margaret," he whispered, "you were made for pleasure." He took her mouth surely then, and felt her sway into him as a small moan arose from her throat.

If he could have made himself part with the taste of her at that moment, he would have thrown back his head and laughed out loud. She would be his! This would be no gradual teaching of the art of love, but the opening salvo in a full-fledged sharing of mutual passion. His heart was beating so hard it hurt, and he swept her into his arms, never letting go of the contact between their mouths. He angled through the door to his cabin and pushed it closed with his back.

She twined her arms around his neck, taut with longing. Oh, the urgency to have her! He laid her on the berth, covering her with his body and already feeling the need to drive into her, the muscles in his hips and thighs bunching.

He wanted to be gentle—oh, how he wanted to be gentle—but she whimpered and clung to him, urging him on. The wild, sweet love he felt for her fought with the last rational thoughts in his mind. My God! A virgin—she had to be. He'd never, to his knowledge, even had a virgin. He *had* to slow down, *had* to say the things she should hear this first time.

But his fingers continued their ferocious assault. Gripping her waist, he rolled half over, bringing her to lay beside him as he undid the fasteners at the back of her skirt.

"Oh, Margaret, forgive me," he murmured, nipping urgently at her throat, "I want you too much."

She tipped her head back and let out a throaty laugh. "I love being wanted by you," she said, her voice husky. "Want me, Richard, want me as much as you like."

A monstrous, fiery lust roared through him. He stared at her, panting. Her skin, fair and fresh as new milk, gleamed in the soft light of the bedside lantern, her eyes heavy-lidded and brilliant with desire—how could a man stay sane in the face of this? Other times, many times lay ahead, he told himself ruthlessly. Be careful to make this time right!

She shredded his momentary control by taking the top button of his shirt and undoing it, and then the next, and the next, all the while with her eyes locked on his and a soft, knowing smile on her lips. His frenzied breathing didn't deter her as she worked her way down, keeping her hold on the shirt unerringly as his chest moved rapidly under her fingers.

"I want to see you," she whispered. "I love your body."

Richard felt for the first time a very real fear that he might explode before he could even undress her, never mind himself. He captured one of her hands and kissed it, trying to slow her down. His sense of irony was not buried so deep beneath desire that he didn't appreciate the incongruity of having to slow *her* down. He pressed his lips to the pad of each of her fingertips as she watched him with languid delight.

But her other hand continued its exploration, sliding over bone and muscle, and over skin exquisitely attuned to her touch. She traced lightly over his nipples and he sucked in a knifelike breath as she slowed and circled one. It ached and tautened and he saw that his response kindled sparks in the deep purple eyes that watched him so closely.

"Oh, Margaret, you can't know what that does to me," he groaned.

188

"Then tell me," she said softly. "You're the teacher."

Richard wasn't so sure. She pulled her hand free and rubbed his chest with both hands, positively glowing with desire as she traced the muscles there, not lightly, but with sensual intent.

It was too much for him. He pulled her shirt apart, careless of the buttons—there were plenty in the slop chest—and drew a ragged breath at the sight of tender, full breasts straining toward him through the fine cambric of her camisole. With a groan, he buried his face in the valley between them.

"Oh, Richard, that's nice," Margaret whispered above his head. She twined her hands through his hair as he eagerly pulled the fabric away to free her breasts.

"They're beautiful," he murmured, "so beautiful."

"Take them then," she said, pulling his head toward her.

What remnant of self-restraint Richard had still possessed was shredded with those words. Deftly and efficiently, he stripped first her and then himself. He was careful to be sure that haste didn't turn to roughness, but a lingering, sweet seduction no longer played any part in his intentions.

She loosened her hair and lay back with a smile, a most unvirginal smile that made him wonder, in the several heartbeats it took him to reach her side, whether she truly was inexperienced. He took her in his arms, not caring. She was here, she was his.

He gazed down at her for a long moment. That precious face—how he adored it. He would make himself take his time, if not for her sake then for his. The heavy, waving gold cloud of her hair spread out around her head and spilled across the forest green blanket on his berth. Funny how a simple, utilitarian wool blanket had suddenly become a frame for a work of art. He laughed, low and deep.

"What is it?" she asked, her eyes merry but her voice thick with arousal.

"Nothing, love, nothing," he said. She'd think the

189

thought odd and unromantic if he shared it. "Only that you're beautiful."

"Don't lie to me," she said, her expression sharpening.

The knowledge that she was so unsure of her own beauty distracted him from pure lust as nothing else had. "But you are beautiful, Margaret," he said softly, "and I love you."

There! He had said it. Now all he could do was to try and make her believe it. He traced the arching golden brows with his lips, dimly registering the surprise and disbelief in the violet eyes beneath. The full mouth parted with denial but he covered it quickly with his own, just long enough to feel her respond, her body yearning upwards to him.

The frail, slender shoulder felt good under the palm of his hand. He bunched her hair with his other hand and dipped his face into the shadowy hollow beneath her ear. "So sweet," he murmured as her scent filled his nostrils, "so sweet."

Her hands moved across his back, slowly, taking pleasure as her body relaxed from the tension of denial and began to tauten again with desire. Now his arousal was more constant, steady and sure as the beat of his heart. He kissed her slowly, confident that he could savor her mouth without his control being shattered.

He drew his hand down the slender arm and took her waist, his thumb spanning her stomach and his fingers arrayed across her back. A faint dew moistened them as she arched against him.

"Richard, love me," she said breathlessly, "please love me." The taut urgency in her renewed plea mirrored the astounding response of her body.

"I will, love," he said, gazing into the hungry violet eyes. "I'll love you, but slowly." She whimpered in protest and he felt even more in control. "I'm the teacher," he whispered in her ear, "remember?" He took her ear lobe between his teeth and rolled it gently. She bucked beneath his hand and he firmed his grip on her waist.

"Oh, please," she said, straining to rub her breasts

across his chest. Richard felt dizzy with satisfaction, master of himself and the situation. He had no doubt what she was asking for, though he wondered briefly if *she* did.

"Oh, love," he murmured, "you want me so soon?"

"Yes," she said raggedly. All the earlier playfulness was gone from her face, supplanted by urgency. He truly would be the teacher now.

"Then you'll have to wait," he said, softly triumphant, "until *I'm* ready." The painful throbbing between his legs made it a grotesque lie but he didn't care. All that mattered was that before he entered her, *she* was truly ready.

He raised himself on one elbow and gloried in the sight of her pale, full breasts, the nipples rosy with longing. Gently, slowly, he took one in his mouth and stroked it with his tongue. She gasped and her hands clenched on his back as it tautened fully in his mouth.

By God, but she responded sweetly! With his hand, he cupped the fullness of flesh which his mouth could not reach, and he felt it firming under his fingers. He shifted so that his other hand was free and he could mold both breasts in his hands, pushing them together. He buried his face between them and then drew his tongue along the faintly salty line where they met.

Margaret tipped her head back and thrust herself into his hands as a low, deep moan rose from her throat. Her hands scrabbled at the back of his head, twisting through his hair. Satisfaction ripped through Richard at this proof of her pleasure. To create such arousal in her thrilled him more surely than his own arousal, but he felt the fine edge of his control slipping as he kissed her other nipple and heard the throaty sounds grow louder.

"Richard! Oh, please . . ."

It was amazing, his beautiful Margaret so abandoned to desire, and so ardently begging him for the very thing he longed to give her! He laughed softly, the sound muffled against the ripe heat of her breasts. He drew his weight off her and saw the glorious breasts fall back, but only a little, despite the withdrawal of his hands. A man could make love to her breasts alone, so full and taut and high.

191

She reached out desperately, seeking him but finding only air. He had gone from sharpest lust to profound arousal and now found himself at the brink which had no name. Margaret had clearly reached that stage, too. The tension in her body and the mute, beseeching look in her eyes told him that beyond any doubt.

To deny themselves any longer would be unthinkable. He parted her thighs with first one leg and then the other and settled between them on folded legs. Whatever shyness he may have expected was totally lacking. She opened herself fully to him, her eyes wide with expectation and her mouth tense. She stretched her hands out toward him eagerly.

"Yes, love," he murmured, stroking her spread thighs, "now." But he didn't want to lose sight of her beautiful breasts, or miss the expression on her small, exquisite face. Her hips moved erratically and Richard quivered. He spread her knees apart, opening her further, and reached around to seize her buttocks.

He stared in fascination at the glistening wetness between her legs, and was struck forcibly by a hundred desires at once—to touch, to taste—but she wrapped her fingers around his forearms and pulled herself firmly against his shaft, her face avid. It forestalled any response in him but the obvious one.

Fire curled through his belly as he felt her heated flesh lapping at his own. A ferocious need to sink deep inside her consumed him. He pushed against the flushed, moist flesh and it parted easily, slick with arousal. He groaned as heat now licked at him from within and without, and he saw her eyes closing, her chin tipping up as she arched her back to accommodate him.

A last, frantic thought assailed him. Had she really meant for it to go this far? Or had her own passionate nature carried her beyond a boundary she had not meant to cross? Pain stilled him for a moment, and he knew that his real fear was that she did not love him as he loved him. He felt the pull of her hands on his forearms and roused, as if from a dream.

MORE PASSION AND ADVENTURE AWAIT... YOUR TRIP TO A BIG ADVENTUROUS WORLD BEGINS WHEN YOU ACCEPT YOUR FIRST 4 NOVELS ABSOLUTELY *FREE* (AN $18.00 VALUE)

Accept your Free gift and start to experience more of the passion and adventure you like in a historical romance novel. Each Zebra novel is filled with proud men, spirited women and tempestuous love that you'll remember long after you turn the last page.

Zebra Historical Romances are the finest novels of their kind. They are written by authors who really know how to weave tales of romance and adventure in the historical settings you love. You'll feel like you've actually gone back in time with the thrilling stories that each Zebra novel offers.

GET YOUR FREE GIFT WITH THE START OF YOUR HOME SUBSCRIPTION

Our readers tell us that these books sell out very fast in book stores and often they miss the newest titles. So Zebra has made arrangements for you to receive the four newest novels published each month.

You'll be guaranteed that you'll never miss a title, and home delivery is so convenient. And to show you just how easy it is to get Zebra Historical Romances, we'll send you your first 4 books absolutely FREE! Our gift to you just for trying our home subscription service.

BIG SAVINGS AND FREE HOME DELIVERY

Each month, you'll receive the four newest titles as soon as they are published. You'll probably receive them even before the bookstores do. What's more, you may preview these exciting novels free for 10 days. If you like them as much as we think you will, just pay the low preferred subscriber's price of just $3.75 each. *You'll save $3.00 each month off the publisher's price.* AND, your savings are even greater because there are never any shipping, handling or other hidden charges—FREE Home Delivery. Of course you can return any shipment within 10 days for full credit, no questions asked. There is no minimum number of books you must buy.

4 FREE BOOKS

TO GET YOUR 4 FREE BOOKS WORTH $18.00 — MAIL IN THE FREE BOOK CERTIFICATE T O D A Y

Fill in the Free Book Certificate below, and we'll send your FREE BOOKS to you as soon as we receive it.

If the certificate is missing below, write to: Zebra Home Subscription Service, Inc., P.O. Box 5214, 120 Brighton Road, Clifton, New Jersey 07015-5214.

FREE BOOK CERTIFICATE

4 FREE BOOKS

ZEBRA HOME SUBSCRIPTION SERVICE, INC.

YES! Please start my subscription to Zebra Historical Romances and send me my first 4 books absolutely FREE. I understand that each month I may preview four new Zebra Historical Romances free for 10 days. If I'm not satisfied with them, I may return the four books within 10 days and owe nothing. Otherwise, I will pay the low preferred subscriber's price of just $3.75 each; a total of $15.00, *a savings off the publisher's price of $3.00.* I may return any shipment and I may cancel this subscription at any time. There is no obligation to buy any shipment and there are no shipping, handling or other hidden charges. Regardless of what I decide, the four free books are mine to keep.

NAME _____

ADDRESS _____ APT _____

CITY _____ STATE _____ ZIP _____

TELEPHONE ( ) _____

SIGNATURE _____ (if under 18, parent or guardian must sign)

Terms, offer and prices subject to change without notice. Subscription subject to acceptance by Zebra Books. Zebra Books reserves the right to reject any order or cancel any subscription.

"Love me, Richard, please . . ." she pleaded, her eyes smoky with wanting.

By God, he *would* love her, and bring her such pleasure that she would say the words he longed to hear. Doubt vanished, superseded by determination.

"Yes, love, I will," he said hoarsely, nearly strangled by the fierceness of his desire to please her. He took her hips and slowly pushed against her. He felt a faint resistance and she moaned. He stopped in shock, afraid that he had already sabotaged his cause by hurting her, but she clutched at his arms and locked herself more tightly in their intimate embrace.

Relieved, he took a deep shuddering breath. He carefully withdrew his shaft the small distance between them and gently delved into the tender flesh again. In and out, with minute strokes, focusing on the way her tender, overheated flesh stretched and released with each incursion. Sweat trickled down his temple, and his jaw ached with the effort not to feel what he was feeling.

Margaret let out a silky sound, deep in her throat, nearly purring. It sent a flame through him and he could restrain himself no longer. He pulled her hips to him in one swift motion, burying his shaft deep against the soft, golden curls, and she cried out. He butted softly in and out, restricted in his movement by his awkward position. He clenched her buttocks with his hands, pulling her to him and letting her slide back. With each small thrust, he felt her grasping at him with her innermost flesh.

God help him, but he had never known anything like it! Margaret's eyes were wide open now and fixed on him in wonderment, shining with the first tendrils of pleasure he felt pulsing within her. Before long, she tried to push harder at him but failed. Unable to oblige her, he cursed his lack of mobility. Panting, her hips coiling with desire, she solved their dilemma by wrapping her legs behind his back and pulling herself against him forcefully.

Her full breasts trembled with each stroke, and her mouth widened as her breathing became more labored. Sweat ran down his back as waves of excruciating pleasure rolled through him. He wanted to open his mouth, say sweet things to her about how he felt, but he couldn't. Any slight break in his concentration and he would lose the last, razor-thin control he had. Margaret gripped his arms, her fingers tightening urgently.

"Oh, Richard!" Ecstasy lit her voice and he was undone.

He rapidly unfolded his legs, momentarily losing his place deep within her. She cried out and he threw himself forward, finding the heated sanctuary again and plunging into it as he kissed her. Blinded by pleasure, he plumbed her mouth, too, and great, rolling waves of ecstasy crashed over him without warning. He stroked on and on as the ungovernable tide swept through him, great foam-flecked breakers that tossed him at will.

The surging tide gradually ebbed. His heart still hammered and the faint glow of the lantern made misty reflections in the sheen of sweat across Margaret's shoulder, undoubtedly his own sweat, he realized. He slowly regained possession of the soul which had deserted him at the height of ecstasy and he realized that he hadn't even the strength to lift his weight off of her.

Margaret! Stunned, he realized that he had failed her utterly, taken her on a great voyage and then been swept overboard, leaving her behind. Remorse knifed through him.

"Margaret, dearest one," he whispered brokenly, "I'm so sorry. I couldn't help myself."

There was no sound from her except deep, rapid breathing, and he could feel her straining for air beneath him. With a huge effort, he unwrapped his arms from around her and managed to push himself off to one side. Freed of the bulk of him, she took in a huge breath and subsided. Her lead lolled drunkenly against his shoulder, one delicate cheek resting on his arm.

"Sorry about what?" she mumbled, not even opening her eyes.

A faint, wonderful suspicion touched his heart. "Margaret?" Her eyelids fluttered but didn't open. "My darling, are you all right?" He didn't know how else to ask.

Her eyes still didn't open but her lips curved upward in the sweetest of smiles. "I'm fine, I think." She sounded sluggish, like someone awakening from a deep sleep, and he wanted to laugh out loud. "Is my heart supposed to be doing this?"

He shifted his weight and tenderly laid his head next to hers. "That depends," he said, watching her face with delight. "What's it doing?"

"Mmmm." She nuzzled her cheek against his face, finding it like a sightless, newborn kitten. "Pounding."

He chuckled and found the strength to curl his arm around her waist. Her economy of words certainly suggested a state of satiation. "Pounding, hm? Pounding is good." Needing that last iota of assurance, he asked, "Do you want to go on?" Though what in God's name he would do about it if she did, he didn't know.

She opened her eyes halfway to look at him sleepily. "Go on? Do you mean to tell me there's more?" Before he could answer, she sighed deeply. "Oh, Richard, I couldn't. I've already died once from pure joy. Please, couldn't it wait until later?"

He let his head fall back out of sheer weakness as he had been wanting to do all along. "Oh, Margaret," he laughed. "Yes, my love, it can wait." He wished he had the strength to raise his head and kiss her.

"Oh, good. I do love you Richard, and thank you."

What in the world could he do with such a woman except cherish her? Richard Jensen, habitué of a thousand dens of pleasure, relaxed fully at last, satisfied that he had not failed her after all. "And I love you, dearest one."

Darwin turned out to be not much more of anywhere than the coast of Sumatra had been. Margaret knelt on a coil of rope by the starboard bulwark and squinted at the dusty, coastal town. How very dreary it looked, and yet Richard assured her that to the Australians who wrested a living from the bare outback, Darwin was Mecca. She had

195

no desire to go ashore, because she didn't want to interrupt the fantasy she'd been living.

It was a fantasy of ocean waves and a sleek clipper cutting through them, windy, clear days of brilliant sun and fresh air, creaking rope and rippling canvas. And the nights—that was the heart of the fantasy. She was a princess, cherished by her dark, handsome lover. He existed for her and her alone, and his ship and all his sailors, too, to ferry her endlessly around the world on a cloud of sensual pleasure.

No, dusty old Darwin would bring her back to hard reality with a thud. Margaret smiled. What a child she was being! As if the feel of Richard Jensen's body holding her at night weren't the most substantial kind of reality, and the sometimes tender, sometimes ferocious lovemaking not the most real of all human experiences.

The *Java* rolled gently at anchor, and she rolled with it, torporous with contentment. Her body had metamorphosed from the stiff, aching, bony shell of a few months ago, to a ripe, lithe receptacle of pleasure. Whenever she thought of Christian now, she understood, a least a little better, what compelled him to do what he did. The things she did without shame with Richard Jensen in the night had forced on her the knowledge that she, too, was a very sensual creature. If Christian's tastes had been normal, and hers the unacceptable, she knew she would have gone on seeking out pleasure in Richard's arms anyway, even if it meant debasing herself.

She sighed. The moment when that thought had solidified in her mind had been something of an epiphany, just as shattering in its way as the realization that she loved Richard, not just for now, but for always. His strength strengthened her, gave her the courage to embrace life without many of the scriptures that she had always accepted without question and to accept that Christian truly made his own decisions, that Pensleigh would not, by sheer grit or any determination on her part, be made the repository of another generation of Belleweathers.

It was a relief, pure and simple, to set aside the burdens and duties that had constituted the fabric of her life. The world had shrunk to Richard Jensen and the *Java*, and yet was incomprehensibly bigger, full of a different kind of promise. Not that she had entirely left the past behind—that she could never do. A thick portfolio of drawings waited to be bound into a booklet and mailed back to Reverend Childers, so that he could share her travels with the children at the orphanage.

No—obligations remained, only now she felt freer. If she devoted herself to useful, worthwhile things, it was with a happy heart, not the cranky, tense rendering of duty that had passed for selflessness before. Reverend Childers was a kind man, a sincere man, but she doubted she could adequately explain the difference to him. Richard, on the other hand, seemed to know her better than she knew herself. He took pleasure in her stumbling attempts to express these nascent ideas.

There seemed a time in the darkness of night when only the two of them existed. Richard would hold her and listen patiently. He admitted that most of the time he simply dealt with things as he found them. Margaret still squirmed at that, trying to integrate new ideas with one another, just as she had always been taught facts and figures, in an orderly way. He was a man who lived on his instincts, and her need for order and his deliberate casualness seemed destined to remain unreconciled, except by kisses and loving.

"Heads up!"

Margaret jerked. There stood Richard, grinning madly up at her from the gig. He looked almost respectable today, freshly shaved and with his thick, blue-black hair tied back in a sailor's pigtail. Undeniably handsome, the scamp!

"Goose!" she teased. "Why have you come 'round to this side instead of to the ladder?"

"No reason in the world," he said, "except to see if you were awake."

"Silly," she chided him with a smile. It was true she

often slept long past the time he arose, or fell asleep at odd times of the day. No matter how well she felt, their loving left her longing for more sleep than he ever required. "How did you fare?"

"Better than I'd hoped. By the time we get to Sydney, I'll have her nearly empty and ready for wool. Meet me at the ladder and I'll show you how I keep the books."

"Why at the ladder?" she asked suspiciously.

He started pulling at the oars, back watering to cut under the bowsprit. "Come see and you'll find out," he yelled.

She waited, feeling dodgy and springy as he came up the ladder. The air of suppressed excitement about him didn't inspire confidence for some reason. Nevertheless, she was prepared to welcome him with a kiss.

"Belay that," he said, holding out one hand. He fished in his shirt and she noticed an odd bulge at his waistline for the first time.

"Behold!" he said with a flourish. A snippet of sound emerged from within his large hand.

"Behold what?" she inquired, mystified.

"A cat!" he said triumphantly. He opened his hand, revealing a kitten. It looked wretched, with big, watery eyes, huge ears, like a bat's, and a wobbly head far too big for the emaciated neck. "A pet for you—and a ship's cat for the rest of us."

"Phew! What *is* that smell, Richard?" An awful suspicion crossed her mind. "It's not the cat that smells, is it?"

Richard shrugged. "It was tumbling around the chandler's. Who knows what it got into?"

"It smells . . . rancid," Margaret protested.

"Fine talk about a gift," he snorted. "I wasn't looking for overwhelming gratitude, but *this* . . ."

"*This*," she said, gesturing at it, "isn't a cat. It's a perversity of nature."

"My, I *have* caught you in a tender and nurturing mood," Richard said with a crooked and slightly dangerous smile.

"You have no right to heap guilt on me for pointing out

198

the obvious," she declared. The bedraggled, smelly creature distressed her unbearably. "Besides, have I ever said I even *liked* cats? *And* you've already bought me a bird. To think I'd want to keep a cat and a bird in the same quarters is . . . is . . ."

"Perverse?" He quirked an unfriendly eyebrow at her. "As in a perversity of nature?"

"Yes!" she cried. Her desire to put distance between herself and the cat was urgent in the extreme. "It's just like you to think I'd want it!"

Richard's face went a little colder. "I suppose it's because I'm a perversity of nature, too," he drawled.

The crew gathered around what was shaping up as an interesting confrontation, gazing pop-eyed from Richard to Margaret and back again, all except for Harkay. He was rooted to the deck, and his gaze hadn't shifted from the scrawny, orange tabby since its appearance. The smell, some weeks-old shade of green bacon, carried on the breeze to her.

"Richard, it's making me queasy. Do let's stop arguing and decide what we're going to do with it."

"Fine," he growled. "I'll amend the offer. It's not for you. It's a ship's cat, and cheap at twice the price. Do you have any idea how hard it is to come by a cat in a portside city?"

"You actually *paid* for it?" she squeaked. She hastily withdrew a handkerchief from the waistband of her skirt and covered her nose and mouth.

"Yes," he gritted. "Now suppose we do something useful with it? You did say you wanted to be useful, didn't you?"

"Oh, Richard," she cried, her eyes watering with the stench, "it's really too bad of you to fling that in my face over something like this."

"Useful is as useful does," he said, his lips thin.

"Very well, but I refuse to be gracious about it," she sniffed. And instantly regretted it—how could anything so little smell so enormously bad?

"No need to waste time stating the obvious," Richard

199

retorted. "I suggest you wash it. Dogsmeat can bring you a bucket of soapy water."

He held the cat out toward her. Margaret leaped back as if she'd been stung. "Wash it? I should say not!"

"Then what *do* you suggest?" he asked drily.

"Maybe if we just leave it . . . somewhere, it will air out. Then perhaps in a few days, I could . . ." She trailed off dubiously.

"Do you hear that, Darwin?" Richard addressed the cat. "She wants to peg you out on a laundry line." The kitten's oversized head swiveled around, like a cannon on a pivot. At least it wasn't unintelligent, she thought—it knew when it was being spoken to. Richard turned back to her. "Well, where would you recommend we put it to air out?"

Faintly mollified that she would not, at least for the time being, be expected to wash the dreadful creature, Margaret glanced around. Richard followed her as she walked forward, past the apprentice's deckhouse, redolent of other smells she didn't much care for either, past the narrow, cramped carpenter's shop filled with sharp, woodworking tools, past the sailmaker's shop, stuffed to the brim with canvas, and stopped by Tony's galley, set apart from the other deckhouses for safety.

"Here?" Richard said disbelievingly. "You want to leave it here, to romp through our food?"

She swung on him. "Ha! Then you admit the thing smells foul! It would quite put you off your food, wouldn't it, to have that horrible odor clinging to something you had to eat?"

"Nothing 'quite puts me off my food,'" he said grimly, and she thought for a minute that he was going to add "*. . . Miss Belleweather*," in that scathing way he could when he was really annoyed with her. "My objection to leaving it here is that it could get burned too easily. Added to its other . . . afflictions, it could spell the end of the animal."

"And a mercy to all of us *that* would be," she declared with feeling.

"Nevertheless, we will not set out to deliberately murder the thing," he said, his eyes like green flints.

The cat's ears began to twitch violently. "Speaking of afflictions," she said, "I believe it's infested with mites."

As soon as the twitching subsided, the kitten began to survey its surroundings uneasily. The wind rippled and its ears began to twitch again. The cat shook its head frenziedly and meowed, not a thin, pitiful cry, but a full-bodied howl of protest. A bizarre thought struck Margaret and she started laughing, unable to restrain herself even though it meant inhaling more of the putrid, cat-scented air.

Richard glared at her. "And I suppose mites are hilarious?"

"No," she said, gasping for control. "It's just that . . ." She started laughing again as the wind twirled her skirt around her legs and the cat began its Saint Vitus's dance anew. Richard's lack of amusement was in inverse proportion to her wealth of it. He stood watching her stonily until she finally regained control.

"Some ship's cat," she managed to sputter, "it doesn't like the wind!"

Richard stared at the cat, which was subsiding from another bout of twitching precisely as the breeze diminished. His face darkened and the brows compressed over his eyes most unattractively. Glaring at the cat and then at her, he said defensively, "It's meant to live below decks anyway."

"Good," she said, wiping tears of laughter from her eyes. "Then that's where it can air out, though how we'll tell it apart from the rats, I don't know."

"Harkay!"

The giant shambled over. "Yeah, Captain?"

"Take it," Richard said, ungraciously thrusting the kitten at him. "Wash it, peg it on the clothesline—do whatever you want with it."

The big Polynesian hesitated, darting a look at Margaret. "But it is a gift for *her*," he said uneasily.

201

Margaret giggled. "Take it with my blessings, Harkay. I'm sure you and it will be very happy together down in the cargo hold."

"You sure?" he rumbled. Margaret detected an odd light in his eyes, a sort of wistfulness. She sobered. Sarcasm didn't become the situation.

"Would you *like* to have it?" she asked.

He pursed his big lips. "Yeah," he said slowly, "would."

"Then please, do have it," she said.

"Sure?" he asked again. The wind shifted and Margaret was upwind of the cat, allowing her to think clearly. Harkay, she decided, was positively itching to lay claim to the cat.

"Yes, absolutely and incontrovertibly sure," she said. To make her point, she reached out and pushed Richard's arm so that it swung like a boom toward Harkay. Harkay still hesitated. "Please, I insist," Margaret added, feeling as if she were pressing a family heirloom on a casual visitor.

The Polynesian's hands were up and around the kitten in a flash, as if he feared that the offer might be rescinded at any minute. He lurched off without another word and his mammoth body soon disappeared through the cargo hatch. Everyone on deck seemed to take a deep breath at once, perhaps out of relief that the fracas was over, or perhaps just because the smell was gone.

"There, Richard," Margaret said smugly, "now the *Java* has its ship's cat and we're all spared the necessity of breathing that ghastly aroma."

He shot her a black look. "No thanks to you."

"Oh, please, don't be that way," she said. With the animal out of sight, she was already feeling remorse for the way she'd spoken to him.

Richard thrust his hands in his pockets and turned aft, his feet scraping the deck irritably as he stalked away. Margaret hurried after him. "It's not that I don't like cats," she said to his back, "really. It's just that . . ."

"Don't feel you need to apologize," he said into his

chest, but his tone argued for apology and a great deal more.

She hastened along, up the quarterdeck and down into the saloon after him. "Really, Richard," she said, "it was a lovely thought, only if I have one vice, it's too great a fondness for cleanliness."

"None of us has just one vice," he said, turning to look at her resentfully.

Oh dear, thought Margaret—he really was very hurt. "I'm certain I shall like it once it doesn't smell so," she said optimistically, "and . . . and . . ."

"And what?" he snapped, but she could see that her attempts to make up for her earlier scorn were having an effect.

Casting about frantically for something complimentary to say about the cat, she added in a rush, "And it will be a splendid mouser, I'm sure."

"And why is that?" he asked, the corner of his mouth beginning to twist up. "Because the rats won't know him from their own kind—he'll be in their midst and pouncing before they realize he's not their long-lost cousin?"

Margaret smiled. "Well, once he gets rid of the smell anyway. Until then they're bound to notice him. Lord, but what in the world *did* he get into?"

"He was in a bale of wool when I saw him," Richard said, his shoulders relaxing.

"It must have been shorn from particularly nasty sheep," Margaret commented dryly. "Now that I come to think of it, there's a bit of that smell lingering about you."

"You don't say?" Richard's face lit up and she perceived an instant too late what he was going to do. She whirled to run but he grabbed her from behind. "Darwin may be catching mice sooner than you think," he said in her ear with an evil chuckle. "The smell didn't keep *you* from getting caught!"

"Richard!" she shrieked. "Get away from me this instant—you stink!"

He pinned her tighter. "Only one vice, eh?" he said, nuzzling her neck. "We'll see about that."

"Oh, no! Please, Richard!" Margaret began struggling clumsily against his iron embrace. She'd wanted all to be forgiven, but nothing else until after he'd had a bath.

He nibbled at her neck. "I smell, do I?" he murmured. "Maybe if I just take the shirt off."

He let her go and she fled, but he cut off her only avenue of escape, leaping to block the companionway. He gleefully ripped his shirt off, grinning at her. "And now the pants . . ."

"Richard!" Margaret howled. She scurried behind the table, putting it between them. Torn between scandal and amusement as he dropped his pants, she panted for breath. "What if Dogsmeat comes in, or Daniels or Dekker?" she asked quickly, trying to make him stop.

He pushed the pants off his ankles, hopping from one foot to the other with a wicked grin. "They won't," he said confidently. "They won't want to come any nearer this caterwauling than you did to that cat." He started around the table, completely bare.

"Oh, no . . ." Margaret sprinted for their cabin door, hoping to slip through and bolt it against him, but he was on her in a flash. He seized her wrist and she spun around, like a dog run out to the end of its lead. Giggling wildly, she tried to push him away with no discernable effect.

"Naked in the light of day and everyone up top listening!" she exclaimed. "Please, Richard . . ." she said breathlessly. He kissed her, his eyes black with mischief.

"Please what?" he asked. "Please do it again?"

Before she could answer, his mouth came down on hers again. He pulled her tight against him and she could feel his arousal through her skirt. The hot, heavy kiss and the lean length of him pressing her from head to toe could not be resisted. With an aching cry of mingled exasperation and arousal, she softened against him.

Later, very much later, she was forced to concede that under the right circumstances, one might almost come to *like* the smell of rancid wool and other assorted items in a chandler's shop.

Chapter 13

Margaret pushed a tickly lock of hair off her forehead. Now that the early morning sun had shifted around, she no longer needed all the strays to cast some shade over her eyes. She flexed her cramped fingers and hoped her face wasn't burning too badly in the Australian sun. A straw hat with a wide brim, like the one she wore while strolling through the rose garden at Pensleigh, would have been helpful. The light was strong on Circular Quay, reflecting off the water and the dry, dusty area around the docks and warehouses. Her parasol was a sad shambles from having been used to beat Harkay over the head with it in Singapore, so it wouldn't have done much good.

Harkay sat on the ground next to the bale of wool where Richard had left her to her sketching. His beefy face was slack, his eyes half-closed in the midmorning heat. Darwin lay draped across his shoulder, abandoned to sleep in the way only the very young could be, trusting Harkay to keep an eye out for danger. As if Darwin need fear any danger while Harkay was his guardian!

For herself, Margaret had accepted Richard's edict that Harkay stay at her side while he tended to business. For her protection, he'd said, but so far, Sydney harbor was all business. Not a soul had bothered her, as long as one discounted the men in drab, cutaway suits, and linens in varying states of cleanliness, who tipped their hat as they passed by. Somehow, the issue of chaperonage seemed quaint in this setting, and Harkay an unlikely duenna.

Countless carts and wagons clattered by, stirring up dust as the drivers jockeyed for space around the loading docks of the warehouses. On the return journeys, the horses strained against the traces, pulling loads of coal and wooden crates. The teamsters cast more than a few glances her way, and she suspected it must be because she wasn't yet dust-covered, like everything else in sight.

It was altogether a scene of mayhem, its backdrop an endless succession of brick and wooden buildings blanketing the low, sloping hill leading up from the harbor. Uniformly nondescript, they fairly shouted 'boom town,' a place big and getting bigger each year. Hardly a patch of earth showed between them, as each business vied for a position nearer the heart of commercial activity.

It made her think longingly of Bath, where the press of hillside topography was even greater than here, but the careful hand of architects was evident in the lovely symmetry of homes organized around gracefully curving streets. By contrast, this panorama was raw and crude, but it exuded enormous energy. She'd watched Richard striding off into the dusty town and thought how thoroughly he belonged to this rough, vibrant world.

It had occurred to her to wonder lately how well he'd fit into *her* world. The answer that had come back wasn't reassuring. Picturing him among the occupants of a drawing room, or at a fancy dress ball, was like imagining a wolf in a dovecote.

The brash self-sufficiency, the reckless flamboyance that she admired in him would undoubtedly make high society nervous. It wasn't that he couldn't be tamed—it was that she was quite sure he *wouldn't* be tamed. He didn't suffer fools gladly, never mind politely, and he had the power to use words like fists when it suited him. It was altogether a daunting prospect, the idea of Richard Jensen in society. Margaret sighed. She loved him utterly, but where it might lead, she didn't care to speculate.

Harkay rumbled and snorted, caught in a dream, and Darwin tumbled off his shoulder. The kitten looked around dazedly before orienting himself to the mountainous heap of man he called home, and flopping down on the bulging lap. How simple it was for some to know where they belonged!

Margaret glanced around. Richard had promised to come back for her once he'd arranged for fresh water to be loaded, and he had seen to it that the crew smoked the hold. He'd set them a challenge. The length of their shore leave was dependent on how fast they could light the smoke pots and then shinny into the rigging with tar pots, to coat the fore rigging while the smoke did its work. A raucous cheer had greeted this announcement from the quarterdeck, with half the men sprinting away to start the job even before he'd finished speaking.

Activity on the quay was increasing, but still there was no sign of Richard. Sailors began disembarking from gigs waterside, to mingle with teamsters, businessmen, stevedores, and the occasional bobby. A few women in dark, demure dresses, wives of merchant ships' captains, were being helped ashore and escorted toward the chandler's district. The roads of Sydney were as packed with waterborne traffic as any London street with carriages. They'd arrived late the evening before, adding their green and red running lights to the fairyland of others across the water.

Steamships and clippers jostled for space in the water the way the buildings seemed to on land, all waiting for this year's wool to be released from auction houses and sped to waiting holds. The fastest clippers would reach Deal or Antwerp or Scilly in just over three months, which would have secured top price for them in years gone by. Now, with the Suez Canal open, the steamers could beat them, because the lack of wind through the canal forced the clippers to continue going around the Horn.

Richard's plan, he'd explained to her the night before, was to use the *Java*'s superior speed over blue water to carry wool to Singapore, then tranship to a steamer bound for London via the shorter canal route. That way he and his silent partner hoped to bring their wool to market first, and see the best return. Richard freely admitted the plan was risky. Timing was critical, the wool markets being open only three months out of the year, but the lure of making a year's profits for one month's work was too tempting. The only surprise was that no one else had thought of it first.

Margaret's stomach growled and she wished Richard would come back. The sun was high overhead now, and the quay was becoming so crowded that she discarded the idea of setting off in search of lunch for fear of missing him. Waiting for wool was a holiday of sorts for the sailors, a break from the fearsome four-hours-on, four-hours-off routine aboard ship.

They strolled the quay, laughing and joking, insulting one another's ships good-naturedly, boasting of good time made in foul weather, and laying bets as to who would win this year's wool run. Margaret picked up her sketch pad again to distract herself from hunger and began drawing the lively scene. Harkay awoke and filled a pipe, though, blessedly for her empty stomach, he didn't light it. The smell, coupled with her intense hunger, would surely have nauseated her.

He nodded companionably to several tars who greeted him as they passed. One or two stopped to glance over Margaret's shoulder but Harkay growled and they moved on hastily. It really was too funny, she thought, how he had managed to ignore her completely before but guarded her like some precious jewel now, all because of Darwin, and almost certainly, too, because Richard Jensen made no secret of his feelings for her.

She concluded that the smoking and tarring must be done, as she saw more and more faces from the *Java* among the crowd. Only a skeleton watch would remain on board. In the throng of sailors, she began to focus on familiar faces, picking them out of the crowd and lightly sketching in the blur of activity around them. Sailors paused more frequently now to watch, made bolder by a few tots of rum and less inclined to heed Harkay's rumblings. Three or four stopped as a group and Harkay lumbered to his feet as they made approving remarks.

"It's all right, Harkay," Margaret said soothingly. "They're doing no harm."

"I should say not, ma'am," one volunteered. "That's some right fine drawing. Wish I had a picture of meself like that fer to send home to me family."

Margaret set aside the drawing she was working on and laughingly obliged him. He took it when she was done and it passed from hand to hand.

"Cor, that's lovely!" one exclaimed.

"Lovely!" said another, cuffing his mate. "He's about as lovely as a barnacle!"

"Mebbe," said the subject of the portrait, "but me ma'm'll like it just the same. What do I owe you, ma'am?"

Margaret started to say 'nothing' but she realized there were more sailors crowding around and she might be stuck there all afternoon if she gave her services away for free. She named a sum she hoped would discourage all but the most serious and the sailor held out money.

Harkay grunted and held out his hand. "Yes, thank you, Harkay—you hold it," she said hastily, sensing his desire to exert some control over the situation.

As time passed, more seamen clustered around, until Margaret couldn't see beyond them. The novelty of a lady portraitist was a unique diversion to pass the idle hours on Circular Quay. Margaret found it entertaining in return, from the grizzled oldsters who sat stoically, to the youngsters who preened and struck a pose obviously calculated to impress a girl back home. The onlookers joked with her, and she felt light-hearted, and a little guilty, too, for her paltry talent didn't merit the kind of praise the sailors heaped on it. They could have had a photograph, a true likeness, made for only twice what she was charging them.

A faint dizziness troubled her for a few minutes, and then her hunger finally disappeared as she worked quickly and carefully to capture each man. She expected the demand to abate but the line grew longer instead. Harkay settled on the ground again, lighting his pipe as the pile of money in front of him grew. Margaret found it comical, for to a stranger Harkay would seem threatening indeed. No one even suggested not paying, however, and she saw that for these proud, hardened men, dignity required that they pay hard-earned coin for what they wanted.

When Richard finally shouldered his way through the crowd, she was getting tired, and she saw that it was well into the afternoon. Richard took in the scene at a glance and his mouth twisted in a wry smile, his dark eyes shining with amusement. She shrugged sheepishly and handed over the sketch she'd just finished.

"Here now!" the subject of the drawing said loudly. "That's mine, so's me son knows what I look like afore I sees him for the first time."

Richard handed it to him and watched the by-now routine deposit of money on the pile in front of Harkay. Daniels, who was at his side, inclined his head toward it.

"Miss Belleweather's done well for herself," he said, grinning. "Puts me in mind of that little side bet we never got around to."

Margaret stood up and stretched. Most of the *Java*'s crew had joined the crowd and looked in puzzlement from Daniels to their captain. Daniels looked slyly at Harkay and turned to Margaret.

"I think an even better opportunity has presented itself. Are you game, miss?" he asked with a wink.

Margaret cast her mind back to the original proposition, herself against Harkay in an eating contest. She was quite sure she'd lose but just thinking about food brought her hunger roaring back. Where was the harm? She nodded, and Daniels surprised her by turning to the crowd.

"*Java*'s got a bet for all you scurvy sods," he bellowed. Voices stilled and seamen leaned forward, their faces eager with anticipation.

Richard moved to Margaret's side and said in an undertone. "I'm not sure what Mr. Daniels has in mind, but I hope you're prepared to go along with it. These boys are up for some sport."

"The *Java* challenges any ship to an eating contest, your

best eater against ours, one-on-one," Daniels said loudly before Margaret could think to wonder what Richard meant.

"Har!" said a voice. "No doubt you'll be talking about that mountain there!" The speaker gestured toward Harkay. Harkay heaved himself to his feet and leered. Grumbles passed through the crowd.

Daniels affected a wounded look, his glossy chestnut curls and high color giving him the look of a wronged cherub. "Well, fair's fair," he said. The grumbling increased and he spread his hands out placatingly. "Very well," he said mildly, "I'm willing to make an offer so fair that no one can refuse it." He paused. "Any member of the *Java*'s crew against any other ship's challenger—can't be fairer than that."

"Our choice?" said a skeptical voice in the crowd.

"Of course," Daniels said with mock innocence.

"*She's* from the *Java*!" one cried, pointing at Margaret. "The *Ferriera* will take up the bet—our best eater against *her!*"

Harkay growled menacingly and the crowd fell back.

"But gentlemen," Daniels cried, "I said a member of the *Java*'s crew. Miss Belleweather is a passenger, not a member of the crew!"

Several of the *Java*'s apprentices shouted, "Hear! Hear!"

"*Java* don't carry passengers—everyone knows that!" a gravel-voiced sailor shouted. Cries of agreement rippled through the crowd.

Daniels hung his head. "You've taken unfair advantage of a technicality, lads," he said, his face a picture of boyish dismay.

But the challenger from the *Ferriera* stood his ground. Margaret eyed the sea of rough faces and hoped that Daniels would concede defeat. It was all very silly anyway, and besides, the sooner they stopped their carrying on, the sooner she could eat.

"Fat's in the fire now," Richard whispered, leaning down. He angled his wide shoulders so that the sailors

211

couldn't see her face. "Can you go through with it?"

"Oh, of course," Margaret said, quite certain there was no need for all the fuss.

Richard grinned, the corners of his eyes creasing in amusement. "Then I'll try and see to it that there's *some* common sense used." He turned to face the onlookers again. "Men, I know you want a fair contest, so I have a suggestion or two."

"Since when did a captain ever *suggest* anything?" yelled the *Ferriera*'s spokesman. "Especially you, Jensen!" Muttered assent ran through the crowd.

"Hey! Steady on!" yelled Toby, one of the *Java*'s able-bodieds. He blanched when the sea of hostile faces turned in his direction. Margaret recognized him as the burly youth Richard had carried down out of the rigging so long ago, the one who'd broken his nose. An apprentice elbowed him and he found the courage to resume speaking. "Captain Jensen's hard but fair, a captain any of you would be proud to sail under! You should hear him out."

The *Java*'s crew had been working their way through the throng since the challenge had been issued, and now stood behind Toby, daring any to take exception to his words. Margaret held her breath, expecting Richard to take umbrage on his own behalf, but he stood relaxed and calm next to her. The sailors quieted and looked expectantly in his direction.

"We're all betting men, right?" he said genially. Each man looked at his neighbor and then back again, nodding hesitantly. "Then what we want is to make it an even enough contest so that those who've got some silver in their pockets can make a decent wager."

"So let's have them *suggestions*," the mate from the *Ferriera* said scornfully.

"Very well," Richard replied, the soul of amiability. "We put a time limit of five minutes on it. Each of them starts with exactly the same amounts and kinds of food, and when it's over, whoever has the least left is the winner."

"Now there's the sweet voice of reason," Daniels said cheerfully. "Is there a man among you who sees trickery in that?"

In a matter of minutes, all the terms were set. Men were sent flying in every direction, to fetch tables and chairs and food from a hotel called the Pig and Whistle. Tony was all for rowing out to the *Java* and bringing back some of what he had on hand, things he knew Margaret liked especially, but since it smacked of favoritism, the idea was dropped.

Dogsmeat had whispered instructions to the *Java*'s crew and when they returned, laden down like participants in a scavenger hunt, he took charge. He briskly ordered the laying out of two tables, snapping out clean, white linen cloths on each to hoots of derision from the crowd.

"We'll have some dignity here," he said sternly, eyeing the louder ones. "Miss Belleweather's not a deckhand, y'know."

Margaret giggled. She was certainly in the wrong place if she was going to stand on ceremony. The *Ferriera*'s challenger was led forth and Richard muttered a curse under his breath. Margaret glanced at him in surprise.

"He looks harmless enough," she said, looking the gangling youth over. "Look at him—his bones are too large for his muscles and his hands and feet are too big for everything else."

"Damn!" Richard said again. "That's just the problem," he said out of the corner of his mouth. "He's like all apprentices, still growing and impossible to fill, and what's worse, they can't get on the outside of food fast enough."

"At least I'll get a good lunch out of it," Margaret said happily as the aroma of freshly baked bread assailed her nostrils.

Dogsmeat appointed himself steward, seating Margaret and gallantly laying a napkin across her lap. The fresh apples alone had her salivating, and she didn't need a menu to tell her that other lovely things waited under the cloths. The boy from the *Ferriera* sat down, ill at ease

213

competing against a woman, judging by the look he shot in her direction.

"You can do it, miss!" Dogsmeat hissed in her ear. "I've wagered a month's wages on it."

"Oh, Dogsmeat!" Margaret cried. "You really shouldn't have."

"I have faith," the dwarf said stoutly. "Harkay's got your earnings handy by—d'ye want me to bet'em for you?"

Margaret shrugged lamely. "Why not?" If the *Java*'s men were going to lose money on her, she'd seem a poor sport not to bet on herself. The laying of wagers was approaching pandemonium now, and she watched as Dogsmeat beat his way to the back of the crowd. He returned with a triumphant smile a few minutes later and gave her a thumbs up.

Daniels shouted for order and the *Ferriera*'s spokesman came to stand next to the tables with him. The *Java*'s crew assembled next to Margaret's table and the *Ferriera*'s crew gathered around their contender, each group eyeing the other suspiciously. A last, quick check to satisfy everyone that the portions were equal, and the signal was given.

Margaret had been gulping back saliva the whole time and the chance to actually begin eating took her by surprise. Her opponent wasted no time, however, seizing an apple and stuffing it into his mouth whole. Margaret sniffed. Behind her back, she could feel the *Java*'s crew watching her, tense with expectation. She didn't mean to disappoint them.

She sliced an apple neatly into quarters and essayed a somber expression as she pushed one into her mouth, leaving the skin side out in a caricature of a smile. The trick had always worked on Christian and it didn't fail her now. The *Ferriera*'s apprentice stopped in midbite, gaping at her with his mouth hanging open. Margaret knew what a ludicrous sight she was—she'd checked in a mirror once when she was ten.

She resisted the temptation to laugh at her competitor's stunned countenance as the *Java*'s crew cheered. She grinned, though, a red, apply grin, just to keep the

214

apprentice off-balance. She started chewing with gusto, keeping her eyes on him.

So he'd never seen a woman eat like an adolescent boy, had he? Well, just let him keep watching! Filled with merriment and feeling much better just having the taste of food in her mouth, she swallowed the last of the apple and picked up a hard-boiled egg. The apprentice's mouth still hung open, filled with half-chewed apple, but he shadowed her movement anxiously. She plopped the whole egg into her mouth and exulted as she saw that his hand was frozen in midair as he gawked at her bulging cheeks. Only the fear of choking on the egg stopped her from laughing outright. If only he'd close his mouth, he wouldn't look so unspeakably silly!

Well aware of what a hum she was perpetrating, she decided to shift tactics to keep him off-balance. She paused and looked over the selections on the table like a finicky debutante deciding whether to have caviar or a hothouse pear. The loud exhortations of the *Java*'s crew drummed in her ears as she picked up a piece of buttered bread and devoured it daintily. Louder even than the *Java*'s crew were the cries of the hapless apprentice's shipmates. He'd have a lot of people to answer to if he didn't stir his stumps soon!

She delicately wiped her lips clean with the napkin, just to strengthen the impression of frail femininity. The apprentice goggled at her and only belatedly seized his own slice of bread. He tore off a hunk and began chewing as Margaret did her best imitation of one of Christian's riper prepubescent burps. It worked magnificently. Her competitor forgot the bread in his hand altogether, and the piece he'd torn off dangled forgotten from his mouth.

Oh, really—this was too easy! Margaret picked up a dish of custard. She'd always adored custard, even in the nursery when it was served virtually every day. Spooning it into her mouth, she nearly melted. No acting required here, she thought—it was delicious!

A mate from the *Ferriera* jarred their champion by screaming in his ear. "Gr'up, ye great ninny! Eat!" The boy dropped the slice of bread and hastily picked up his own custard, but he couldn't take his eyes off Margaret, who was making *her* custard disappear at an astonishing clip. He made a stab at his bowl with a spoon but missed it entirely. He jerked in surprise as the bowl tipped and smashed to the table, spattering custard and broken china over the remaining food.

A huge groan went up from his backers. Now he'd have to eat shards of glass to win. Several sailors lunged forward and it was clear from the black looks on their faces that they expected him to do exactly that. Margaret allowed herself a quick glance in Richard's driection. His face was alight with unholy amusement, his eyes crinkled into slits by the force of his grin.

"She's gulling you, lad!" cried a man standing over the bemused apprentice.

If anything, Richard's grin got wider. His hands were thrust deep into the pockets of his black pants, and he rocked back on his heels, vastly entertained. Suddenly she noticed Tony at his side, jumping up and down and screaming unintelligibly. Margaret followed the direction of his wild gesticulations.

The *Ferriera*'s crew was frantically picking bits of broken china out of the remaining food on the apprentice's table, and shoving it in his mouth as they judged it edible. Margaret realized that the contest had overtones of the tortoise and the hare legend—while she gloated, the other side was soldiering on. Startled out of her complacency, she quickly picked up a slice of roasted mutton.

Although the atmosphere didn't lend itself to calm contemplation of the food, her mouth watered as she smelled the aroma of the meat. Tearing off a piece with her front teeth, she savored the lovely taste of it. She hadn't had mutton in ages, not since leaving home, and it was another nursery food she'd always relished. The din of the sailors faded as she took another bite, and another, thinking all the while that the Pig and Whistle must be a really splendid establishment to have produced such a marvelous roast.

Creamed potatoes and onions came next, followed by more mutton and some mint jelly. Margaret peered hopefully around the table, hoping to find another custard, but she spied a molasses and corn pudding with cream instead. A jurisdictional dispute broke out at the apprentice's table as Daniels remonstrated with his supporters for putting the food in his mouth as they picked it free of glass. Margaret couldn't have cared less—participating in an eating contest was now running a distant second to enjoying the lunch she had waited so long to eat.

"You can stop eating now," Richard said in her ear. "Time's up."

She glanced up distractedly and saw that the crowd was breaking up as money changed hands. Harkay made an apron of the front of his shirt and accepted the losers' money with the nearest thing to a smile she'd ever seen on his face.

"Oh," she said, surprised, "must I? I'm not allowed to finish what's here?"

Richard chuckled. "You've been living on love these past few weeks, and no mistake. You haven't eaten like that since you first joined us in Singapore."

"Oh, really?" she asked, drawing a blank as she tried to remember.

"Yes, really. I'm just glad I had the foresight to bet on you myself. Now, do I have to take you to the Pig and Whistle for seconds?"

Margaret giggled. "Actually, now that you mention it, the custard really was terribly good . . ."

"You have prodigious appetites, Miss Belleweather," he said, smiling. Margaret felt her heart go still, for it was the kind of smile that spoke of things other than food. "I'll not only take you to the Pig and Whistle, I'll see to it that your other . . . appetites receive a suitable audience."

"Oh." Margaret felt her mouth go slack at the look on his face. She set her napkin aside and rose a little unsteadily to her feet. The dark, sensuality in his face set her blood rushing.

217

They left arm in arm, though not before every member of the *Java*'s crew had pumped her hand in congratulations and thanks. Harkay skulked along behind them and only belatedly did she realize that he was trying to turn her winnings over to her. Richard put them in a leather purse after counting it and telling her the rather startling total.

The dusty streets now seemed invested with a kind of magic as she strolled along them with Richard. Her mouth was dry with anticipation as he shot her the occasional look of unmistakable lust. High good humor tempered the unabashed want on his face, but when they stopped outside the Pig and Whistle, Margaret stared into his eyes and found she wasn't hungry anymore.

"Then it's on to the surprise I've arranged," Richard said. His lips curved in a mysterious smile, and Margaret felt a familiar lassitude seeping through her bones. His upper lip, like a cupid's bow, mesmerized her, heavy and sensual with promise.

"What is it?" she said, moistening her mouth.

"You've heard what they say about surprises," he said tucking her hand over the hardness of his forearm. "If I tell you, it won't be a surprise."

Even if he'd told her what was to come, it couldn't have prepared her. He took her to a white, three-story building trimmed in red. Once inside, Margaret stared in amazement, blushing as she realized it was a brothel—clean and well-decorated—but a brothel. A cheerful bawdiness permeated the place, from the blowzy bleached blonde who pounded on a piano in the corner, to the madam in a peach, bombazine dress who greeted them. The clientele seemed more interested in playing cards and drinking than going upstairs, but the women didn't appear to be upset about it. Several waved to Richard and shouted loud hellos.

"Richard," Margaret whispered, "do you know them?"

"Sure," he said cheerfully. "I haven't gotten my nasty reputation without some effort. Hello, Esther!" He waved back to a pretty woman dealing cards at a low, baize-covered table.

218

"But Richard," Margaret stuttered, "why have we come here? You don't mean to . . ." She positively couldn't finish the thought.

"What I mean to do is take you upstairs to one of the cleanest, nicest rooms Sydney has to offer and while away the afternoon in a bed that doesn't force me to be creative about where I put my arms and legs, or yours for that matter—unless we *want* to be creative."

Margaret felt a little dizzy with scandal. She'd only dimly realized that his berth aboard the *Java* wasn't as spacious as he might have liked, but *this* . . . "Richard, I hope you won't think me too . . . too prudish, but a . . . a . . ."

"Whorehouse?" He laughed, drawing her close to his side even as Margaret tried to wiggle away, resisting giving the appearance of a perfectly decent woman who was about to go upstairs, take off her clothes, and do wildly indecent things with a man. "Dearest Margaret, would you like a huge, hot soapy bath? And with fresh water, not sea water?"

Margaret stared at him. "A bath? We've come here to take a bath?"

"Only among other things," he said grinning. "Daphne runs a first-class establishment and I've taken her best room, one with a bathroom the likes of which you won't see anywhere else south of the equator."

Margaret took a gulp of air. She tried to speak but failed. The madam was sailing toward them. Margaret felt her ears turn scarlet as she handed Richard a key and wished him a pleasant afternoon.

"Come down and play cards after, why don't you?" she said jovially. "Wouldn't be like a regular visit if you didn't."

"Thanks, Daphne. Maybe I will, if I have the energy." Margaret choked and Richard patted her arm with a bland smile. "You run an honest table and I like that."

"Well, we like a man who knows how to hold his liquor and treat a girl decent, so that squares us. I wish to God they were all like you."

219

Richard guffawed. "Now that's laying it on too thick! Come on, Margaret—when Daphne starts to flatter people like that, she's after something." Daphne smiled at Margaret with a penetrating glance up and down the length of her. "Next thing you know," he added, "she'll be trying to talk you into working for her!"

It was so preposterous that Margaret giggled as Richard led her up the staircase. It was really very attractive, with polished banisters and Turkish runners on the treads. No taint of evil attended any of what she'd seen since they walked in, and yet it was undeniably a brothel. Clearly, there were brothels and then there were brothels. Trust Richard Jensen to find one that resembled a hotel, except that the denizens of the lobby were for sale!

The bathroom was everything he'd said it would be, and the fresh water heavenly. Only rarely had there been enough rain water to spare on the *Java* for her to bathe in it instead of salt water, and she'd had to be content with one bucket of fresh water to rinse off with after the saltwater baths. The bed she scarcely looked at, fighting for composure when Richard threw himself across it and pronounced it good. Stretching out to his full length and spreading his arms wide, he smiled a beatific smile. She turned away, suppressing laughter. He looked like a child let loose in a candy store.

As Margaret soaked in the bath, she eyed the pink wrapper Richard had bought for her and put on a hook in advance of their arrival. It was a lovely light cotton, with extravagant amounts of lace trimming. It was then that she realized that *she* was the candy. She hooted with laughter.

"What is it?" Richard yelled to her through the open door.

"Oh, nothing," she called back. His shadow fell across the bathroom floor and she looked up to see him leaning against the doorjamb, a glass in one hand.

"Do you realize that this bathroom is bigger than my cabin on the *Java*?" he asked. He was right, of course, but she felt a stab of loyalty for the place where she'd shared so much love with him.

"I can't argue with that," she said, "but I do like your cabin, Richard."

He looked at her fondly. "I do, too. Maybe I can get Sanders in to do some refitting though."

"Sanders?"

"Tall, reddish haired fellow—our carpenter."

"Oh." She stared at him, his lean body so elegant and yet so feral. His dark skin, the jet black hair, the piercing green eyes—everything about him was exciting her at this moment. Her body felt pale and inconsequential when compared to this masculine power. She had to pull herself back with a wrench when she realized he was speaking again.

"Hurry up, will you? I have something even better waiting in the other room."

The 'something' turned out to be ice. Margaret sat on the bed and combed out her wet hair, taking blissful sips of iced lemonade every now and then while Richard took his bath. She tried but failed to avoid looking at herself in the mirror on the vanity. She wasn't as unattractive as she'd been the last time she'd dared look in a mirror. Her face was less rounded than before her illness, her neck and shoulders more angular, but not revoltingly so. Best of all was her hair, fully restored to its former brilliant sheen. At least she was not too ugly for Richard. She smiled as she listened to him in the bath, splashing like a narwhal and bellowing a chantey about saying farewell to the Barbary pirates, the streets of Gibraltar, and all of the Spanish grandees.

What a very odd day it was turning out to be, and how she loved Richard Jensen! How could he have captured her heart so thoroughly, this rough-mannered, autocratic, lunatic of an American? She thought of his idea to refit his cabin and wondered if it meant that he expected her to go on sailing with him after Singapore. It was a disquieting thought. Would she? She put the question in the same category as thoughts about Christian's future, as things which only the fullness of time would disclose. As well try to swim back to England as try and answer now, she thought.

The passage of time had softened the horror she felt when she remembered that night in Atjeh, although the occasional nightmare still brought it back with sickening clarity. She would awaken sobbing, and when he was there beside her, Richard would take her in his arms and shush her softly. He had never even asked her what she dreamt about that saddened her so, but she suspected that he knew.

For the most part, though, she could put it aside, and think of Christian as he had been, as she loved him best— home at Pensleigh—and that was something she would never have credited that time could do. What insight time would provide regarding Richard Jensen remained to be seen, but she knew beyond question that he had become just as important to her as her brother.

Builders of empires manipulated people and events to their own ends. Margaret did not know whether it was a sign of maturity or cowardice that she no longer felt sanguine about doing so herself. She liked to think that she had acquired some humility, had recognized that she barely had the right of it when it came to making decisions for herself, never mind for others. She unworked a particularly troublesome knot with her fingers. Let the passage of time tell the tale. Cowardice or maturity? Perhaps a little of both.

"You're far too pensive."

Richard's voice brought her abruptly out of her reverie. "Oh, sorry," she said, smiling. "How am I supposed to be acting?"

"Well, for one thing, you're supposed to be showing a little curiosity about that silver bucket in the corner."

Margaret looked over and noticed it for the first time. Richard moved across to it in that soft, cat-footed way of his, as if he was walking across dry twigs without breaking any of them. With just a towel around his hips, he was heart-stoppingly beautiful, impossibly taut and slender through the torso and hips, widening out above to the

222

shoulders, and below to the powerful thighs.

She heard ice crunching as he withdrew a green bottle, pale drops of water running off it in rivulets. He turned to her with a sly grin. "I don't care for the stuff myself, but I thought if we were going to do this right, I should ply you with champagne."

"Oh, Richard! You're so very silly sometimes!" she laughed.

"We'll see who's silliest when you've put a bit of this down the hatch," he said wickedly. "I'll be drinking my usual, but you . . ." He gave a sharp twist of his wrist and the cork popped out with a hiss. ". . . *you'll* be drinking this." He took a glass from the vanity, its triple mirror reflecting his bare chest and strong hands.

"This is really very wicked, Richard," she giggled.

He looked at her reflection in the mirror, his eyes glinting with amusement. "Be thankful for wickedness," he said. "It's what makes the world go around. It's the things that strike us as wicked that have the most potential for pleasure." He poured the champagne slowly, watching her out of the corner of his eye. "If being naked with me didn't strike you as wicked, then it wouldn't thrill you like it does."

"What an astounding thought!" she declared. She sat up straighter and the pink wrapper fell open. The hazy, golden sunlight that filtered through the muslin curtains played across his face, and she saw that his gaze was drawn to her bare breasts. It felt wicked, and it *did* give her a thrill.

"Astounding but true," he said, handing her the glass of champagne. "Maybe you don't feel up to having a drink on top of all the rest of the wickedness I have planned." He returned to the vanity and filled a shot glass with rum. He took a swallow staring at her reflection over the rim.

Her breath quickened. The gauzy light defined his body with shadow, deep shadows under the long, lean jaw, and darker shadows at his armpit when he raised his glass to drink. The dark hair trailing down his belly looked, in this light, as soft as she knew it to be to the touch. The high

223

prominences of his shoulder and chest muscles glowed golden in the late afternoon light. Every inch of him carried some special memory for her fingers, and heat flushed through her veins as she remembered the feel of him.

He laughed softly at the expression on her face, and he turned his back to her to pour another rum. The flat hardness of his belly gave way to the sloping contours of his buttocks and the lean ropes of muscle that curved upward from his waist. Just below his waist were the two small clefts where muscle attached to bone. Margaret could remember the moment when she had learned that pressing there aroused him, and made him push deeper and harder into her. Her breath caught in her throat as she felt an echo inside of what it felt like when he did.

A glint of light caught her eye, and she saw in the mirror that a ray of sun had pierced the shot glass in his hand and split into rich, amber sparks. But there was another, more compelling sight in the mirror. Richard's eyes. He raised the glass to his lips and drank. He watched her as he swallowed, his eyes heavy with desire.

"Wicked, isn't it?" he said, with a rich, sardonic smile. "Drinking champagne and being naked in the afternoon?" Turning, he displayed all the fearsome grace of his male body.

Margaret swallowed. "Very."

"And if I came over and touched you, and held your breasts in my hands, that would be wicked too, wouldn't it?"

Margaret's throat went dry. "Yes."

He walked slowly toward her, sensual mischief gleaming in his eyes. His own arousal became more evident under the towel with each step. "And out of all this wickedness, comes pleasure," he said. He stopped in front of her, his face growing taut all of a sudden. "Be wicked with me, Maggie," he said, his voice low and urgent.

She opened her mouth but nothing came out. His eyes darkened as he took the untouched champagne from her. He set the glass on the floor and knelt at the edge of the bed. She felt a pulse in her throat raging out of control as he reached out and slipped his hands beneath the pink wrapper. Molding his hands over her shoulders, he caressed them with his palms and then slowly slid the wrapper down her back. A shudder passed through her, with heat burning in its wake.

He kissed her breasts with quiet hunger, his breath coming rapidly. Desire coursed through her and she put her trembling hands on his shoulders. The hot, sweet rage to have him burst into her as it always did, with frightening intensity and speed. A look, a touch, was enough sometimes. She wanted to slow it down but she never could, not until the second or third time, when he grew sleepy and only lazily passionate. Then her hunger fed only off her own thoughts, and was not fanned by his own into something over which she had no control.

"Oh, Margaret, I've been thinking about this for weeks," he murmured as he burned a path to her throat with his tongue. "Nothing to think about except making love to you, nothing to distract me."

A sob of mingled pleasure and amusement bubbled up from deep in her chest. She combed her fingers through his damp, sleek hair. "You mean you haven't given it your full attention up until now?"

"Not like I've wanted to," he answered, running his hands down her sides. "The ship's always in the back of my mind." He cupped her hips with his fingers and brushed his mouth across her breasts.

"I'm most certainly in trouble then," she managed to say as he bent and nipped at the soft skin of her thighs. "I won't last the blink of an eye if you arouse me any more than usual."

He chuckled, a husky rasping sound, and looked up, his eyes almost black with arousal. "Then we're both in the same boat," he said, "but a problem shared is a problem halved."

Margaret thought it the most bald-faced lie she'd ever heard—his arousal only doubled her own. He stroked the curls at the juncture of her thighs, sending a frisson of pleasure through her. She'd have to prove to him just how wrong he was. She leaned over and kissed his upturned face to distract him as she worked her feet around his hips and pushed the towel off with her toes. "Your problems have only just begun," she whispered.

In the deepening twilight, she saw the reflection of his bare buttocks in the mirror, pale and muscular, and a thrill chased down her spine. She slipped her hands under his arms and down below his waist, to cup the fullness of the pale flesh, her breath quickening as she watched it happening in the mirror. He took a ragged breath and turned. His eyes caught hers in the glass.

"Oh, Margaret," he said, his jaw taut with desire as he saw the look on her face, "this is too wicked, even for me."

She laid her cheek against his head and pulled at his buttocks. "Come to me then," she said, her voice unsteady with longing. The heat between her legs was painful now, threatening to dissolve her if she didn't satisfy it. Later, when the first storm abated, they could be more leisurely. Now the need was too urgent. He surged up and over the edge of the bed, taking her with him in a rush.

She welcomed the hard, heavy maleness of his body on top of her, opening her legs to take him in greedily. She saw the dim reflection of his darker body over hers, his pale hips between her outstretched legs. Wickedness coursed down the length of her at the sight. Who was that strange woman in the mirror who made Richard Jensen want her so, and who wanted him so badly in return?

Richard found her mouth and took the thoughts away, replacing them with the smell and touch of himself. A dark, hot storm of desire swirled through her as he pushed into her, lifting her hips away from the bed with the force of it. She gasped and rocked against him, falling into the rhythm of his thrusts. Everything she needed centered on him, the fullness of him deep inside and the high ridge of bone above his shaft driving against her.

He groaned and called out her name hoarsely, then sought her mouth. She heard the hard rush of air through his nostrils as he filled her mouth with his tongue. The

226

sensation of being filled by him above and below sent dark shivers of pleasure rippling through every part of her. She heard another groan coming from deep in his throat, a long helpless groan of unbearable pleasure, and, just that swiftly, she was climbing to join him at the peak of pleasure.

There was nothing of tenderness in either of them, just taut, desperation in every muscle as they locked their bodies together. He gripped her tightly and she felt the bruising strength of him driving against her. She welcomed it, sliding her hands up to hold his hips, but it was her own hips that answered each thrust of him. She returned the powerful strokes with unquestioning trust in the surrender of self.

He pushed deeper and harder until she was blinded by pleasure and the boundary between her skin and his blurred and merged in a paroxysm of physical release. He held her afterward, trembling and breathing harshly. She tenderly kissed his temple where it lay next to her face, left sharp-edged and exalted by the magnitude of her own pleasure.

After a long period of holding her, he moved to one side, and she saw the short tendrils of hair around his temples plastered to the skin by sweat. He smiled, his eyes a frosted green from pleasure. She had never noticed it before, but in the last light of day coming in through the curtains, the change was startling.

"I love you, Margaret," he said softly. "I never manage to tell you that when I'm inside you, but I do."

Touched by his earnest expression, she smiled. "I know you do, and I'm quite sure I couldn't manage to say it either, not then. It's too much, isn't it, to have all that pleasure and still make one's brain work?"

"Do you know what a gift that is for a man, Margaret? For a woman to give herself up to pleasure in his arms the way you do?"

"Is it?" she said softly. "I don't know much about all of this, only what you've taught me."

He rubbed a lazy arm across her belly. "I haven't taught

you a thing," he said. "That was all a part of you, even before you knew me. It's just my good fortune that you chose to discover it with me."

Margaret felt vulnerable suddenly, spent desire replaced by shyness. She curled into the space between his arm and shoulder. "It really is special, isn't it? I mean, I suppose it's nice for everyone or people wouldn't write about it and talk about it so much, but surely it can't be this wonderful for everyone?"

Richard laughed and gathered her into his arms. "I don't know, love, truly I don't. I haven't asked them and I don't care. All that matters is us. I've never had such pleasure before, and I've never loved anyone like I love you."

Margaret sighed with contentment. "Do you know that apart from my father and brother, you're the first man who ever kissed me?"

"The world is full of fools, little Maggie," he said softly. "The world is full of fools."

Chapter 14

Richard stared out to sea. The future lay ahead out there somewhere. It was a disconcerting thought, but there it was. Ahead lay Singapore. past Timor, past Makassar, past Bali, past Borneo. None of it was visible now. They wouldn't see land for a while now, but still it was there, just like the future. He'd never cared much for the future. It had never held out the promise of anything he wanted so much he couldn't walk away from it.

Now it was different. Now there was Margaret Belleweather. She nestled deep within him, something precious and remarkable that filled all the spaces inside he'd never known were empty. He'd spent thirty-one years incomplete. He'd always laughed at men who blathered on about the woman they couldn't live without, and he had been convinced that Ezekiel Bursey was the only one of them who wasn't a nincompoop. At least Ezekiel would be kind enough not to rub his nose in the fact that he, too, had become a nincompoop.

He watched Margaret—his Maggie—up on the bow. No, he wasn't a nincompoop. Loving a woman like her made sense. He'd thought he loved Emma, though even at the time he'd known it had a lot to do with Jack. Someday he'd have to tell Margaret about Jack. The hunger for children had always been a burning need deep in his gut, to raise them with all the love and security he'd never had. Even though Margaret Belleweather couldn't have children, somehow she would fill that void like she'd filled all the rest.

She was so easy to love, so different than she had been before. He knew she thought he'd been instrumental in opening her mind, but she'd had that in her all along. He wished he could take credit for it, but pride had played the biggest role—the false pride that had stiffened her back and her mind before. It had deserted her at the height of her need to help Christian and left her defenseless against the truth.

No, there was little enough that he could give her. All he had to offer her was his love and a place in his life, such as it was. Money was always a worry, money to pay the crew, money to keep the *Java* in good order, money to buy the next cargo. If he could have stomached a partner, made deals with trading firms, it would have smoothed the way, but it would have robbed him of the autonomy he craved. More money in exchange for freedom seemed a poor deal. This voyage marked his first venture with any outside connection. It was the only way to exploit the idea he'd had for transhipping.

When he'd asked his prospective partner whether he could be trusted, the man had laughed long and thoroughly. "I don't know. Can I be? You will only know at the end, my friend," he'd said. "That is the nature of trust—you can only know when a thing is over whether trust was a part of the deal."

And Richard had been satisfied with that. Any man shrewd enough to speak the truth so plainly was a man he could deal with. That and the fact that the man was something of an outsider, like himself, convinced him that it was time to make this move. Still, the sooner he brokered the wool through this man's auspices, and emerged unscathed and richer for it, the better. He never wanted to captain for anyone else again, and to keep his independence meant building a fat bank balance. Not for the first time, he mused on the irony that to fortify his independence, he had to relinquish part of it first.

The ship's clock chimed and he stretched, satisfied that

he could go below, have lunch, and maybe catch a little sleep. He'd kept the room at Daphne's two extra nights so that Sanders could refit the main cabin. His berth was twice the size it had been, and the floor space was reduced accordingly. Now Margaret would have to be really determined to take a bath, but the most important thing, the place where he made love to her and held her and listened to her heart's secrets, was big enough now to hold them both in comfort.

It felt fine, it felt right, all of it. He'd wrested the *Java* out of the grip of men who didn't deserve her and made a life for himself. Now he'd make Margaret Belleweather a part of it. The wind was tugging at the brim of the straw hat they'd bought for her, pink ribbons flying from it like sail ties. He took it as a good omen, those pink ribbons, that and the new, dark purple skirt that matched her eyes. It replaced the bedraggled lavender one she'd cut from her dress, but much more significant was the fact that she'd given up wearing mourning. It wouldn't be right to begin a new life wearing mourning.

The starboard watch was lining up at the cookhouse for their food. Dogsmeat was casting odd glances in his direction. Let him wonder. If the captain didn't feel like eating lunch right on the watch change, he wouldn't. Right now he preferred to watch Margaret. Toby had foregone lunch and was handing her a shirt he'd fetched from the fo'c'sle. Richard could see the small, perfect silhouette of her face under the shade of her hat as she smiled up at him. Toby hunkered down and Richard felt an unreasoning stab of jealousy.

Suddenly he was hungry, and he wanted to see Margaret across the table from him. He was tired, too, for no particular reason he could discern, and he hoped she would come and lay next to him while he slept, perhaps reading a book—anything, just so that he could reach out and touch her as he slept. It was one of his chief pleasures in life these days, holding her, looking at her, touching her. How perfect it had been at Daphne's, having her all to himself.

231

That couldn't last. He'd have to share her with the *Java*, and with the *Java*'s crew. Still, it wouldn't hurt to remind her that lunch was waiting in the saloon. He braced his arms on the quarterdeck rail and swung over it to the main deck, feeling like a boy as he landed with a solid thud. He grinned. It had caught Toby's ear and the young sailor took himself off quickly. Good.

"Not hungry, eh?" he asked, strolling up to Margaret.

She looked up, putting her hand to the brim of her hat to shade her eyes against the nearly equatorial sun. "Oh, Richard! I was just coming."

He held out his hand and she took it, rising gracefully. Silly how just her smile and the touch of her hand had the power to make his heart skip a beat. "You're back to living on love," he said, not letting go of her hand. "I won't have that. I like my women round."

She laughed. "That, I fear, will never be the case with me, but if those are captain's orders, I'll do my best."

"The captain insists," he said.

She didn't take him very seriously, not that he'd meant her to, looking out over the water instead of replying to his comment. "The sea makes more noise up here," she said. "Have you noticed?"

He chuckled. There wasn't anything about the *Java* he didn't know. "The bow cuts the water here." He gestured toward the wakes of foam streaming back from both sides of the bow. "If it wasn't louder up here, it would mean we weren't making good time. We're riding heavier now, too. Each of these bales weighs upwards of five hundred pounds, and we're full to the hatches with them."

"Still, she's flying isn't she?"

"Set the canvas right and give her a bit of wind and I think she could actually leave the water," Richard said.

"I love the sea," she sighed, "and I love the *Java*."

He felt a tightening in his chest. The *Java* was his first mistress. For Margaret to love her too was another bond between them. "It used to be part of sailor's superstition that having a woman on board meant bad luck. I suppose if you love the *Java* though, I'll have to let you stay."

232

She smiled up at him merrily. "It's a good thing I know better than to take you seriously most of the time."

"Come back and have lunch and then lay down with me. You'll find out how seriously I take you."

"No doubt," she said dryly.

But when lunch was over, she declined his offer, much to his disappointment. She seemed very mysterious, saying only that she wanted to sketch, and that she could do it better with him out of the way. Richard lay down alone, and for once his well-honed ability to fall asleep the instant his head hit the pillow deserted him. Tossing restlessly, he found the berth far too large without Margaret, which was ludicrous, of course. She was so small that she filled only a corner of it. Sleep came eventually, but a fitful sleep driven by uncomfortable dreams that made no sense.

Margaret smiled, remembering the sulky set of his shoulders when he'd gone off to their cabin a minute ago. Ordinarily, she was glad to oblige him by lying down when he slept, but she had conceived a wonderful idea in Sydney and she needed to work on it. She would paint the *Java* for Richard in oil. It would take some collusion with Dogsmeat, but the diminutive steward was happy to help keep her secret.

She'd seen the *Java* under sail from shore for the first time in Sydney, and realized how beautiful the clipper was. She'd sat on Circular Quay while Richard and the crew brought her in from the roads under sail, swooping with breathtaking elan to within a short distance of the steam tugs waiting to nudge her the rest of the way to the quay. They'd backed the mainsail abruptly in a display of nautical virtuosity, and she'd heard the other ship's crews cheering for the bravura performance.

The *Java*'s bow had dipped briefly as they'd reefed the other sails, men and boys strung out along the yardarms. It had looked for all the world as if the clipper was taking a bow before she graciously allowed the pygmy tugs to

233

elbow her up to the dock. She'd loved the picture the *Java* had made tucked up against the quay, Harkay with Darwin standing topside to supervise the winching of the bales on board, and all the men working to maneuver burlapped bales through the hatch.

It had been a long, hot afternoon, but she'd liked watching Richard, his white shirt soaked and clinging to him as he oversaw the operation, even riding a bale once, his teeth a flash of white in the swarthy face as he swung high above the dock. With his hair tied back in a sailor's pigtail, he'd been powerful and lean, too carelessly masculine for words, and the sight had made a funny little place inside of her twist tight.

But he didn't care for his own appearance, and she didn't think she could do it justice anyway, so she decided to do a view of the *Java* underway. The ink drawing had gone quickly, and as she'd drawn she'd felt the warm wooden rails under her hands, and the nearly white deck, with its long striations of oakum forced between the planks, under her feet. The sound of taut rigging and the rich, raw power of canvas catching wind had hummed in her ears as she'd drawn.

She'd taken out the one piece of art canvas she always kept carefully rolled in the back of her traveling desk, and a thick, cream-colored card had fluttered to the deck. She'd looked at it and smiled, thinking what an odd train of events An Wu had started when he'd given her the card. Tucking it back in her desk again, she'd checked that her oils were supple. Dogsmeat had helped her knead them, to remix the linseed oil separated from the pigment by disuse. Each day she was adding a bit more, spreading the oil paint carefully and then letting Dogsmeat carry it off to dry in his quarters in the fo'c'sle. She wasn't sure she'd have it done by the time they reached Singapore, but she wanted to. It seemed symbolic, somehow—a journey come full circle.

Margaret glanced up uneasily from a letter she was

writing to the Reverend Childers. The sky had never lightened substantially at dawn, and now the frame of the skylight was shuddering with the force of the ship twisting around it. So far it just seemed as if the sea was running high, with no particular storm in view. She finished the letter with difficulty and then decided she'd better secure the bird's cage. It swung madly from side to side, and she regretted having brought the poor sparrow along for such an awful ride.

It was all she could do to keep to her feet, and she had just finished wedging the cage in a corner when Dogsmeat appeared with a plate and mug.

"Won't be any proper lunch served today, miss," he said. "Captain Jensen won't be down—he said you was to eat without him."

"It's very rough, isn't it?" she asked hesitantly. She grabbed for the table.

"Nah, and you're not to worry," the steward said cheerfully. "Nothing but a bit of a blow, about what we expect this time of year." He uncovered the plate. "It's cold—can't light the fire when it's like this—but you'll find it fills the bill."

"Will Mr. Dekker or Mr. Daniels be coming down?"

"Shouldn't think so," Dogsmeat said, "except maybe to kip out for a bit." He saw the apprehensive look on her face as the *Java* groaned and swung up and about. "*Java*'ll ride it out, never you fear, miss. Has done many a time, and us all safe at the other end. No, she's safe as houses, the *Java* is."

Margaret managed a tepid smile. "I'm sure you're right."

"'Course I am. Now when you've eaten, you might want to just cozy up in the berth—won't be so like to get slammed about. We can keep the gimbal lanterns lit, but down low, so you'll have a bit of light to read by," he said. The bird cage went flying suddenly, and Margaret watched helplessly as it bounced across the deck. "And I'll see to that," Dogsmeat said. He fielded it like a ball batted long on a cricket pitch.

"You're very good at keeping your feet under you,"

235

Margaret said shakily.

The steward laughed. "And so would you be if you'd been at sea as long as me. There's a bit of a trick to it, but mainly it's just catch as catch can. Now you snug down and don't worry if you don't see me for a while. I've got to help Harkay man the pumps so we doesn't get all our lovely wool wet."

Margaret ate a little of the cold chicken then, and tried to forget how afraid she was. This was much worse than she'd imagined a storm would be, and yet it wasn't really a storm yet. There was no thunder, no lightning, no rain. By midafternoon, she thought she'd go mad if she didn't have some fresh air. She made her way to the top of the companionway, clinging to the rails on each side. When she broached the deck, the wind nearly took her breath away, and the dull groaning of wood under stress was replaced by the sounds of the pounding sea and wind screaming through the rigging.

Not wanting to venture further, she stopped only half out. Huge waves slapped the *Java*, spewing angry-looking water across the bow. It sluiced across the main deck and poured out the bulwarks. By just turning her head, she could make out two figures by the helm, one fair and the other dark. She'd have known Richard by the width of his shoulders alone. He seemed to be faring well enough, she thought, though he was hunched sharply against the wind.

The sky was darker now, nearly black in every direction. If she hadn't known it was only three o'clock in the afternoon she'd have sworn it was nearer midnight. Tiny drops of rain stung her face and far ahead of them she could see sheets of water being swept along from the clouds. Her heart flip-flopped abruptly as lightning sawed across the sky, painting everything an odd, iridescent green.

"'Scuse me, miss!"

Margaret jumped as Dekker yelled above the wind to be heard. He waited to one side of the companionway for her to let him pass. She turned and started down again instead, hoping she wouldn't be flung face down on the deck before she reached the saloon. Dekker took a turn into his cabin and appeared again soon after, suited up in oilskins.

"I need to get Captain Jensen's oils from his cabin," he said over the creaking of the ship. "Dogsmeat can't be spared from the pumps. Do you mind if I go in?"

"No, of course not," she said, and then realized that her polite reply was all but lost in the *Java*'s protests. She waved toward the cabin door instead, tasting the coppery flavor of fear in her mouth as she stumbled across the deck. She wished Richard had come down for the oils himself. Dekker gave her an attenuated salute as he passed by again.

"Thanks, miss. Captain says you're not to worry about a thing." He shut the cover over the companionway behind him, dimming the sound of the storm somewhat.

It was all very well for them, Margaret thought. At least they had something to *do*, some useful part to play which would keep their minds off the increasing ferocity of the storm. Fear was at the heart of her irritability. She lurched to the aft cabin and blessed Dogsmeat for his habit of tucking sheets and blankets down tightly on the berth. She slipped between them and they kept her from pitching about.

The groaning of the ship's timbers increased until she was sure the *Java* would grind itself to pieces and be lapped up by the sea like so much tinder. Pumping the bilges usually took place only once on each watch. Dogsmeat had made it sound as if it was going on continuously now. The ship's clock chimed four o'clock but she couldn't hear the watches changing. Maybe no one got to rest when it was like this. She shuddered as the *Java* let out a particularly high-pitched squeal, one timber crying out as it rubbed another. How much strain could mere wood endure?

She took a book from the top drawer next to the berth and stared at it dully. Her hands trembled and the words were only blurred ant tracks in the feeble light cast by the lantern mounted on the bulkhead. She imagined all that might happen in the next hours, including the spector of

237

drowning, until her imagination was wrung dry and only fear remained. Even fear had its compensations, however. It drained her, and she was able to drift into an uneasy doze.

When she awoke, she immediately perceived that the storm had increased considerably. She licked her dry lips and wondered if she had the will to cross the cabin to where the jugged water was kept by the sink. She could see it, swinging tantalizingly in its gimbal. Her stomach growled and she knew it must be past dinnertime. Why hadn't Dogsmeat come to wake her?

Stupid woman! Because we're all about to die and no one has time to wait on you! The rebuke sounded as cleanly in her head as if it had come from an outside source. She supposed it was some atavistic survival trait, for it made her angry enough to overcome her fear for the length of time it took to rise and stagger across the cabin. Drinking greedily, she made herself breathless. She was about to make a run back to the berth when she saw a huddled shape in the wild shadows cast by the lantern swinging in the saloon.

"Richard?" Black hair plastered to his head left no doubt that it was Richard who was clinging to the doorjamb from the alleyway into the saloon. She shouted, louder this time, "Richard!"

The *Java* groaned and shimmied as Margaret stumbled to the cabin door. Richard made no sign at all that he'd heard her, but then she wasn't sure he *could* have heard her over the cacophony of the tormented ship. She waited for him to move, or look up, and saw that he was shaking from head to foot.

"Richard!" She reeled into the saloon and grabbed for a chair. At first, she thought the moisture on his face must be rain, and then she saw that his oilskins were nearly dry. "Richard!" She screamed so loudly that it hurt her throat.

He didn't even look up. Her heart hammered with terror. What in God's name was wrong with him? His eyes were squeezed shut, his face rigid. For once, the scar on his cheek wasn't visible, the whole of his face being the same vivid white as the dead tissue. The muscles in his jaw

238

and neck were corded, and he clutched one arm tightly around his waist. Was he hurt? She wanted to go to him but the ship was pitching so badly that she hesitated.

What are you waiting for? He needs your help! The same primal voice that had taunted her before now prompted her to work her way to his side by fits and starts. He clenched the doorway so tightly that she could see the cartilage in each knuckle beneath skin made transparent by the force of his grip. Dread clawed at her.

"Richard?" He slowly opened his eyes and stared hard in her direction. The green there was a glittering parody of their usual color, and his pupils failed to focus on anything in particular. She reached for his hand and felt searing heat beneath her palm.

"Oh, Richard!" she cried. "Please tell me—what's the matter?"

"Hurts," he gritted through clenched teeth. "Hurts bad." His gaze traveled vacantly around the general vicinity and came to rest on her at last. "Margaret."

It was said without expression or recognition. His eyes closed again and his brows drew together, creating deep ridges across his forehead. A fresh spasm of trembling shook him and the bleached knuckles whitened still more. Margaret looked around helplessly. It was obvious he needed to be gotten into his berth, but how?

You! You'll have to do it! Margaret wondered with a touch of hysteria why the hateful little voice in her head hadn't surfaced until this moment in her life. She wished it would go away. *Not until you start thinking clearly!* it shouted. She would have covered both ears with her hands if it hadn't meant giving up her precarious hold on the doorjamb.

"Go away! I'll do it!" The whispered words seemed to satisfy the voice, for it fell silent. Margaret thrust her shoulder beneath Richard's armpit and disengaged his hand from the door.

"Let's go, Mr. Jensen," she muttered to herself. She bent his arm so that she could tuck his hand in front of her and use all her strength to tow him along. Without stopping to think how impossible it was for her to do it, she struck out across the saloon. Richard shambled along in her wake, leaning so heavily on her shoulders and back that she was sure her legs would buckle.

Miraculously, they did not, and the *Java* remained still for a long minute. She knew that it must have just crested one of the huge waves it had been skating up and down for hours. Next would come a soul-sickening swoop down the other side. It began just as they entered the cabin. Richard's dead weight added to the angle of the deck combined to slam her against the bulkhead. The pain was nauseating, and the taste of fear in her mouth became real as blood swam in it.

Margaret beat back the desire to simply collapse to the deck. She let the *Java*'s motion roll them forward along the bulkhead until it tumbled them onto the berth. The ship nosed down and then reared up abruptly as she hit the bottom of the trough. Margaret used the relative calm as the ship climbed the next swell to push Richard to the far side. He curled into a ball, shaking violently, and the sweat on his face glistened in the flickering light of the lantern. She saw his lips move and bent over.

"What?"

"Hurts. Cold." His voice was nothing but a rasp.

"What hurts, Richard?" she asked urgently. If only she knew, she might be able to do something!

"Everything," he said hoarsely. He doubled over, his eyes squeezed shut so hard that only the tips of his lashes showed between the folds of skin. Each dark whisker stood out on cheeks the color of ash.

Oh, Mother of God, help me! Margaret clung to him helplessly. Had he broken a bone? Been knocked across the deck by the boom? What? With panicked fingers, she pried the oilskin jacket off his shoulders and wrenched it down his back. He was soaked beneath it, and hotter to the touch than Tony's stove.

Dogsmeat! She needed Dogsmeat! He'd know what to do. Tears of anguished fear spurted in her eyes as she realized the impossibility of going to find him. Her

240

shoulder and hip ached horribly from having crashed into the bulkhead, and she knew she could easily be swept overboard if she went up on deck.

"Oh, Richard," she pleaded, "tell me what to do."

An instant too late she remembered the tyrannical little voice. *Don't be a ninny!* it snarled. *Get him under the covers!* With hands shaking only slightly less than Richard's, she wrestled him the rest of the way out of the oilskin coat and pulled off his sea boots. With a strength she hadn't known she had, she pushed him beneath the sheet. After that, she simply didn't know what else to do. Richard was clearly in agony, but why?

He mumbled and she bent down to hear him. "Cold," he croaked.

Cold. She pulled the blanket up over him and he clutched at it like a dying man. No! Not a dying man! It wasn't the voice this time—it was Margaret's own thought. She nearly slapped herself for the stupidity of the notion that there was anyone in her head but herself. Anger displaced fear. The *Java* jibed viciously and she was furious. How dare the storm take them in its grip and subject them to such terror? Margaret screamed out a curse that had never passed her lips before.

If Richard was cold, then he would have all the blankets he wanted! She slipped over the edge of the berth and opened the drawer beneath it, pitching the extra blankets there up on the berth. The *Java* nosed downward and began a long slide, hitting a wall of water at the bottom as solid as concrete. She was thrown against the bureau so hard she bounced off of it.

"Damn you!" Margaret screamed, pulling herself up. Richard needed cold compresses for his head, and hot water bottles to ward off the chills, and the damned ocean wouldn't even let her put extra blankets on him. She clambered up on the berth and arranged the blankets over him with manic determination.

Richard stirred. "Oh, God," he moaned. "Sick."

She took his face in a relentless grip. "What is it, Richard? What should I do for you?" she demanded.

"Sick," he rasped again, and made a retching sound.

She looked around the cabin. There was a basin under the fixed sink, and towels. She lurched across the cabin and grabbed them, and snatched the water jug, too. Her back and shoulder hurt and she became an automaton, moving persistently as she reeled back to the berth and pushed the basin under the side of his head. There wasn't much to come up and she knew he mustn't have eaten in hours.

She let numb practicality guide her, alternately holding his head up so that he could retch into the basin and wiping his face. Sweat beaded up like liquid ash over his skin, and he took only scant sips of water. She used him as an anchor, hooking her arm under his neck and letting his weight keep them both in place. Whispers of prayers learned at Reverend Childers's knee made their way to her lips, the earliest, simplest ones, coming up from that young animal deep inside, the one that had feared death more than anything.

After a while, she couldn't feel her legs anymore. The intensity of Richard's chills came and went, peaking with such violence that she held him with all her might to keep him from hurting himself. Whenever the shaking stopped, he lay limp and unresponsive, the dull tinge of sweat and a faint pulse at the base of his neck the only signs of life. His pallor shocked her, the bloodless lips already the color of death.

Don't die, please don't die. Her soft litany didn't even include a mention of God, or an amen. Amen—Latin for 'so be it.' No, no 'so be it.' As *she* wanted it—don't die. Not God's will—*her* will. *Don't leave me, Richard.* She lay her cheek across the hot-smelling hair. *Don't leave me.*

She tipped the water jug onto a cloth over and over, wiping his face and pressing the coolness to his neck. Her limbs were taut with fear, her ears attuned to the ship and her eyes on Richard. The tenor of the ship changed as time wore on, screaming in protest as it reached the top of the waves and then charging down again with the speed of a locomotive. Dogsmeat suddenly appeared in the door—

was it hours or only minutes later?

"Here!" he cried sharply. "What's to do?"

Margaret found she couldn't unclench her jaw to speak. Dogsmeat briskly handed her a small loaf of soggy bread and bent over Richard. She took the loaf and stared at it. The staff of life? Could she make Richard eat it? Would that save him? She looked at Dogsmeat again and opened her mouth.

"Malaria by the looks of it," he shouted over the din. It was followed by a rush of Cockney patois so thick she could only understand the curses.

He pushed Margaret back and she barely noticed the brusque familiarity. Like a diminutive doctor called to a patient's bedside, he stripped away the blankets and went over Richard inch by inch. He lay unresisting, limp and stunned as a fish panting its last on the shore. She watched with a remote curiosity as the steward pulled off Richard's shirt and pants, his brows beetled in concentration, and pressed his stubby fingers to one wrist.

"Damn! It's took him bad this time," he said, his mouth taut. "I'll get some medicine. Stay here."

And where would I be going? she thought wildly. And why didn't the medicine work before? Dogsmeat rolled back through the door. Her thoughts were close to her lips. "Why didn't the quinine work?" she demanded as he poured some of the whitish liquid down Richard's throat.

"Could be it's tropica," he said without looking at her. He wiped away a trickle on Richard's chin. "Nothing's proof against that." He let Richard's head fall back into her lap. A drop of sweat collided with another and rolled down into his ear. Margaret wanted to stop it but her hands were trapped by the weight of his head. "Can't do nothin' more for him than that now."

Dogsmeat looked at her at last. She noticed the color of his eyes for the first time, a dark hazel. Was that good or bad? Everything was an omen now; only magic could save Richard. "Why can't we do any more for him?" she asked petulantly, although she already knew the answer. Only magic.

243

"You eat that bread," he said sharply. She looked around vaguely and saw that the bread had coasted toward the pillows and lodged there.

"Why? Will that help?"

"Listen to me, miss—we've got our hands full topside," he snapped. "We're near down to bare poles, with every sea anchor we can rig and all the oil we can find overside. Don't take this as cruelty, because I love him and I know you do, too, but he'll either live or die and there's nothing more we can do for him now. The other twenty-odd of us, that's another matter. I don't look to see another sunrise meself, but we ain't going to quit trying. You hold tight here, eat that bread, and I'll come to you as I can."

Margaret nodded numbly, staring at him. She felt Richard's slow, hot pulse under her hands. Someone had to know what was what, and it certainly wasn't her. Dogsmeat pulled a few of the blankets over Richard again.

"Just two or three, y'ken?" he barked. "And all the water he'll take."

"Yes."

He left and she looked at Richard, burning away in her lap. She freed her hands and stroked him to the beat of his pulse. The rhythm edged her into sleep after a while. Her head slumped forward until the muscles knotted in protest and she jerked upright again. Over and over, she dozed off and awakened to the pain, the one constant the creak of tortured wood around her each time she awoke. Richard tossed his head from side to side and mumbled, lost in fevered dreams whenever the chills subsided.

Margaret came awake with a start as a terrible shriek cut into her unconsciousness, a hideous cry as wood twisted and cracked. The *Java* rolled and kept on rolling, heeling far over, so that Margaret's spine was rammed against the wall behind her. Richard rolled with the ship, his heaviness nearly crushing her as they continued the long, slow, death roll. The lockers and bureau drawers gave way, spewing their contents as the ship heaved. A sound like a giant ram battering at the ship's hull hammered into her brain. They were going down.

Margaret welcomed Richard's weight over her. They would die together. She wrapped her arms around his trembling body as several strands of his damp hair fell against her cheek. All the prayers with God in them came back with a rush. The paltry events of her life streaked by—eating strawberries on midsummer's eve, a rolling coach ride into London and her first memories of the city, foot races at the church fete, the face of the first suitor she'd fallen in love with.

"Cut away!" Impossibly, she heard someone up on deck. It would be Dekker, or maybe Daniels, at the helm not too far away. The ungodly thumping lessened bit by bit and then disappeared entirely. She felt the ship roll back slowly, a little at a time, until she centered over her keel again. Richard subsided to the berth and she lay over him, the smell of his skin and suffering rising to her nostrils as his heart beat softly under her ear. Let the drowning be quick. She waited and waited and waited. The sound of water rushing in didn't come. She opened eyes puffed with exhaustion and saw Dogsmeat.

"We're dismasted!" he shouted, braced in the doorway. "Keep yer wits—it's maybe the end. I'll come fer you if we're abandoning ship."

"Not without Richard," she said slowly. Expecting to be dead and finding she wasn't exacted a toll. All her thoughts ran slowly, as if to make up for their speed before. "I won't go without him."

Dogsmeat made a growl of disgust, distorting his normally kind face. His hair dripped in his face and water spackled his lashes. He looked like some angry troll of death. "Aye, and did'ye think we wouldn't take him?"

She blinked at him. The etiquette of abandoning ship hadn't been covered at finishing school. "I . . . I didn't know."

"Well now y'do." He turned and left abruptly.

Margaret looked down at Richard. Glazed, insensate eyes sought hers. "Bring me a priest," he said in a hoarse whisper. The green there was fey, only half of this world. He could easily lose his grasp on this side.

245

"Hush," she said, smoothing the damp, tousled hair back from his burning face. "Hush. You're only dreaming." If he believed he was only dreaming, then he could only dream that he was dying. Maybe she could save him that way. He sighed and turned his head away impatiently. *Don't think about death,* she pleaded silently. The mere thought could carry him away. His long, blunt-tipped fingers clenched a piece of sheet. She reached out and pushed her fingers through the spaces between his knuckles.

The force of his answering squeeze shocked her. "Marry me, Maggie," he rasped. "When I'm gone, you'll be free again, but at least I can die having you."

The words crackled like dry leaves through his blistered lips. His breath on her cheek was hot, straight from the furnace of death. It crisped the words and set them smoking.

"No," she retorted, afraid that he would give up once he had what he wanted. "No dying requests." She snatched the water jug and held it to his lips. "Water? That's all you'll get from me."

"Oh, Maggie." It was vaguely regretful, faraway enough to make her even more fearful.

"What else do you want?" she demanded. "Tell me something else!"

He tossed his head fitfully, buffeted by her words. "Crucifix," he said suddenly. "In the bottom drawer."

Margaret worked herself free of him and stumbled over the edge of the berth. Scrabbling through the clothes strewn across the deck, she bit back a sob. She'd been too harsh. He would die just to put distance between her hard words and his tired mind. She rooted frantically, anxious to satisfy his request.

At last she found it, in a small black jeweler's sack. She pried apart the drawstring and slipped the fragile gold piece into her hand. The raised carving had been reduced to soft humps, defined only by blackened lines where dirt had settled. It was fragile with age and use, but fragile by design, too. His mother's? She rolled it in her fingers, revealing the other side. All trace of any inscription or jeweler's hallmark had long since worn away. It slid along a frayed, black cord that showed its white core in spots. One violent rent showed the whitest, as if someone had once tried to tear it from his neck, or from his hands, and nearly snapped the cord.

She lurched to her feet and the sea heaved up under the *Java*, spilling her across the cabin and up against the hard edge of the berth. She sank to her knees, dizzy with pain. "Here, my love," she said when the worst of it had passed. She reached for his hand and pressed it into his palm. He fingered it with growing awareness and took it to his lips with shaking hands. She closed her hands over his arms to steady them. "Pray," she said fervently, "pray to stay with us." *With me*.

Long moments passed and she wondered if he knew he still held the gold pressed to his lips. Then he let out a soft sigh that turned into a murmur, half Portuguese, half oddly-accented Latin. She put a finger to his cheek and felt the hot, tautness of his skin moving beneath it. At last the words became a whisper and faded away.

"Oh, dearest love," she whispered as his face relaxed into sleep, "if I could bring you a priest, I would." She lay her head down on the edge of the berth. As it was, he would probably just be the first of them to die. Tiredness swept through her bones, the drudgery of unceasing fear dulling her wit to accept it. Her last thought as she subsided to the deck was that she would have married him if there had been a priest there.

Chapter 15

He dreamed that he was in a native village, up in the interior. Everything should have been green but all around him the fields were on fire. Behind him, the trees were burned to stumps, collapsing and sending out great sheaves of sparks. Ahead the trees were just beginning to catch fire, writhing like human beings without feet, burning, but powerless to run from the pain. He plodded along the desolate path, his mouth like dust and his tongue too dry to wet it. He saw a jug by the roadside, its surface rippling with diamonds of sun. Water.

But when he picked it up, his teeth were chattering too hard for him to drink it. The water poured past his mouth and spilled down his chest, and then, suddenly, it was dust—hot, choking dust. He let the jug fall. Away on the horizon, he saw a line of bearers, with Atam Datu and Christian Belleweather riding in splendor before them. They shimmered in the heat, like phantoms. They would have water. And Margaret would be with them. Margaret and water. It was all he needed.

His feet began moving and the heat of the road singed them. He walked faster. The heat intensified. He looked down and saw flamelets erupting from the road and lapping at his ankles. He shook them off but they multiplied, so he began to run. Now he could see the glint of Margaret's gold hair. She was sitting next to Christian on a palanquin, laughing, and he was handing her pieces of mangosteen. Even from this far away, Richard could see the juice dripping down her chin. She didn't seem to notice him and he began yelling.

The flames were licking higher now, consuming his knees and thighs and making it almost impossible to run. He could see the purple of Margaret's eyes, cool and welcoming, the stuff of salvation. Why couldn't she see *him?* He waved and went on trying to outrun the fire. The whole world was on fire. Someone grabbed his elbow and he spun around. Margaret? Or was it Emma? A wall of flame gushed up around them, and the heat seared his eyes closed. Had it been Emma or Margaret who shook him and offered to lead him away from the hellfire? He yelled, over and over, asking for someone, anyone, to answer him, for the owner of the hand on his elbow to speak, and then he awoke.

It was night. He lay stiffly, in a bed, with a compress off to the side of his head. The room was unfamiliar—gritty outlines in the low lamplight. He was alone. His body felt like a hard piece of wood, and he hoped it would not start burning again. As bad as they were, the shaking and the helpless shivering were better than that. His pulse hammered in every point of his body, building until it hammered in his head. He had a terrible headache, and behind his eyes, the worst pain of all.

The pillowcase was sodden beneath his head. He turned his face to find a cool, dry spot, but soon that area was as hot and wet as the other. He turned again, irritably, but there was no relief that lasted more than a minute. At length, he lost the strength even to turn his head away from the heat. He lay and stared at nothing until he sank back into darkness and flames.

Margaret stopped to mop her face off. Down by the docks it was much hotter than up on the hill where the cottage lay. Thank God for her earnings in Sydney or there would not even have been that, or money to pay the slatternly girl who was only slightly better than no one to stay at Richard's bedside while she dealt with the shipyard. Decent women were hard to come by in Makassar. She hoped this girl would at least have the sense to come running for her if Richard took a turn for the worse. Each time she left him, she took his hot, dry hand and told him she was going away for a short while but that she would be back. He never seemed to notice but she hoped that some part of him heard and knew that he was not abandoned.

It was malaria tropica, as Dogsmeat had suspected. The doctor Dekker had unearthed in a bar was sure of it. Margaret wouldn't have trusted him to vet a horse at Pensleigh, but here she had no choice. Choices had been few and far between for weeks. She had become sharp-edged, a harpy, pushing the men and driving herself. The shipyard had received the worst of her temper and determination. It was cash on the barrel head for repairs. With its captain near death, a wild woman claiming to be wealthy, and a crew just back from the edge of hell, the *Java* hadn't looked like the most promising of jobs.

In desperation, she'd toughened, haranguing the owner until he locked his office against her and refused to come out until she left the shipyard. She'd screamed and beat on his windows until the glass threatened to shatter. Richard would live, and when he recovered, the *Java* must be waiting for him, whole and hearty, not the sad tangle of ripped decking and tattered lines that rocked at anchor out in the bay. They'd held a council of war in the curiously untouched saloon, Dekker and Daniels, Margaret and Dogsmeat, Tony and Harkay, Toby, Sanders, and anyone else who cared to crowd in.

The money they'd pooled hadn't been a tenth of what was needed. The promise of the profits from the wool run in exchange for the repairs hadn't moved the shipyard owner. Richard Jensen was a penny ante trader in his book, and the wool wouldn't even get to England in time for this year's market. Margaret had tried in desperation to explain Richard's plan, but the owner had guffawed. Singapore's trade firms wouldn't participate in a hare-brained scheme like that, he said, and certainly not with a reprobate like Jensen.

250

That's when she'd thought of Charles. The man only laughed harder when she told him she was half-owner of Townsend and Townsend. It was stretching the truth since that investment had been made in Christian's name, but she didn't care. She telegraphed to Charles and asked that he send a letter of credit by the fastest means available, guaranteeing the funds through Townsend and Townsend. She'd brandished the return telegram under the shipyard owner's nose. Only then had the man stopped laughing. The formal letter, on the firm's letterhead, had arrived today on a Dutch mail packet, along with a more personal one from Charles expressing his concern for her welfare and a desire to help in any way he could.

Now she could afford to let herself feel, but as the hot sun beat down on her, she leaned against the gate to the shipyard and felt nothing but exhaustion. The crew had already cleared the wreckage away on the *Java*, and the sound of hammers and the smell of freshly cut wood should have lightened her heart. But as long as Richard still lay so dangerously ill, there was no room in her heart for hope. She turned and started up the hill, leaden with lack of sleep.

One night he awoke dripping with perspiration and got out of bed. He clutched the edge of the mattress, making his way dizzily to the wash basin. He rubbed himself dry with a towel in the dim glow of the lantern and had a drink of water before he wove his way back to bed. He saw a shimmer of gold in the depths of the corner and stopped, holding the bed post for support. It was Margaret, huddled in a wrapper he hadn't seen before, slumped over in sleep. He fell into bed. Was it really her?

He would have liked another blanket but he didn't have the energy to rise again. Thought came with difficulty. If Margaret was here, did that mean he was dreaming, or had she been real all along? His face felt tight and he was deadly tired but he fought to think it through. And what about Emma? He hadn't seen Jack so that meant she was probably a dream. Or would they keep a child away from a sickroom? He wished they wouldn't. He really wanted to see Jack. The thoughts loosened and flew every which way in his head. He went to sleep again cold.

"Any change?" Dogsmeat worried the hat in his hands as he stood in the shade on the veranda, turning it around and around by the brim.

Margaret sighed. "Just a bit, for the better I think. But if he doesn't start eating again soon . . ."

"Tell him the lads is all askin' after him, if you can. Or maybe better, tell him they're not doin' a lick of work till he gets back on his feet."

She let a tired smile lift the corners of her mouth. "If he wakes up for long enough, I will."

"Right then—I'll just be off." He took two steps away and Margaret was about to close the door when the steward stopped. "Oh, and miss—tell him the *Java* looks grand. She's ready to sail when he is."

Margaret nodded. If anything would help, that would. She took the basket of food that Tony had sent along and put it on a rickety table in the bedroom. Richard lay just as she had left him. A tatty tree outside the window shaded the room from the midday sun, leaving it in shadow, and a light breeze stirred the faded, disintegrating curtains at the open window.

The abandoned trysting place of a European doctor and his native girl, the cottage was an odd mix of good, solid furniture and tasteless, shoddy pieces. Margaret wasn't even sure the man who'd rented it to them had the right to do so, but she'd been too anxious and tired to argue fine points. They'd carried Richard there in search of the doctor and found only the empty house. They'd taken possession without so much as the need to break a lock, and the 'landlord' had shown up the next day.

She took out the jug of soup which would probably go uneaten like all the others. Fresh bread—Tony must have been half-cooked himself by the time it finished baking in the cookhouse—and fruit, even cold tea, and, at the very bottom, the little jeweler's bag with Richard's crucifix.

Dogsmeat must have found it when they'd finally cleaned up the main cabin.

Margaret felt a stab of guilt. She hadn't even thought about finding a priest in Makassar. A more godless place on the face of the earth would be hard to imagine. If there *was* a priest here, it was an accident of fate.

"Do I get some of that or are you going to eat it all?"

Margaret spun around. Richard's voice was weak, somewhere between a croak and a rasp, but definitely lucid. Dogsmeat had shaved him the day before, revealing the gaunt lines of a face ravaged by illness. Still, with his eyes open and seeing her, definitely seeing her and not the shapes and shadows that he'd been speaking to for countless days, he looked wonderful.

"That depends," she said slowly, not quite daring to believe that he was truly there in spirit. She kept her hands locked together, her feet in one place. He could start to babble again any minute. "It depends on whether you like broth made out of stringy old chicken and questionable potatoes."

His eyes slid shut and her heart sank. He wasn't going to rise to the bait.

He took a small, shivery breath, his rib cage lifting the sheet and subsiding again. "I've had worse."

"Oh, Richard! You're really awake."

He didn't open his eyes but his mouth twitched. "Not for long if I don't get some of that soup."

Margaret felt buoyant, inexpressibly light. Not only was he awake and talking, but his cranky sense of humor was in evidence. She uncorked the soup hastily and snatched a spoon and napkin. "Open up then," she said, settling gently on the bed next to him.

He opened one eye. "You're going to feed me like a baby?"

"Wits are not the prerogative of rude, American clipper captains," she said sternly. His other eye opened. "Kindly allow me the dignity of using mine. You cannot possibly sit up so I will feed you." She waited breathlessly as his face wrinkled in confusion.

At last he said weakly, "I think I've been paraphrased."

"Oh, yes," she said happily. It had been a test, a reminder of the day he'd insisted on carrying her to the coolness of his cabin after the spiny anemone had stung her. "Now, open your mouth."

His wakefulness lasted only a few minutes more, but in that time she managed to spoon nearly a whole cup of broth into him. He closed his eyes halfway through but she persisted until he stopped swallowing and the broth dribbled from the corner of his mouth. Then the tears came, a storm of release that wouldn't stop coming once it started. Margaret tottered into the front room and sagged into a wildly out-of-place wing chair so as not to risk disturbing Richard with her crying.

At nightfall, he awoke again, this time for a little longer. He slowly chewed the bread and had some of the tea. She sponged him clean and rolled him over so that she could put a fresh sheet on the bed, chatting to him about nothing in particular so that he would stay awake until she finished.

"S'nice," he mumbled.

"What's nice?" she asked, gently pulling him by the shoulder so that he settled onto his back again.

"Everything," he said. "Glad you're here." His face relaxed into unfocused lines and she went to the other side of the bed to pull the sheet over and tuck it in.

"And *I'm* glad you're awake to appreciate it," she said, grunting as she lifted the mattress with his weight on it. She turned and saw that he had fallen asleep again just that fast.

Hard lines ran from his nose to his mouth, though the heavy, Cupid's bow mouth itself was as full as ever, blistered by the heat of his own body, but beautiful just the same. She softly traced the outlines with the tip of her finger. The lean muscles of his upper arms and across his chest had been stripped of all extraneous flesh, laying bare the cording and deepening the hollows at his throat. Each rib pushed at the skin, a row of undulating depressions down his sides. His nose was sharper, the long sweep of lean cheek more shadowy below the proud cheekbones.

254

No part of him had escaped the wasting, except his lovely, full mouth.

A fine pair we make, Margaret thought tenderly. She would ask Dogsmeat to bring more food, and she would invite the steward to come and bully his captain into eating more. With the two of them badgering him, Richard would be well again that much sooner. The razor edges that tension and fear had put on her soul began to soften. He would live—it was no longer a prayer but a certainty.

"Richard, who is Emma?"

He pulled the pillow more firmly under his neck and stared up at the ceiling. She took several stitches in the blouse she was making just to keep her hands busy and glanced through her lashes to see if he had fallen asleep again. She had grown used to that, talking one minute, sleeping the next. Sometimes he had trouble focusing on the train of conversation, so she tried not to tax him, but late in the evening seemed to be his best time of day for concentrating. She had deliberately saved this question for then.

The small lamp on the bedside table picked out silver reflections in his eyes so she knew he was still awake. "You mentioned the name when you were ill," she said casually.

"She was someone I knew in Charleston," he said at length. "She was Jack's mother. I nearly married her but she took off with another man."

"Oh." Her heart took an odd beat. Did he still love her? How could she ask? She couldn't, so she tried to draw him out on a different tack. "Was that a long time ago?"

"Six years," he said shortly. He still stared fixedly at the ceiling. "Jack was so little then. I made my deal for the *Java* and went to break the good news, but they weren't there."

"There?"

"Home."

Margaret sewed on in silence. *Their* home? *Their* child?

If he wouldn't tell her himself, she couldn't bring herself to ask.

"They stripped it bare," he said after a long pause. "The neighbors were quick enough with the details. Another sea captain. He brought a cart and they emptied the place. There was the *Java*, waiting for all of us. I was captain of my own fine ship, and then the pleasure of coming home to tell them turned to ashes."

"You loved her very much then," Margaret said quietly, laying the blouse on the incidental table next to her chair.

"I didn't hold out for love," Richard said, a bleary bitterness in his voice. "She was comely, pleasant. I was alone in the world and she had no family so we drifted together. But Jack . . . Jack. I never knew how much it was possible to love a baby." He was silent for a moment. "They said the other man carried him off on his shoulders. He was two by then. He would have thought that was fun." His voice was raw now. "And he loved carts and horses, too, so I'm sure the whole thing was a big adventure to him. At least, I hope it was."

Margaret no longer pretended not to watch him. His jaw trembled and his neck was taut. He closed his eyes and she saw his hands curl into fists on top of the sheet. He made a sound in his throat and a tear slid down from the corner of his eyes and zigzagged through the day's growth of whiskers on his cheek.

"Oh, Richard," she said softly. "I'm sorry. I didn't mean to make you sad."

He didn't answer. Another tear streaked its way unevenly down his cheek and his chest shook. Margaret clenched her hands together. To see his anguish hurt so much that her own eyes watered. He rolled away abruptly and buried his face in the pillow, the choking in his throat matched by the shaking of his exposed shoulder. Margaret slipped onto the bed and laid a hand on his back.

"Richard, I'm sorry," she said. She felt like crying for him, with him.

He shrugged at her hand and turned his face farther into the pillow. "Not your fault," he said in a choked voice.

"It's just the damned fever."

She stroked his neck, pulling his newly washed hair back off his face. It slipped through her fingers like velvet, heavy, black velvet, and she felt moisture at the hairline where a tear had run into it. His reserves were so low that he quieted before long. She curled along the length of him and held him gently, afraid that he would shrug her off again.

"It's in the past," she said as his breathing grew more steady. "I'm sorry I made you remember it."

"You didn't make me remember it," he said, his voice rough from tears and tiredness. "I think about it anyway. It's just that the fever's left me so damned weak, I . . ."

Margaret held him tighter. "I know, I know," she said soothingly. "Daniels and Dekker wanted to know if you'd like to play cards tomorrow, did I tell you? They said they'd see if there was an unmarked deck to be had in Makassar and come up with it right after lunch. If you're sleeping, they said they'd wait."

He slowly relaxed against her and his arms softened their grip on the pillow. When she was quite sure he was asleep, she trimmed the lamp back to nothingness and lay in the dark for a long time.

"Here, here!" Dogsmeat cried. "You'll be takin' it easy on him!"

Harkay rumbled and darted a black look at the dwarf as he backed away from setting Richard on the seat of the dogcart. Richard let out a deep sigh as he leaned back and closed his eyes. Even to dress with his steward's help and be carried out of the house was almost beyond his strength.

"My money's on the dwarf," he murmured.

"There'll be no betting on such things," Margaret said with asperity. "The very idea!"

Richard felt himself melting like hot tallow against the seat of the cart. He hadn't realized how hard this was going to be. He let himself feel Margaret's strength, the way she gently clucked the Cockney and the big Polynesian into submission. He realized he'd always wanted that—a woman who could be strong without being a virago.

"Come along, then," he heard her say. The cart began to rattle down the hill.

He hoped he didn't embarrass himself by sliding down off the seat, or falling asleep before they reached the docks. He was anxious to see the *Java*. Daniels had told him how, when the storm had passed, they'd managed to rig a jib sail and limp into Makassar. It was all a blur to him, a faint memory of being jostled up a hill and no more. Just the thought of the *Java* dismasted, the splintered mainmast leaving a hole between the mizzen and foremasts like a child's missing tooth, had tugged at his gut.

He dozed off, but lightly, not into nightmares or the deathly grip of total depletion, but only a restorative nap. The next thing he knew, the cart had stopped and he heard the cry of sea birds, scavengers of the docks. He smelled the sea, his first breath of it in how long? Longer than he'd been away from it since he'd first smelled it at sixteen. He kept his eyes closed for another long minute, almost afraid of what he'd see when he opened them. Could the *Java* really be whole again?

"There, that's the last of it," he heard Margaret say. "Plates, bedsheets, everything. You take them to the gig, Dogsmeat. I'll sit with him until he awakes and then Harkay and I will follow you." He felt the cart tip slightly as she stepped up to sit next to him.

"I'm here," Richard managed to say. He struggled to a sitting position. His spine felt like jelly.

"You can see the *Java* now, Richard," Margaret said with quiet anticipation.

He gazed across the water and had no trouble picking out the *Java* in the welter of other ships at anchor. She looked the same as she ever had and he released a tight breath. "I can't see anything different."

Margaret laughed softly. "Do you feel up to going out? Everyone's excited to have you come aboard."

"That's the object of this whole exercise, isn't it?" He felt a fresh energy and swung his legs over the edge of the seat. Harkay jumped nimbly to his side. Just as well, Richard realized, as his feet hit the ground and almost went out from under him.

As they rowed out, he felt a tight knot of tension in his chest. The *Java* looked beautiful. The new mast, new rigging, and fresh paint—she looked even better than before. Daniels and Dekker had told him it was so, told him all that Margaret had been through to make it happen, but he still couldn't quite believe it. The whole crew was lined up in their best, grinning like banshees as they stood in military precision on deck. Dekker waited until the gig was within earshot and led them in three cheers for the captain.

"Stop a minute," Richard barked. Harkay shipped the oars as Richard struggled against the tears that came to him so easily in the aftermath of his illness. He turned to Margaret when he was sure he was in control. She was watching him with cautious expectation. "By God," he said, "I didn't think I could love you any more than I did already, but . . ."

Her face lit up. "Then you like it? It's all the way you would have ordered it?"

He laughed weakly, still teetering between tears and elation. "She's perfect, and you know it."

Margaret smiled. "She wasn't, but she is now that *you're* going to be on board again."

He submitted to riding aboard in the bosun's chair and made a brief tour. It was all first-class, the best, just as Dogsmeat had told him that morning as he shaved him. How in God's name he would repay Margaret, he didn't know, but the knowledge that he had lived and that the *Java* had lived was enough for the moment. Below in the saloon, he begged off lunch. His legs felt like rubber and he could barely keep his eyes open.

Margaret helped him into their berth and he fell asleep immediately. When he awoke it was dusk. He felt the peace that only the motion of the *Java* beneath him could bring, and a new vigor surged through him. Margaret came in to light the lantern and saw that he was

259

awake. She had never looked so beautiful.

"I have one more surprise for you," she said, "but you'll have to come into the saloon."

He would have gone anywhere just to be within sight of her. The saloon seemed well within reason. "Just give me a minute," he said. "Sit down and let me look at you. You're so lovely. I dreamed about you when I was sick, you know. You were always there, but I could never touch you, and I wanted to so much."

She ducked her head shyly. "You're being fanciful."

He smiled. She was softer now, in little ways, but so much tougher, too. He loved her unreservedly, pulled into her orbit like the earth to the sun. "Are you afraid I'll ravish you? Let me set your mind at ease—as much as I'd like to, I'm afraid I don't have the energy. Maybe tomorrow."

"And maybe next month," she admonished him. "When you're well enough, we'll talk about it."

"Then you don't object to the part about being ravished? We're agreed on that?" He watched her honest confusion with delight. He loved it when she couldn't quite decide if he was being serious or not. She wasn't usually this easily fooled. Ravishment began to seem an attainable goal.

She surprised him by laying down next to him and nestling against his shoulder. "I hope when it comes to that, I'll be allowed to ravish you in return," she said.

He'd been joking before but her words set in motion a train of thought that began with love and ended in lust. His body, indifferent to almost everything but sleep for so long, stirred. "You're a witch, Margaret Belleweather. I've said it before and I'll say it again."

She looked up at him, her nose wrinkling at the bridge as the delicate gold brows drew together. "You never! Called me a witch, that is. I should have remembered if you had, because I wouldn't have liked it."

"Maybe I only thought it then," he conceded, "but it's true."

"Then I cast a spell on you," she said, looking him straight in the eye. "When you can walk three times around the deck, we'll talk about ravishment, and not before.''

"Hm. Is that the quarterdeck?"

"Certainly not!" she declared. "The main deck, and let's make it five times just for good measure."

"Damn." He stared at the ceiling. The white gloss paint was freshly scrubbed. An idea struck him. "Wait a minute. I have a compromise offer. Make it twice and then I'll let *you* do the ravishing while I lay here. That won't take as much energy on my part."

"Richard!" She giggled and pushed away from him, sitting up to frown at him with feigned severity. Her hair, which had been pinned up on top of her head, had loosened, creating an enchanting gold halo around her face. "Really," she said, "sometimes you remind me of nothing so much as a small, naughty boy."

"Naughty. Yes, that's what I had in mind—naughtiness—but small, never." He grinned at her and grabbed for her wrist an instant too late.

She twirled across the cabin, laughing. The high color in her cheeks suggested that she would willingly be naughty with him once her conditions were met. "Five times," she said merrily, "and the main deck. Otherwise you won't be up to your usual . . ."

He saw the color flood her cheeks as she caught her own unintended double entendre. "Is that so?" he asked lazily. He glanced to a spot below his waist. She followed his look and saw the swelling of desire there. "I think I'm up to it," he said.

"We can't," she whispered, her body going still, her expression frozen in sudden longing. "You're not fit enough. You couldn't even walk two times around the quarterdeck."

"Since that wasn't what I was proposing to do, it doesn't matter," he said softly. "Close the door and come be with me. I swear I'll let you do all the work."

Her mouth went round with desire, the purple eyes wide in the smooth, white oval of her face. "It can't be good to . . . not in your condition."

He looked down again and back at her. "Just offhand,

I'd say there's nothing else that would suit my condition better."

She drifted slowly toward the berth, her hair cascading down on one side, completely undone by her escape attempt. It made her look like a lopsided angel. He held out his hand. She absently pushed the cabin door closed on her way past, her solemn gaze never leaving his face.

"Oh, Maggie," he whispered when she sank down beside him, "I never feel so alive as when you're near me."

"And if this kills you, how will you feel then?" she breathed, running her hand experimentally over his chest.

"Wonderful," he said on an intake of breath. "Never better." He took her by the hips and urged her over him. "Kiss me, Maggie."

Her lips came down softly and he was engulfed by warm tenderness as he felt her thighs straddling him and he tasted the sweetness of her mouth. It was like the sea, something he couldn't live without. He slid his hands up to span her small waist and felt a tight curling in his belly. The hunger was gentle, slow, more a measure of weakness than desire. He let her take the lead, as he had promised.

She kissed the corner of his eye. Her lashes brushed his, and she moved on, inhaling deeply when she reached his temple. "You smell like you did before, like the sun and the sea," she said breathlessly.

"If that's the secret of my attraction for you, I'll have to spend all my time up on deck," he answered, letting her special fragrance float over him. She braced her hands on his shoulders and sat up.

"You can't even get out of your clothes without Dogsmeat's help," she said regretfully, wiggling her hips gently so that his desire rubbed against hers.

He closed his eyes and pushed harder into the sensation. "Do you want to call him in or shall I?"

"Neither," she whispered. She pulled at the fastenings on his pants. They resisted her efforts. "Oh, damn!"

"Such language," he said with a smile. He pushed her fingers away. "Here, let me." She slid off of him and pulled away his pants when he lifted his hips.

"You're still so brown," she said, stroking his leg as she pushed his shirt up. She bent over and kissed the skin of his exposed belly. "And so soft."

He sucked in a deep breath as her hair trailed over his manhood. "It's good thing you're not prejudiced," he managed to say as he pulled her blouse free of her skirt. "I hear European women in Singapore won't even dance with a man with sallow skin."

"I wouldn't know," she murmured, pushing his shirt higher.

"That's what I mean—you're not prejudiced." He gasped as she trailed the soft, moist tip of her tongue up his side. "Are you going to take off that shirt or am I going to have to?" he said in a rush, urgency building with every inch that shivered under her tongue.

She paused and lifted her head. Her purple eyes glowed in the lantern's light. "I thought I was doing the ravishing here," she said softly.

"Only for as long as I can stand to be ravished." He reached out to twist a strand of her hair around one finger. "Kiss me again, Maggie," he said, drawing her to him.

She resisted the pull. "The ravishee is in no position to give orders," she replied, her expression a mixture of amusement and desire.

She sat back on her heels and slowly unbuttoned her blouse. He stared at the sweet fullness of her breasts as she freed them from her chemise without haste, watching him all the while. The slender, graceful look of her arms fascinated him as she let her hair down the rest of the way. He moistened his dry lips as she undid her skirt and passed it over her head, leaving her in nothing but the silk stockings that ended above her knees, secured by pink garters.

"Don't take them off," he said hoarsely.

She smiled seductively, her face incredibly beautiful in arousal. "You certainly do give a lot of orders for someone who's being ravished," she replied. Her eyes were heavy-lidded, sparkling with desire. "You really must remember to play by the rules." She slipped one silk-covered calf across his thighs and put her hands on his sides.

"I'm not a well man," he murmured, cupping her breasts and letting their pendulous weight caress his palms. "Chalk it up to that."

"No excuses," she whispered, planting herself firmly atop his manhood. She arched her back and came down, taking him partway in, her eyes half-closed. His hips rose to meet her but she pulled back, arching and returning again. Desire built as he let himself be encased in the wet heat of her, drumming a demand into his blood for more, but she would not be rushed.

He could never recall such a slow, sweet building between them, and decided that there was a lot to be said for ravishment on her terms. He closed his eyes and let the pleasure of the lingering strokes wash through him. To be allowed in by such slow degrees was agonizing bliss. His impatient hands found the pink garters at her thighs, and he rubbed the backs of her knees through the silk stockings.

She made a low purr in the back of her throat and settled over him, slowly, slowly, slowly, until he finally lost the will to accept it passively and thrust himself into her the rest of the way. Her lips parted and she threw her head back with a soft cry. His chest nearly burst with the pleasure of filling her. He gripped her waist and stilled her for a moment.

"I love you, Maggie," he whispered. Her eyes opened slowly, a drugged passion burning in the purple depths. The rich cloud of gold hair cascaded down her shoulders and flowed around her breasts, the ends sweeping across his belly. She stared at him, frozen in desire, the full, pink mouth trembling.

"I love you, too," she said softly, "and I love having you inside me."

Hot need twisted through him and he pushed deeper into her. Her spine went stiff and then curled as she melded herself to the tautness between them. He gave himself up to the sensation as she dipped and rose over him. The feel of her hips butting against him sent him into a dark maelstrom of pleasure. He held her hips, watching her face as soft cries built in her throat.

She spread herself wider and he felt his shaft enter her to its fullest, so deep that he felt as if the rest of his body might follow and be consumed in the hot center of her. He half-hoped it might actually happen. She impaled herself on him over and over, crying out softly, her expression tense with pleasure and her mouth slack. Her lashes sank down until her eyes closed in fierce concentration on the swell of sensation between them.

She drove on, the beat of her thrusts slower than his would have been if he had been in charge. Weakness forced him to accept her rhythm, gliding into and out of her in matched strides. The final run toward the peak built slowly but with shattering force. He surrendered to her pace, and her small moans of pleasure filled him with unbearable excitement. He strained upward under her and felt sweat begin to bead on his upper lip.

After so long, after so long. He threw his head back, exulting in the sweet pleasure he hadn't thought he'd live to share with her again. Her full, pale breasts trembled and swung as she mounted him, higher and higher. He felt the first pulsing of pleasure inside her and grabbed her buttocks, pulling her hard against him. She thrust faster, rocking them both as she cried out. He felt the edge of sanity blur but he clung to it for long enough to keep pushing inside her until he was sure she was well over the precipice, crying out his name in long gusts of pleasure, and then he let himself follow her into the vortex.

She fell forward, all weakness in the aftermath of pleasure, and he held her to him fiercely as her breath came in great, shuddering gasps. His limbs shook with the remnants of his own pleasure as he savored the weight of her cheek against his. What a gift she was! Fire and life and laughter. He wanted this for the rest of his life, to hold this precious gift and be a part of her.

"Oh, Maggie," he said, when his breathing had steadied, "I love you so much."

She made a drowsy sound of acknowledgement that

hummed in his chest and tickled his ear. He quivered deep within her, nerves still raw and tender with pleasure, and her murmur turned into a lazy giggle.

"I can feel that you do," she said.

He hugged her tighter. "I want to stay like this all night. I want to fall asleep inside you."

"I'd like that, too," she said sleepily, "only I'll die if I don't have a drink of water soon."

He laughed softly. "Ah, but which of us has the strength to move?" She came a little more awake and he could almost feel the earnest wrinkling of her brow as she considered the problem. She sighed.

"I suppose it will have to be me as I'm the one on top," she said a little sadly. She slowly peeled herself away from him and he saw that her eyelashes were flattened to her cheek on one side, battened down by perspiration where she had lain against his face. He laughed as she blinked to free them.

"You look like a baby bird," he said.

"And you look like a great, lazy hunk of man," she retorted, but she smiled and stretched luxuriously, still sitting astride him. "If I weren't so thirsty, life would be perfect at this moment."

He watched her breasts lift and settle again as she raised her arms over her head for a long, catlike stretch. "Marry me, Maggie," he said suddenly.

She stopped in midstretch and stared at him. He felt his heart thudding as hard as it had been just a short time ago. The words had come without thought but he found that as soon as he said them, nothing mattered but that she should say yes.

"Are you sure, Richard?"

He felt a disquieting jolt. He should have led up to it more gradually, explained how much she meant to him. He would try now. "You mean everything to me, Maggie. I want you to stay with me forever."

She cast her eyes down and braced her hands at his sides, shifting to withdraw her weight to one side. He felt himself slipping out of her and wanted to seize her to stop

266

it. But the moment was too delicate, too fragile with unspoken words. He stifled the groan of disappointment that rose in his chest and watched her anxiously. Emotions he couldn't even guess at swirled around her.

"I'd need some time," she said hesitantly, lifting her face and glancing at him through her lashes without precisely looking at him.

He felt a dirty, mean sensation in his throat, a choking. "You can have time," he said, his voice flat with tension. "As much as you need."

She studied her folded knees. "There's Pensleigh to be thought about, and the people who depend on me for their living," she said, speaking to her knees. "And I must think what's to be done about Christian's investment in Townsend and Townsend. It's up to me to see that he has funds to live on."

He felt a nasty chill at the mention of Townsend and Townsend—if Christian was connected to them, it might explain how he had come to be Atam Datu's guest. Nothing else she said reassured him either. It was all about other people, other places. What about them? He tasted a dark, bittersweet flavor in his mouth, like unblanched aniseed. "I didn't realize it would be so complicated for you," he said, working hard to keep his voice light.

"Oh, Richard," she cried, her eyes flying up to meet his, "I do love you! I want to marry you—truly I do, only I must think it through."

She seemed so contrite that he felt some of his misgiving ease up. "Go get your drink of water," he said gently. He'd gone about it all wrong. He should have waited for a different moment.

She put the candy pink wrapper on and tied it loosely. It reminded him of Daphne's, how uninhibited she could be, but the fact that she put it on when she arose reminded him, too, that she could be shy when the passion between them subsided. He pulled the sheet over him, hating the shaking weakness that wouldn't go away now. The future had looked so bright in Sydney. Could that have been only two months ago?

He'd lost so much time. "Come back to me, Maggie," he said. He drew the sheet back to make a place for her.

She looked up and smiled, an elfin smile in the small, lovely face. He was sure he must have misinterpreted her first reaction to his proposal. Of course she had to think about the effect marrying him would have on her life.

She raised one eyebrow. "Any more ravishments or unexpected marriage proposals?"

His mood lightened. It had been the unexpectedness of it. "Maybe not tonight," he said. "Let's be decadent though, and have dinner in bed."

She laughed and put the water jug back in its holder. "I should have thought you'd had enough decadence for one day."

"Never—it can never be enough with you." He reined himself with an effort. There was more he would have liked to say, about how he much needed her, but he wanted to be sure of his timing. He'd said enough for tonight. She slipped in beside him and he knew there was one more thing he must say now.

"I haven't thanked you yet for saving the *Java*," he said. He kissed her forehead tenderly. "I can't tell you what it means. She's so much more to me than a ship or my livelihood."

"I know," she said softly. "That's why I had to save her, because she's a part of you."

"You were strong, Maggie, very strong." He felt a trace of awe as he thought about it. She stroked his chest lightly and he looked at the neatly trimmed nails, the fragile fingers—such strength in so fragile a shape.

She reached up and turned his face with the tips of her fingers, regarding him earnestly as she said, "It wasn't just me, Richard—it was all of us. We were strong for you, because you're always so strong for us."

He kissed her temple and settled back, passing his hand over her hair absently as he stared at the beams overhead. She thought he was strong. How little she knew that his strength resided in her.

Chapter 16

Richard sat at the saloon table, staring at the figures. He idly scratched in the amount he'd thought to make. It had been a nice dream. Instead, they would arrive in Singapore a week after the last wool auction took place. Now the best he could hope for was that his partner would have the space to warehouse the wool until next year. He buried his tired face in his hands. He'd gambled everything on the wool run, invested every cent he had. The crew hadn't even been paid while they'd idled in Makassar. The devil just waited for fools like to him to make their move.

He pulled the title to the *Java* out from under the ledger. It was the only thing he had to offer, one piece of his heart to another. He would put it in Margaret's hands as security against the debt he owed her. She'd assured him that the debt was personal and not to Townsend and Townsend. That had been a formality to satisfy the shipyard in Makassar. He didn't like being indebted to her, but being indebted to Charles Townsend would have been far worse. He'd have had to work off the debt running the kinds of dirty cargo Townsend liked to deal in under the table, an offer he'd refused more than once.

It made him think again about Christian Belleweather. He'd never have found his way to Atam Datu without Charles Townsend's involvement. Nothing could have come of it, however, or the rajah wouldn't still be looking to buy guns from Richard. He passed a hand through his

269

hair, shoving it off his face impatiently. Whatever was going on, he prayed to God he could stay clear of it. His only concern was paying Margaret back, to keep his pride. With hard work, he might be able to do it in a year. He'd even haul coal for the lousy steamers if he had to. Even if she married him he would feel the need to pay her back. Especially if she married him.

Two signatures on the deed of sale flanked his own. Samuel Coit, agent for the owner, and Herbert Higginbotham, witness. One a lying dog and the other the most loyal friend a man could have. Coit was the incompetent son of a bitch who'd commanded the *Java* when she'd been taken by the United States Navy, and just by luck he had regained his command when the Royal Navy showed up. No man deserved the luck fate had dealt out to Coit, and only luck and Richard had kept the clipper in one piece after they resumed running the blockade. It was Richard who'd seen to it that whiskey was loaded in London by the case, so that Coit was never sober enough to lash the men over imagined slights and for failing to obey his ludicrous orders.

And then there was Herbert Higginbotham—Dogsmeat. He'd been one of the few pieces of good fortune in Richard's life. He'd waited in the shadows and watched as the surly, red-faced Coit counted the money and then signed the title over, acting as agent for the timid Southern gentleman who'd decided that blockade running wasn't worth the potential profit once insurance was no longer obtainable toward the end of the war. Coit's cowardice had been another of the few, inexplicable high cards fate had dealt Richard. If not for that, he'd never have been able to afford a ship like the *Java*.

It had taken two years of slow, careful subterfuge under Coit's nose, carrying off-list cargo. If Coit hadn't been so obliging about drinking himself into a nightly stupor, he'd have never gotten away with it. Some men would have called it dishonest. Richard had thought of it as survival, a way out of servitude. By God, he'd earned every penny of what he'd made on those side deals, and in the process, he'd learned everything there was to know about false decking, camouflage packing, and artful bookkeeping. When a captain reeled ashore too drunk to know, or even care, which side of the Atlantic they were docked on, you learned to be a thoroughgoing taker. Richard hadn't even had to think twice when the chance came.

Coit was never satisfied unless the *Java* was overloaded. He called her a lazy old scow and yearned openly to fulfill his true destiny, to captain a steamer. To Richard had fallen the task of husbanding the *Java* through fair weather and foul, with worn rigging and sails strained to the breaking point under the load. When even Coit could no longer deny she needed refurbishing, Richard had seen his chance. It had been a simple matter to order the load lines repainted, and one tier of copper plating removed in Charleston, so that to Coit's bleary, alcohol-hazed eyes it had seemed as if the *Java* was overloaded. Richard had managed to carry even more off-list cargo after that, and still keep them underloaded in the interests of avoiding powder burns as they ran the blockade.

Richard let his gaze come to rest on the painting of the clipper Margaret had done for him. It was magnificent. Sanders had fashioned a frame for it, stained and rubbed to match the paneling in the saloon, and hung it over the mantle of the small, cast-iron firebox that hadn't seen any use since they'd arrived in the East. A ghost of a smile passed over his face. She'd given him the *Java* on canvas and in reality. He was grateful, but he felt uneasy when he realized how much he was beholden to her, how much he owed her in every way.

The closer they got to Singapore, the more apprehensive he got. The obligation warred with his love, leaving him feeling slightly tainted. He made love to her every chance he got, and that too felt dishonest, repaying her with the physical passion she craved. It was a way of keeping her, binding her to him, because with each passing day, he grew more troubled over what might happen when they reached Singapore.

He knew her well. The utter stillness of her face teased

271

him at times. He sensed her withdrawing, a retreat to some part inside where he couldn't follow. Luxury, sophisticated company and beautiful clothes awaited her, if she chose them. She belonged in a different milieu. Had she stepped too far out of it when she'd come aboard the *Java* and become his lover? He'd left behind a life he hated in a frontier town, and found the sea. It had fitted his soul, but he'd still had the occasional twinge of longing for some of what he'd left behind—the smell of rain approaching over rich, brown earth, the easy cadence of Swedish mingled with the staccato sounds of English in his stepfather's store on a busy Saturday morning.

How far could she move away from her accustomed life and still be comfortable? He tried hard to fight the tide of desperation that swept through him when he thought of her leaving him. He would be reduced to nothing more than an amusing, pleasurable episode in her life, something that provided her with exotic stories to tell her friends at dinner parties.

He rubbed his fists into tired eyes. If she left, she left. It wouldn't be the first time a woman had found him wanting. He'd offered all he could—his love, his passion, a place in his life. For now, he would struggle against the demons that said she would leave, and try to give her no reason to want to go.

Margaret leaned on the rail and watched the water slipping past the *Java*'s hull. Singapore was only a few days away. She meant to marry Richard, but distance had created a new perspective on the standards she had been raised to embrace. Now that the distance was closing, she felt the old standards crowding in on her with unexpected power.

Singapore society wouldn't welcome Richard Jensen into its midst. Neither did she have a mother to plan her wedding with, nor a father to give her away. Richard was Catholic and she was not. It need not concern anyone but the two of them, but who would consent to perform the ceremony? And she would not be a blushing, virginal bride, either. She felt the pull of tradition enough to regret that they would probably have to settle for a civil ceremony.

She had been hoarding these last days and hours, trying to be sure of her mind before society exercised its own form of censure. She could not bring herself to disregard it entirely. She felt split in two, Lady Margaret Belleweather on the one hand, and the future Mrs. Richard Jensen on the other. But it was Richard's Maggie who stood at the rail of the *Java* now, wrestling with the pull of two worlds.

Never in all her years as a woman had she dreamed that there could be so much more to life, the separate identity of her body that closed all the windows and doors to the other world she had grown up in. She'd thought that what she saw and thought was the whole of it, but the pleasures of the flesh she'd shared with Richard had shown her that another realm existed, where feeling and touch reigned. Had it clouded her judgment, seduced into accepting a life she would not otherwise choose?

So many questions remained. She didn't think she could stand to sail through another storm like the one they'd encountered, a typhoon Richard had called it. He'd assured her that he'd never seen anything to rival it, nor would they probably see its like again. Few sailors did, he said, and Margaret had resisted the temptation to say that those who did most likely perished and were never able to share their stories. Would he mind if she wanted to keep Christian's house in Singapore and wait for him there during typhoon season?

And always, always, there was Christian. For someone so indolent as Christian to have traveled all the way to northern Sumatra defied logic. Why he had done so concerned her now only insofar as it might provide a clue as to the likelihood of his ever returning. Might he still come back to Singapore? Would he ever want to return to Pensleigh? Any financial arrangements she made on his behalf must take all possibilities into consideration.

She could not ignore her own fortune either. Generations of Belleweathers had nurtured it and built Pen-sleigh into what it was. She would gladly have put it all in trust for Christian and his issue, but for the doleful fact that Christian was unlikely to *have* any issue. The irony was that she must do *something* about the management of it, for she knew from passing remarks Richard had made that he wanted no part of it. Ever since she'd first thought about boys as beings she might one day marry—and not simply as creatures who liked to get dirty and could run faster—the idea that a man might be attracted to her for her fortune had repelled her. Now she faced the opposite problem.

But the deepest, most unsettling consideration of all was her inability to have children. She had not found the courage to tell Richard yet. That, more than anything, had kept her from saying yes to his proposal right away. He'd made no secret of his love of children, and she remembered him talking about Jack with a tightening in her chest. Had he fathered Jack? The likeliest answer was that he had. When time went by and she did not conceive, he would know it was not his fault. It must not come to that. She must tell him now, before he committed himself to her in marriage.

Margaret let the serenity of the night stars soothe her. At sea, they were a heavenly carapace that wrapped her in their brilliance. They restored a sense of simplicity to the universe. To exist was sufficient, they seemed to say, and tomorrow was only that—tomorrow. She pulled her shawl around her shoulders and breathed in deeply. In two days they would be in Singapore. She must not wait any longer.

She found Richard in the saloon. A glass of rum sat unregarded on the table as he pored over paperwork, a dead cheroot clenched in his mouth. He glanced up briefly as she came in and gave her a half-smile indicative of thoughts far away. How well he looked! His recuperative powers had been astounding. His arms and chest were fully rounded again, taut with muscles as they had been, and his face gleamed with health. He had taken to shaving at night, for reasons which had become all too apparent to

274

her, and she smiled as she saw the faint blue tinge over the deeply tanned cheeks. His face would feel delightful to the touch.

"Richard?" She hated to disturb him but she must, before she lost her courage. "There's something we must talk about."

He looked up, caught by her tone, and set his pen aside. She gripped the back of a chair, too apprehensive to sit, and let another long moment go by while she grappled with the impulse to turn and run. The Sumatran sparrow twittered softly in its cage, none the worse for having been through the typhoon with them.

"Surely it can't be that bad," Richard said at last. He looked uneasy and she knew she must speak quickly.

"I want you to know that I would be honored to marry you," she said in a rush, falling back on the polite form society dictated.

He smiled at her, a slow smile of encouragement that spread across his face, touching everything except his eyes. "But?"

"You know me too well," she said with a shaky laugh. "There is something I must tell you, and if you wish to withdraw your offer of marriage once you've heard me out, I'll certainly understand."

His expression became carefully neutral. He leaned back and crossed his arms over his broad chest. It made the muscles of his upper arms bulk up against the sides of his chest, and she had a momentary vision of the small V of skin that formed at his armpit when he did. She loved to tease it with her fingertip when he was naked. She dismissed the distracting thought with an effort and went on.

"When I was recovering from my illness, the doctors told me that I would never be able to have children." She held her breath, waiting for his reaction.

He frowned. "And you thought I wouldn't want to marry you if I knew?"

"Well . . ." She was startled into speechlessness by what sounded very like anger in his voice.

"I already know that, Margaret," he said abruptly. "It

275

makes no difference to me."

Margaret let out a sharp breath. "You knew?"

"I overheard you telling Mora Bursey that night in Anjer. How could you possibly think it would make any difference to me?"

"It would to most men," she said nervously, "and I know how you feel—felt—about Jack."

He sighed and she felt rather than saw some of the tension leave his body. "Oh, Maggie, I've traveled a crooked road to arrive at this moment. All the twists and turns made me what I am, but I'm powerless to go back and change any of it. Yes, I loved Jack. I still do, even though I have no expectation of ever seeing him again. I probably wouldn't even know him if I did, and he certainly wouldn't remember me. I love you, Maggie, and that's all that counts. The rest is gone, behind us. Let's look to the future."

"And you truly don't mind that I can't have children?"

"I'd like it if you could," he said candidly, "but I'll take what comes. Doctors don't know everything. I'll bet they'd have told you to write me off when the tropica had a hold of me."

Margaret smiled. "They did. I mean, he did, but I didn't believe him. His breath reeked so of alcohol that I swear it could have cauterized a wound."

Richard laughed and a thick shock of his blue-black hair fell forward. "Anyone who lets a doctor in Makassar treat him doesn't really want to live. I take it Dogsmeat kept him away from me?"

"Once we paid him, he staggered off into the dark. I doubt we could have found him again even if we *had* wanted his help."

"Good. So I lived despite him. I'm healthy. You're healthy. And maybe you *will* be able to have children." He saw the dismay on her face and added, ". . . and maybe you won't. Let's let nature take its course."

Margaret relaxed her grip on the back of the chair. He had made it so easy, and he had a point. She knew the doctors had despaired of her life at one point, and yet here

276

she was, healthy, as he had said. "Take things as you find them, is it? The Richard Jensen philosophy."

"Exactly. Now, since we're talking about the future, there's something I have to say." She watched as he withdrew a document from under the pile of papers on the table. "I owe you some money." He waved aside the beginnings of her protest. "I want you to know that I take the debt seriously. I don't care if you throw the money overboard once I give it to you, but I *am* going to pay you back. In the meantime, I want you to hold the title to the *Java* as security."

"But Richard, if we're going to be married, it hardly matters whose money is whose," she protested.

He looked at her with the piercing green stare that had so intimidated her when she first met him. "It does to me, Maggie," he said, a note of warning in his voice. "Let me do this." She found the stare still had the power to leave her defenseless.

"Very well, Richard. And what am I supposed to do with it?"

"Just hold on to it. I'm going to endorse it so that the *Java* is, in effect, yours to do with what you will. You could sell it to satisfy the debt if it ever came to that."

She sat down carefully. "You know that I would never do that."

He ignored the remark and handed her the document. "You sign the bottom and we'll have Dogsmeat witness it. And while we're about it, why don't we have a drink to toast our marriage?" His face softened. "That's the most important thing, you know. I don't want your money and I'm not going to worry about whether we'll ever have children. It's you I want, Maggie, just you. I love you. The rest can take care of itself as long as we have each other."

Margaret smiled, loosening her taut posture. "Yes, of course." It would all be all right, she thought. The woman she had become in the last few months loved this man far too much for it to be any other way.

*   *   *

The mangrove swamps gave way to wider, clearer shipping lanes as they made their oblique approach to Singapore harbor. It all seemed to go so fast. The little steam tugs came out and jostled the *Java* efficiently through the ships anchored out in the roads, and suddenly they were at Tanjong Pagar Dock. Margaret felt a nervous rustling in her stomach as she saw that Charles Townsend was waiting with a carriage. His mother and sister sat in the open conveyance, parasols in their gloved hands.

Charles spotted her and waved. His warm smile lightened her heart. He looked so solidly, wonderfully English! She loved him for his loyalty in meeting her when all S'pore must be scandalized by the return of Lady Margaret Belleweather. She supposed that Mrs. Townsend and Susan had come out of loyalty to Charles.

Seeing their immaculate dress, she glanced at the plain blouse she had made and the modest purple skirt. Dogsmeat had played lady's maid, packing her case, steaming her straw hat into shape, and brushing her skirt clean, but Margaret was vividly aware that she arrived looking a good deal less well turned out than when she had left. For the woman who swam naked with her lover, engaged in eating contests, and spent nights at a brothel, the outfit had been more than adequate, but for being met by Charles's mother and sister . . .

Charles came striding down the quay. His bearing exuded welcome. She was so genuinely glad to see him that she met him at the bottom of the gangplank, smiling. Somewhat to her surprise, he embraced her fondly.

"By Jove, my dear!" he exclaimed. "You look marvelous!"

Margaret let him lead her away from the *Java*, chatting as they walked. He drew her to a halt just short of the carriage. "Margaret, there's been some rather bad news in your absence."

Margaret felt a chill. Something about Christian? Before she could open her mouth, Charles gestured toward his mother and sister. "We knew you would need the support of us all when you hear what I have to say."

Margaret nodded nervously toward them, her throat too tight to speak. Their answering nods were pale, the faint smiles just the bare minimum that politeness required.

Charles took her hand gently. His face was all kindness and concern. "Your father's solicitor sent word through the firm that there was a dreadful downturn in the stocks he had invested in for you. To put it bluntly, my dear, your fortune is lost."

Margaret felt relief that nothing worse had been heard about Christian, and then the enormity of what he *had* said sank in. "All of it?" she whispered. He nodded. "But there's Pensleigh, too!" she cried. "How shall I pay for its upkeep?"

"Do not think about it for the moment," he suggested. "I particularly wanted to break this news to you in person, so that you would not be overset by it. You can communicate with the solicitor in due course, and together, we shall make a plan for your future." He took her elbow and assisted her to step into the carriage. "In the meantime, you shall come and stay with us. You will always have a home with us. Driver!"

"No . . . wait! I must go back and speak with Rich . . . with Captain Jensen!"

Charles's mother made a strangled sound in her throat while Susan coughed and looked away. "Do you think that wise?" Charles murmured. "Please, come with us now. We'll send the driver back for your trunk later. We have tried to lend respectability to your impulsive action in sailing with that man but we cannot protect your reputation if you continue to have contact with him."

Margaret lowered her gaze. How could she explain that she meant to marry Richard? Not here, not now—it would fly in the face of their kindness. They knew him only by reputation, and they had laid their own reputations on the line to protect her. No, she would explain later—somehow—that he was not what they thought him to be. But still, she had to speak with Richard now, let him know what had happened.

"Please, I only require a few minutes," she said urgently.

Charles took her hand and smiled. "Very well, my dear. I'm sure we have enough currency of respectability to sustain your reputation through one last encounter with the notorious Captain Jensen."

"I won't keep you waiting long," she said. God bless him, Margaret thought as she hurried back up the gangplank. Could there be a kinder, dearer man in Singapore?

Richard watched it all with a sense of frustration and a sick knotting in his stomach. Seeing her welcomed by Charles Townsend, and seeing her enthusiastic response, he could only suppose that she was coming back to say that it had all been a horrible misunderstanding and she had no intention of marrying him. Damn her! His whole heart belonged to that slender, impossibly beautiful creature. He ached to enfold her in his arms and keep her by his side forever. Whatever she wanted of him, he would do, only let her be his unequivocally.

The news was bad enough, but not as bad as he'd feared. She did not say that she wouldn't marry him after all, but that she would need more time than she'd thought.

"Charles says he knows none of the details, but the money which was invested for me had been lost through some turn in the markets. I'll have to write to the solicitor and await his response. I have no idea how this can have happened, but I must see that Pensleigh is preserved."

"I understand," he said coolly, "but I won't sit in port while you see to your business. I have to get this wool unloaded and find another cargo. I hope you'll be ready by then."

"There's Christian's investment in Townsend and Townsend to be thought of, too," she said guardedly. "I must be especially careful to look over the figures and see whether he is provided for."

"Of course." Margaret was transparent to him—she could no longer shutter those pansy eyes against him. He saw that her thoughts were far away from him. He remembered the sight of her in Charles Townsend's embrace and his hands itched to seize her and lock her away in the saloon for as long as it would take to cast off the lines and sail away from Singapore. "You asked for time before. I said you could have it, but I'm not a patient man by nature. Remember that."

Margaret heard the coldness in his voice and saw the rigid posture in his back and legs. She loved him and she had no doubt he loved her, too, but there was a sense of finality in his expression. If he could not bend even a little, she would have to bend that much more. Could she?

"You're asking for so much, Richard," she said softly. "You must realize that when I came and asked to sail with you, it was because I had certain duties, certain obligations. That hasn't changed. I would never ask you to shirk your duties for me. Please don't ask me to shirk mine for you."

"I won't," he said. A muscle jumped in his cheek. "I'm not. But we have a chance to build something together. Unless you can put that first, there's no hope for us."

"I've said that I would." He seemed so hard, so unlike the loving man who held her tenderly in the night, that she found herself wanting to turn away. "In any case, you needn't worry that I'll sell the *Java*."

He made an impatient noise. "It's possible I may find another lender who could advance me the money so that I could pay you off," he said. "Be sure you hold on to the papers. If I can, I'll send someone with a check and ask that you hand the papers back to him."

Margaret started to tell him that she didn't have them, that she had slipped them behind the canvas of the painting she had done for him, but she checked herself. The scar on his cheek stood out white against his tensed cheek. No, let him think that she still had them, a link between them to ensure that he would return.

"Yes, all right, I will," she murmured and turned away.

"You have interesting enemies, my friend," the China-man said.

"I've always managed to excel in that regard," Richard replied bitterly. "A man can be as evil as he likes but as long as he's careful to appear righteous, he has nothing to fear. Refuse to dance to their tune and you're branded as evil without proof."

"As long as you're sure no proof will be forthcoming . . ." The Chinese merchant leaned back and signaled for a servant to pour his guest another rum.

Richard sighed. "There can't be any." He took a swallow and closed his eyes, inhaling the scent of the shadowy godown. It was filled with merchandise destined for every corner of the world, his ill-fated cargo of wool included. "I never double-crossed anybody. And I've got papers to prove it," he added as an afterthought. Of course, those papers were with Margaret now. Would she prove true to him, to their love, or would she unwittingly put them into the hands of his enemies?

"Still, when so many would like to believe, one must be cautious." An Wu leaned forward and set his cup on the low table. "You stole the first shipments of tea out from under their noses at Foochow, you refused to carry their cargoes when it didn't suit you. No, the traders of Singapore have no love for you. They are most eager to spread the news that you stole the *Java* and brought her to this part of the world to escape detection. It could prove troublesome even if they have no proof."

"The authorities can't watch me any more closely than they already do," Richard countered.

"Still, you must play your hand carefully. As you say, the appearance of wrongdoing alone may undo a man. They might try to impound your ship while an investigation is conducted—if enough tongues wag in the right corners."

"So I'll keep my bow into the wind and ride it out," Richard said roughly.

"Very good, my friend." An Wu shifted his massive body, and a servant was there instantly to reposition the pillows behind him. "I'm sorry our little venture did not work out as we had hoped. Nevertheless, we will find another cargo for you now, as you have asked. About the other . . ." He opened his hand with a regretful expression. ". . . I wish I could help, but I cannot. Just at the moment, I have had to put all my cash into the hands of my various captains, and I have not yet received payment for the last shipments they delivered."

Richard shrugged with an attempt at nonchalance. "I'll get by."

"Just keep your eye out for this man, Coit. He means to do you harm, and we both know that a certain trader would like to obtain a fast clipper for him to captain. He's already lost the first one he was given."

Richard stood up. He tossed back the last of the rum. "I'll anchor out off Pagar Spit," he said. "Send word when the cargo's ready and I'll come in."

"A wise precaution." An Wu lumbered to his feet. "It may be that those who trade in contraband will be too greedy and reveal themselves. Be patient. Remember, if you wait by the river long enough, the body of your enemy will eventually float by."

"Thanks," Richard said. "Thanks a lot. I'll remember that."

Chapter 17

It was intoxicating, purely intoxicating, to handle the silks and satins and Swiss cottons as Eliza brought out the dresses one by one. Margaret felt almost giddy as she looked them over. How insightful of Eliza to have anticipated that they might still be in Singapore when her period of mourning ended! And the ribbons! A rainbow of them was strewn across the bed, amidst laces as airy as gossamer. Gloves, parasols, lovely stockings, dainty shoes—how glad she was to see them all!

But the corsets—Margaret eyed them with distaste. She didn't think she'd resume wearing them. And then there were the chatelaine bags—embroidered, appliqued, beaded—and the jewels. She hadn't brought even a tenth of what she owned, but seeing them after months and months was like looking on the contents of Aladdin's cave. She let a strand of pearls shiver across her palm. They reminded her of home, and of the pale debutante she had been, a mere copy card of the woman she was now.

"Pardon, miss," said Eliza. "I don't wish to hurry you, but Mr. Townsend will be here in less than two hours. If you'll make a selection, I can ready it while you bathe."

Margaret spun around gaily. "Yes, yes, of course. What fun this will be! The blue and gray striped silk, I think."

Eliza smiled. "You're blooming, miss. John and I are very glad to see it, if you'll excuse me saying so."

"Oh, Eliza, when I see these dresses, I could forgive you

anything! Oh, and the hats! I cannot tell you how I longed for more hats when I was at sea." She picked up a straw shepherdess-style bonnet and eyed the ribbons critically. "I think we should retrim this one, don't you?"

"Indeed, miss. Perhaps in apple green, to go with the walking costume?"

"There! Exactly what I was thinking! I really am so very pleased to see all these things."

"It gladdens my heart to see you so happy," Eliza said, "and after these months of idleness, it's a welcome thing to be kept busy. Have you given any thought to which dress you'll wear for the Townsend's ball?"

"The rose satin, I think, with the opera mantle—not that I'm likely to need *that* in this heat. Still, it suits me, and I do want to look good for my first formal event in . . . why, it must be almost a year!"

"Yes, a year come April. The rose satin will be the very thing," Eliza said happily. "It will take only the smallest of alterations to make it fit you, what with the weight you've regained. The neckline is very revealing but I don't believe your measurement has changed there, so it should fit admirably. You're still a bit smaller in the waist and hips, but not so much that we need a dressmaker. I can turn my hand to it easily."

"What a treasure you are," Margaret exclaimed. "Oh! That reminds me—is the servant that An Wu lent us working out?"

Eliza's mouth tightened ever so slightly. "For a foreigner. I expect that with five or ten years in a proper household he might be turned into a reasonable footman."

Margaret laughed. "By which I assume you mean he's helping out a great deal."

"It goes against the grain to work side by side with a Chinaman, miss, and that's the truth, but I see that he lightens John's load a great deal, and for that, I'll willingly put up with him."

"Very well. Tell him to prepare my bath and knock when it's ready."

Margaret watched Eliza's retreating back with a smile. She had far too much good sense to let prejudice stand in the way of running Margaret's household the way it should be run. She and John had been unreservedly delighted to see her, and Margaret suspected they had thought themselves abandoned in a foreign land. Of course they'd have been snapped up in a minute by one of Singapore's European families if she hadn't returned, and probably at double what Margaret paid them. An Wu's houseboy was impeccably trained but the prestige of European servants could not be overestimated. She was grateful for the use of the houseboy however, since she had resumed a full social schedule.

An Wu had sent him over with an invitation to take tea, and she had gone. The Chinese merchant had expressed pleasure over her return to Cluny Road, complimenting her on her boldness in daring to take up residence there again. Margaret had merely laughed. It had been so easy to slip back into the old familiar role as Lady Margaret Belleweather, a role her mother had trained her for so rigorously, but she could not relinquish the person Richard Jensen had freed her to become either.

Two people existed within her skin: the Margaret who said and did all the proper things and was enjoying enormous success in S'pore society, and the other Margaret, who did as she pleased. She could never be sure which would predominate, but she was not blind to the fact that the dichotomy made her more interesting to Charles. The daring, self-determined Margaret said things, did things, he did not anticipate. The unpredictability made her appealing to other men as well. Opinions which would have drawn nothing more than a grunt from Richard Jensen widened eyes in S'pore society.

She made no secret of the fact that she called on An Wu regularly, or that she had taken to praying at the most beautiful of the Chinese quarter's temples, in Telok Ayer Street. It solved a religious dilemma for her, as she did not wish to answer to a spiritual advisor who would offer advice she didn't want, which would happen if she at-

286

tended services at St. Andrew's. Owing to the language barrier, no such advice could be forthcoming at Tean Hock Kiong. And since the subject of most her prayers, Christian, seemed to be in the grip of Eastern influences, she reasoned that it would be as well to pray in the presence of the Eastern gods.

Each day she went, and afterwards strolled to Johnston's Pier, along the seawall, and back to Telok Ayer Market. Not a soul spoke English but she found it no obstacle at all. It was rather tranquilizing, in fact. An Wu, Captain China, acted for British authorities, none of whom spoke Chinese. He organized their relations with the huge Chinese labor force, and Margaret slowly realized that he was the highest authority in Singapore to them. It was doubtful they even realized there *was* a higher authority than Au Wu, she concluded. Whatever words he had whispered regarding her had made her life marvelously simple.

Fresh water appeared daily, the *Singapore Times* arrived, already ironed, on her doorstep, and anything she pointed to in the market was delivered to the back door on Cluny Road within the hour. In fact, she'd had to learn not to point to things she did not mean to buy, and Eliza always expressed delight over the quality of what was sent, and for half the prices she'd paid in Margaret's absence. Sometimes Margaret suspected they sent goods not even displayed where she could see them, substituting superior items for the ones she'd actually pointed to.

Shortly after the shot fired at Fort Canning every morning at five o'clock, she would arise and loll about, drinking tea and writing letters. During the heat of the day, she retired to the bathroom and poured cold water over herself from a huge Shanghai jar. If she chose, she could sleep through the afternoon and take a late tea with An Wu. She had met his numerous children and acceded to his oblique request that she speak English with them and teach them the English form of writing, which An Wu himself had never mastered.

Unfailingly polite from youngest to oldest, but ever

watchful of her every mannerism, they studied her as rigorously as they studied English. In a few short weeks, they emulated her almost perfectly, and she was highly entertained to watch herself reflected in their dark-haired, dark-eyed selves. The girls did very well at it, but something about the boys struck her as strange until she realized that they, too, imitated her feminine manners precisely. It made her giggle to see how completely they could mimic her, but she showed them the gruffer, blunter way a man would do the same things. There was no doubt in her mind that they were under An Wu's strict orders to learn how to behave with the English, against the day they would become master merchants like their father.

If she ever faltered in remembering exactly how it was that men did things differently, she thought of Charles, though she kept that information to herself. He was the quintessential English gentleman and she was quite sure he wouldn't care to know that he was the pattern for An Wu's male offspring.

She had ample opportunity to observe Charles. At least every other day he arrived at Cluny Road in the late afternoon, to escort her to a dinner party or a musicale, or more often just to drive to the esplanade, where the men played fives, or cricket, while the women and children gathered to chat and watch. A regimental or naval band played twice weekly, too, and Margaret enjoyed sitting in the carriage as S'pore society, notorious for being restrictive about admitting newcomers, paraded by and paid her their compliments.

They were fascinated by her transformation from the sickly woman who'd arrived in Singapore so many months before, with nothing but a fortune and a title to recommend her, to the irrepressibly gay, beautiful woman who had disembarked from the *Java* a month ago. Even the rumor that her fortune was greatly diminished couldn't overshadow the effect she had on them. It was so strong that it seemed she might even inspire a fashion for freckles, and faintly tanned skin. She found it all very

288

comfortable and gratifying, from the polite rituals to the subdued flirtations.

The only fly in the ointment was Richard. He had appeared at her door one night a few weeks after their arrival, looking haggard and angry in the light of the veranda lamp. He had informed her curtly that he was taking a cargo of coal to Sydney. Knowing how he felt about steamers, she'd found it somewhat surprising that he'd carry coal for them, but she'd refrained from saying anything, calling to Hoc Sing to bring them refreshments instead. It would be a long run to Sydney and back, but he made no mention of her accompanying him.

Puzzled and yet secretly relieved, she invited him to sit in the small parlor. He barely looked at her, gazing out into the night through the doors open onto the veranda. She wasn't quite ready to make good on her acceptance of his marriage proposal. It had seemed, as the days went by, a little absurd, the idea of returning to the *Java* and living at sea. She didn't stop to analyze why but the answers came to her in small ways. The pleasure of walking out and wearing attractive clothes that drew compliments, arranging the fresh flowers that grew in her garden, enjoying the company of other women at the evening socials, having Eliza bring in her breakfast tray with the mail each morning, visiting the subscription library, even being able to move about her bedroom without the floor rolling under her—all these things brought her pleasure and contentment.

Margaret sat opposite Richard in silence, belatedly realizing she had no whiskey or rum to offer him. His face was tight and withdrawn, like a man with more than a few unpleasant thoughts on his mind. He didn't seem inclined to talk, and offered no accounting of where he'd been since their arrival, or what he'd been doing. He sprawled irritably in the chair with his legs stretched out, his broad shoulders fanned across the back without regard for how the chair was meant to be sat in. His black boots were dusty, his beard grown out to rakish-looking stubble.

289

"I'm sorry I haven't any liquor to offer you," she said at length. He glanced over at her in surprise, almost as if he'd forgotten she was there.

"I don't need a drink," he said brusquely.

Margaret recoiled from his tone. "I didn't mean to suggest that you did. It's only that I feel a poor hostess not having what you prefer."

"And appearance is everything," he snapped. He sighed and shifted his weight toward her. "No, I'm sorry. I didn't mean that. Tell me what you've been doing."

She twined her hands in her lap. She didn't think he wanted to hear that she'd been to a bridge party at the Townsends last night or that she'd enjoyed the bright conversation. "Nothing particular," she said. Hoc Sing arrived with a tray gracefully laid out with the tea service and she welcomed the distraction.

"Everyone is well on the *Java?*" she asked as she handed him a cup.

He eyed her skeptically. "They're fine."

Margaret flushed. It sounded stilted and it was, but she couldn't seem to think of anything else to talk about. Charles or any of the other men in Singapore's social set would have understood the necessity to make some other remark, to cover the awkwardness and keep the flow of conversation going, but Richard merely watched her for a long moment.

"You're having second thoughts, aren't you?"

Her eyes flew up. "Second thoughts?"

"Yes, second thoughts. As in, why should I marry Richard Jensen? He was good enough in his way when I needed him, but now that I'm back where I belong, he doesn't seem worthy of me."

"No!" The vehemence that tinged the word revealed all too clearly that she *had* been having second thoughts, and it was all too clear that he had been thinking about it for some time, delving into her thoughts, as he was so adept at doing at times. Margaret fumbled with the cup in her hand, wishing he wouldn't look at her so keenly.

He shrugged. "Don't bother to deny it. 'Love is not love

which alters when it alteration finds.'''

"You need not quote Shakespeare to me," Margaret said peevishly. "And besides, which one of us has changed? Not me. It was you who went all cold and sullen when I told you my fortune was lost."

"That has nothing to do with it. You're enjoying being back among your own kind, aren't you?" he said calmly, coolly. "You've taken Singapore by storm. The daring, the incomparable, Lady Margaret Belleweather lives in the Chinese quarter, visits with Captain China, went off sailing with that American pirate. All the eccentricities only make you more glamorous, don't they? I imagine it's hard to resist being lionized."

The bitterness in his face and voice frightened her, and the very accuracy of his observation made her indignant. "That's simply not fair! You're blaming me for other people's opinions and reactions."

"But you're enjoying it." His mouth twisted into a mocking smile. "They're all wondering if I'm your lover but no one has dared to ask, have they? After all, you're so beautifully mannered, and so fashionable. It just adds to the cachet as long as no one is absolutely certain that I was. Besides, you *didn't* lose your fortune entirely, did you? That leaves you titled, beautiful, and eminently marriage-able."

"Of all the low, disgusting things to say! As if I were on display at Covent Garden!"

"So you didn't lose your entire fortune?" He was relentless in his determination to talk about it.

"No!" she cried, stung by his scorn. "The trust my grandmother left me is unaffected, and it appears that the home farm can be made to pay for Pensleigh's upkeep, with care."

"Ah, with care. That would mean you'll want to go back and live there, see to it yourself."

Margaret drew an irate breath to reply and then choked on it. She gulped another, bracing her hands on the arm-rests of her chair. "How I choose to manage my finan-cial affairs is . . ." She stopped, appalled by what she had been about to say.

". . . is none of my business?" Richard raised a sardonic eyebrow and when she didn't respond, he stood up. "You're right, of course, but then I never wanted you for your money. I wanted Maggie, not Lady Margaret Belleweather, but I see you've reverted to type. Maggie's gone. The tide has turned."

Margaret rose half out of her seat. "You're making unwarranted assumptions. It doesn't become you."

"I never cared much whether something became me or not," he declared smoothly, "unlike others to whom appearance is all." He turned and started toward the door before pausing, raw tension in every lean line of him. "Since you're not indigent, just do me a favor and hold onto the papers for the *Java*, will you? I'll be paying you back as soon as I can." He strode out into the night.

Suddenly she didn't want him to go. "Richard!" She caught up with him at the steps to the veranda. He turned and stared at her, his eyes dark and unreadable by the lemon glow of the lantern. His blue-black hair was severely straked into a sailor's pigtail, exposing the bones of his face, unEnglish in every detail, and his long, thin nose cast a sharp shadow along his cheek.

Her steps faltered and her breath came in short, uncomfortable gasps. "*You're* the one who's judging by appearances," she said. "Did it occur to you, even once, to *ask* me how I was feeling?"

"I did. The answer wasn't very satisfactory. It was a very guilty 'no' if you'll recall."

"You don't know the meaning of the word compromise, do you?" She was almost hysterical with anger now. "You're just like you were when I met you—it's all your way or not at all. Well, I didn't like you for it then and I don't like you for it now! It's just not fair. I'm expected to give up everything, walk away from my life as if I had only been born the moment I met you!"

His eyes narrowed, gleamed in the light. "What's it going to be then? You stay here, think about it some more, maybe see if you get a better offer?"

"Stop it! Stop it! You're being cruel!" Margaret bunched her fists at her side, rigid with fury. "I haven't asked you to give up the *Java*, to stay ashore and live with me here, but that's no different than what you're asking of me."

He felt the pull of the tide. It would turn in another hour, clearing the way to skim down the channels and out to sea. He could feel the painful prickle of new sisal across his palm, the bulge of the high tide beneath the hull. It was the highest tide there'd be this week and he'd overloaded by a quarter to increase the profits. He needed the tide and he needed the money. The *Java* would understand why he'd burdened her past the true load line. He beat his black captain's cap against his thigh in utter frustration a few times.

"I can't offer you what I don't have," he finally said. "All you can see is what you're giving up. I thought that what we had would be an adequate replacement." His chest hurt and he stopped for a moment, jamming his cap on his head and adjusting it to buy a minute. "If it's not, it's not."

Her mouth opened. He wished she didn't have her back to the light, so that he could see what was in her eyes. "I'm not going to be your lover anymore, so make up your mind if you're going to be my wife." He thought he could feel her unbending toward him in the dark. "I love you, Margaret. At least I loved the woman I thought you were. If you don't want to be that woman, I can't do anything about it. When I come back, I'll look you up. You can tell me then how it's going to be."

"Richard . . ." The soft, pleading note devastated him. He sucked in a breath and glanced away. Through the sheltering trees, he could see lanterns moving along Orchard Road, syces running in front of English carriages. "Richard, if you could only meet me halfway," she continued, "let me have some of what I've had. I made myself a part of your life. Can't you at least pretend to be a part of mine, stay ashore sometimes, let me have some of what's important to me?"

293

"I don't know. Not here—maybe somewhere else. I think I've worn out my welcome here."

"But Christian may come back here. I don't want to close up this house."

"He's not coming back, Margaret." He said it flatly, with no margin for doubt.

"Oh, it's too much," she said, her voice thin and sad, "too much."

He knew what she meant. He had wished at various times in his life that someone would take a belaying pin and beat him senseless with it, and go on hitting him after he fell to the deck, so that he would never have to wake up and deal with all of life's insuperable problems again. Why couldn't he make her see that their love was the one thing that *was* worth fighting for?

"Don't settle for a facade, Margaret," he said tiredly. "You can never be satisfied with what others see, only with what's inside. You're scared. I understand that. I'm scared, too, but not of what's between us. That's the best thing that's ever happened to me. That's why I won't push you. Either you come freely or it means nothing."

"Be safe, Richard."

His heart sank. He couldn't force the rest of what he'd been about to say out of his mouth, an urgent plea for her to come with him now. Maggie would have come but it was Margaret who stood poised on the top step. He turned and walked quickly into the darkness.

Margaret didn't move, watching what she thought was the shape of him walking down Cluny Road through the shadows. A bright orange flare marked his arrival at the end of the road, a brief spark as he paused to light a cheroot. He seemed determined to make it as difficult as possible for her to act on her love for him. He'd talked about love but there had been no love in his face, and he hadn't reached out for her, hadn't touched her with love. That would have made it so much easier to do what he asked. She slowly walked to the end of the veranda and rested her cheek against the carved column that supported the corner of the thatched roof.

His power over her was frightening. Being apart these few weeks had underscored a realization that had come to her in Makassar when he lay near death. She lost a part of herself whenever she was with him, something far beyond the mere trappings of her life. She needed some sign from him that he understood that, and that he would not ask more of her than she could give. He needed so much— unquestioned loyalty and love. Only she knew how much he needed that, deep down inside. His strength was a peculiar illusion. The veils had been stripped away as she watched his face tonight. At the very core, he was empty. The thought that he expected her to fill it scared her.

Chapter 18

It was all well and good to talk about Christian's investment in Townsend and Townsend, but Margaret decided the next day that she ought to do something practical about it. Charles was pleasant, assuring her that she need not worry about the specifics, and pledging that when Christian returned, he would not want for anything.

"Just as we mean for you to be secure, my dear. We hope we can persuade you to stay with us here. Nothing would give us more pleasure."

She passed over his remark concerning her future. "You seem very certain Christian will return." The thought warmed her immeasurably.

"Oh, he'll come to his senses eventually," Charles said comfortably.

Just the fact of his saying it made the possibility more real. "I've thought of hiring someone to bring him back bodily," she said hesitantly, "since I do know his whereabouts now."

Charles coughed. "Oh, my, no—that would never do, my dear. Your brother is not the first young buck to go amok upon coming of age. Experience teaches that it must be he who puts a period to it. If we drag him back before he's ready to settle down, he'll simply bolt again."

Margaret loved him for his kindly tone and his certitude that all would come right in the end. She remembered Richard's cold, unfeeling assessment, that Christian

296

would never return, and disliked him heartily for it in retrospect.

Margaret smiled at Charles. "Then you think it may do some good for me to remain here in Singapore?"

Charles smiled in return, his pale blue eyes lighting up. "All the good in the world, yes, and not least of all for me."

"I *do* intend to stay on in the bungalow," she said.

Charles laughed. "Oh, yes, yes, I've quite given up on the notion of seeing you remove from Cluny Road."

"Good," Margaret said. "I'm very comfortable there." Behind her she could hear the soft flutter of cards in the drawing room. The long, elegant veranda that swept around the Townsend house was in semidarkness, leaving her in cozy intimacy with Charles. He placed no demands on her and she found she could relax utterly in his company. His mother had unbent towards her, mostly, Margaret suspected, because the rest of S'pore had, and his sister Susan had attached herself to Margaret whenever possible, for much the same reason.

"Ah, there you two are!" Susan's voice came from behind them. "We're changing partners and you really must come make up a foursome with Mr. Hornsby and me." She lowered her voice. "Mrs. Beesom is becoming excessively nit picky about Mr. Beesom's bidding, and she went so far as to imply that he didn't know East from West!"

Margaret laughed as she accepted Charles's hand and rose. "Well, I suppose she may have a point. However, I can see that you need rescuing."

"That's my girl!" Charles said genially. They moved indoors, away from the scent of the clove and jambu trees, and arrived in the drawing room just as Mrs. Beesom leaped from her chair, overturning it.

"A chikchak!" she screamed.

Margaret glanced up indulgently. A tiny green house lizard was walking upside down across the ceiling. They were ubiquitous in Singapore.

"So it is, Mrs. Beesom," she said calmly. She went to take a seat at a card table as the other guests gaped from her to Mrs. Beesom to the little lizard. Charles hastily pulled out a chair just in time for Margaret to sit in it. She picked up a deck of cards. "There is a chikchak that lives on my bedroom ceiling," she remarked as she shuffled the cards. "I've grown quite fond of it." Mrs. Beesom shuddered but the rest of the room's occupants relaxed.

"I daresay you've even named it," called out one buck with an admiring glance.

Margaret cast him a sideways look as she rifled the cards expertly. "I daresay I haven't," she said with a half-smile, "but I find that I am inclined to now that you have suggested it. How does Rupert strike you?"

A laugh went through the room as the owner of the name pulled at his high collar, nervously happy under her scrutiny. "You're certainly welcome to the use of my name," he said, adding quickly, "provided I may have the honor of the first dance with you at the ball next month."

Margaret dealt the cards around once as everyone awaited her answer. The honor should have gone to their host. Margaret looked up at Charles. "Provided Charles has no objection . . . ?"

No one missed the familiarity and there was a satisfied murmur. Expectations ran high that Lady Margaret Belleweather was amenable to Charles Townsend's obvious infatuation with her.

"Well, I should think that a jolly steep price for lending one's name to a chikchak," he said, a little sternly. "Perhaps the second dance . . ."

"Well said!" cried a man at the next table. "Don't let Rupert fox you out of what's rightfully yours, old man."

Charles smiled and winked at Margaret as he sat down. "Couldn't let him get away with such a piece of cheek," he whispered.

Margaret smiled back. It was exactly what she had expected he would do. How nice to send an unspoken signal and have him pick up on it so deftly. Being with Charles was so comfortable. He nodded his handsome head at a passing servant and turned to her.

"Can I interest you in some coffee, my dear, or perhaps a sherry?"

"Thank you, no, Charles. I shall concentrate all my attention on this last rubber. I intend to join you at the office tomorrow so I must leave immediately after we've finished it."

Charles did a double take and waved the servant off again. "I say, do you think you should?" he asked in an undertone. "It's really not quite seemly. I could bring all the papers home if you like."

Margaret smiled up at him. "I don't care a whit for what's seemly, Charles. Besides, I find myself longing to see what it is you do all day."

It was only a small exaggeration and Charles softened visibly, flattered, as she had meant that he should be. Boredom was tapping at her door, and she had decided that a visit to the offices of Townsend and Townsend would be her remedy for it tomorrow.

She arrived before Charles the next morning, inspiring a flurry of bowing and barely concealed expressions of shock. It was silly, really, the idea of protecting her brother's investment. She pulled off her gloves and looked for somewhere to set her parasol. Ignoring the startled looks from the clerks, she matter-of-factly hung the frilly thing next to her hat on the rack provided for gentlemen's wraps.

In the crowded outer office, tall stools faced slanting desks of account keepers, and there were also massive desks, dusty and messy, above which hung maps, faded pictures, and calendars from enterprising ship's chandlers. She went down the long line of desks, past a cashier's cage and through a narrow door, until she came to the larger offices, one with Charles's name on it, the other with Christian's. She sat down at her brother's desk and went through the papers there methodically. Silly, really—after all, she had plenty of money. Charles had misunderstood.

The reverses in the market had merely reduced her fortune from staggering to bountiful. She could easily give Christian all the money he needed. There was no need to protect this tiny corner of it.

And yet, she went every day after that, absorbing the details of trading like a fresh wick. None of it made sense at first but it flowed readily into her mind. Freed of the impediment of Richard Jensen, her mind was clear, her thoughts precise. It was as if her mind welcomed the exercise after months of inactivity while her body was in sexual thrall to him.

The clamor of life in Singapore was a distant murmur, glimpsed dimly through the dusty windows that lined the street side of Townsend and Townsend. Precision and neatness counted for something here, and Margaret felt herself grasping to become a part of it, and to let the orderliness order her. She had confessed to no one that she rarely slept at night anymore, that she lay awake watching the chikchak on her bedroom ceiling until close to dawn. A part of her missed Richard desperately and tried to convince the rest of her that she should be gratified to be needed so much by him. She often awoke still dreaming of him so vividly that she almost smelled him next to her. The damage to her peace of mind was so great that she satisfied her need for sleep in the afternoons, when dreams did not have the same impact.

Margaret attacked the ledgers with increasing ferocity, never giving orders to the clerks, never attempting to alter the way business was conducted by so much as a raised eyebrow, but simply riding the office routine, much the way she had ridden the sensibly predictable and well-scheduled trains back home. Bit by bit, by dint of repetition, the details in the ledgers formed themselves into discernible patterns, and brought her comfort by that very fact.

She was well aware that what brought her comfort brought an equal measure of discomfort to Charles, no matter how hard he tried to conceal it. Like a hound baying and panting on the trail of a hare, he pulled up short when he found her there each morning. Anticipating a hare, he would find that the trail had gone cold, and he whiffed and puffed around Margaret agitatedly, the spot where he'd last scented the quarry. He did his manful best to accept her presence, though, and she took pity on him.

She let him nose around her, greeting him with a smile that concealed a growing suspicion that someone at Townsend and Townsend was not quite honest, either that or incompetent. She made a pet of the chief clerk and when Charles went out, as he inevitably had to during the day, she would ask Mr. Coggins what this or that meant. She wished she'd paid more attention when Richard had offered to show her how he kept the records on the *Java*. It would have been a useful cross-reference.

She was not looking to find skulduggery, but she could not escape the conclusion that it was taking place right under Charles's nose. Rather than upset him with vague accusations, she bided her time, waiting until she could prove her suspicions so that he could confront the culprit. The discrepancies were substantial enough to concern Mr. Coggins, but he was at a loss to account for cargo that seemed to go missing, or ships that consistently sailed underloaded. He seemed confident that Mr. Townsend could explain it if she would only ask him, for as he explained, the son did business differently from how the father had, but Margaret chose not to disturb the delicate tolerance Charles was exercising by challenging him on points she did not comprehend.

As in any mathematical proposition, she reasoned that either there was a flaw in the calculations, or a flaw in the numbers being fed into the formula. While she waited for an exact accounting of her finances to arrive from England, she could enjoy the challenge of discovering which it was. And she reminded herself of her father's first principle, that a mathematician without humility and patience was no mathematician at all.

*　　*　　*

"Are you enjoying yourself?"

"It's lovely, Charles, really lovely!" Margaret let herself sway to the strains of the music as Charles guided her around the floor. He felt solid and masculine beneath her fingers, and his starched shirt front was so polished that it reflected the light of the numerous argand lamps hung from the ceiling of the great room. She had seen him in his flannels on the cricket pitch and knew that he had a handsome figure, and she let herself admire him at the same time she knew he was admiring her. She let the music and the mood divert her thoughts from the unpleasant confrontation with Richard that had taken place that afternoon.

She had gone to the temple on Telok Ayer Street, seeking serenity beneath its cylindrical roof tiles, scarlet lacquered posts, and tiered pagodas. The glazed porcelain dragons surmounting it all suggested a ferocity of spirit at odds with the gentle smiles and kind acceptance that the temple's keepers offered their by now familiar visitor. She had been on her knees, deep in her devotions, when Hoc Sing had arrived to say that the 'captain-tuan' had arrived at the house on Cluny Road.

He repeated it over and over again in an urgent hush, until she comprehended that he meant Richard. She levered herself to her feet and followed the Chinese servant out into the sunlight. Though she went unmolested in the Chinese quarter, her movements never went unremarked, so it did not surprise her that Hoc Sing had found her so easily.

Richard. Her heart beat faster. She was almost afraid of him now. The dark, intense man she'd last seen over a month ago still haunted her dreams, frightening her with demands she could not hope to meet. Only rarely now could she remember the gentle lover, the bold and life-loving spirit she had fallen in love with. As she hurried along, she did have one pleasing recollection of him, of a day when they had been anchored off Sumatra. He had stood on the bow, nearly naked in a sarong. He'd yelled and dived into the water like a plummet and disappeared

302

completely, only to erupt joyfully again, grinning, his teeth white against the oak-colored face as water streamed down it and over the perfect arms and chest.

The memory only intensified the sense that he existed on some other plane, one that was far beyond her capacity to share. She was frantic when she arrived at the house.

He looked well, a taut, well-oiled machine whose muscles uncoiled like springs as he arose from a chair. The green eyes searched hers, his expression unwavering. The boldness of it was unnerving, especially to one whose nerves were already stretched thin. Curiously, it was he who dismissed Hoc Sing. He handed her a check without comment. It represented nearly a fifth of what he owed her.

"You didn't have to come with this," she said, looking up at him. "I don't expect you to . . ." She faltered. Something in his eyes told her that he had no interest in discussing the payment with her.

"I want you to have dinner on the *Java* with me tonight," he said. "We're taking on a load at Collier Quay but once we're finished, I'll anchor out in the roads. It will give us a chance to talk."

Margaret experienced a momentary sense of surprise. "Another load of coal?" It was inconsequential to the matter at hand and he showed no inclination to answer her. She looked down at the floor. "I'm afraid I can't. I have another engagement tonight."

"Charles's grand ball," he said flatly.

She looked up, startled. "How did you know?"

"I make it my business to know what's going on in Singapore. Someone's out to get me. I don't know who and I don't know why, but I mean to find out."

"Well, it's certainly not Charles!" she said indignantly. "In any event, he's giving the ball in my honor, so I must attend."

"Send him a message. Tell him you're sick."

Margaret felt a surge of exasperation. "I'm not one of your deckhands," she snapped. "I don't care to be ordered about."

His tone changed abruptly. "Margaret, I'm begging

303

you. You're letting yourself be lulled further and further from what's real and what's right. Come and be on the *Java* with me, talk, and then you can decide what you want to do, only give me a fighting chance."

She felt a shiver run down her spine. The voice was smooth and persuasive, but he had the air of a desperate man. She didn't want to make a choice about him. "I can't do that," she said. "If I plead illness, Charles will want to come and sit with me, or at least visit to see that I'm being taken care of."

"Tell him to keep his damned hands to himself!"

Margaret stiffened and then she saw the distress behind the words. She touched his arm lightly. "Richard, you don't know what you're talking about. Charles is a gentleman. He would never touch me without my consent."

Richard glared at her and let out a sound halfway between a snarl and a curse. She withdrew her hand nervously and he took an agitated turn around the room, his grace and power barely contained within the civilized cage of her small drawing room, like a tiger that had blundered in from the outskirts of town. He finally came to a halt.

"I'm always going to be there, you know, in your mind. I won't go away."

Margaret stared at him, unable to make sense of his words at the same time that she knew perfectly well what he meant. She felt a sudden, unbearable longing to be held by him, but he merely stared at her, as if willing her to obey him.

"You were happy on the *Java*, with me. I know you were. We planted a seed, you and I, and it grew into something, only now you want it to stop growing because you're afraid of it. Damn it, Margaret, where's all that courage that got you through the typhoon, that got the *Java* repaired? Where's the woman who wasn't afraid to face the truth about her brother and could still find love in her heart for him? Are you just going to melt back into mediocrity?"

"I don't call it mediocrity to live the way I live," she

protested angrily. "You can't win me over by denigrating the things I value. I won't give it all up for you. I don't want to."

"What are you saying? That if you had a house on shore with a little white picket fence, you could be happy?"

"I need something, some piece of . . . of *something* that's mine," she said desperately. Her anger muted as she searched for the words to explain what wasn't even clear in her own mind. "I enjoy dancing, I enjoy going to parties. I like to live in a world where all the talk isn't about wool and coal and cargoes and . . . and what the wind's like today!"

He looked at her, his face expressionless. The white, untanned creases radiating from the corners of his eyes made him look vulnerable, pointing up the fact that he was a man who had spent most of his life at sea, squinting against an unforgiving sun. He still wore a neckerchief, and it was limp with sweat. Margaret felt a swell of tenderness for him as she saw a smudge of black dust at his temple and knew that he was carrying the coal for her sake, sullying the beautiful clipper and himself with the hated cargo.

"Richard . . ."

He didn't let her speak. "All right," he said slowly, "all right. I'll see what I can do about that." The words carried as much threat as promise. His gaze shifted and she saw a distance opening up between them, as his thoughts were elsewhere. He turned and left without another word, a sense of purpose in his stride.

"Good God!"

Margaret felt Charles stiffen and miss the next step. She stumbled against him and he immediately collected himself, as the strains of the music bore in on her again. "I'm so sorry, my dear," he murmured, but his eyes were focused on something across the room.

She twisted in his arms to see what had arrested his motion.

305

"Don't look," he warned sharply.

But it was too late. Her heart thumped painfully as she caught a glimpse of the newcomer who had already set voices buzzing in the room. Richard stood just inside the door, immaculate in evening dress. She nearly lurched as Charles forcibly turned her so that she could no longer see Richard. Faces swam in her vision, blurred with the lanterns' light and animated with the hint of scandal. Her mouth went dry and she felt the pressure of Charles's hand, urging her to look up at him.

His face was relaxed, though with a tangible effort. "Do you want me to ask him to leave?" Charles asked. "I will if you want me to. Otherwise I think it would be best to act as if nothing is out of the ordinary."

Margaret stared at him, aware of Richard watching them. The other dancers around them were bobbling steps, too, as if they had all had too much to drink, but it was only avid curiosity that made them falter, so that they could watch the drama that was unfolding. Only the musicians were unaffected, playing on unaware that the deeply tanned man accepting a glass of champagne from a passing servant was not an invited guest.

"Yes," she finally managed to say. "I mean, I think it would be best to simply pretend that he was expected." Charles let out a dry laugh and Margaret looked at him in surprise. "I must say, you're taking this very calmly."

Charles smiled down at her. "I was just thinking whether that meant I had to acknowledge him. I think not. Rumor has it that he was fired on by Dutch cruisers as he made his run past Java coming back. He's an awful black-guard, you know. Heaven only knows what he was carrying."

Margaret started to say "coal" and then checked herself. He was carrying off a difficult situation with great grace, and all for her sake. It would be better not to let him know that she had seen Richard that day, alone, at her house. The orchestra played on and Margaret was sure it must be the longest dance of the night. At last they stopped.

"I suggest you stay at my side," Charles said in a low

voice. "I can't think what he means coming here."

Margaret fanned herself anxiously. "I think it may have something to do with me, with something I said to him . . ." She trailed off, uneasily aware that she had nearly told him what she had already decided not to, that she had seen and talked to Richard just that day.

Charles drew her hand up over his arm and patted it gently. "Then I should think a deal more highly of him than I do, my dear, for he would have that in common with every decent man in this room. We are all under your spell."

She laughed politely, a tight little laugh that died in her throat as Richard began walking toward them. He looked supremely relaxed, responding to stares of shocked fascination with pleasant nods as he made his way across the shining parquetry. He had a lithe quality, the broad shoulders and narrow hips framed to perfection by the short-waisted black evening coat with swallow tails. His shirt front was a brilliant white, the wing collar fitted by a master hand to just graze the lean, blue-shadowed jaw. He was undeniably the handsomest man in the room.

Out of the corner of her eye, Margaret could see that despite his unconventionality, or perhaps because of it, he was having an effect on the women which could only alarm their mothers and husbands. It was as if a jungle cat had appeared in their midst, speaking flawless English and nibbling at canapes, rendering them all speechless with amazement.

Margaret felt a reawakening of feelings that had been submerged by fear. If he could do this for her, then perhaps he had understood after all. His expression seemed neutral enough as he drew even with them, but there was a cunning in his eyes that reminded her of the day Atam Datu had barged onto the *Java*.

"Mr. Townsend? Your servant, sir." He made a small, elegant bow to Charles.

Charles responded with a nod and a stiff tilting of his torso that took Margaret's hand with it. "Captain Jensen."

Richard withdrew a gold case from the breast pocket of

his jacket. "This is a splendid affair," he said, proffering the case to Charles. "You are to be congratulated."

After a moment's hesitation, Charles took one of the cheroots, releasing his hold on Margaret in order to do so. "Thank you," he said, "though I admit I am somewhat surprised to see you here tonight." He leaned forward to accept the lit match that Richard held out, puffing the cheroot to life. It gave Margaret an odd sensation to smell the odor she associated with Richard coming from Charles. Richard, she noticed, did not light one himself.

"I thought that as one trader to another, you would not object," Richard said. His eyes, on a level with Charles's pale blue ones, carried a challenge.

"As one trader to another, my surprise at seeing you has less to do with the lack of an invitation and more to do with the blue peter I saw hoisted on the *Java* today."

"Ah, so you do keep a close eye on your competitors then," Richard said smoothly. "Yes, I mean to leave, but with the early tide."

"Then you will not want to stay long, I'm sure," Charles said, his meaning unmistakable.

Richard smiled as the music began again. "Perhaps just long enough to have one dance," he said silkily. He turned to Margaret. "Lady Margaret, will you do me the honor?"

Margaret started, jerked out of her role as mere spectator. Charles's mouth tightened as he perceived that he had been outmaneuvered with the offer of the cheroot, leaving him encumbered. Margaret flashed him a bright, nervous smile.

"Do go enjoy your cheroot, Charles. I shall dance this one dance with Captain Jensen and rejoin you."

Charles's aplomb slipped noticeably but he managed a truncated bow. "Very well."

Richard held out his arm and waited patiently as Margaret slowly turned and placed her gloved hand in his. She felt dizzy as he stepped closer, settling his hand lightly at her waist. It was too familiar a touch, too low to be completely acceptable. He moved into the dance without warning and she quickly put her other hand on his shoulder.

To follow his lead seemed as natural as breathing, and the fluidity of his steps reinforced the impression of a jungle cat. The steel beneath his sleek hide asserted itself deep in her consciousness. His outstretched arm was like a spar on the *Java*, his back as straight and unyielding as the mainmast, and she was the sail stretched taut across the span. She billowed and swayed in an invisible wind as he swept her past the confounded gaze of S'pore society. He reefed her in and she pulled for breath from lungs that defied her efforts to inhale.

His expression was smooth, pleasant, with no hint that they were more than casual acquaintances. "Allow me to tell you that you look exceptionally lovely tonight, Lady Margaret."

Margaret stared up at him, aware that she must look like an imbecile as she grappled with the turn of events. His hair was trimmed and styled fashionably, though still unfashionably long, but the fact was that he looked like the standard by which every other man in the room ought to be judged. She caught a glimpse of Charles out of the corner of her eye. He disposed of the cheroot and made a feint in their direction, as if he intended to cut in. Richard maneuvered her adeptly away from him and toward the far side of the room without seeming to do so.

"I had no idea that you even owned an evening suit," she stammered.

He looked down at her, the straight, thick lashes obscuring the amused glint in his eye from everyone but her. "I have friends," he said shortly.

"How? I mean . . ."

His hand tightened on hers impatiently and she could almost feel the roughened palm through her glove. "Clothes do not make the man, which is a lesson I thought you had learned. I'm damned if I can understand how you can have been through so much and still be impressed by show."

309

"It's not just show," she said defensively. "It has to do with manners and conversation and . . . and . . . and interests."

His eyes bored into hers implacably. "I'm interested in *you*, Maggie. There's nothing in this world that interests me more. Is that worth less than whatever it is you find to talk about with Charles Townsend?"

Margaret felt a queer wobble in her heart at his use of the name Maggie, and his straightforward declaration of interest in her. The way he said it made it seem even more important than love. She had a sudden remembrance of her mother's bedroom at Pensleigh, how she had felt excluded from the conversation her parents conducted through their connecting dressing rooms as they prepared to go out. They had always been so absorbed in one another that she had felt secondary, and had been forced to rely on Christian for the closeness she craved.

"Your interest means a great deal to me," she murmured, lowering her lashes.

"But not quite enough?"

Margaret did not answer, feeling she had already admitted too much. She nearly lost her balance as he swung her abruptly toward the outer doors. She had never felt so clumsy on a dance floor in her entire life. The cool evening air coming in from outside caressed her bare neck and shoulders. She was afraid to look up, certain of what he would do next.

With a few effortless steps, he danced her out through the doors. Lamplight gave way to darkness and he broke from the dance. Her heart tripped uncontrollably, leaving her breathless. Without a word, he shifted his grip on her hand and led her down a path. He kept moving, penetrating farther into the extensive grounds where only the intermittent glow of fireflies illuminated the night. Margaret kept her eyes on the grass in front of her as they went on and on until the house was far behind them and the music nearly inaudible. Her delicate evening shoes made a pale blur below her hem as she struggled to keep up.

When he stopped, the suddenness of it took her by surprise. He took her shoulders and pushed her against a tree, effectively trapping her between the wall of his chest and the smooth trunk. Tiny slivers of moonlight darted through the abundant foliage above, but she did not need much light to see that he was looking down at her, his lips thin with tension and the scimitar-shaped scar on his cheek standing out.

"You belong to me, Maggie. We belong together." His voice had lost its smooth, magnetic quality. It was raw with intensity instead. "I'm not going to let you run away from it. I can play a decent hand of bridge, I like to read, I can go to the races and not be such a dunderhead as to leap the rail if my horse loses, I've got more than a little interest in music, and anything else I don't know, I can learn. I'm a quick study, Maggie, and I could enjoy doing all those things if I did them with you. But what we have goes much deeper. It's something that would sustain us on a deserted island. It doesn't depend on fine clothes or French chefs or having the right people around us."

Margaret stared up at him, feeling the heat of his body radiating through the fine black wool of his evening suit and flowing over her breasts and face. She put her hands on his shoulders to keep a distance between them, afraid that his overpowering physicality would swallow her up. Wetting her lips, she said, "There *is* something between us, Richard, but I'm not sure it's as substantive as you think. It may be that we've confused animal passion for true attachment. I never knew about that side of myself until I met you, and while I certainly . . ."

His mouth came down on hers without warning, swiftly, recklessly. It startled her and she almost panicked to find her breath cut off so precipitously. Then she felt the raw passion in the stoking of his lips and forgot the panic. Her first protest died as his scent rose in her nostrils and the rough cheeks grazed hers. His mouth moved insistently across her lips, and a hot, coiling desire burst to life inside her. She returned the kiss ravenously, even more hungry for his passion than she had known.

311

He pulled her tighter and she felt the proof of his own desire through the thin satin of her ball gown. She wanted him so much it induced a sob of frustration. The sheer masculine bulk of him lost its power to threaten and became a temptation instead. His body pressed against her with barely contained power, and she twined her arms around his neck to pull him closer. A groan ripped upward from deep in his chest and his hands found places on her that hadn't been touched for far too long.

He worked one thigh between her legs and Margaret felt a shock of sensation as he pressed it up against the soft flesh between her legs. He began rubbing there with hard muscle, making her swell with desire. She let out a strangled cry as he pushed harder, mercilessly pleasuring her with the rhythmic motion. She felt weak with it, and her head fell back. The tree bark didn't feel as smooth against her bare back as he forced her harder against it. He deepened his kiss, a wholesale taking of her mouth that sent a pulsing wave of sensation through every part of her. The wave tightened and furled into throbbing need. She clutched at him and strained upward, lost to all decency as she felt the pleasure mount. He pulled away and she sagged within the confines of his hands.

"You like it, Maggie," he said in a rough undertone. His own breathing was ragged. "I know you like it, but that's not what I meant. You can get this anywhere. Plenty of men would be glad to give you this."

She tried to twist away, shocked by his crudity, but he gripped her tighter and bent to kiss the swell of her breasts. They strained against the bodice of her dress. She was breathless with desire and unable to find the words or the will to stop him. He cupped one breast and pushed it up, nearly out of the dress. His tongue reached for the nipple just below the neckline and she wanted to tear away the fabric, anything, just so that he could massage the ache there.

"Oh, yes, you like it, even this way," he murmured. With an expert turn of his wrist he brought her flesh out of its confines and into the open air. Margaret clutched at his shoulders, straining upward.

"No, I don't," she gasped, appalled at the force of her lust.

"You're a fluent liar," he said, the words raspy with the force of his own breathing.

He freed her other breast, leaving the bodice of her dress limp against her ribs and her breasts pressed up full and high in the night air by the neckline. A bolt of pleasure shot through her as his hot, wet mouth sucked at her nipple and his hands forced her hips to move against him. She heard her own panting as if from a distance as he ground his thigh into the vulnerable flesh between her legs. He found her mouth again and took it greedily, filling her senses with hot sand and salt and sea air as he gripped her bare shoulders. The roughened skin of his hands was a powerful reminder of his strength, but he exercised only enough of it to mold her body to him.

She closed her eyes and let him do what she knew he would do anyway. She was helpless with pleasure and soaked in need for what he brought to her, the fierce tenderness that always characterized his lovemaking. His stiff shirt front and the silk lapels of his jacket chafed her swollen breasts, making her tauten. She pulled at his hips, too far gone in desire to deny it, and opened herself wider to him.

He groaned and his inhalation sucked the breath up out of her lungs. He took his mouth away long enough for both of them to draw fresh breath and then plunged back for more, his tongue making the same circular motions in her mouth that his thigh did, rocking her with building waves of pleasure. Desire hammered in every pulse point of her body and she slipped her hands beneath his jacket. The muscles at his waist strained beneath the silk cummerbund, knotting beneath her fingers. She let out a breathless cry and he parted from her mouth, kissing his way urgently along her cheek and burying his nose in the hair at her temple.

"Maggie," he said hoarsely, "Maggie."

It meant nothing and it said everything, it gave her the

313

freedom to lose herself to him. She surrendered the last vestige of self to passion, and pleasure ripped through her with almost painful intensity. Her cries rent the stillness around them as he held her, secure in his arms.

When it was over she fell back against the tree, limp and dazed, gasping for breath. She felt his hands loosen their grip, and he rested the weight of his head on her bare shoulder. His forehead was damp. His hair felt like dark satin draped across her skin. His own breath came unsteadily, fanning her neck. When he raised his head at last, she saw through heavy-lidded eyes that his mouth still glistened wetly from kissing her, but his gaze was sharp and seeking.

"Anyone can give you this," he said on a harsh exhalation. "I'll give you this—as much as you want—but I want more. I want to hold you afterward, I want to hold you when you're sleeping, I want to wake up next to you every morning. Everything, Maggie—I want everything. Come with me now, before it's too late."

Still shocked by what had happened and stunned by pleasure, she could only look at him. She heard Charles calling her name from far away, and as he got closer, it started a bulbul into a burst of song. The notes died away in midphrase as it realized it was still the middle of the night, and she could almost feel the bird's sleepy puzzlement as it subsided again.

Richard still held her firmly between his hands, watching her intently. She didn't want to go away with this raw, violent stranger who could drag her into the darkness and strip away her soul so effortlessly, turn her into an animal, "I . . . I want you to go . . ." she whispered.

"Oh, I'm going—that's certain. The question is, are you coming with me?" When she didn't answer, he withdrew. A shock of dark hair fell across his forehead. "I sail at dawn. Come with me, Maggie."

She could hear Charles coming closer and closer. Would he find her or some depraved stranger? "I can't. Not now—not tonight."

Something like despair flashed across his face and then was gone so quickly that she thought she must have been mistaken. He took another step back, into shadow. His voice when he spoke again was little more than a growl. "Hoc Sing will know where to find me if you change your mind." There was a soft crunch underfoot and a blur of white, and then he was gone. She felt the emptiness around her like a yawning pit.

"Margaret! Are you there?" Charles called again, off in another direction. She didn't answer immediately, needing time to compose herself. She felt the dampness between her legs and a flush spread from her still-tender breasts up her neck. Dear God—she must get command of herself and not let Charles suspect what had taken place. Margaret hastily rearranged her dress, pushing and pulling until she was covered again.

"I'm here, Charles," she said, but her voice was only a thin thread. She tried again, with more success. "I'm over here, Charles."

He found her quickly enough then. "What's going on?" he asked, distress in every syllable.

Margaret held herself upright with an effort, her knees weak and her whole body trembling. "It's nothing. Captain Jensen was merely taking his leave."

Charles peered suspiciously into the darkness. "Damned impertinence! He didn't offer you any . . . well, he didn't do anything improper, did he?"

Margaret managed a tepid smile she hoped would pass as genuine in the dim light. "No, he merely wanted to tell me that he was leaving in the morning."

"Can't imagine why he thinks you're interested in his whereabouts," Charles grumbled. "Besides, he already told me that in your presence."

His anger had turned to irritation. Margaret breathed a sigh of relief and began walking, slowly and carefully, back toward the house. Charles fell in beside her.

"Charles . . ." Margaret faltered, feeling faintly light-headed. "Charles, I'm not feeling terribly well all of a sudden. Would you mind awfully if I left now?"

315

He was all solicitousness. "Of course not, my dear." He put a gentle hand under her elbow. "I'll gladly drive you home, but if you're not feeling quite the thing, why not stay the night? I know my mother has rooms prepared."

"No, thank you." She felt his kindness, in his voice and in his touch, but she didn't want him to be touching her at just that moment. She softened her voice as she disengaged her arm. "I've had a marvelous time, really, but I should prefer to wake in my own bed tomorrow morning, especially if this is the beginning of some illness."

What was it Richard had called her? A fluent liar. Well, she was proving him right, but she told herself that it was to spare Charles any unnecessary upset. She had an intense need to be alone, a need that was creeping toward mania. She walled the emotion away with a supreme effort, the legacy of years of masking her feelings in the name of politeness.

She took her leave of Mrs. Townsend and a servant brought her wrap. A faint dew of perspiration clotted on the back of her neck. She knew without benefit of a mirror that her face was chalky, but of course it was only the aftermath of Richard's loving, which usually left her prostrate for hours. She counted herself lucky to be able to walk and talk with any clarity at all, and resisted the vague nausea that movement induced. Charles handed her into the carriage and she made idle chat on the way home, the gist of which she couldn't remember afterward. When John and Eliza appeared on her veranda, prepared to see her safely to bed, Charles reluctantly let them lead her away and drove off.

Moving mechanically, she let Eliza undress her for bed. She stepped out of the rustling rose satin dress and accepted a loose wrapper. Eliza brought her a cup of tea, clucking over her lack of color. With a weak wave of her hand and a few reassuring words, Margaret was able to allay her concern. When she was finally alone she started shaking so hard that she had to set the cup of tea on her dressing table and sag onto the chaise near the window.

It felt as if a small wound was bleeding somewhere deep

316

inside of her, leaving her weak and unable to think. Her mind clouded over and she saw Richard's face in front of her. He had said that any man could bring her the physical satisfaction he did, but she knew he was wrong. Unalterably, indisputably wrong. Not just any man could do that to her. The very reckless intensity in him that frightened her also ignited a streak in herself that she would never have known she possessed if not for him. She knew without benefit of other experience that he and he alone had the power to arouse her spirit, and that the rapture he brought her body was only an extension of that. He forced her to be more, do more, than she had ever thought possible.

In return, she brought him a gentle peace, a love which was not afraid to approach and see his demons. Her love and trust was like a hand held out to a savage beast, a beast with a power so great that it frightened even itself. As long as she did not bolt or show fear, she was safe. He would hurt neither himself nor her if she stood firm. It was the fear that had triumphed when she walked away from him—fear of his brashness, fear of storms, fear of watching him nearly die, fear of all that was new and different from what had gone before. She was struck by a profound certainty, that he was a wellspring of life for her, a place where she could go and be nourished and sent back into the world stronger than she had been, if only she kept the fear at bay.

Just as an anchor was cast off the cat's-paw and dropped into deep water, she realized that she had been thrown into a stormy sea when she met Richard Jensen. Now she had no more choice than the anchor. She must hold him to the limits of her strength or perish with him. The simplicity of it defied argument, and the knowledge brought a profound calm.

Chapter 19

Richard awoke with a blistered, foul taste in his mouth. He wondered where he was, and why in the hell he'd had to wake up before the hangover wore off.

"Come on, Captain. S'time you were up and about."

Richard groaned and swatted at the air around him. It was pushing on him uncomfortably. "Go away. Leave me for dead."

Dogsmeat let out a mirthless chuckle. "You been out for so long, I might have thought you *was* dead, only dead men don't snore."

Richard cracked one eyelid open and instantly regretted it. It was still dark outside and Dogsmeat had turned up the lantern. The steward shook him with no regard for his delicate state of health.

"If you do that again, I'll vomit on you," he warned the dwarf softly.

He rolled over and buried his face in the pillow and was sorry he'd moved. The violent rocking motion could have been the *Java* under sail—in a gale, waves at least thirty feet high—but it wasn't. They weren't due to sail until first light so the motion had to be in his head. He groaned again. He vaguely remembered looking up at the underside of a table at Proctor's Pub. It, too, had been rocking.

He'd left the ball and headed straight down River Valley Road, past all the stately homes of all the stately English. He'd have liked to have their stately English hearts skewered on a gaffer's hook. At least that pompous ass Townsend hadn't managed to make him look foolish, though God knew the potential for that had been enormous. Maybe the conniving son of a bitch had known that all he had to do was step back and Richard would take care of that himself. Richard ripped off his white tie as he walked, flinging it into the bamboo hedge lining the road.

Margaret wasn't going to come, he thought. Not tonight, not ever, not after what he'd done. He'd started off well enough, but that was about as far as he ever got. It was always a lick and a promise ahead of disaster with him. He'd been doing well enough until he took her into the garden and she'd started with that drivel about it just being sex between them.

He pulled the studs out of his shirt front and angrily flung them into the bamboo without breaking stride. She'd had to remind him of how much he liked to touch her, and how he craved seeing her rise under his hands. And that dress! It put the luscious breasts that drove him mad with desire up and on display for everyone, including that pig, Townsend.

He stopped at the intersection with Orchard Road, belatedly remembering the hired carriage still waiting in the drive back at the house. He'd hired it for the evening on the outside chance that Margaret would leave with him, run like Cinderella from the ball, but with her prince at her side. Some prince! He slammed his fist into a white pillar marking the corner. Self-disgust replaced every other emotion as he relived the scene in the garden. Oh, he'd won her over, all right. She'd expressed concern that it was all physical between them, and what had he done? Had he talked to her about love and happiness and growing old together?

No. He'd pushed her up against a tree and done things to her he'd never even done to a whore. He felt a wild laugh well up in his chest and knew that if he let himself think about it anymore, he'd lose his mind. Then he decided that losing his mind wasn't such a bad idea. He struck out toward the docks, intending to find the seamiest bar he

319

could and get on the outside of more liquor than he'd ever drunk in his life. With luck it would kill him.

Proctor's wasn't the seamiest but it was the closest. He made a good start on a bottle of rum before he even looked past the mahogany bar that shone like a mirror under the oil lamps. Eurasian girls roamed the place, stopping at curtained booths in the back and occasionally disappearing inside them. Around the tables sat sailors, traders, ship's chandlers, Chinese merchants, tea planters, silent Moslems sipping at nonalcoholic drinks, and Malay boatmen. The spawn of the East, in short. Hawkers, thieves, and pimps circulated between the tables, adding to the riotous, lawless atmosphere, as sensual as it was salty. Richard pushed his stool back, feeling marginally better, though still not nearly drunk enough.

"You look real nice," a girl said, smiling up at him with dark red, bee-stung lips that were about as different from Margaret's as lips could get. She fingered the silk lapels of his evening jacket and he looked down at her fingers caressing the material. His head felt weighted, like a fisherman's pot. It bobbed uncertainly at the end of his neck and he knew he was already drunker than he'd realized.

"Thanks." Her cheongsam was slit high up on her hip, and it didn't take a sailmaker to know that the fabric would burst under the strain of her voluptuous hips if she so much as bent over.

"You want love, maybe?" she asked.

Her eyes seemed dark, hypnotically beautiful, and he was pretty sure it wasn't just the liquor making that judgment. She slipped her hand inside his shirt front, left conveniently open by the absence of studs, and her fingers did some professional stroking that reminded him of how uncomplicated it was just to pay for it. His gaze slowly traveled up to her face again and he realized she was patiently waiting for a reply.

"Nobody loves me," he said thickly.

"I could, maybe," she said with a beguiling smile. She bent her head toward the back. "We go find an empty booth, or maybe a toff like you, I take you somewhere else,

320

you spend the night with me?"

The smell of the sea mixed with her heavy jasmine perfume, making him dizzy. He took another drink and closed his eyes for a minute.

"No," he said, "I don't think so."

She pouted a little, alluringly so, and smiled again, looking up at him from under her lashes. "I think I could fix whatever problem you got."

Richard cringed. "Not tonight."

The girl wandered off with a promise to come back later, in case he changed his mind, but he knew he wouldn't. He wanted to stay right where he was, and get blind, stinking drunk. Here was a good place, right by the bar, where he could be sure to get deeply involved in any serious brawls that developed.

Something started around midnight, precipitated by a racial slur that condemned the sexual prowess of every nationality except the speaker's own. It was good enough for Richard and just about every other man in the bar, although fifty against one made for a waiting line. Just to pass the time, the rest of the patrons warmed up on each other. It didn't last long, at least not for Richard. He took a nasty uppercut, about the best he'd ever felt he thought admiringly as he hurtled backward into a wall. The impact knocked one of the pictures of naked women down off the wall and onto his head.

The next thing he knew, a Norwegian bosun was scraping him up off the floor and apologizing. The fight was over and someone was buying a round of drinks. The big Norwegian propped Richard and the downed picture up on two chairs and went to take advantage of the largess before it ended. When he came back with two glasses, Richard was amazed to find that Norwegian was a lot like Swedish, at least to two drunks, and they took turns toasting the bovine beauty in the picture in an outpouring of international goodwill.

There was another fight later, but he didn't remember that one as well, although he suspected it had been a better one. It involved knives, which was a pity, since An Wu's tailor hadn't thought to equip the evening suit with any. He gave it up as a bad job and let an apprentice's first punch send him under a table, where he obligingly stayed. By then he was feeling magnanimous. It was his gift to the apprentice, letting him take a swat at an officer without retaliation.

"Sir, it won't accomplish nuffin' for you to ignore me."

Richard smelled hot coffee and promptly threw up into the pillow. By the time the dwarf got him cleaned up, his anguish knew no bounds. There was no doubt he was going to be sick a lot more and he staggered up on deck so as not to foul the air belowdecks.

The sun was just coming up and the sight of open sea almost cleared his head. "Where the hell is Singapore?" he demanded.

Harkay was sitting on an overturned crate below the poop rail, nursing a black eye. He shrugged and pointed back over the stern. Richard spun around, scanning the empty horizon, and tumbled to his hands and knees for his trouble. He retched a few times and staggered to his feet again.

"Where the hell is Singapore?" he roared. It came out as a whisper but inside his head the effect was just what he'd intended, enough volume to reach the fore royal. He staggered to the binnacle and sagged over it, wishing it were a coffin, and that he could crawl into it.

"That's why I've been tryin' to wake ye, Cap'n," Dogsmeat said behind him. "We had to get out o'there."

Richard waited for the cannons in his head to stop firing. "Why?" he whispered.

"A longboat come up on us, captain, about four this morning, all quiet like. It was Harkay what heared'em. He went overside and popped their stopper, but not before he seen they was carrying a load of guns. Me and Mr. Daniels, we hightailed it for shore and rounded up the crew. Some big brute with a funny accent told us where to find you."

Twenty pounders were still going off with monotonous and painful regularity but Richard understood enough of the story to figure out the rest. All well and good, so they'd

322

had the sense to cast off before worse could happen. Wouldn't that have been a dandy present for the Dutch, he thought.

"Beware of Greeks bearing red herrings," he muttered.

"Sir?"

"Nothing." He stayed where he was. It wasn't any worse than any place else. "Get me Mr. Dekker. He knows a thing or two about running blockades."

"Yes, sir!" The steward seemed delighted to hear something sensible out of his captain.

Dekker was distinctive in that the habit of naval service had never quite left him. Richard would have recognized his highly polished shoes anywhere. He spoke to them in an earnest whisper.

"Get us to Sydney, Mr. Dekker."

"Aye, sir."

Richard silently blessed his first officer for his brevity. Satisfied that the chain of command had functioned like it was supposed to, Dogsmeat rolled his captain off the binnacle and rewarded him with a hair of the dog. Richard awoke many hours later, grateful for small things, like being left to lie flat on the deck, and the wet towel someone had thrown across his face.

The *Java* creaked and groaned around him, bringing him as much comfort as anything could. It didn't really matter that they'd sailed a little early. Margaret wasn't ever going to sail with him again.

He dragged himself into the shade of the companionway and thumped on the deck to summon Dogsmeat from below. Something stuck out in front of him and he realized it was the front of the previously elegant starched shirt. He yanked it off. What had happened to the jacket was anyone's guess.

He leaned back and stared morosely at the silk cummerbund and black dress pants. His bare feet poked out the ends. He looked like a civilized savage. Or a savage civilian. Dogsmeat appeared, carrying the bottle Richard had been going to ask for.

He took a swig from the bottle and noticed it wasn't the

good stuff. Friends didn't have to be told when all you needed was rotgut. Through the porthole, he heard the twittering of Margaret's sparrow in the saloon. Blackness settled into his soul and around his heart. Steadily and with forethought, he drank himself into oblivion, congratulating himself on doing it up on deck where they could easily sluice away the consequence with a bucket of sea water.

Margaret turned away from the telegraph counter and found that the sense of urgency that had propelled her here was gone now that the telegram was sent, and she didn't quite know what to do next. She wandered out onto the street with John behind her. She heard a familiar voice and looked up. Charles sprang down from his carriage, undoubtedly on his way home out of the noonday heat, like every other right-thinking resident of Singapore.

"I say, you're looking very well," Charles said, smiling. "I'm so glad. You did look a bit peaky when I left you last night."

Margaret hoped the shade cast by her poke bonnet would hide the faint blush that rose to her cheeks. "It was just temporary," she assured him.

"May I give you a ride somewhere?" he asked.

"No, thank you just the same." She gestured toward the elegant pony trap An Wu had sent around for her use.

"Ah, of course," Charles murmured. He glanced up at the marquee. "You had a message of some importance?"

"I did." Margaret swallowed. She might as well get it over with. "I've sent a telegram to Captain Jensen, via the pilot's office in Anjer. He asked me to marry him last night, you see, and I've consented."

Charles looked so thunderstruck that Margaret's first thought was that she'd better lead him out of the sun and make him sit down. He stared at her and swallowed hard.

"My dear, you can't be serious. That . . . that *bounder?* How did he even work up the nerve to ask you?" He sputtered and drew another breath. "By God, he should be

324

thrashed for even daring to ask!"

She sensed something else behind his outrage—betrayal or disappointment or hurt feelings. She couldn't be sure which, but he deserved an explanation. "I'm afraid I haven't been entirely candid with you, Charles. Won't you come back to Cluny Road and have lunch with me? Perhaps I can explain."

"I won't. That is, I can't. I'm expected elsewhere," he said. He took out a handkerchief and mopped the perspiration that had suddenly appeared on his face. A dull red flush crept up from his shirt collar.

"Charles, please, you mustn't be distressed. I came to know Captain Jensen rather well during my time on the *Java*. In all honesty, he had asked me to marry him even before we returned. I would have sailed with him this morning but he had already left by the time I arrived."

"No! Oh, Margaret, what a disaster that might have been!" He looked as if he wanted to reach out and sweep her into his arms. He glanced around hastily. "I can see that we must talk. My other engagement can wait."

He went with her to Cluny Road but turned down any offer of food. Margaret decided it was just as well, given his agitation and the heat. He insisted that she send John and Eliza off on some errand so that they could speak in privacy.

"There are things I would not care for the servants to hear," he said as they sat down in the small parlor, "even at the risk of compromising you by being alone with you."

"Oh, Charles," she said with a gentle smile, "as if I should fear anything untoward from you."

Charles cleared his throat and looked away. When he turned back, he had a faintly ill look, and Margaret suddenly perceived that his distress stemmed from his own feelings for her.

"I'm glad to hear you say it," he said, "for I hold you in too high a regard to ever want to . . . to risk offending you."

Margaret began to feel quite sorry for him. "Charles," she said gently, "you have never offended me, nor are you likely to. I'm only sorry that my acceptance of Captain Jensen's marriage proposal should have shocked you so."

"Margaret, how can it not?" he snapped. He shook his head. "I'm sorry. Perhaps I'm too overwrought by the idea to be able to discuss it rationally right now."

"I know what you think of him, Charles," Margaret said, "but I must say that I know him rather better than you."

"I wish that were true," Charles said. "Regretfully, I am in possession of certain facts regarding him which must cause you to reverse the course you're on. It's as well that he almost certainly won't receive your telegram."

Margaret felt an anxious jolt. After arriving at the docks that morning and discovering that the *Java* had already sailed, she'd been furious. Hoc Sing had listened without comprehension to her ranting and railing, his smooth face apologetic, and then she realized that she had no one to blame but herself. She had given Richard no reason to hope she would come. Of course he had left without her. She sat down on her trunk, nearly sick as she thought of the raw hurt in his voice when she had asked him to go. She grew weepy with self-pity and guilt, and Hoc Sing sat beside her, baffled, his intelligent eyes mirroring her distress. Only after hours of anxious pacing had she hit upon the idea of sending a telegram to Richard through the Burseys, begging his forgiveness and asking him to return for her.

"He's bound to go through the straits either on the way out or on the way back to Singapore," she said nervously.

Charles stood up and went to a window, clasping his hands behind him. "There was some unpleasantness before he sailed this morning. I'm afraid Captain Jensen may have worn out his welcome in Singapore. In fact, in this part of the world. I daresay he will not try to go through the Straits of Sunda and therefore, blessedly, your message will not reach him."

"What unpleasantness?" Margaret asked. She twined her hands together nervously and then hid them in the folds of her skirt to conceal her agitation.

Charles sighed and turned back from the window. "He took on a load of guns, which as you may know, is perfectly legitimate cargo here in Singapore, but he apparently declined to pay for them. His crew badly beat the men charged with making the delivery and then scuttled their boat."

"But he was carrying coal, Charles! Not guns!"

Charles shrugged, making his frock coat shift up. "I received the information from a very reliable source, my dear. It was common knowledge by midmorning. We traders have an uneasy alliance with independent captains as it is. When there is a bad egg among them, the word spreads quickly. To order goods and then, well . . . do what he did, it's unforgivable. The system depends upon the integrity of all the participants."

"Well, I don't believe that story," Margaret declared. "With all due respect, Charles, I know that Captain Jensen does not deal in guns. He told me so himself."

Charles smiled a little patronizingly. "Naturally he would tell you that. No one will give him a distance charter because he is too disobliging to forge the necessary relationships. Therefore, he has become an uncomfortable half-breed, trying to sustain a blue water vessel and its large crew on island trade when he really requires the longer, more profitable runs to do so. Naturally, he turns to the cargo which will produce the highest return."

"But he *does* manage it," Margaret insisted, "and without running guns."

"Your defense of him reflects well on your tender-hearted nature, my dear, but the facts simply don't support that view. I'm afraid one or more of my colleagues has alerted the Dutch authorities that he was known to have left here with munitions. They will undoubtedly board him if they can, and confirm the truth of it. He is no fool, however, and will probably take a circuitous route to wherever it is that the guns are expected, most likely through the straits of Malacca up to northern Sumatra."

"I was on board when Dutch officials searched his ship once before," Margaret said stoutly. "I believe they have long suspected him of wrong-doing. It was reflected in the thoroughness of their search. However, they found nothing before and I believe they will find nothing this time."

Charles sat down opposite her again, his blue eyes glowing with sympathy. "Margaret, I admire your loyalty but we must be practical. Given what we know, he is not likely to stop for the Dutch and they will fire across his bow, or more likely, simply attempt to hole him, which would be a waste of a perfectly good ship. At the risk of being crass, he owes you a good deal of money which will not be forthcoming if that happens. Your only chance to recoup the debt may be to claim the *Java* as payment."

"I needn't claim it," Margaret said bravely. "He signed the *Java* over to me so I do, in effect, already own her."

Charles sat back, blinking in surprise. "Did he, by God? Then the man has at least a trace of honor in him." He shook his head gravely. "Unless the Dutch know that, they will be at no pains to spare the ship, though. If you will give me the papers, I will present them to the local Lloyd's agent and obtain insurance on your behalf, to protect your investment until this is resolved."

Margaret felt her irritation rising. "I know you mean well, Charles, but I do not wish you to do that. The *Java* belongs to Captain Jensen and he has already begun repaying me. Besides, what there is between us far exceeds a mere business relationship. In fact, the money is of little or no concern to me."

Charles lowered his eyes. "I'm sorry to press the issue, my dear, but have you considered that if you are the owner of record and you do not obtain insurance, it will seem suspect?"

Margaret checked her rising irritation with effort. "In what way, Charles?"

Charles jiggled the fob on his pocket watch uncomfortably. "It may create the impression that you do not, in fact, hold a title which would bear official scrutiny."

Margaret kept her back straight, her shoulders held tightly back, radiating disapproval. "I trust Captain

Jensen and I do not care for your implication that he is somehow deceiving me. I will take no action with regard to insurance. In any case, the papers are aboard the *Java*."

Charles withdrew his pocket watch, his face reddening. "I am terribly late. Please, consider what I have said. It is not just that the man will be an outcast in Singapore, but that Java and Sumatra will no longer be open to him either. I cannot help but think that you would not wish to ally yourself with such an individual, quite apart from the difference between your stations."

"I have thought about that, Charles, quite a bit as it happens," she said stiffly. "I have decided that if my rank and money do not buy me the freedom to marry whomever I consider worthy of me, then they are of little use."

"I wish I had known that was the case," Charles replied. He looked down at his finely formed hands for a moment, twisting a gold signet ring on his third finger. "You see, I have a great deal of affection for you. It cannot have escaped your notice. My first thought when you told me you'd nearly sailed with Jensen this morning was that you would have been in terrible danger." He glanced up at her quickly, and the alarm in his eyes was palpable. "I admit that when the news of your . . . financial setback reached my ears, I experienced a momentary pleasure." He made a deprecating gesture with one hand, his eyes seeking hers. "Please, do not misunderstand me—I did not relish your misfortune. It was only that it left perhaps less distance between us, although I still did not seriously hope that you would marry so far beneath yourself as to consider me."

Margaret found the speech curiously moving. She softened her spine and leaned toward him slightly. "I am most appreciative of your regard, Charles. If I had not become attached to Captain Jensen, I am sure I would have looked kindly on your suit."

Charles stood up, looking flustered. "I wish I could have dissuaded you," he murmured. "I'm sorry, but I really must take my leave of you now."

He hurried out the door. Margaret heard the jingling of the harness and then the clop of horse's hooves as his carriage moved off down the drive. She hugged herself tightly, feeling as if she had begun the turning away from one world and toward another. And she was fearful, too, fearful for Richard. She stood up resolutely. She would return to the telegraph office and send a message to him care of the harbor master in Sydney, reiterating her desire to marry him, and warning him of the dangers Charles had outlined.

Chapter 20

Richard surveyed Circular Quay with painfully blood-shot, light-sensitive eyes. Where to now? He crumpled the papers in his hand. One was a bank draft for the coal now destined for some steamer's belly. He owed An Wu most of it in payment for the front money to buy the coal in Singapore. The rest he owed to Margaret, after he paid the crew and took on stores.

Harkay would see to the stores. He had a very effective negotiating technique that moved chandlers to give him their best price—he growled. Darwin, perched on his shoulder, added his own growling. In combination, they were intimidating and odd in the extreme. Dekker and Daniels would see to moving the *Java* to a mooring in the roads once the stores were on board. He saw them on the quarterdeck conversing regularly these days, but they kept their own counsel. Their talk over meals ceased if, and when, he staggered in to join them. A drunken captain was never a pleasant thing. Sunk in grief for what might have been, he still had enough of a toehold on the world to remember that.

He stood in the dust and the noise, aware that carters were going around him, shooting angry looks in his direction. Maybe they were even shouting at him to get out of the road. They might have been. He wasn't sure. Even when the liquor wore off, as it occasionally did just because he got so drunk that he passed out and couldn't drink anymore, even then he felt as if a gauzy blackness draped everything around him. It was like walking through a closed-up house, all the furniture covered with dust sheets. There might have been a party going on there, with lights and laughter, and the smell of warm food, but it was all lost on him.

He shoved the papers in his pocket, fumbling and missing several times. All the bother over docking and unloading and mooring, and payment for the coal, all recorded on paper. He'd signed it all, paid all the fees, and now it bored him worse than it had then. None of it mattered.

Margaret. The pain rose up out of his gut and never stopped coming. It clawed through him, marvelously inventive in the ways it tortured him. There were whole years of his life he could scarcely recall except for this port and that cargo and maybe a particularly ruthless storm. How the hell had he built up such a storehouse of vivid memories in the few short months she'd been with him? When he managed to suppress one thought, another, more painful one, would rise and take its place. They swirled through his chest, hideous ghouls that could only be dimmed by liquor or unconsciousness. Now he had benefit of neither.

He decided to go to Daphne's. He could get drunk there as well as any place. They'd swaddle him in kindness, commiserate over his lost love. He could almost feel the soft breasts cradling his head, a hand stroking his hair, and a voice murmuring comforting things. And when he got sick, or passed out, or both, Dogsmeat wouldn't have to take care of him for once. That was only fair. A sailor expected his shipmates to put up with all his vagaries, but a fair-minded captain spared his crew, at least some of the time. Dogsmeat would know where to find him later.

He sat in Daphne's parlor and poured the rough, Australian bootleg liquor down his throat. He remembered walking up those steps with Margaret, her small, pointed face rosy with embarrassment and amusement. He remembered drowning in those violet eyes when he lost himself inside her, straining to go as deep as he could, and wanting to stay there long after the pleasure had peaked. That hadn't been just here, though. That had been always, everywhere.

He rubbed his open palms across his face, blotting out Daphne's parlor and the sunlight for a minute. He had seen paradise and lost it. The angels that had hovered over him when she had been by his side had fled. He'd taught Dekker how to reckon line of position, and he'd taught Daniels, too, so that they wouldn't be adrift in the sea of bloody misery with him. They thought he'd gone mad but he saw the hope in their eyes that he was coming back, that it was only temporary. Richard didn't think it was. He felt like a badly trimmed sail, flapping in the wind and unable to grab onto it.

Dekker was what? Twenty-four? And Daniels was younger than that. Neither of them knew what a berth on a hellship was like. But Dogsmeat knew, and Tony, and a few of the other, older men. They knew the *Java* was one in a thousand, lucky in her captain. Trouble was, the *Java*'s captain was her problem now. Reviled by the Dutch, framed by the British, deep in debt, Margaret gone. Even stalwart An Wu would be afraid to consign cargo to him now, for fear of offending his overlords.

Some nameless, faceless force was pushing him under. He didn't know why, but it had always been there, waiting for him. It had dogged him from his first day of existence, born a bastard, half Portuguese, half nothing, to a mother who couldn't or wouldn't love him. In a town full of Swedes who were unalterably convinced that he was the seed of the devil.

Richard let out a raw laugh. Maybe he was. Maybe that was what the other half of him was—it would explain his bloody-minded perversity. Pure bloody-mindedness had gotten him through most of his life, out of Ohio and onto the clippers. He hadn't minded the unrelenting work, the grinding routine with never enough sleep, and always being either too cold or too hot. With the strength and the arrogance of a young man, he'd taken it on and thrived.

Then there'd been the war and the Royal Navy. Waking up in the stinking fo'csle of a British blockader instead of the clean-smelling arms of the tavern girl had been a steep downturn for the worst. They'd had to beat him to make him do the turn, but even that he'd survived. Then had come the *Avenging Angel*, retaken from the American Navy. It had been a ray of light to be put off on her, out from under the thumbs of British officers, and to leave behind the hovering charge of a murder he hadn't committed.

But An Wu's mention of Samuel Coit had brought things back into perspective. All the old ghosts were here tonight, Richard thought darkly. He closed his eyes, trying to force away the vision of men being dragged through an ice cold sea in a bosun's chair, all for looking at Coit cross-eyed. Sometimes it hadn't even taken that much provocation.

Richard shoved himself to his feet. It wasn't going to work. Being here was no better than on the *Java*. The papers in his pocket tumbled to the ground and Daphne came over as he swayed on his feet, trying to find the horizon.

"Here, lovey," she said, "you're losing all your bits and pieces." She refolded them and put them inside his breast pocket. "Taking yourself off home, then are you, lovey?" She grabbed his arm as he lurched to starboard.

"May as well, Daphne," he muttered. "I'm not good company tonight."

She eyed him and the acumen of years was evident in her appraisal. "I'll send the cook on along with you," she said. "You won't find home without some help, state you're in."

"No, don't want'im. Can't look for home anyway. Don't have one." Richard heard the thick blurring of his speech with an observer's clarity. Good. He sounded drunk. Maybe he'd start to feel drunk soon. He made his way to the docks with an occasional shove from another drunk along the way. By sheerest luck, he tumbled into the *Java*'s

334

gig, manned by a sleepy apprentice at the south end of the quay.

The last rays of the sun glossed the *Java*'s polished rails, and gave a kind of majesty to her. It gave him a momentary pleasure as they approached. He was vaguely surprised to see the whole crew aboard and realized he hadn't given orders regarding shore leave. By God, they were a good lot. Any other crew would have gone anyway and failed to leave even a watch.

There were one or two murmured greetings that died as he toppled over the side rail and fell to the deck. The wood was still hot, and smelled of sun-softened pitch between the planks. The odor cleared his head briefly. He looked around him. Men—all men—and knew he could not want for better shipmates. They ate together, suffered storms together, sang chanteys to a ripping turntide together, and tolerated one another's foibles. But they were men, with hairy backsides and loud, rough voices.

He longed for the softness of a woman, but not just any woman. Sometime in the past few months, he had passed the point where he wanted women in a general sense, where any body in the night would do. No, it was Margaret. She folded him in understanding. He had given his heart into her safekeeping, and the rest—the touching and the holding—just put the seal on it.

Oh, he wanted it all back, with a yearning that was painful. To find safe harbor with her, to be loved by her, had been the fulfillment of dreams he'd not even known he still cherished. The loneliness and the hurt of having had it and not having it anymore filled him with inconsolable loss. He wished with all his heart he'd never met her. It had been doomed from the start. Hellspawn like him didn't win angels. And she was. An angel. Maudlin grief inundated him, and knowing it for what it was didn't help him fend it off. She was all sunshine and beauty.

"'You are all light and I am all shadow,'" he said out loud. "Who the hell said that?"

Toby and one of the apprentices nearest him glanced at

335

each other and shrugged. Richard picked himself up off the deck. "Who the hell said that?" he repeated loudly.

Dekker appeared at his elbow. "I believe it was Cyrano de Bergerac, sir." He took Richard's elbow. "Can I help you find your berth, Captain?"

Richard peered at him. "Wise man, Cyrano. S'true, y'know."

"Yes, sir," Dekker agreed politely. Daniels appeared at Richard's other elbow and they maneuvered him aft, gently but firmly.

"Whole crew should read'im."

"Yes, sir," Dekker agreed.

"But first they should go ashore, have some fun," Richard said in sudden inspiration. He tottered and Daniels took more of his weight.

"Yes, sir, as soon as you're in your berth."

"By God, you're obsti . . . obstinin . . . stubborn," Richard pointed out.

"Yes, sir," Dekker said quietly.

"You're a good man," Richard persisted, "but stubborn."

Harkay appeared in their path. With a slow rumble, he stepped in front of Richard and slung him over his shoulder. Richard's belligerence went out of him in a heartbeat.

"You're a good crew," he said brokenly as Harkay thumped down the stairs into the saloon. "A damned good crew." Dogsmeat looked up from the table and set aside his copy of the *Illustrated London News*. Richard wanted to ask if he'd missed anything especially exciting, display a bond of friendship with another fine member of his crew, but the impulse was lost as Harkay passed him by and dumped Richard on the oversized berth in his quarters. There was barely room for the Polynesian to turn around and leave.

"Fine crew," Richard muttered. He felt unwell, like eels were swimming around where his brain ought to be. Dogsmeat came in and pulled his clothes off and Richard tried to tell him about the time after he'd been so sick, when he'd almost called the steward in to undress him so that he could make love to Margaret.

It knocked his thoughts back onto the course they never left for long. To be in love with her had been like having the breath sucked out of his body. She would breathe air back into him with a look, a touch, but now that she was gone, the void went unfilled. He went on breathing—air in, air out—but it wasn't the same. It didn't mean anything. And then he couldn't stop crying. He covered the length and width of the berth with his nakedness and sobbed with the frustration of not having her there.

It was hours later that Dogsmeat softly pushed the door open and saw the heavy, inert body laying in drunken stillness, twisted in the bedclothes.

"Captain?"

No answer. Dogsmeat looked at the battered telegram in his hand and back at the motionless body sprawled across the berth.

"Sir? There's sumthin' here you should be readin'."

The steward smoothed the paper between his fingers and read it again. He knew the captain hadn't read it—the envelope hadn't even been breached. It had been carelessly folded in with the paperwork required by the harbor master, a declaration of ship, of captain, of cargo.

Dogsmeat pursed his lips. How much chance was there of getting through the haze that surrounded his captain these days? It was almost visible, an aura that defied anyone to come closer. He was like a plague ship, something to be skirted, something that would take any who offered succor down with it. It frightened Dogsmeat, and he knew from their faces that it frightened the rest of the crew. He'd seen him in his cups before this, but never day after day, week after week, and all black humor in between. The very core of Richard Jensen was imperiled, crumbling bit by bit, leaving his skin drawn taut over the bare shell that was all that was left of him.

Would this message turn the tide? Dogsmeat sighed.

Not tonight, it wouldn't. Tomorrow he'd hide the liquor, all of it, and brave the storm long enough to make sure that the captain read it.

Margaret picked up the letters on the breakfast tray Eliza had set on the bed between her and Mora Bursey. Outside, down on Orchard Road, the merchants were coming to life, and already there were impassioned cries as drivers of bullock carts berated pedestrians meandering with early morning leisure down the center of the road. She shuffled through the envelopes as Mora spread jam on a rusk. She smiled. Jam on a rusk—it was a peculiarity she had grown accustomed to in the week Mora had been there. She smiled softly. What a good friend she was, and how welcome it was to have her here, no matter that her desire to lend aid and comfort was futile.

One letter caught Margaret's eye, and she pried the envelope open, cutting herself slightly in the process. She winced and wiped the speck of blood away with a napkin as she scanned Charles Townsend's neat, careful script. His message so confounded her that she lifted the letter and held it so that the morning light illuminated it more fully.

Finally she conceded defeat and said to Mora, "Listen to this and see if it makes any sense to you."

"May 14, 1870

My dear Margaret,

Bearing for you a great deal of affection—as you know—I could not help but want to learn as much as possible about your Captain Jensen, to assure myself that your decision to marry him would be a happy one. As your devoted friend, I could not do less.

Your spirited defense of him gave me cause to hope that he was, indeed, worthy of your love, and that I would be reassured by what I learned of him outside trading quarters. Regrettably, I

338

have learned some facts regarding him (unrelated, I hasten to add, to those which I conveyed to you on the occasion of our last meeting) which must alter your intentions.

I ask that you call on me at Townsend House at four o'clock today so that you can meet the informant who has brought these new facts to my attention. Knowing the strength of your feelings, I am sure you will be persuaded by nothing less than a direct interview with this informant. At Townsend House, at least, you can be assured of complete privacy.

Please send word if this will not be convenient. I remain your faithful servant, etc.

Charles"

Mora looked thoughtful. "I can think of no deep, dark secrets in Richard's past that would prevent you from marrying him," she finally said.

"I don't imagine there are any," Margaret sighed. "Charles is inclined to be very strict in his interpretation of what is proper. No doubt this is something which may alarm him but which won't concern me."

"So you'll go then?"

"Oh, certainly. Charles means well." Margaret picked listlessly at a bun. "I'm afraid that the only serious impediment is the one I created. I drove Richard away, Mora. How could I have been so weak?" The last words came out cracked with despair.

"It's not weak to falter before taking a big step," Mora said gently. "As long as you're clear in your mind that you mean to marry Richard now, the rest can be put straight. Even if your message doesn't reach him in Sydney. Ezekiel assured me that the pilots in the straits will pass the word that an M. Belleweather is attempting to reach him. Eventually Richard is bound to receive the message."

"But how can he forgive me?" Margaret said unhappily. "I sent him away—practically ordered him to leave." Margaret felt a tight welling of misery inside. "I wouldn't blame him if he never wanted to see me again."

"I sincerely doubt that that's the case," Mora said dryly. "My guess is that Richard will be so glad to hear that you've changed your mind that he'll come back as fast as he can." She sipped at her tea. "All the explaining can come later."

Margaret twiddled the handle on her cup, making it revolve around the saucer with a faint screech. "I feel so foolish, so everlastingly foolish. I know him well, Mora. It was the worst thing I could have done. He was always ready to turn his back on love and kindness, in some mistaken belief that those simple, ordinary things might come to others but never to him."

"You could be right, but that doesn't mean he won't see sense," Mora said firmly. "Let me tell you something. When I first met Ezekiel, I was at least as frightened of him as I was fascinated by him. He was so big, and hearty, and his voice was so deep. I loved to watch him across the room but whenever he got close, I got nervous. When I was quite sure I was falling in love with him, I felt nothing but terror." She laughed, a soft faraway look in her eyes.

"But Ezekiel is a lamb around you," Margaret protested. "It's obvious he adores you."

"He's not a complete lamb," Mora said with a flash of amusement, "but my mother told me something that changed the way I looked at him. She said that men needed women more than women needed men. It calmed me down to think that, even though I didn't believe her. Still, it was something to cling on to, and when Ezekiel first tried to kiss me, I managed not to be afraid by telling myself that he was as afraid as I was."

Margaret smiled in spite of her own heartache. "I can't imagine Ezekiel ever being afraid of you."

Mora's eyes grew warm and tender. "I couldn't either, in my heart of hearts, but it got me through that first kiss, and then I discovered that I liked being kissed by him so much that I was never afraid again."

"Then what a good thing your mother told you what she did, even if it *was* a hum," Margaret declared. "Look

340

what a wonderful marriage you have!"

Mora's expression softened. "Well, that was the funny thing—it wasn't a hum. My mother was right. Ezekiel confessed to me after we were married that he nearly didn't propose to me for fear I would turn him down. He said he almost walked away without asking, thinking it would be better to go away knowing he *might* have had me than knowing he couldn't."

Margaret stared at her, sobered by the thought. "I find that very nearly impossible to believe. Both of them— Richard and Ezekiel—seem as if nothing can scare them. I'm quite sure Richard had no such doubts when he proposed to me." Her face warmed as she recalled the love-making that had preceded his proposal.

Mora looked directly into Margaret's eyes. "Don't you believe it. I've come to realize that men don't have the least clue about women, except they know that they want them badly, and they want to be loved by them. Richard needs you as much as any man ever needed any woman, Margaret. Don't be fooled. They fight it, that need for love, because it leaves them feeling helpless. Most anything else they want they can get by brains or brawn, but they can't demand that you love them, and the more they need it, the more they'll fight it."

Margaret tracked the sound of a passing carriage with her eyes and then looked down. "I need it, too," she said softly. "I can't think why I ever thought otherwise, even for an instant. I was frightened, but I only started feeling weak once I walked away from Richard. When we were together, on the *Java*, I felt almost invincible just being near him."

"That's how I feel with Ezekiel," Mora said. "Being with him makes me strong. I've never felt, since the day we married, that there was anything I couldn't do as long as we were together. I could have been frightened—moving halfway around the world, leaving my family, having two children, facing all manner of trials and tribulations—but every night, when we're together, I know that I'll survive, and I'm happy, Margaret—truly happy."

Margaret felt the strength of Mora's love for Ezekiel in the room, like a living presence, and was touched by the intimacy of her revelation. "I think . . . that is, I'm sure it could be that way between Richard and me," she said quietly.

Mora reached out and covered Margaret's hand with her own. "I know it could, only you've got to remember that deep inside, he's not as sure of himself as he seems. You've got to be strong enough for both of you. If you aren't, you'll regret it for the rest of your life."

Margaret let a soft smile tug at the corners of her mouth. "Richard said something like that. He said he'd always be in my head, even when I wasn't with him."

"And he will, but it can either be as regret for what might have been, or as joy, for what is. You must be prepared to fight, Margaret. Use whatever means you can, but don't give up!"

"I won't," Margaret said. "I need him too much, and I know he needs me."

"Yes, he does," Mora said firmly. "Keep that fact firmly in your sights." She withdrew and straightened her back, as if the deed was as good as done. "Now, as much as I wish I didn't have to go, I must. I swore to Ezekiel that I wouldn't stay more than a week, and that means, I simply must catch the noon packet, else he'll be fuming and storming up and down the dock in Anjer until I *do* disembark."

"I'm sorry to have kept you away from Ezekiel and the children," Margaret said. "You didn't really have to come."

"Don't be silly! After that second telegram, wild horses couldn't have kept me away. Ezekiel says you can leave it to Richard to sort out all that other nonsense, about running guns and bilking chandlers. It was you I was worried about, and truth to tell, I've enjoyed this time away."

"Pardon, ma'am."

They glanced up to see Eliza in the door.

"I've finished packing your things, all but the outfit

342

you've chosen for today. Shall I have Hoc Sing draw a bath for you now?"

"Yes, please," Mora replied. "Thank you, Eliza."

As soon as Eliza had gone, Mora turned to Margaret with a conspiratorial smile. "Besides," she said wickedly, "I've never had a lady's maid to wait on me. How could I pass up the chance?"

Margaret thought later, as she grasped the wrought iron fence that ringed the dock and watched Mora's boat steaming away, that her friend was far too wise to have her mistaken dross for gold. She might enjoy being waited on by a proper ladies' maid, and wearing nice clothes, but she would never have done as Margaret had done, and let fear and habit stand in the way of love. Instead of letting the thought further demoralize her, Margaret raised her parasol with determination and got back into the pony trap. She was firmly resolved that Richard would never have cause to doubt her again.

When Margaret arrived at Townsend House, the veranda was conspicuously void of servants. Charles himself descended the stairs and escorted her into the front salon. A woman rose nervously from the striped settee by the window, but the small child with her remained seated.

"I am sorry if it distresses you to hear it," Charles said without preamble, "but this woman—Emma Jensen—is Captain Jensen's wife. And this boy here . . ." He swept a careless hand toward the solemn-faced child. ". . . is his son, Jack."

Margaret didn't want to believe it. The woman was slight and pale, her hair an unbelievable shade of yellow, but the resemblance to herself sparked an uneasy frisson that trailed down her spine. And the boy. She let herself see him only through the corner of her eye. It was just as she had imagined Richard might have looked as a small child, watchful and withdrawn, too much weight on little shoulders for any lightness of spirit.

Charles seemed impatient for some kind of response but

she had none. If it was true, it was true. Only a fool argued with facts. The boy more than the woman convinced her that she was staring an unpleasant truth right in the face.

"Have you come to find him?" Her voice was emotionless. In her core, feeling wrestled with feeling, a veritable emotional melee, but toward the top, which was all she allowed herself to feel, there was nothing but calmness.

"Aye, miss. He left us behind in Charleston, but I've searched for him ever since, as far as my purse would allow." Her flat American accent grated on Margaret's ear; it was nothing like the soft, easy sound of Mora Bursey's. "Word was that he was drunk at the time, so maybe he misunderstood."

Charleston—true. Drunk—another truth. Richard had admitted to that.

"Misunderstood what?" Margaret asked. If she was to deal in facts, she must have them all.

The woman faced her, with her chin up, her eyes wide open. "I went off to see my mother, miss, and stayed longer than I'd intended. It may be he was told, and then again, maybe he didn't get the message. Things were bad in Charleston, then. That's why I went, to get Jack away from it for a bit."

"Your mother?" Margaret was on the verge of saying that Richard had said Emma was without living family, but that would be tantamount to admitting she'd had some inkling of this woman's existence. It was a high fence, this—truth on one side, lies on the other. She chose to walk along the edge of it anyway, contribute nothing herself, until she knew which side Richard's story fell on. Humiliation hammered at her heart, too. Charles's expression said that he was prepared to humor her, be a gentleman about this whole sordid mess, even if it should prove that Margaret *had* known Richard Jensen was already married.

Charles's intuition failed him in little. He *knew* she'd had some knowledge of this woman before she walked into the room, ferreted it out of the simple question, 'Your mother?' Perspicacity was all well and good but she

344

wished it had deserted him on that one small point. Of course she knew. Else why question the existence of someone's mother? Everyone had one.

The woman—Emma—looked at her in mild anticipation. "My mother, miss? What about my mother?"

"Your mother lives some distance from Charleston?" Margaret asked. Play it out, she thought. "Someplace Rich . . . Captain Jensen wouldn't have come looking for you?"

The woman lowered her head, looking at the tips of the cheap shoes that peeped out from under her gray dress, "He didn't know about my mother," she said hesitantly. She looked up again, clear-eyed. "I told her I'd married a fine gentleman. Richard was—*is*—no better than he has to be, as I expect you know. I loved—*love*—him, but I knew she wouldn't think he was grand enough. I figured it would be better to tell a little lie to both sides."

"Yes, of course," Margaret said dully. Another piece of Richard's story dropped neatly into the puzzle. She hadn't told him about her mother so why would he have gone looking for her? Truth and lies. Whose truth and whose lies? She looked at Emma again. "Miss . . . Mrs. Jensen, would you care to have tea with me, you and Jack?" The title 'Mrs. Jensen' burned like lye on her tongue.

Emma looked over to Charles and raised her eyebrows in mute interrogation. Why did she look to *him* for permission? Charles cleared his throat, well aware of the unspoken question. "Shall I have tea brought to the garden?" he asked Margaret.

Emma looked back toward Margaret. "Since Mr. Townsend has no objection, yes—I'd like to take tea."

Margaret repressed a shudder. *Take* tea—an affectation of the lower classes, vulgar in the extreme. "In the garden would be fine," Margaret said. She felt the tension in the room like palpable clouds, billowing around them. They seemed a strange triumvirate, each aligned to the other in uncertain ways, their conversation seeming disjointed unless one knew that. "Please," she said to Charles, "don't let us detain you any further from business."

If she hadn't been distracted by thoughts running deeper, it would have sounded like the dismissal it was. As it was, it sounded like sincere concern for Charles's convenience. He crossed to her and took her hand, brushing the backs of her knuckles with a kiss.

"Of course, my dear. I'm sorry to have been the one to bring this to your attention."

Just when she thought she would burst into tears at this offer of solicitude which she so desperately needed, he withdrew his hand and put on a bluffer facade, also intended to ease her distress. "Only don't lose sight of the fact that there is the musicale tonight. I'll send the carriage back from the office for Mrs. Jensen, but I'll need it to come round for me again by six o'clock."

"Of course. Thank you, Charles." His tolerance and sensitivity inspired a rush of gratitude in her. She found she could rise above her own concerns long enough to smile up at him and mean it.

As soon as he was gone, Margaret led the way to the garden, feeling nearly as at home at Townsend House as she did at Pensleigh. Little Jack was like a shade, unchildlike in the extreme, so quiet and still as he sat on a garden bench. The watchful brown eyes gave Margaret an uneasy sense of being spied on by Richard's young self. Emma, too, seemed to have nothing to say, although she looked around and seemed reasonably at ease. It wasn't that Jack seemed ill at ease precisely which bothered Margaret, only that his eyes never left her, those huge brown windows on the world.

Margaret turned suddenly. "What color are Richard's eyes?" she asked Emma.

Emma looked at her in blank puzzlement. "His eyes?"

Margaret felt the wind go out of her sails. Emma didn't seem the least bit distressed by the question, as if the answer would be easy enough to give once she knew the cause of the question.

"I imagine you know the color of his eyes well enough," Emma said. "Why do you ask?"

Margaret felt a little breathless, as if she were skirting

the edge of a shore where rocks lay concealed just below the water's surface. "I see that Jack's eyes are brown, and that your eyes are blue," she said. "I'm a student of inherited traits. Pray tell me, what color are his father's eyes?"

Emma lowered her eyes for the second time that day. Margaret felt her rib cage straining at the contours of her bodice. Either she knew or she didn't. One could not forget those cat's eyes, not in three lifetimes. She allowed fair time for memory to do its work and when no answer was forthcoming, she sat down and folded her hands in her lap calmly.

"Who are you really?" she asked.

Chapter 21

She got to the door before either Eliza or John, wondering which of her nightmares was going to come to life, which of them lurked on the other side and would become reality as soon as she opened the door. It was the middle of the night and deceptively cool-looking moonlight had been playing over the rose-patterned rug in her bedroom while she lay in the still, hot night, fending off sleep. She had arrived in the vestibule first, the only one in the house without sleep to brush out of her eyes.

She stood there so long, afraid to find out what was making the faint rustling and scraping on her veranda, that John appeared, his face bleary with dreams. He was tying a dressing gown around himself. It had been one of her father's, a handsome maroon and gold striped one, and she had not wanted to see it go moldering in the master's dressing room at Pensleigh.

The insignificant thought was a delaying tactic and she knew it. She stood poised with her hand on the warm brass doorknob, unwilling to go forward or back. Nightmares came in the night, and bad news. Her nightmares had proliferated in recent weeks, populated with strange, unearthly demons that pulled her this way and that with gaunt, ferociously strong arms. She knew who they were for all their inhuman appearances. One was Richard, the most demonic of all, his face tortured and his shade insistent on drawing her down deeper into the flaming, smoking pit he called home. Another was, must be, Sarah Coit, long hair streaming out behind her, never the same color for long, but each color it shifted to less plausibly human than the last.

And then there was Charles, in a garishly checked suit, like some tout at the seamier entrances to a racecourse, with a wooden case propped against his chest and suspended from his neck by a worn leather strap. The case shifted every now and then, revealing a black stain spreading across his shirt front. Margaret did not know what it signified but the emotion it provoked was undiluted horror. She closed her eyes, a shiver of terror walking down her neck and across her back.

She opened her eyes again as John paused beside her, giving one last tug on the tasseled cord at his waist. It had not taken as long to feel all those nightmare figures as she had thought. They were so familiar that they seldom left her. Only Jack and Christian were exempted from the suffering, wandering through the flaming cesspool without apparent torment, although she suspected that it was because their waking moments were as bad as anything the pit could produce. Jack merely watched, the same in her dreams as by the light of day, always watching, never giving away his thoughts by so much as a quiver or a blink. Christian had begun to fade of late though, and his was the only figure that never came close enough for her to see clearly through the looping, sulphurous mist.

"Miss? Do you mean to be opening the door?"

"Yes, I do," Margaret answered tiredly. She knew that anything that awaited on the other side of the door at this hour could not be pleasant. The knock came again, soft and urgent. John, perhaps thinking he had misunderstood her, removed her hand from the doorknob ever so delicately and opened the door himself.

"Master Christian!" he cried. He pulled the door open wide so abruptly that he nearly knocked Margaret over. The light behind them in the entry way sputtered and flared as Eliza's hand faltered in the act of adjusting the flame, making shadows leap and dance over the odd assortment of characters within its reach.

It was the pit. Margaret recognized it a second too late to shut out the vision in front of her. The shadowy, flaming abyss of her nightmare had come to life. Richard stood in the farthest recesses of the lamp's scope, his face strained with the effort of holding the burden in his arms. Margaret felt faint, weak with an appalling sense of déjà vu as she saw the near-corpse in his arms, with its untidy cap of shining gold hair, head lolling back and eyes closed.

John rushed to take Christian from Richard's arms but Richard warned him off with a violent throw of his head. "He's not as light as he looks," he snapped. "Just show me where to put him."

Margaret clutched the edge of the door and fought off the white spots swimming in front of her. Sweat ran down Richard's face, a cold, cruel-looking face that neatly paralleled the nightmare figure in her dreams, and Christian— he, too, looked as she had seen him, except that now she was close enough to see the sores and lesions that the smoky shadows had hidden in the dreams.

They were frozen in the moment, looking to her for guidance. She managed to unstick her tongue from the roof of her mouth. "Show him, John," she said.

John hurried down the hall toward the third, and only unoccupied, bedroom in the main part of the bungalow. The dressing gown flapped around his bare white legs and Eliza turned and followed him, her face distorted by the light from the unevenly trimmed lantern. Richard brushed past Margaret without a glance and she heard his heavier tread and the hushed, anxious voices of the two servants as they rushed to make accommodation for Christian.

Margaret followed reluctantly, stopping to adjust the turnkey on the lantern with slow deliberation, until it burned exactly as it should. She went on past the bedroom door and the murmuring inside, down the hall into the kitchen, with slow, carefully controlled steps. She lit the lantern in the kitchen, too. Sanity came out of small things, like lighting the gas flame on the stove and setting

350

water to boil for tea, and her hands knew it.

She heard John and Eliza rushing up and down the hall, fetching linens and towels and basins. Margaret sat down with elaborate care, like someone with aching muscles, and lay her hands on the table. Without something purposeful to do, they flopped lifelessly, palms up. The news about Christian, such as it was, would find her soon enough.

Richard appeared in the doorway. His expression was grim and dark, and his fists were curled at his sides. His shirt was still askew where Christian's weight had pulled at it. She looked up and met his eyes, narrow and green, and filled with some terrible combination of fury and bitterness and fear.

"Should I go to him?" she asked, her voice sluggish with dread.

"He's out," Richard said curtly. "Maybe in the morning."

"Then he won't die tonight?" It came out as an emotionless whisper.

Richard shifted his weight and the hard edges of his face softened as the light filled the contours of his cheeks. Sweat still glistened around his temples. He took a breath and exhaled sharply. "Not tonight."

"Do you want some tea?" It sounded callow, like a young girl belatedly remembering the first stricture of etiquette.

Richard merely looked at her, his gaze drifting across her face and loosened hair, and down the front of her pale yellow wrapper. He wiped his open hands across his thighs uneasily. "No," he said, "I have to go."

That penetrated. "Did you get my message?"

He went so still that she knew he had, and she also knew it was the kind of stillness that precedes flight.

"Stay," she said suddenly. It fell into the deepening silence between them and she panicked. Standing up so quickly that the chair nearly tipped over behind her, Margaret unleashed her only weapon. If he could not find it in his heart to forgive her for pushing him away, maybe

351

she could hold him a little longer with Jack.

"I want you to see someone," she said.

With hands not calm and efficient anymore, she lit a small oil lamp, fumbling with the match as Richard stood motionless in the door. She started toward it and he stepped back into the hallway so quickly that it wrenched at something inside her, speaking as it did of revulsion and rejection. She walked blindly down the hall, tears blurring the flame in front of her. After a moment in which she heard only the swishing of her own wrapper, she heard the creak of floorboards behind her. She took a deep breath and clenched the lamp tighter as she stopped by the second bedroom.

She felt Richard's heat and breadth behind her but she did not turn for fear of making him draw away. Raising the lamp, she let its light fall on the small, sleeping shape on the bed. At first Richard did not move but then, slowly, he came around her. She forced herself to remain still, only raising the lamp higher as he skirted her. The smell of sea and salt and tar touched her as he passed, and she inhaled deeply, forgetting where she was for the moment, until she heard the stifled sound in his throat.

"Jack?" It came out a hoarse, disbelieving whisper.

Richard moved across the room with his smooth, rolling gait and dropped to his knees by the edge of the bed. His large, dark head shadowed the smaller one on the pillow, and Margaret lifted the lamp still higher so that he could see Jack. He reached out a trembling hand to push the hair off the boy's face and then stopped, burying his head in his hands instead. Jack murmured and rolled toward him, deep in sleep, his mouth working softly. The short, thick lashes fluttered briefly and then sank down again. Another minute passed and Richard raised his head, his broad back tight with concentration. Margaret saw his head move, and she imagined the penetrating look in his eyes as he took in every detail, from the dark, shining brown hair that was brushed into ruthless order each morning and went its own disorderly way in the night, down to the small, blunt hands relaxed in sleep. At last

Richard stood up, not even bracing his hands on the bed, but rising out of his own power straight off the floor.

Margaret led the way back to the kitchen, trying not to read too much into the haunted look on Richard's face that showed briefly in the flick of lamp light before she turned her back. His footsteps sounded dull and heavy behind her, and she held her breath as she entered the kitchen, half expecting him to simply continue on down the hall and out the front door into the night. But he followed her.

There was so much to say that she could not say any of it. Without looking behind her, she gestured to the table and heard the scrape of a chair as Richard sat down. She released her taut stomach muscles as she brewed tea, setting a cup in front of him and then another opposite, for herself. Richard was staring straight ahead, the bridge of his nose pinched and deep lines curving around from his nose to his mouth, outlining some deep distress. Too frightened to sit and begin the talk that might be their last, Margaret went to the sitting room, feeling the bite of the straw matting under her bare feet as one would feel cold water dashed in one's face. She returned with a glass of whiskey and set it next to the tea.

Richard had let his head fall forward into his hands, running strong brown fingers through his disheveled hair. His shirtsleeve fell back, revealing a dirty strip of cloth covering his forearm.

"You've hurt yourself," Margaret said dispassionately. "It wants a clean dressing." She filled a bowl with hot water left in the kettle and assembled scissors, clean cloth, and disinfectant. He resisted only a little when she pulled his arm toward her.

Touching him gave her renewed hope. His scent rose to her nostrils and the feel of the hard muscles overlaid with the thick, dark hair reminded her of how very much she loved him. Strength and determination took root as she cut the bandage away. Little as it was, this service she could do was something tangible, something to show she cared, and also, just possibly, a way to gentle him into staying a while longer, until the important things could be said.

The injury itself was curious, a long, curving gouge of flesh from one side of his wrist up and over the soft skin of his inner arm to the inside of his elbow on the other side. It had been cleaned before but there wasn't much else to be done for it, a deep channel of missing flesh so profound that stitching together the sides could not even be contemplated. She swabbed it gently, satisfied that it had not reddened though it looked days old.

Richard sat without moving or speaking but Margaret was undaunted. Make it plain and natural, she thought, as natural as it had been between them on the *Java*. "How did you do this?" she said conversationally. She was pleased to hear that the strain she was feeling didn't show in her voice.

"Rope," he said. "A line snapped."

It was said somewhat churlishly but Margaret felt satisfied that at least he was talking. "All that lovely new rope," she said idly, wrapping the fresh bandage around and around. "I suppose it has to get seasoned or something."

"No, I just wasn't paying attention. It was a stupid mistake," Richard said. Margaret braced his arm against her hip and snipped the bandage end lengthwise so that she could secure it. "We had to cast off in a hurry," he added in a mumble.

"Oh?" Margaret tidied the supplies on the table and sat down. "Did it have anything to do with Atam Datu?"

He looked up at her sharply. "How did you know?"

"It didn't take any great leap of intelligence," she said. "You had to have gone there to get Christian. Why, Richard?" She saw his brows draw together. "I'm appreciative, of course, but why?"

He stirred restlessly, his gaze sliding away. "I had to go see who's been trading in guns up there. Naturally, I looked Christian up. He was in no condition to stay there."

354

"What's wrong with him?" Margaret toyed with her spoon, tracing the ivy pattern on the saucer with a sense of dread. She stared at Richard's dark, hawkish profile, waiting for an answer.

"Something that's probably going to kill him sooner or later," he said shortly. "That's all I can tell you."

Margaret digested that, surprised to find that it didn't surprise her. The dreams had somehow prepared her. She felt a certain numb inevitability that kept her from wanting to go to Christian, knowing that the living issue, the future, was here at this table. "You said you 'naturally' went to see him. Is it because he has something to do with the guns?"

Richard sliced a penetrating look at her. "I never got an answer to that. Maybe, maybe not."

Margaret felt a ripple of impatience. It wasn't what she wanted to be talking about. "The message I sent, Richard—I meant it. I'm sorry for the way I behaved before. I don't expect you to understand, or even to forgive me. It was really unforgivable, but I do hope it's not too late for us to at least talk about it."

He shrugged without looking up. His hand found the glass of whiskey and jiggled it, making the liquid slop over the edges. "Where did you find Jack?" he asked.

"Charles found him, actually," Margaret said, and regretted mentioning Charles's name the instant she'd said it. Richard flinched and drew away from the table. "His stepmother doesn't want him."

"His stepmother?" Richard's eyes held confusion and pain. "What happened to Emma?"

"She died, Richard. He hasn't really anyone left, except you. I thought that you would want me to keep him here until you could . . . well, make some arrangements."

"I can't offer him anything," Richard said bitterly, "except a berth as an apprentice, and he's too young for that."

"But he's your . . ." Margaret stopped. She saw the legacy of the past in the sadness in his eyes. "Surely you

355

don't mean to disown him, not now?"

Richard looked up wearily. "He's not my son, you know."

"No, I didn't know," Margaret said carefully.

Richard sloshed the whiskey around in the glass, staring at it. "He was already three months old when I met Emma. I came off the *Java* one night, just looking for a place to get away from . . . everything. It was wet and cold, with a hellish wind coming off the harbor. I was heading toward a tavern when I saw a woman who'd taken shelter in a doorway. I couldn't believe that any human meant to take shelter there and then I saw a bundle at her feet. It made a mewing sound, like a cat, and I realized it was a baby."

Richard's face went tight, his eyes distant and vague. "I was forced to conclude that she not only meant to take shelter there, but that she meant for the baby to as well. You can't imagine how I felt." He stared at the wall and Margaret saw desolation on his face. "I took them to the tavern and before they'd even warmed up properly, I knew what I would do. Emma told me her story, abandoned by her husband, no way to support herself, short of the thing she'd been on the verge of trying."

He ran his finger around the top of the glass and licked the whiskey off it. He grimaced and set the glass aside. "Don't think I didn't appreciate the irony," he said with a harsh laugh. "I was following in Gunnar Jansson's footsteps, and no mistake. But I fell in love with that baby, so help me God, I did. I'd never even held a baby until then. He was warm and soft, and he just molded himself to me, no matter how I held him."

He put his elbows on the table and leaned forward, resting his forehead on his hands. "I found them a little house on the waterfront, set Emma up with enough money to last each time I went away. And Jack started to know me. He was glad to see me whenever I came, and always smiled at me, even if I'd been gone two months . . ."

He trailed off, leaving Margaret sitting alone in the silence of her own memories. His grief was evident in the set of his shoulders, the loss overwhelming even now.

356

Margaret could not begin to summon the words which would justify intruding on it. She stood and lit the stove to make more tea.

At last she said, hesitantly, "Can you not love him still, even though he *is* another man's son?"

Richard pushed away off his hands and threw his head back with a mirthless laugh that bared his teeth. "Don't you see the dilemma? I do. It doesn't matter whose he is."

"Then there is no dilemma," she said quickly. "This woman, his stepmother, says her husband is not Jack's natural father either, though he *was* Emma's husband. She said they would gladly give over custody, sign any necessary papers. He is unwanted, Richard, and that is surely the cruelest fate of all. You could make a home for him now, and I . . ."

Richard went still, his eyes narrowed. "Could you love him?" he asked.

Margaret looked down. "As absurd as it may sound, I already do."

"Then make a home for him, Maggie." His voice was brittle, the suggestion peremptory. "You can do that, can't you?"

"Me?" Margaret was filled with bewilderment. "Why could we not, the two of us . . ."

"Because I can't be a part of it, Maggie," he said tiredly. His expression was rueful and strained in the pale light. "There was a time, not long ago, when I had something to offer him, and you. Now all I have is a ship that's fired on by every pirate and Dutchman from here to Papeete. Even if I handed the *Java* over, it wouldn't be enough. They want my blood now. I'm like a spider to them. They want to step on me so they don't have to look at me anymore."

"Then there are other places," Margaret said carefully, afraid of frightening the tiger away when he was so close to eating from her hand. "We can go back to England. We could live at Pensleigh."

Richard shook his head. "I can't do that, Maggie. Trouble follows me, always has. I go along well enough for a while, but sooner or later, it all comes crashing in.

357

I'm cursed, Maggie, I'm bad seed. Jack's lucky not to be my son. The farther I stay away from him and you, the better off you'll both be."

Margaret felt an icy uncertainty in her veins. He seemed prepared to fend off every possible avenue of happiness. "But that's superstitious nonsense," she said. "We could be a family, you and I and Jack. We could take the *Java* and go anywhere you like. We don't have to live at Pensleigh."

"I like the idea of Jack at Pensleigh," Richard said slowly, his eyes vacant as he pictured it. "He'd grow up knowing he was loved. I know you'd see to his education. He'd have a fine future with you."

She felt him slipping away. He seemed to have left the room already, although he sat there, solid and real in a chair in front of her. The skin on his hands was dry, with white scratches across the backs, and the smell of sun and sea hung on him, all proof that he was there in the flesh, but he was like a ghost. It was as if she were casting lines to a ship, one after the other, but no one was on board to catch them. The ship was drifting away, covered with lines, none of which found a hand to take it, a hand to wrap it securely to a cleat.

"Why, Richard?" she cried desperately. "Is it because of me? Because of what I did? I'm sorry, terribly sorry, but please don't punish me for it, or Jack!"

He stood up slowly and looked down at her, tiredness creasing his face. He motioned toward the bedrooms where Jack and Christian lay. "You go to Pensleigh," he said. "Take them with you. Make them a home. I'm sorry to put it all on you, Maggie, but I just can't do it. I've tried and I've tried, but whatever it is that a man needs to make a home, I don't have. I'd just take you down with me eventually."

"No! That's not true!" Margaret leaped to her feet, cold with anger and fear.

"I'll come see you sometimes, if I can," he said as if she hadn't spoken. "I'm sorry, Maggie."

Margaret watched him go, weighed down by a mantle of

defeat. She was nearly helpless with fury and afraid to open her mouth, afraid that if she did, she would call him unspeakable things that would only drive a bigger wedge between them. Coward was only the first of them.

Jack needed her, Christian needed her, but she needed Richard, and he had turned away. Damn him! She sat down again, exhausted by the struggle. His demons had won.

Christian did not last long. He wasted away gently, with good humor, another ghost ship in her life. He was glad to see John, happy to talk about Pensleigh, and even asked Margaret to read to him from the Bible. The doctor who came took one look at the lesions covering his torso and limbs and left the room. Margaret pursued him as far as his carriage, snatching his medical bag from him to make him stop and talk to her.

The rude unexpectedness of it offended him as much as Christian's disease. He rounded on her and told her, in sharp, swift strokes, what ailed Christian and why he would die of it. Margaret covered her mouth with her hands as he added his own moral assessment of the situation, and said that under no circumstances would he treat a bugger for the consequences of sin.

Margaret reeled away and collapsed on the steps as his carriage rattled down the drive. Tight, painful contractions gripped her chest and she only gradually recognized them as dry sobs. Eliza came out and tried to draw her inside, out of the noonday sun, but Margaret waved her away. She gripped the edges of the wooden steps, dragging her fingernails over the grain of the wood, again and again, until they bled. It was Jack who finally persuaded her to go in.

He came and sat by her, silent and grave, as she stared at the treetops beyond the garden. The sea breeze rifled through them and made a bland picture of randomness that trapped her thoughts and held them still. When Jack took her hand and dabbed with his small white handkerchief at the blood there, she looked down at him in surprise. When she saw in his large brown eyes that her pain was causing him pain, she was overcome by remorse and she let him lead her into the house.

Christian was very sweet to all of them, accepting their ministrations with patient gratitude, but most of the time he was adrift in another world. He declined food, all except for tea and the buttered bread that Eliza baked fresh each morning to tempt his appetite. He said it reminded him of Pensleigh, and of being a child.

Jack took on the task of carrying the trays in. Eliza resisted at first, wanting to serve the master herself, but Jack would meet her at the doorway of the kitchen and put his hands on the tray. When she refused to relinquish it, he merely stood there without a word, looking up at her with sober implacability. The quiet struggle for possession of the tray took less and less time each day, until Eliza conceded defeat, merely setting it on the kitchen table. Jack would come to get it, always seeming to know exactly when she had just finished steeping the tea and buttering the bread.

He read to Christian, too, from the Bible. Margaret paused outside the door the first day he did it, surprised into utter stillness by the confidence in the childish voice. He stumbled over some of the words, sounding them out awkwardly until Christian supplied the word in a voice which became a whisper as the weeks passed. Jack would resume reading, clearly and confidently, until the next word that he couldn't parse, and they would start the process all over again.

Margaret could imagine Richard at the same age, reading just the same way. From the sound of it, Jack had taught himself to read, just as Richard had once confessed to her that he had, early on, at an age when no one would have even thought to try teaching him. They were so alike, Richard and Jack. The physical resemblance was not astonishing in and of itself, but the similarity in temperament was. She had been so sure they were father and son, but now the similarity seemed to be just an odd coincidence.

It didn't matter anymore, Margaret thought. It was only one of the many unanswered questions that revolved through her tired mind. Jack was as much her child as Richard's now—more really, since Richard refused to be a father to him whereas she was quite willing to be his mother. She loved him fiercely, and was determined that he would lose some of his unnatural, unchildish gravity, and feel some of the carefree happiness all children deserved to have. She would love him, and give him the security to lay down his adult burdens.

But not at Pensleigh. She had given up on that idea for the time being. Christian would not survive a trip of that magnitude, and she had no other reason for going there if Richard would not come with them. She would simply stay in Singapore and hope that Richard would leave his private hell every now and then, just long enough to come and see the boy occasionally. Just as in Makassar, Margaret found that her choices were few and simple. She went to the offices of Townsend and Townsend nearly every day, to exercise her mind and to keep herself apprised of what ships came and went. The *Java*, she knew, had left with another load of coal. She knew that Richard could go on sailing, of course, and never return to Singapore, but she locked him in her heart and willed him to stay nearby. All the while she wrestled with ledger columns that would not balance, and fretted over them with an increasingly agitated Mr. Coggins, or watched Jack at play in the garden on Cluny Road with An Wu's children, she schemed quietly, weighing what she might do to win Richard back.

His pride was an issue, but soon enough his debt to her would be paid. It suited her to think that once he was out from under it, he might feel free to come to her again, but then she would agonize over the reverse possibility, that he would sail away, never to be heard from again, once he had discharged the obligation. As for his demons, she could not fight them for him. All she could do was stay solidly where she was, proving her steadfastness by being where he could find her, and welcoming him with open arms if he did come.

Charles she kept at arm's length. He apologized over and over for having been the unwitting dupe of Sarah Coit, admitting that he had offered a reward for information regarding Richard Jensen's past. It was that which had brought her forth, but Margaret could not escape the obvious, that she *had* known about Emma. Charles castigated himself for believing her, and for having paid her the promised money, and seemed so sincerely overwrought by the false accusation he had brought against Richard that Margaret forgave him readily. She, too, had nearly been persuaded, but she could not help harboring a lingering distrust of Charles long after she had accepted his mea culpa. That it had more to do with her nightmare visions of him than hard fact was so irrational that she pushed it to the farthest recesses of her mind.

Christian died, sweetly and quietly, in her arms one night, as a light rain pattered on the thatched roof. So much of her went with him that she simply sat there, motionless, until morning, when John came in and found them. She sat through the night, mentally ticking off all the memories she had shared with Christian and no one else. Without him to remember them with her, it was as if half her life had never happened. Paper kites made in a rainy day nursery against the certainty of bright, windy days to come; hot cocoa cadged from the cook and drunk under the stairwell to the servant's quarters, lest their nurse discover them and complain that they were ruining their supper; a cherished cat run over by a delivery man's cart and buried with full honors in the rose garden.

Christian had been so beautiful to look at. She avoided looking at him again when the mortician came and took away the body, preferring to remember him as he had been, with the face of an angel. Anything he'd said had had the power to enthrall her, coming from those beautiful lips. The sparkling blue eyes, always full of amusement,

362

and the gilt hair, a shade lighter than hers—to be with him had been complete nourishment of her eyes and of her soul. He had liked to comb her hair and she had let him, knowing she had the best of the bargain as she watched his handsome face and clever fingers in the mirror.

She tried to turn Jack away from the final trip to the cemetery, high on Singapore Hill, but he stood imperturbably at the carriage until she was seated and then climbed in beside her, his lips set firmly, his back straight and unyielding. Charles came and made a small sound of disapproval and Margaret shrugged. Her heart was too miserably sore to make an issue of the matter.

The day was extraordinarily, indecently beautiful. It grieved her to see how lovely the world looked on the day when she must put Christian into the ground. How unjust that he should not be living and breathing in it! But as the carriages climbed the hill and passed the botanical gardens until the whole of the European quarter spread out below them, she saw a certain balance in it. From the sea, Singapore looked utterly English, with tidy church spires and monumental public buildings, but now she could see the Chinese kampong over her left shoulder, and, down to the right, the flashing domes of mosques in the Arab kampong and gilded cupolas in the Indian quarter. It was all beautiful, and yet not quite what it seemed, like Christian.

She found some peace in the thought, and she let Richard's words come back in force, too. Christian had made his own choices. His choices had been antithetical to his heritage but it was not for her to judge him. *Oh, Richard,* she thought. *I wish you were here.* She wanted so much to draw on his strength, to feel his arms around her, but instead it was Charles who steadied her across the open ground and stood at her side by the gravesite. She held Jack in front of her, clutching his insubstantial shoulders under her gloved hands.

Mrs. Townsend and Susan were there, and though no one else came who would bear testimony to their proximity, they distanced themselves from Margaret, standing stiffly on the far side of the plot. The story was all over Singapore by now that Lady Margaret Belleweather had taken in her lover's bastard, and they did not seem to think that even she could weather such an infamous undertaking. It did not concern Margaret nearly as much as how Jack might be feeling, but he maintained his composure throughout. She hoped that in the days and nights to come he would talk with her about Christian, and she found a measure of satisfaction in knowing that in some way, Christian and Jack had struck up a bond that had comforted them both.

Mr. Coggins, fussy Mr. Coggins, with his ink-stained fingers and flyaway ginger-colored hair, arrived at the last minute, bringing with him several of the clerks from the offices. Margaret acknowledged them with a quiet smile that proceeded from a warm glow deep inside. They had come out of respect for her and she felt tears rise to her eyes. A few other men milled in the background uneasily— friends of Charles, she supposed, doing him a favor by preventing the service from being embarrassingly devoid of mourners.

The minister Charles had engaged was terse, bringing the barest civility to the standard words, and Margaret let her eyes drift out over Singapore bay as he delivered the clipped and frozen eulogy which had nothing whatever to do with Christian Belleweather. The wind was strong up on the hill, and Margaret felt the way she had on the *Java* at times, as if the next gust might carry her away. The sheen of water in the channels stretching away for miles toward the open sea dazzled her, and she wished with all her heart that she was a bird and could fly over them and find the *Java*.

And then she saw it. She blinked hard, sure that it was the product of her intense longing to see it, but when she looked again, it was still there, out beyond the three-fathom shoal line. The sun caught the narrow gold stripe that lined the hull near the bulwarks, and she saw the unmistakable mix of newer white sails and the creamier old ones that had survived the storm. She averted her glance quickly, hoping that no one had noticed.

Something that had escaped her until now suddenly dawned on her with stunning impact. Richard had brought Christian back to her. The price of taking him away from Atam Datu must have been the promised guns. If he'd been running guns, it was because of her!

She nearly forgot the rest of the funeral party, wandering dazedly to a tree and stopping in its shade. She stared blindly at the ground. She knew for a fact that Richard had not been carrying guns when she sailed with him. All his troubles were her fault. Well, not all. Even in her distress she had had enough presence of mind to realize that there were other issues: his pride, her money; his demons, her fears.

Charles's voice interrupted her train of thought.

"He's back, isn't he? That's his ship out beyond the quarantine mooring."

Margaret stared up at Charles, startled. "I . . . I don't know," she stammered. It didn't sound very convincing. She tried again. "I mean, I thought it might be, but . . ."

Charles smiled, gently, sadly. "You've got to stop trying to protect him, Margaret. It's a losing battle, I'm afraid."

A bubble of protest formed in her throat and lodged there. Charles took her hand and massaged it through her glove, softly rubbing his thumb across the pleats on the back. His pale blue eyes searched hers, his expression regretful but firm.

"Information has been lodged with the magistrate, Margaret, to the effect that Richard Jensen stole the *Java* from her rightful owner in the United States. He repainted her and renamed her and sailed as far away as he could, but the witness is quite sure of the facts. The authorities in this part of the world can overlook a great deal, but the theft of a ship is something which cuts across all the lines. Jensen will be taken into custody if he drops anchor, and the *Java* impounded while the matter is investigated."

"But . . . but . . ." Margaret felt as if all her blood was draining out through her feet. It left her head first.

"Oh, dear," Charles murmured. He whistled sharply

and took her elbow, putting his other arm around her waist. The piercing sound of his whistle rattled her ears and replaced the angry buzzing inside her head.

His carriage was brought up onto the grass without ceremony and he lifted her in. "Here, have a little of this," he said, putting a flask to her lips.

Margaret let her head be tipped back and she tasted the hot, malty taste of good whiskey, warmed to nearly tea temperature by the heat of the day. It burned down her throat but she was too stunned to even cough.

"I'm most dreadfully sorry to have to upset you, especially at this moment," Charles said.

"But it can't be," she whispered, hoarse with the whiskey and disbelief. "I've seen the papers. He *paid* for the *Java*, Charles. I *know* he did."

Charles signaled the driver to pull around onto the road again. "Please take a bit of advice, my dear. Distance yourself from this whole affair. Tell me precisely where on the ship the papers are so that I can retrieve them to present them to the magistrate on your behalf, to substantiate your claim to the *Java* should Jensen be found guilty."

"But I don't wish you to do that," Margaret protested. "I mean to say, I can hardly be concerned with . . ."

"Margaret, really, I must insist," Charles said.

Margaret felt her blood return with a rush. "You presume too much on our friendship, Charles."

Charles made a soothing noise. "Yes, of course I presume, my dear, but I do it out of concern for your welfare. If you do not present the papers, it may suggest that you have somehow colluded in the theft of the *Java*."

Margaret picked herself up briskly, anger replacing the weakness she had been feeling before. She stepped out of the carriage without waiting for assistance and turned to Charles.

"You may be certain, Charles, that at such time as the papers may be required for official scrutiny, I will be only too pleased to present them."

Gathering her skirt, she made her way across the open grass and collected Jack firmly by one hand. She ignored

Charles as she walked briskly back to her own carriage and waved to Hoc Sing to depart, leaving behind a dismayed minister and a baffled Mr. Coggins. For the rest of them she cared not at all. Her thoughts were on fire as they descended the hill and for once she was glad that Jack was not a talkative child, for all her attention was turned inward. Richard had said that someone was out to discredit him and now she was sure of it. Her most pressing concern was to get a message to him, warning him of the new, and potentially far more serious, charge facing him.

Chapter 22

"He may simply disappear," An Wu said, wagging his broad head.

"Yes, I've considered that," Margaret replied. "Still, I wish him to know where the papers are, so that he may adequately defend himself. I also wish to sign the papers back over to him so that he can go in freedom if he chooses. I will not bind him to me with mere monetary obligation."

"Ah, freedom," An Wu sighed. "A precarious state at best. He may go as far away as he likes, but I fear our friend will not be free."

Margaret studied the Chinaman's eyes. "I wish you will explain that statement."

An Wu tipped his head back and peered thoughtfully at the ceiling. "It has nothing to do with possessions, this state of being free, but rather with the heart. Captain Jensen lives by his heart, you understand. Most European men lack the courage and spend much time pushing aside their feelings and replacing them with facts and figures. I have observed this in the English. They do not pay sufficient attention to their instincts, their . . ." He made a sweeping gesture across his ponderous belly. "I do not know any English for it, but to we Chinese, the heart tells us what is true. Captain Jensen is truly a man of the East. He listens to his heart."

Margaret followed the merchant's idea carefully. "Yes, I

believe I know what you mean, but in what way does that affect his freedom?"

"Why, very simply. His heart is with you," An Wu said.

Margaret looked at the merchant reflectively. "And mine is with him," she said slowly, "but that avails nothing if he will not take it. He seems to have succumbed to some idea that he is cursed. I, on the other hand, believe there is some very definite human agency at work here and he must take steps to fight it."

An Wu smiled meditatively. "I concur. Nevertheless, that is a European response and not necessarily the one Captain Jensen will adopt."

"But then how am I to assist him?" Margaret demanded impatiently.

An Wu spread his hands. "Why, we will send a message. The rest is up to him."

Richard wiped his hands dry impatiently and blotted away the drops of sweat scattered across his ledger, even as another dripped off the end of his nose. It was blistering hot in the saloon and he was in a filthy temper. They had dropped anchor less than an hour ago and already the air had turned to unbreathable steam. He felt like flinging the ledger across the saloon, or landing his fist in someone's face. Whose face and why didn't matter, but he needed something to wreak his mood on.

The figures in front of him were not to blame. If anything, they were better than he'd hoped, but there was a sickening rage in his veins that no amount of liquor had tamed. It had to do with Margaret, and with Jack. They were so close and yet so far away, much farther than the mere two or three miles of channel between where the *Java* lay anchored and Tanjong Pagar Dock.

He buried his face in his hands. He wanted to see them so badly it was making him physically ill. He wanted to unload the horses he'd bought in Sydney and head straight for the house on Cluny Road. Oh, God, he'd taunted Margaret for wanting a house on shore, one with a white

369

picket fence, and now all he could think of was how perfect that would be. He'd arrive at sundown and swing Jack up on his shoulders, and play with him a while before taking a cool bath and having drinks on the veranda with Margaret. They could eat dinner late, in the freshness of night, and tuck Jack in together before going off to bed themselves.

Richard squeezed his eyes shut with the pain. Her skin would be soft and cool, like chilled velvet, and she'd whisper his name in the dark. He'd find her lips and drink deeply, feeling her breath quicken as she pulled him to her eagerly. She'd twine around him and take him deep inside, all the while telling him how much she loved him, and her violet-scented skin would perfume the night air around them. Richard dug his fingers into his scalp as a deep, choking misery settled in him.

He couldn't do it. His life was in tatters. He scarcely even dared to go ashore. He might not even be able to unload the horses and then he'd be forced to peddle them somewhere else for half what he'd paid for them. He eyed the bottle of whiskey sitting just out of reach and found it had no appeal. No answers lay within its amber depths.

Buying the horses had been a tacit admission that he would return to Singapore, where Australian horses were always in demand. The need to come and be at least this close to Margaret was a compulsion, a deep, dangerous compulsion. If he walked through the door she had opened, sought her out and made himself a part of her life, he would drag her down as surely as if he had sold her to Atam Datu.

"Ahoy the *Java!*"

Richard's head came up abruptly and he heard the soft thrum of a steam engine.

"*Java*, my name is James Philpot and I represent the magisterial power of the Straits Settlement. Prepare to be boarded on official business."

Richard rose and thrust a pistol into his belt. This was a free port. They'd board the *Java* over his dead body! He sprinted up the companionway and caught the worried

370

glances of the crew as he rushed to the boarding ladder. Three men stood below in a pilot's tug, rocking uneasily to the swaying motion of the boat.

"State your business," Richard shouted.

"My name is James Phil . . ."

"I heard your damn name! I asked your business."

"We are here to impound the *Java* pending a hearing on charges that she was stolen. You and your entire crew are to come off peacefully. You will be bound over to the . . ."

"What the hell is Charles Townsend doing here?"

The official stiffened. "He is here to assist us. He will examine your books and check the cargo against your records. All your property will be returned to you, just as he finds it, should you be proven innocent."

"Like hell it will," Richard jeered. He stilled his body and felt the complete absence of wind. The *Java* sat limp, nearly atop her own anchor chain. It was no good trying to make a run for it. The crushing black cloud that had been closing in on him now surrounded him completely.

"Will you cooperate?" Philpot called out.

Richard tugged at the pistol at his waist. At least he could have the satisfaction of blowing Charles Townsend away. As well be hung for a sheep as a lamb.

"Don't do'er, Cap'n."

Richard felt the hand on his wrist and looked down. Dogsmeat looked up at him intently.

"Go with'em," he whispered. "It's the only way to settle this whole rum mess. Miss Margaret'll bring your papers and I can testify that I saw the money change hands."

Richard stared at his steward through a murky veil of unquenched hatred, but the urge to shoot Charles Townsend began fading at the mention of Margaret's name. It would only bring more notoriety down on her if he gunned down her protector in cold blood. He let his hand drop to his side. Dogsmeat reached up and took the pistol.

"Come aboard," Richard said dully. He was hemmed in on all sides, damned if he did, and damned if he didn't.

The officials were no more officious than they had to be,

371

but Charles Townsend was another matter. He circled the deck as if he owned the *Java*, and quickly ascertained that the *Java* carried a live cargo.

"We'd best unload these animals and then you can put the ship at a secured anchorage, in close," he said imperiously to the magisterial officials.

The anchor was weighed and the tug nudged the *Java* up the channel, past slimy, stinking mud flats with mangrove roots exposed by the low tide. They writhed up and over each other, like huge serpents, and seemed to Richard to round out the whole, lousy picture. When he saw Charles Townsend making for the saloon, he followed him, shaken out of his stupor by anger.

He found Charles rifling through his papers with impunity. "Get your hands off those," Richard growled.

"My dear fellow, I'm simply doing the job I came here to do," Charles replied without bothering to look up. "As one trader to another, I'm doing you a favor. Those nitwits up on deck wouldn't even have thought to unload your horses."

"You don't give a damn about me or my cargo," Richard snapped. "We both know what this is all about."

Charles smiled indulgently. "You're an impudent rascal, Jensen, but your impudence will do you no good with me or with the magistrate."

"Then maybe your fellow traders would like to hear how you tried to corner the market in gun running to Sumatra." Charles paused in the act of perusing a ledger. "Maybe they wouldn't think it was sporting of you to report that I was running guns when all the time it was you. Being sporting—that counts a lot with them, doesn't it? Reminds them of the old school and all that."

Charles slowly closed the ledger and tapped the table with the edge of it. "I don't think anyone is going to believe such a crack-brained theory, Jensen. Under the circumstances, such an accusation could only be perceived as wildly self-serving. You'd be better off to think on how you intend to defend yourself from the charge of theft. Margaret tells me you have the papers of ownership

372

aboard. I doubt that they are genuine but she could not be expected to know that."

Richard controlled the trembling rage in his chest with an effort. "You're a black-hearted beggar. You know perfectly well she has them! You've talked her out of them and now they'll disappear so that you can make *me* disappear. First you used her brother as a pawn and now you're twisting Margaret around your little finger. I'll make sure she knows the truth before this is over, that it was you who arranged for Coit to take Christian up to Sumatra."

The skin around Charles's mouth went white. "You're spouting a lot of nonsense. No one will listen to a story like that!"

Richard allowed himself a brief, sardonic smile. "How do your books look these days, Townsend? Not too good is my guess. With Christian out of the way, you could keep his investment, but now that the sister's come along, you've got to account for it, don't you? Of course, if you marry her, all her money comes to the rescue. That's your aim, isn't it—to marry her? It's a neat scheme, Townsend, only I'll see you dead first."

"You aren't in a position to threaten me," Charles said with frightening confidence. "I'll see you clapped in irons and committed to the brig of a pirate ship before I'll let an upstart bastard like you tell me what I can and can't do."

Richard gripped the back of the chair to keep himself from lunging for Townsend's throat. "It's too bad Coit lost the ship you bought for him. That really put you in the hole, didn't it Townsend? Enough guns and you could have made up the loss, become the undisputed king of gun runners, instead of merely a decent merchant, like your father. Sad to say, though, you won't be doing any more trading with Atam Datu."

"Honestly, Jensen, you're mad as a hatter," Charles said disdainfully. "I haven't the least idea what you're talking about."

Richard laughed, genuinely pleased to be able to say what he was about to say. "Atam Datu's dead, Townsend. I killed him myself."

It elicited all he could have hoped for. Charles went still and the color drained out of his patrician cheeks. "That's not possible. You wouldn't have made it out of there alive!"

"I nearly didn't, but it was worth it. It was marvelously inventive of you to send Christian to him to do your negotiating. Or was he just a human sacrifice, a bribe for Atam Datu? I didn't have the heart to tell Margaret about that, but maybe Christian's figured it out by now and he'll tell her."

"Christian's dead," Charles said stiffly.

"Ah." Richard felt a momentary sadness for Margaret's sake, and then he let it drop, an issue for another place and time. "Christian was determined to ruin himself, but you! You were unscrupulous enough to exploit his ruinous tendencies. I'll see that Margaret finds out why. Bet on it, Townsend."

"Save your posturing for the magistrate," Charles said coolly. "Once you're convicted of theft, I don't believe Margaret will put much stock in anything you say."

Richard felt sweat wending its way between his shoulder blades. "I should have killed you when I had the chance," he snarled. "I may not be in a position to marry her, but I'll be damned if I'll stand aside and see her marry *you*. You're scum, Townsend, godless, conniving scum!"

Charles set the ledger down and blotted at his brow with a handkerchief. "Damnably hot in here, eh what?" he said without any evidence of discomfort. He tucked the square of white linen back into his pocket. "Now see here Jensen, you've admitted you can't marry Margaret and she's indicated that if it were not for you, she would favor my suit." He paused and laughed. "What an extraordinary idea, *you* marrying Lady Margaret Belleweather!" He shook his head. "Ah, well, that's neither here nor there now. The fact of the matter is that if you wish to see her adopt your bastard son, you'd do well to keep your mouth shut. I'm prepared to respect her wishes—although I think

374

it's an enormous error—but I'm in a position to place certain obstacles in her way, if I choose."

Richard glared at him. "What obstacles?" he demanded.

"Coit is the boy's legal father, Jensen, since he was married to Emma at the time Jack was conceived. Of course, I didn't know that until very recently, but the estimable Coit is a man who seizes the moment. It was he who concocted the idea of passing his second wife off as his dead first wife. How Margaret saw through the deception, I can't imagine. However, Coit wants another chance to captain for me and I'm inclined to give it to him, provided he does as he's told. He may be forced to withdraw his consent to the adoption of the boy, and then, well . . ."

It was the last provocation. Not only could he not have Margaret but now he could not even unmask Townsend without jeopardizing Jack's future. Richard had a brief, intense vision of the day on the docks when Margaret had flown into Charles Townsend's arms. The vision merged with Townsend's smirking face in front of him. The deck lurched under Richard's feet as the *Java* bumped up against the dock and without an instant's hesitation, he snatched his last chance to settle accounts.

The saloon was a red blur as he leaped across the table and began pummeling Charles Townsend. He felt the skin on his knuckles split as he landed punch after punch into the hated face. He heard his own savage, animal-like grunts as he put the force of his entire body into each blow. Charles raised his arms and cried out to the men above decks to come to his aid but it barely registered with Richard. He felt a primitive pleasure as Townsend's blood spattered across his white shirt front. He doubled his fists together, preparing to drive a ruthless, killing blow into the center of Townsend's chest.

He felt only the first swing of the belaying pin and then blackness descended. The rest of what had been done to him he only came to appreciate many hours later, when he came to in the darkness of a cell, hurting in every fiber of his body. Most of what they'd done to him had been done from the back and sides, gallant sods that they were. It hadn't been enough that they'd knocked him cold with the first blow.

Richard tried to lever himself to a sitting position but the pain stopped him. He tested gingerly for broken bones but found none, although the left side of his face felt curiously numb and heavy. Sweet mother of all seaman, what he wouldn't have given for a drink of water! His head throbbed and the taste of clotted blood in his mouth nauseated him. The *Java* was gone—Townsend would see to that—and Margaret would never know the truth. To move was unrelieved agony, but the pain inside more than rivaled the pain outside. Richard let his eyes close to try and stop the room from spinning. He heard the scrape of a door nearby and then footsteps.

He opened his eyes again and realized that the curious heaviness in his face must be swelling. He lay perfectly still when the footsteps stopped nearby. There was a creak and then an excruciating stab of light as the door opened and a guard looked in. Richard started to speak and discovered he had nothing to say.

"Waking up, are you?" the guard asked warily. Richard blinked painfully against the light. "Reckon you could use some water. If you won't be hurting me, I'll give you some." In answer, Richard shook the chains that bound the manacles at his wrists and ankles together.

The guard still hesitated. "You're a rough customer," he said, "assaulting officers of the court and all. You're in for it, and that's certain."

Richard nodded in agreement. He wanted the water and hated being reduced to meekness to get it. He wondered what would happen to him. All he knew for certain was that if he kept his mouth shut, Margaret would get Jack. God, from drinks on the veranda to this—if ever a man invited disaster by dreaming, he was it!

"Keep yourself still now," the guard said, cautiously holding out a ladle. He showed no sign of helping his prisoner to sit up so Richard had to tip his head to the side and gulp as much of the water as he could as it passed his mouth. By the light, he could see more of his surroundings. It was a rough sort of cell, not nearly secure enough to hold him if it hadn't been for the manacles.

The guard saw his gaze wandering and backed away warily. "We don't see too many hard cases," he said, peering at Richard from a safe distance. "Most of'em just gets shipped out on the next boat. Don't know what's so special about you that they're going to all this trouble."

Richard let his eyes sink closed again. He knew very well why they were going to all this trouble. When the door closed again, he lay in the darkness, oppressed by pain and frustration. Townsend had picked his ally well. Coit would happily perjure himself in front of the devil himself. By the time they finished the hearing, Richard Jensen would be a villain and a bogeyman, the name used to threaten every misbehaving child in Singapore for years to come.

The pain of it sliced cleanly through his heart. He could only pray that Margaret would evade Charles Townsend's clutches and take Jack back to England. If she didn't, Jack would grow up living with the stigma of being the son of a criminal and a misbegotten misfit. As exhaustion claimed him, Richard felt the bitter twist of history repeating itself.

Margaret laid aside her sketching pencil when she heard the knock at the door. Hoc Sing would answer it but she needed a moment to compose herself. It was probably Charles. He had rushed down the hill after her that morning but she had not cared to stop and hear anything else he might say. It was cold, it was senseless, but she had understood the impulse to kill the bearer of bad tidings in that moment. Now he would be coming to smooth things over between them.

Jack looked at her solemnly, his pen poised over the page of cursive writing he had been practicing so diligently. They had eaten a desultory dinner, neither of them having much appetite after the events of the day. He had taken her hand in the carriage and held it tightly, his eyes bright with unshed tears, and she had hugged him to her fiercely, wishing he would say what was in his heart. But he had not.

Margaret smiled at him gently, nodding to indicate that he could be done with his work if he liked. It seemed to be taking a long time for Hoc Sing to come and announce her visitor and she felt a sudden flame of hope in her heart. Perhaps it was Richard! Perhaps An Wu had succeeded in getting the message to him! She hurried to the door and stopped short as she opened it.

The entire crew of the *Java* stood on her veranda. Dogsmeat was attempting to persuade Hoc Sing to let them in but he stopped when he saw her.

"Miss Margaret! Thank God you're here! The captain's been arrested!"

"Oh, no!" Though she had been forewarned, Margaret felt the worst sort of shock that it had actually happened. "Where is he? What have they done with him?" she cried.

"They've tossed him in some little bit of a ramshackle jail. We tried to see him but they wouldn't let us. We've been thinking for hours how to find you but no one would give us your direction."

"Yes, yes, but you're here now," Margaret said impatiently. She could well imagine the reactions to a band of nearly twenty men, roaming the streets and inquiring after her address. Darwin clung to Harkay's massive shoulders, peering suspiciously up at her, Toby glowered at the head of the apprentices, all of them looking ready for a fight, Dogsmeat was clenching a pistol in one hand, and Tony clutched a frying pan. Only Dekker and Daniels looked remotely safe to be spoken to. "Come in, come in," she said quickly. "We must talk about what's to be done."

Dogsmeat shuffled his feet and looked over the crew. "Thanks just the same, miss, but we're awfully dirty. Maybe just a few of us."

"They are Captain Jensen's crew, aren't they?" Margaret heard Jack's clear young voice say at her elbow.

"Yes, dear," she said quietly. "They've come to us for help."

"Then we must help them," he said. He looked up at her anxiously. "They look as if they must be hungry and thirsty. Shall we feed them?"

Margaret felt a burst of love for Jack. "Of course, dear," she said. "How very clever of you to think of it. Why don't you fetch Eliza and John and tell them to prepare something?"

Jack hurried off and piece by piece, Margaret heard the whole story of the boarding. Her first thought was to go to Charles, but when she heard he had been there helping the officials, she discarded the notion. That Richard had been carried off, unconscious and in chains, distressed her horribly. She wanted to run to the jail and demand admittance but Dekker counseled against it.

"They mean to prosecute him immediately," the fair-haired officer said. "They've seized the ship and sealed her up. The best thing is to find a legal advisor for the captain right away."

"And the papers, miss," Dogsmeat said urgently. "We must have the papers the captain signed over to you."

"The papers are on the *Java*," she said. Dogsmeat's face fell and Dekker and Daniels looked at one another uneasily. Margaret felt a ferocious determination to let nothing stand in their way and she dismissed their reactions. Thinking out loud, she said, "And I must go talk to my neighbor. He may have some idea of what else can be done. No lawyer in Singapore will represent Richard, that much is certain."

Dekker, Daniels, and Dogsmeat insisted on accompanying her. They left the rest of the crew gratefully eating and drinking on her lawn, looking like the oddest of garden party guests, overstaying their welcome long after darkness. An Wu did not seem at all surprised to see the *Java*'s officers and steward when they were ushered into his lavish salon. He sank back into his mound of pillows and heard them out, although Margaret felt sure they added very little to what he already knew. When they had finished, he sat back and stared at the punkah being wielded by a servant pulling a string in the corner.

At last he sat up. "Captain Jensen must have a fresh change of clothes and his toiletries. That is the most obvious order of business."

"But . . ."

An Wu cut Margaret's protest short. "He will be judged on the facts, but he must not present a less than civilized appearance."

"If I can get on the ship, I can get what he needs," Dogsmeat said eagerly.

"Just so," An Wu murmured, "just so. Also, someone must go to the constabulary and take an offer of . . . shall we say, a gift? It will ensure that Captain Jensen's needs are seen to while he enjoys the hospitality of the crown."

"I can do that," Daniels offered. "I can wheel and deal, sure enough."

"You should take food and drink for him, too," An Wu added, "and inveigh yourself into the good graces of the guards, so that you can stay, and see that Captain Jensen receives his clothing, and has water to wash and shave. Most importantly, we will need you to send word the instant he is to be taken for the hearing."

"One of the lads can come and stand by for that duty," Daniels said, his dolorous expression lightening notice-ably at the prospect of having something useful to do. "Toby's a reliable one."

Margaret could stand it no longer. "But the papers! Surely that is the crux of the matter. We must have them off the ship."

"Precisely. I could not agree more. However, if the ship is sequestered . . ." The Chinese merchant paused and steepled his fingers. "Perhaps some judicious law breaking is called for."

Margaret sprang to her feet. "Then that is what we will do!"

"Your fervor is commendable," An Wu said. "I believe the attempt should be made tonight. I leave the details to . . ." He inclined his head toward Dekker and Dogs-meat.

"Herbert Higginbotham," Dogsmeat said, proudly

drawing himself up. "It won't be the first bit o' law breakin' I've done neither."

"Ah, it would be a stale life that did not include some skirting of the law," An Wu said, smiling. "Hoc Sing, to whom Lady Margaret can introduce you, will be at your disposal. I think you will find the lack of a common language no impediment to his usefulness."

Margaret was fairly trembling with impatience but the Chinaman seemed in no hurry to see them leave. He reordered his vast bulk on the pillows and sat deep in thought. Margaret hesitated to leave, afraid that they would miss some fundamental detail which An Wu was pondering. At last he spoke again.

"It would be naive in the extreme to suppose that suiting Captain Jensen out appropriately and presenting the papers will answer the entire case. I do have some other ideas, however . . ."

"What?" Margaret said quickly, afire to be gone and aid Richard in some material way.

"If I could have the assistance of someone who reads English proficiently," An Wu said, "it will greatly aid me in my efforts. It would also be helpful if it was someone blessed with patience."

Margaret instantly eliminated herself from consideration but Dekker stepped into the awkward silence.

"I would be glad to assist you," he said, executing a small bow.

Chapter 23

Margaret paced nervously in the ladies' anteroom outside the magistrate's hearing room and wished she were not so craven and useless. Her hands trembled and her heart hammered. Only motion could distract her from the disturbing manifestations of her fear. She clutched the papers for the *Java* securely in a cream-colored folder as she roamed back and forth. Ever since the night before, she had felt disoriented and inadequate to all the odd turns of events.

Not that anyone would have reacted differently, she supposed, anyone except Richard. Richard, if he had been present for the drama that had taken place on the *Java*, would have laughed that loud, whooping laugh of his and fallen to the deck, gasping for breath. Margaret found she could actually smile a little at the thought.

They had arrived at the ship under cover of dark, she and Harkay and Dogsmeat, with the resourceful Hoc Sing rowing the small painter he'd procured from under a dock that smelled to high heaven of some strong, oily-smelling fish. Margaret had insisted on going with them, since only she could be sure of retrieving the papers without marring the painting she had done for Richard. Harkay and Dogsmeat had easily overpowered the two sleepy guards who stood watch on deck, and Margaret had gone below.

She'd had to overcome a wave of nostalgia that bleached

her insides of all sense and purpose when she entered the saloon after such a long absence. Papers were strewn about haphazardly and she was glad that An Wu's messenger hadn't reached Richard before the officials arrived. Surely they would have confiscated the papers and altered or destroyed them. She no longer harbored any illusion that fair play would win the day.

She had pried the frame away from the canvas and extracted the papers when a scraping sound behind her made her turn. A bearded man stood in the doorway to Richard's cabin. "Them papers is needed for the hearing tomorrow," he growled. "Hand'em over and I'll see that they get to the right people."

"No!" Margaret drew a deep breath and screamed. "Dogsmeat! Harkay!"

The stranger leaped around the table and grasped her upper arm so quickly she did not have time to evade him. "Give'em over!" he snapped. The man's fingers tightened on her arm and she stared into his eyes, dazed by the malignant look in them. "Your little helpers'll have their hands full by now and . . ." Suddenly he broke off, his eyes widening.

Margaret twisted around in a panic to see what had arrested his threats. Dogsmeat stood just inside the alleyway, a peculiar expression on his face. "Oh, thank God!" she exclaimed. "Dogsmeat, this man is demanding that I give him the papers, and I think he's already been through everything searching for them, only he didn't find them and . . ." She gabbled on, desperation in her voice.

Dogsmeat eyed her warily, his gaze sliding to the point where the man's hand still gripped her arm. "Step away from him, miss," he said, his voice taut with warning.

"But that's what I've been trying to . . ." The stranger tightened his grip on her arm still further and his other hand emerged from between them with a pistol in it. Margaret felt dizzy with fear.

"Well, well, well, so the midget's still hangin' around . . ." the stranger said, his face twisted with un-

383

disguised loathing. "I always prayed I'd never see you again." Margaret felt brittle, caught in the enmity between the two men.

"No harder nor I prayed you'd gone straight to hell once we left Charleston," Dogsmeat growled. "You stinking sod, you have a helluva nerve settin' foot back on this ship!"

The stranger leveled the pistol squarely at the steward and Margaret could feel the gathering violence. He was broad and square, with a seaman's calloused hands, and even without the pistol, he could undoubtedly make short work of Dogsmeat.

"Where is Harkay?" she asked nervously. "Shouldn't we call him down here to help us get the clothes the captain will need?"

Dogsmeat's eyes flickered briefly from her to the stranger but he betrayed no sign that he thought it an odd request. He nodded slowly.

Margaret twisted around, made careless of the danger to herself out of concern for Dogsmeat. "I think you had better leave now," she said to the bearded man, her voice shaking.

"Not till I've . . ."

The man opened his mouth, his jaw working aimlessly as he saw Harkay emerge from the alleyway. The Polynesian looked balefully at Dogsmeat, unhappy to be called into the confines belowdecks. Darwin balanced on his shoulders and his back stiffened in response to the tension in the saloon. He emitted a low growl, more canine than feline in nature, and the hair along his spine stood up, the orange guard hairs standing proud of the finer down beneath. Harkay's black eyes shimmered with malice as he stared at the bearded man.

"He no like you, mister, that's by damn," he said grimly.

The caged sparrow reacted with alarm to the low growling and jumped agitatedly from the lower to the higher perch and back again. Darwin's head swiveled around in that uncanny way he had and in less than a heartbeat, he had launched himself off Harkay's shoulder. Margaret was hard put to reconstruct events later, save for remembering the distant orange blur and then the stranger's self-protective lunge which threw her clear of the scuffle. Dogsmeat was somewhere in it, kicking the stranger's shins, she thought, and when it was over, Harkay was sitting atop the bearded man. The sparrow chittered in panic as Darwin swung from the bottom of its cage ignominiously.

"Don't move," Dogsmeat said threateningly.

At first, Margaret thought he meant her and then she saw that he was addressing the stranger, who hadn't the wind to answer if he'd wanted to. The dwarf retrieved the pistol which had skittered across the saloon.

"You get clothes," Harkay said to Dogsmeat, settling in comfortably. "You be fast. I maybe have to break a head soon."

"Faster than a barmaid at closing time," Dogsmeat replied with a savage smile. He disappeared into the main cabin.

Margaret stared at the stranger, who lay bug-eyed and red-faced under Harkay's enormous bulk. She still hadn't the least idea who he was and decided she'd lived in ignorance long enough. Dogsmeat emerged from Richard's cabin with a seaman's duffel and edged Margaret toward the companionway.

"Who in the world is that man?" she asked Dogsmeat fretfully.

"Name's Coit, Samuel Coit, and he don't deserve the kindness you'd show a rat. Come along, miss," the steward said.

"Coit! But then you are Jack's . . ." She broke off. The man glared up at her, his head flat to the deck and his exposed eye hot with hatred. It seemed too odd to converse with a man being sat on. She turned and went with a sigh. It was all too much for one day.

A touch at her elbow threw Margaret into a spin that nearly resulted in her landing in an untidy heap on the floor. "Charles!" she gasped. "You frightened me out of my wits! Please, do not come up on me so."

Charles withdrew his hand. "I'm sorry. I spoke several times but you did not appear to notice. Let me call my carriage around to the front to take you home. A few hours rest will put your nerves in a happier state." Margaret shook her head impatiently. "For God's sake, Margaret, you must not have any more to do with this matter."

Margaret brandished the folder. "I mean to see Richard Jensen proved innocent," she declared. Charles reached out to take the folder and Margaret snatched it away. He sighed.

"He's a bad seed, my dear. Nothing's to be gained from exonerating him. Let the *Java* come into your hands, my dear—into *our* hands. I love you, Margaret. This is hardly the time or place to say it, I know, but please, you must know that I have only your best interests at heart."

Margaret stared at him, nonplussed by the declaration. It seemed to her that Charles had a most peculiar look on his face and then she realized it was because his nose was swollen and misshapen, and one eye was puffy. At any other time she would have inquired as to its cause. Now she merely brushed it aside as the probable result of an unlucky brush with a polo mallet. "Charles, I am most appreciative of your regard," she stammered, "but right now I cannot respond to it. My concern is Captain Jensen."

"Really, Margaret, you must listen," he said persuasively, his gaze boring in on her. "We—you and I—can see to it that Captain Jensen is found guilty and then freed. Surely that is what you desire?"

"To see him found guilty?" Margaret mumbled in confusion. She felt as if her otherwise sharp, precise mind were wrapped in cotton wool.

"No, to be freed, of course," Charles said. He took her hands and pressed them together between his own. "This . . . thing . . . this *feeling*, you have imagined there is between you, it must all come to naught in the end. Don't you see? He is nothing but the sorriest rogue. You cannot possibly wish to spend the rest of your life with him. Say you will marry me, Margaret, and together we will have a splendid future."

Margaret felt the upsurge in activity in the magistrate's hearing room behind them, more voices being raised and the shuffle of feet and chairs. She craned around in agitation. "But Charles," she protested, "as you said yourself, this is neither the time nor the place. Besides, it is Richard I love. I *must* see him proved innocent!"

Charles's mouth flattened impatiently and he increased the pressure on her hands, uncomfortably so. "You have only to present the papers and the court will undoubtedly recognize your claim. Then, if we suggest that the matter is best dropped, Captain Jensen will be set free."

We, we . . . Margaret hesitated. All the 'we's' were fogging her brain. Why on earth did Charles insist on acting as if they were of one mind?

Charles mistook her hesitation for agreement. "I know you feel some obligation to him, Margaret, but please allow me to say that it is misguided in the extreme. The most kindness he can deserve in return for what he has done for you . . ." Her mouth opened in protest and he smiled, a quick blur, as he patted her hand. "Yes, yes, he has done you a service, perhaps more than one, but his usefulness to you is at an end now."

Margaret found her tongue at that. "His usefulness has never been the issue, Charles, and it sounds most cold of you to speak of him as if he were no more than a servant. I intend to marry him, if he will have me after what I have done, and if he will not, then I will marry no one."

Charles's expression went blank except for a quick, cold flutter behind his eyes. He dropped her hands and stood with his arms at his sides. "Then I am afraid Captain Jensen will almost certainly go to prison for the theft of the *Java*."

Margaret felt the floor dropping away from under her. "Why?" she whispered in disbelief. "Why?"

Charles sighed. "Because my dear, you are clearly the one with the best claim to the *Java*. If we were able to go in there and present them with the fact that we are to be married, and use the *Java* in pursuit of legitimate trade through Townsend and Townsend, it would present a far different picture than if you stand alone and say that you think Richard Jensen is innocent and should go on having the use of the ship."

Margaret took a convulsive breath of air, steadying herself by focusing for a moment on Charles's lapel. "But that is just what I intend! The papers clearly show that the sale was made to him, and now that I am the owner of record, I do not see how the court can object to me disposing of my property as I see fit."

Charles motioned toward the court and his face took on a mulish cast. "The papers are as false as the man himself. I will not stand by and see you held up to public ridicule for defending a man with no morals. If you pursue this course, the magistrate will doubtless conclude that he has influenced you through unseemly methods. It simply does not make sense for you to give away valuable property to a man like Jensen. The court will feel obliged to protect what is yours since your father did not—and forgive me for saying it—have the wisdom to appoint a trustee for you."

Margaret drew herself up indignantly. "If my father did not appoint a guardian, you may rest assured it was because he knew I would be competent to handle my own affairs!"

She turned on one heel, aggravated beyond her ability to tolerate Charles another minute. Still seething with resentment, she took a seat in the front row of the hearing room. Every member of the *Java*'s crew was already there, looking uncharacteristically tidy and clean. They had slept in her garden overnight and Hoc Sing had done the work of ten men to clean and press the clothing they'd been wearing when they were ordered off the ship. She managed a wan smile for them before turning to face the broad oak table which would serve as the magistrate's dais.

A small florid man came in and peered around uncertainly before setting his sights on the table. He took off his glasses and cleaned them before looking at the table once again. His face brightened with recognition, as if he had found a long lost friend, and he trundled over and seated himself behind it. The perplexed look came over his face again as he leafed through the papers on the top of it. He cleared his throat repeatedly as he adjusted one to varying distances from his face. Finally a clerk came in, and, with a patient look, turned the paper right side up. The magistrate's face bloomed into smiles again.

"Thanks, George," he said happily. "Most kind." He took his glasses off and polished them again and Margaret watched as he set them down. So much of their case rested on the scrutiny of the deed of sale that she feared the whole outcome would be in jeopardy if he misplaced his spectacles. She kept her eye on them anxiously, fully prepared to hand them back to the magistrate herself if he forgot where he'd put them.

"Now, now . . ." The magistrate scanned the room and a rabbity look of confusion replaced the smile. He cleared his throat. "Hmm, hmm." Then he saw Charles seated in the front row and gave him a cheery wave. "Townsend! Good of you to come." Charles nodded graciously and Margaret felt a sinking sensation, since it was all too apparent that Charles would be no friend in the proceeding.

"Hmmm . . ." The magistrate reached for his glasses and dragged the ear pieces on firmly. He craned around to the clerk. "Don't seem to have a prisoner, George."

"Right away, sir, if you're ready."

"Oh, yes, fit and ready," the magistrate cackled. "Fit and ready."

He certainly didn't have the aspect of a hanging judge, Margaret thought, but then she didn't even know if theft was a hanging offense anymore. A near-sighted, disoriented judge who was on close terms with Charles was bad enough without the eccentricity of manner he was evincing. She held the folder tightly, hoping that the promised help from An Wu would arrive soon. Then she heard a jingling.

Like everyone else in the hearing room, she followed the sound. What she saw horrified her. Richard emerged from

389

a side door in chains. His face showed the signs of a severe blow to the side, and he kept his eyes on the floor, even as she prayed he would look up so that she could see his face. What on earth had they done to him? His clothes were clean enough, his shoes polished, but he moved slowly, woodenly, as if he were in pain.

Only the appearance of An Wu and Dekker kept Margaret from flying across the room to Richard's side. The Chinaman's appearance was as much of a surprise as Richard's, though for different reasons. He was decked out in an English suit, his high wing collar gleaming white and tailored to frame his large neck without cutting into it. A gold watch fob spanned his prodigious girth and his hair was neatly parted in the center, brilliantined to perfection. Most surprising of all, he wore spectacles which were almost identical to the magistrate's. An Wu looked almost as English as Charles Townsend. In a lighter moment, Margaret might have laughed at the thought.

The Chinese merchant made a courtly bow toward the magistrate, who immediately straightened and began groping for the spectacles which were already on his face. An Wu turned and bestowed a restrained smile on Margaret. He waddled over and took a seat next to her, or more accurately, two seats.

"Not to worry, Lady Margaret," An Wu said in an undertone. "We shall carry the day—never fear." His black eyes were shining behind his spectacles and Margaret wanted very much to ask exactly what he meant, but a loud throat clearing from the front of the room distracted him.

The magistrate was looking at An Wu with great interest. "I do not believe I know you, sir," he said.

An Wu rose to his feet and bowed again, a small English bow of greatest propriety. "My dearest sir, my name is An Wu. I will not tax your poor ears with the fullest expression of my name, but I am a merchant in this city and am also referred to sometimes as Captain China."

"Are you, by God!" The magistrate looked distinctly

pleased. "Well, this is a rare day. Welcome to my court, sir, welcome!"

Score one for our side, Margaret thought, noticing the decidedly unhappy expression on Charles's face in response to the magistrate's effusive greeting.

"And are you here as an observer, sir, or do you intend to play a part on these proceedings?"

An Wu bestowed a gracious smile on the magistrate. "I beg your indulgence to observe what takes place," he said. "I have the highest regard for the judicial system of Her Majesty, Queen Victoria, but not being a subject of her majesty, I beg you will hear whatever small contribution I may have as to the material facts in this case through Mr. Olin Dekker, Captain Jensen's first officer."

"Nonsense!" the magistrate cried. "I won't hear of it. Please, sir, you seem most able and what you know I will be pleased to hear from your own lips."

"Oh, with the very greatest of pleasure, sir. I thank you most humbly," An Wu said, bowing and beaming. "You honor me beyond all expectation."

"Oh, stuff," the magistrate declared with glee. "I'll dine out on this story for months."

The clerk belatedly set a brass nameplate on the table, proclaiming the magistrate to be The Right Honourable Horatio Smythe-Jones. She decided she felt quite warmly inclined to like Mr. Smythe-Jones. But it was Richard who drew her attention again and again.

He sat stiffly to attention in the chair, looking straight ahead, and not once did he scan the hearing room to see if she was there. Even subdued, he exuded the raw, muscular power that was so fundamental to him. Between the manacles and the formal suit he wore, it was if the tiger had been caught and forced to masquerade as a man. His black hair was tied back neatly and he had been shaved, presumably by Daniels, but the whole impression he created was of a man fully expecting to be found guilty and hating every minute of it.

Margaret gnawed on her lip, wishing she knew what An

391

Wu had discovered that had him looking like the cat that had swallowed the canary. Perhaps it was only a facade, a confidence designed to beget confidence. Would she be better, even at this last minute, to strike a truce with Charles so that she could be sure Richard would walk away a free man? Charles was looking truculent and not at all receptive to such an approach, and Margaret decided to put her faith in An Wu. Dekker, in his extremely quiet, mannerly way, looked confident, too.

"Now, hmm-hmm," the magistrate said, examining the papers in front of him. He looked over his glasses, lifted them, looked under them, and finally settled for looking through them. "We are inquiring into the true ownership of the ship formerly known as the *Avenging Angel*, which is alleged to have been stolen and renamed the *Java*. She is a clipper, gross tonnage of . . . hmm . . . well, the same it appears as the *Avenging Angel*. Mr. Townsend," he said, looking up, "it was you who brought this matter to the court's attention. Would you please tell us what it is that persuaded you to believe that . . ." He peered at the paper. ". . . Mr. Johnson is not the legitimate owner of the ship?"

Charles stood up. "That's Jensen, Richard Jensen, your honor." Charles inclined his head toward Richard, who did not respond.

Mr. Smythe-Jones looked a little put out. "Yes, sir, that gentleman there," he said, "I believe I know well enough who the accused is."

"Of course," Charles said hastily. "I did not mean to imply otherwise."

"Then get on with it," Smythe-Jones said.

"I first became aware that the *Java* was in questionable hands when . . ." Charles launched into a lengthy, detailed account of his shipping business that seemed to have little to do with the case. Margaret found it almost soporific and apparently so did the magistrate.

At length, he interrupted. "Mr. Townsend, you said in your sworn statement that you had a witness who could testify to the theft. I wonder if you will be so good as to bring him forward."

Charles appeared flustered by the intrusion but recovered himself swiftly. "Yes, your honor. Mr. Samuel Coit was captain of the *Avenging Angel* when Mr. Jensen declared his interest in purchasing her. It was he who carried the offer to the owner, the offer which turned out not to be an offer at all, but a theft in the making."

"Well, then, we'd better hear from Mr. Coit, hadn't we?" the magistrate said testily.

Margaret shifted in her seat when Samuel Coit appeared from the back of the court. Several of the *Java*'s crew members looked at him with open contempt as he passed. Just seeing him made Margaret's skin crawl. His beard had been trimmed and he looked more presentable than he had the night before, but the small, dark eyes could not conceal the malevolence she had sensed in him the night before.

"Now, sir, what have you to say?" Smythe-Jones asked.

Coit affected a solemn air. "Well, sir, only just that I was able to work out a price, but the night I went to the *Avenging Angel* to get the money, Jensen told me to go to hell. He took the papers and forced me off the ship at gunpoint and the next morning, he was gone."

The corner of Richard's mouth twitched and he looked faintly amused. Margaret was glad to see some manifestation of his sense of humor, no matter that she didn't understand its source. She moved restlessly in her seat, wondering if she should present the papers which would show that Coit had received the money. An Wu looked placid and not inclined to disturb the proceedings. Margaret tapped his arm hesitantly.

An Wu turned his head slightly and said out of the corner of his mouth. "Give the man enough rope, Lady Margaret."

Margaret subsided uneasily. The magistrate peered at the papers in his hands before finally speaking. "I do not see any papers of ownership here. Surely they should have been presented in evidence and then we could compare the relevant signatures."

Richard's face turned grim again as Coit said, "He forced me to sign'em at gunpoint!"

A voice from the back of the court shouted, "Liar!"

Everyone turned. Smythe-Jones lifted his glasses and tried to find the speaker. "Come forward, sir!" he said peevishly. "If you have information, come forward and make it known. No need to shout it from the gallery."

Dogsmeat walked down the center aisle and the magistrate quickly ascertained his name and connection with the case. Dogsmeat took the papers from Margaret and handed them to Smythe-Jones.

"I was there, sir, the night what them papers was signed, and I can tell you it was no theft. Captain paid in good Union currency, too, not in Confederate scrip. That was one o' Coit's conditions," he added with a sneer. "Most likely planned to bolt wi' it all along."

"Hmmm." Smythe-Jones turned the papers every which way until his long-suffering clerk stepped forward and reversed the paper so that the side which was written on faced the magistrate. "Ah! Much better! Much obliged, George. Hmm, now according to this you were witness to the transfer of money, Mr. Higginbotham?"

"He weren't never there!" Coit yelled. "It was just him and me!" he said, pointing at Richard.

Richard glanced up and his eyes met Coit's. There was a feral gleam in the green depths that said he'd better never meet Coit in a dark alley in this lifetime. Coit looked momentarily shaken and then he puffed out his chest and turned away.

Smythe-Jones looked pained at the outburst. "Mr. Coit, I may be old, and perhaps even a bit daft, as some of my detractors say, but I am not deaf!" His glasses slipped down his nose and with an impatient jerk, he pushed them to the top of his bald, speckled head. "Now," he said testily, "where were we? Oh, yes, Mr. Higginbotham. Sir," he said, peering nearsightedly in Dogsmeat's direction, "would you kindly explain how it is that you were there when this . . ." He paused and glared toward Coit. ". . . this *gentleman* says you were not?"

394

"'appily, your honor," Dogsmeat said. "Bein' a small man sometimes 'as hits hadvantages. Oi never trusted that one. Captain said as 'ow Coit wanted the meeting private-like, another one o' 'is conditions," he said, sneering at Coit. "Oi reckoned Oi'd look out for the captain, like, so's Oi hid in the stateroom. Oi saw it all wif me own eyes."

Margaret thought that Dogsmeat had never looked taller. She silently rejoiced for his stout heart, only hoping that Smythe-Jones could understand his Cockney accent, which had thickened noticeably under stress.

"Hmmm, I see. You saw it all then, without being detected, owing to your fortuitously small stature?" The magistrate angled his glasses down again and looked at Dogsmeat with more comprehension than before.

"That's right, sir, and witnessed it wif a signature after."

"Just so, just so," Smythe-Jones murmured. He looked at the deed and seemed to drift off into a reverie for a moment. "Hmmm, so what we have is one man's word against another's." He seemed to remember something abruptly. "Oh! Mr. Johnson, I presume you subscribe to the version of events Mr. Higginbotham has just outlined? Deal struck, paid in Union currency, papers properly executed, etcetera?"

Richard straightened his shoulders and gazed at the judge with no discernable expression. "No, your honor. I stole the *Java*."

Margaret gripped the arms of her chair and stared in disbelief. Several members of the *Java*'s crew leaped to their feet, shouting. Charles Townsend looked like a man who had heard what he expected to hear all along and Smythe-Jones pounded his fist on the desk and yelled for quiet.

"Mr. Johnson!" he exclaimed. "Do you mean to tell the court you have been wasting our valuable time all along? Explain yourself, sir!"

An Wu lumbered to his feet. "Your honor, if I may interject myself on these proceedings . . ."

"Gladly! What a mish mosh," Smythe-Jones said,

shaking his head in disgust. "If the man's guilty, why didn't he just say so?"

"With sincerest regrets for any embarrassment it may cause to those present, I would like to suggest that Captain Jensen has been coerced into taking an untruthful position," An Wu said. "With sincerest regrets."

"How's that?" Smythe-Jones asked, his face bathed in confusion.

"Sir, it grieves me most terribly to even suggest such a thing," An Wu said, "but if you will just regard the condition of Captain Jensen's face for the briefest of moments, you will surely see that he has been beaten."

"The devil, you say!" Smythe-Jones adjusted his spectacles in every conceivable position and scrutinized Richard as Margaret held her breath. She remembered Charles's bruises and a quick suspicion formed and became certainty.

"Your honor," she said abruptly, "I believe it is Mr. Townsend who is responsible!"

Charles turned to her in amazement, his mouth open. "Why, Margaret, how can you . . ."

"I'll be in charge here, Mr. Townsend," the magistrate said, adding pointedly, "if you don't have any objections." Charles's mouth snapped closed again. "Now, you, miss, would be . . ."

"Lady Margaret Belleweather, your honor," Margaret said fiercely.

"Ah, yes." He smiled genially. "And a belle you are, if you'll excuse an old man for making a personal remark." Margaret smiled uncertainly. Smythe-Jones beamed. "Always a pleasure to have at least one pretty face in the room. But I digress. I was under the impression that Mr. Townsend was representing your interests in this matter. I understand you are the nominal owner of the . . . well, let's just say 'the ship' for the moment."

"Mr. Townsend in no way represents me," Margaret said firmly. "In fact, I am now quite convinced that his interest and mine are at odds."

"Oh! Well, that's a very different matter," Smythe-Jones

said. "Have you anything to say regarding the case before us?"

"I believe Captain Jensen to be the true owner, your honor. Furthermore, Samuel Coit menaced me last night, when I was aboard the ship retrieving the deed."

"Did he, by God?" Smythe-Jones looked Coit over and wrinkled his nose, as if it didn't surprise him in the least to learn that the bearded man had been menacing beautiful young women within the last twenty-four hours. "Humph! Well, we can take that matter up later, Lady Margaret, unless it has some bearing on the case . . . ?"

Margaret moistened her mouth. "I believe the papers which he attempted to take from me reveal that he *did* receive the money for the ship, and that his signature is quite genuine. Not once, but several times, another person . . ." She looked pointedly at Charles who refused to meet her gaze. ". . . another person has tried to induce me to relinquish the papers, all in an effort, I believe, to conceal the fact that a legitimate sale *was* made."

Smythe-Jones nodded several times as he followed her statement. His brow wrinkled earnestly. "Well, then I'd better have another look at them, hadn't I?" he asked, smiling benignly at her.

An Wu stood up. "Your honor, if you would be so very kind . . ."

"Ah! Captain China! Of course, join us in this bafflement."

"If I might put a question or two to Mr. Coit, I believe it may clarify a point, the very point upon which we are unable to decide, namely, whether the papers in your hand are, in fact, genuine, and money changed hands."

"Well, that would be splendid," Smythe-Jones, looking very bucked up at the notion. "As it stands, all we have are questionable papers, contradictory testimony, and a dashed lot of rudeness."

"Mr. Coit," An Wu began, "you represented the owner, Mr. Asa Baker, is that not correct?"

Coit nodded uneasily.

"Speak up, man!" Smythe-Jones barked.

"Yeah, I did," Coit said.

"And upon discovering that Captain Jensen had absconded with the ship, did you communicate that fact to Mr. Baker?" An Wu asked.

"Yeah, 'course I did," Coit said belligerently.

"Then one may assume that the theft was reported to the insurance company so that a claim could be paid and an advisory placed as to the theft in insurance bulletins which, all praise to modern means of communication, traverse the globe?"

Coit screwed up his face as he listened. The gist of the question was not at first apparent to him and then he appeared to understand. "Oh! Well, she weren't insured," he said expansively. "We was at war, see, and not Mr. Baker nor anybody else could *get* insurance, what with the blockade and all."

"Ah, just so, just so," An Wu murmured. "Most unfortunate, but very understandable in the circumstances." He turned to the magistrate. "I have a number of ships myself as your honor may know, so this is something with which I am familiar."

"Dashed lot of them from what I understand!" Smythe-Jones declared. "Very familiar, I should think! Pray go on."

An Wu smiled and bowed, and Margaret shifted uneasily in her seat. Where was An Wu taking this line of questioning? At least Smythe-Jones didn't seem worried about it. Richard was leaning forward ever so slightly, looking interested in the proceeding for the first time.

"Then—correct me if I am wrong—you reported the matter to Mr. Baker and there was nothing more to be done than accept the loss? No recourse to a reward, no circulation of the news of the theft as is customary in shipping circles?"

"Nah," Coit said confidently. "Old man Baker could afford to lose a ship, and he was gettin' on, didn't see the point. I told him Jensen was a crafty devil and we'd never catch up with him."

"Hmmm." An Wu looked thoughtful for a moment. He

turned to the magistrate. "This raises a most curious point, your honor. Pardon me if I digress, but you see, I am an inveterate saver of all reading matter regarding shipping. It is perhaps a regrettable habit, but it is one which I can afford to indulge, having at my disposable a commodious godown in which to store things. Also, in my thirst to master the English tongue, I have found it invaluable to read all publications I can obtain in that language."

"Most admirable," Smythe-Jones said, nodding vigorously. "You are to be commended on your accomplishment in speaking our tongue, sir."

"Thank you most kindly," An Wu said with a pleased smile. "And now to the point of my digression. When the name 'Avenging Angel' was bruited about last night as being the original name of the Java, it struck a chord, sir. It struck a cord. I confess, with all due humility, that my memory is more than adequate to my daily needs. I find that my mind stores away any number of additional facts which I am not likely to need. Well, sir, with Mr. Dekker's help, I spent the whole of last night at my godown perusing old shipping bulletins to find the reference to the Avenging Angel which must have planted the name in my mind."

Smythe-Jones leaned contentedly on his elbows with every appearance of being captivated by An Wu's narrative. Margaret squirmed unhappily. It was all going with affability to spare, but in what way did it serve Richard? The magistrate adjusted his glasses.

"This has the makings of a most excellent mystery which I suspect you are about to solve for us, Mr. China," he said happily.

"Oh, indeed, I hope that is the case," An Wu said. "You have been so extremely obliging, I would hate to think that I had led you down a primrose path."

Margaret wanted to scream. Get it over with, she thought. Say what you have to say and then you and Smythe-Jones can repair to the nearest drinking establishment to further your new friendship.

"No, no, I'm quite sure you haven't," Smythe-Jones said equably. "I await with interest to know the outcome of your all-night search."

"Just this, your honor, and here I will read from the *Merchants and Manufacturers Gazette* for the week of July 20, 1864. It says, '*The Avenging Angel* out of Charleston, South Carolina, was reported lost by her owner, Mr. Asa Baker, having been sunk during a naval engagement whilst the ship was engaged in peaceable business. The ship went down with all hands save her captain, Mr. Samuel Coit, who lodged the report with Mr. Baker. All such goods as were consigned to the *Avenging Angel* were consequently lost, and no alternate delivery should be anticipated.'"

"I never!" Coit roared, leaping to his feet.

Smythe-Jones gestured briefly for the clerk to bring him the gazette. It took him less than a minute to peruse it. He leveled a look at Coit, who had gone beet red with rage. "It would appear, sir, that you have knowingly pressed a false charge against Mr. Johnson," he said sternly. "I imagine that Mr. Baker would be glad enough to know that the man who sold the *Avenging Angel* is here in Singapore. Perhaps he would like to discuss with you how you intend to recompense him for the loss of a ship which is still navigating the seas."

Coit's bravado deserted him. "He's dead now, and he didn't have no kids to inherit his money," he sniveled. "He was old and sick and I figured it was a chance to get on my feet."

"Then perhaps the American authorities would still be interested in pursuing a charge of fraud against you," Smythe-Jones countered. An Wu nodded approvingly.

Margaret stood up, trembling with anger. "Your honor, if I may, I'd like to ask Mr. Coit a question."

Smythe-Jones wagged his head. "With pleasure, dear lady."

"Did you put your wife, Sarah, up to impersonating your deceased wife, Emma Coit?"

Coit went pale, and beads of sweat shimmered on his

brow. "He . . ." He jabbed his finger toward Charles. ". . . *he* thought of it. He wanted the *Java* for himself. All he had to do was keep you from marrying Jensen and he figured he could marry you himself. That way the *Java* would be his."

Margaret drew a deep breath, resolved to stay calm and to be sure of the exact facts. "And so you persuaded your wife to pretend she was Emma?"

"I did, but I never thought of it on my own! It was Townsend who came up with the idea."

Charles drew a strangled breath to protest but the hearing room erupted with shouts from the spectators, the loudest coming from the *Java*'s crew. The unholy alliance between Charles Townsend and Samuel Coit had come crashing down.

The magistrate succeeded in restoring order and looked at Charles with grave displeasure. "*You*, sir, have acted contemptibly in this matter. You have caused charges to be brought, which we now see you knew to be false! Moreover, sir, you appear to have been toying with this lady's affections! I recommend you hold yourself in readiness to answer charges of perjury and collusion."

Charles Townsend went a dull shade of red and pulled at his collar. Margaret felt a fierce surge of joy. Richard was going to go free! She wanted to throw her arms around An Wu and after a moment's hesitation, she did. She broke away from the flustered merchant and sought for a glimpse of Richard's face, but pandemonium had broken out in the hearing room. The *Java*'s crew mobbed the corner where Richard had been seated and by the time she retrieved the ship's papers from Smythe-Jones and accepted his congratulations, Richard was nowhere in sight.

Chapter 24

Richard hefted the sack onto his shoulder and made his way out of the chandler's shop. He paused at the corner of Battery Road and Flint Street when he saw a member of the Singapore constabulary. They were a casual lot, not having much crime to deal with, but having been in manacles only two days before made Richard more than a little sensitive to their presence. The constable moved on without any sign of curiosity. Richard turned his back and cursed himself for a fool—he had no reason to worry. Already the story was all over the city that Richard Jensen was innocent. An Wu had seen to it that the news was spread, no doubt.

Margaret had saved him once again. In her quiet way, she had brought together all the elements necessary for his rescue, just as she had in Makassar. He hadn't even worked his way out from under the indebtedness for the first time yet, and though there was no money involved this time, he felt under a cloud. And there was the question of Jack. Could she successfully complete the adoption or would Coit wreak his revenge by withholding the necessary consent?

He was damned if he could see how he could be anything but a hanger-on, a hindrance to Margaret Belleweather. All the need flowed one way, from him to her, and it left him feeling less than a man. She had become more and more like a dream to him since the night he had taken Christian to her, a beautiful talisman of what had been an unlikely interlude in the life of Richard Jensen, a man with either no luck at all or the worst luck imaginable.

Richard grunted and shifted the sack. No good would come of standing here. He had to leave, had to get back on board the *Java* soon, so that they could load and set sail. He didn't have a full cargo but it was the best he could do on short notice. He desperately needed to put Singapore behind him so that he could think clearly. Time enough tonight to lay and think about Margaret, and whether he dared go to her when he returned. She had looked even more beautiful yesterday than he'd remembered, in an apple green dress softly tailored to her small, shapely figure, and her violet eyes flashing with anger.

"Sir? Pardon me, but would you be Captain Richard Jensen?"

Richard stared down at the man who stood in his shadow, ginger hair gone flyaway in the midday heat and sunlight glinting off his scalp where the hair was beginning to thin on top. "Yes," Richard said reluctantly. What new trouble was this?

"I wonder if you would be so kind as to follow me? I have been endeavoring to locate you all morning. Your crew said I might find you here." Coggins didn't bother to add that the other suggestion had been to look for Jensen at Proctor's Pub.

"What's this about?" Richard asked suspiciously.

"I represent a merchant who wishes to discuss the possibility of chartering your ship for a lengthy term," Coggins said. "If you could spare the time, I think it will be worth your while."

Richard's mind went into high speed, rapidly considering who on earth could be thinking of dealing with him. Not one name came to mind. Still, the possibility was tempting. He squinted painfully up at the sun, his left eye still tender and swollen, before looking down again. "I can spare an hour, no more."

The man beamed. "I'm sure that will be quite adequate.

This way, please."

The ginger-haired man set a brisk pace, leading Richard back through the esplanade at the center of town and then up into the quarter where all the trading firms had their offices, one after another, as regular as daisies in a cutting garden. He made a last, quick turn and ushered Richard through a set of double doors.

"Here, sir, I'll just take that for you," he said, reaching out for the sack as naturally as if it were a gentleman's hat and gloves.

Richard let the sack slide to the ground and glanced with growing apprehension at the door through which they had just passed. It took a fraction of a second for him to decipher the backwards letters. *Townsend and Townsend.* "I think I've seen all I need to," he said, briskly picking up the sack again. "Tell Townsend he can send his thugs out to the ship if he wants to talk. We'll be ready for him. It'll be belaying pins at ten paces, only he doesn't get one this time."

"Sir!" the man cried, looking alarmed. "You misapprehend. It is not Charles Townsend who wishes to speak with you but the new owner of the firm."

"Look, I'm not in the mood for jokes," Richard said sourly. "I don't even want to talk to the man who'd buy him out. Go find yourself another patsy."

The ginger-haired man looked indignant. "On behalf of the firm, I resent the implication that the newly reorganized Townsend and Townsend is not to be trusted. A new day has dawned here, sir, and we will be doing business in a fair and gentlemanly way."

"Yeah, right, with doilies on it," Richard said. He turned and had a hand on the door when a voice called out.

"Captain Jensen?"

He stopped. He had heard that voice in all winds and weathers, in sorrow and in pleasure. He turned. Margaret stood at the far end of the room, in a dress of palest yellow, looking fresh and lovely. Her fair skin flushed a becoming pink as all the clerks looked up from their work.

Margaret gestured toward the corridor behind her. "If

404

you please, Captain Jensen, we can talk privately back in my office."

Richard felt a heavy, painful sensation in his chest. She was so lovely, so small and proper and brave here in this male bastion, and he loved her with an ache that wouldn't go away. How could he go to her and wish more of his demon's luck on her? She watched him, the violet eyes wide and hopeful, her soft, pink mouth set in pleasant lines of expectation. Richard let the sack slide to the ground again.

"Yes, just there will be fine," he heard Coggins say. Richard started down the long aisle between the high clerks' desks feeling like a man walking to his own execution. His hands were shaking and the side of his face throbbed with the force of the blood pounding through it. In a world filled with rampant stupidity and self-deception, surely he was the foremost exemplar of man's weakness. But he could not stop his feet from taking him forward.

Margaret turned and he gazed on her small, upright back as she walked gracefully in front of him, down a narrow corridor and into a large office. He ached deep inside for an excuse to reach out and span the small waist encased in yellow, to touch the shining gold hair bound up in an elaborate coif, to push aside the simple lace collar at her throat and caress the long, slender neck. He would do none of those things. He would keep his pride and his dignity. He would hear her out and go. He would do them both a favor and end what had had no chance from the start.

"Captain Jensen?"

Richard started. Margaret was standing behind a large desk covered with ledgers bound in leather, all open to various pages. She looked at him uncertainly and he realized he had been staring with longing at one pink earlobe, soft and delicate.

"Yes?" His voice came out cracked and strained sounding.

"Will you have some tea or other refreshment while I

outline my proposal to you?" Richard shook his head, unable to speak. Her voice was so sweet and low, so utterly feminine and out of place in this office. He remembered the stupefying and exhilarating moment when that same voice had asked him to teach her about pleasure. His gut twisted and he sat down abruptly. "That will be all then, Mr. Coggins," Margaret said. Richard turned and saw that the man with ginger hair stood in the doorway.

"Very well, Lady Margaret. If you require my services, I shall be just around the corner."

Yes, Richard thought, there's a good idea. Stay nearby, in case I lose control and start ravishing your employer. He planted his hands on the arms of the hard wooden chair and faced Margaret again. She shimmered in his vision, her hair backlit by the sunlight streaming through the wide windows.

"Captain Jensen," she said, "what I have in mind is a long term charter of your ship. I have signed it back to you and the papers are there, in that folder. After consultation with Mr. Coggins, I have determined that the amount remaining in payment for repair of the storm damage in Makassar is more than offset by the fare which I would have paid for my journey with you as a passenger, that is to say, all the way to Sumatra, Australia, and back."

Richard blinked, trying to make sense of her words. They were going to talk about passenger fares? She turned gracefully and picked up a paper from a credenza behind her.

"As to the long-term charter, I would need to know the *Java*'s gross tonnage."

"Six hundred and forty-eight tons," Richard answered automatically.

Margaret's face brightened, whether because the tonnage pleased her or because he had spoken at all, he wasn't sure.

"That would be ideal," she said. "You see, we have recently lost the use of a ship of more or less that size. It was run onto the rocks near Banda and cannot be salvaged."

"Coit," Richard murmured. "It had to be Coit."

"As a matter of fact, that is precisely what Mr. Coggins has concluded. The records are not quite clear on the matter, but it is immaterial at the present time."

"It's a specialty of his," Richard said, as if she hadn't spoken. It made him think with a shudder of all the times Coit had nearly wrecked the *Java*.

"Yes, well I shouldn't think we need concern ourselves with him," Margaret said, her manner brisk and businesslike. "Now, as to the types of cargo I propose to have you carry . . ." Richard watched in fascination as she wet her lips and scanned the sheet in her hand. "I am advised that gutta percha is a cargo which one may reliably profit from, though I believe it has its drawbacks."

"It's sticky and it stinks. Once you've hauled that, the bilge has to be pumped and cleaned and damn near scrubbed down with boiling water before you can carry anything else."

"Indeed?" Margaret said in surprise. "That doesn't sound very satisfactory at all, then. Another consideration is to import horses from Australia as part of a two-way trade, with wool coming the other direction, as per your idea. Of course," she said diffidently, "we should have to work out an equitable split that recognizes that the notion of transhipping was yours initially."

Richard wanted to open his mouth and ask why they were talking about equitable splits. Had she not said that if they were married, it hardly mattered whose money was whose? Then he remembered that it was he who had decided against marriage after all. He tried to remember why he had come to that conclusion and couldn't. Instead he gestured weakly and said. "It's not such a brilliant idea unless it works."

"Well, no idea is," Margaret replied. "Nevertheless, one tries. It is all I can do under the circumstances. I admit that part of my motive in approaching you with the idea of a charter is that I am desperately in need of good advice regarding cargos, and shipping in general. You have a wealth of experience and an intimate knowledge of this part of the world."

A thought that had been bothering Richard coalesced. "Did I understand right, that you've bought out Charles Townsend?"

"Yes," Margaret said carefully. "He found it needful to go abroad rather abruptly. No cash has changed hands, however. Rather than engage in an audit of the firm's books, he agreed that I should have the whole of the company, provided I pay an annuity to his mother and sister which will enable them to stay on in Singapore, though in somewhat reduced style."

"Too bad," Richard said, digesting it. "Rotten luck for them." He gazed at Margaret. He didn't give a damn about the Townsends but he was busy mulling over the idea that Margaret had done a very odd thing for a well-bred woman. "Why?" he demanded. "Why have you done it?"

She pursed her lips thoughtfully. "Well, in point of fact, Jack is keen to stay here, near you, and if I am going to remain in Singapore, I need some occupation, something useful to which I can apply myself. However, I was hoping to make it part of our agreement that you will transport us to England once a year, so that Jack and I may spend Christmas at Pensleigh." She set down the paper as if what she was about to say was committed to memory. "I intend to make Jack my heir and I wish to familiarize him with his legacy."

Richard gaped at her. Jack, his Jack? "But how?" he asked.

Margaret seemed surprised. "Well, I told you I intended to adopt him, didn't I?" She chewed her lower lip for a moment. "Yes," she declared, "I'm sure I did. And so I have."

"I don't understand," Richard said. "I thought Coit was going to oppose it unless Charles got his way?"

"Oh, really?" Now Margaret looked thoroughly confused. "Did Charles tell you that? Really," she said, shaking her head, "that was too bad of him. The adoption has been a *fait accompli* for some weeks now. Coit is not so sentimental as you regarding parentage. Knowing Jack was not his natural son, he willingly signed a consent form relinquishing all claim to Jack in exchange for a sum of money.''

Richard felt a tic developing in his injured eye and rubbed at it distractedly. "The bastard!"

"I thought it showed great good sense," Margaret countered. "He had no feeling for the boy and I do."

"No, I meant Townsend." Richard stood up and shoved his hands down in his pockets to hide the fact that they were curled into fists. He paced the length of the office before turning and facing Margaret, his chest tight with anger. "Townsend told me Coit wouldn't consent to the adoption unless I kept my mouth shut, didn't contest the charge of theft."

"Charles was doing rather a lot of lying toward the end," Margaret pointed out. "I wondered why you perjured yourself. Still, to allow ourselves to be distracted from the present by what has happened as a result of his lies would be to afford him continued power over us." She drew herself up. "I, for one, do not intend to let the past rule the future."

Richard thought about that. It seemed to have a great deal of significance. His head began pounding and he wanted to ask for a bag of ice, but he also wanted to grab Margaret and hold her tight. He wanted to smell her skin and run his hands over her bare shoulders, and brush the soft down just in front of her ears with his lips. It wouldn't do to send Coggins out for ice. Richard felt in far too precarious a mental state to be entirely alone with Margaret.

"So you want my advice," he said with an effort, trying to appear focused on the subject at hand. "I'm to be not only a long-term charter captain but I'm also supposed to help out with other decisions?"

Margaret glided over to the desk. "Yes," she said. "I hope you will consider my offer. I really do believe my success or failure hinges on my having your expertise to draw upon." She raised troubled eyes to his. "I feel a great need to make a success of this venture, to prove to Jack that one can make one's own luck with diligence and patience."

Richard began to feel nauseous with the pain in his head, and his back and shoulders were screaming where the belaying pins had caught him. The tic in his eye was surely noticeable by now. He had to leave before he embarrassed himself. He slowly took his hands out of his pockets.

"I'll think about it," he said uneasily. "Cargoes are easy enough." Another pain chewed away inside him. "Is there anything else?" he managed to ask. "Besides tonnage and cargoes?"

"Yes, as a matter of fact, there is," Margaret said. "I am of the opinion that Jack needs a father, a man to whom he can look up. He has not had much of an example on which to pattern himself so far. I am aware of any number of suitable candidates to be my husband. However, I feel you are the best qualified for reasons we both understand too well to require any discussion. I would be willing to enter into any arrangement you think best regarding his religious upbringing, and would respect your wishes regarding whether we are to be married in name only, or in substance." She leafed through an appointment book on the desk. "I can reserve the use of a Chinese temple on Telok Ayer Street for a marriage ceremony. Would you be free on Tuesday next?"

She looked up at him expectantly, her pencil poised over the page. The vision in Richard's left eye began to blur and the restraint he had been exercising was all used up. Confusion, pain, and need roared through him, inextricable from one another. "Let me think about it," he choked out. "I'll have to let you know."

He turned and strode out of the office, aware that every head turned as he passed down the long center aisle of Townsend and Townsend. Each step jarred his head and made pain dance a vicious rhythm in it. He walked faster and nearly ran over Coggins as he came around a corner.

Richard left the chief clerk awash in his wake and made a beeline for the outer doors.

Margaret sat in the shade of the veranda watching Jack play with An Wu's children by the setting sun. All her evenings seemed so long now, but they were a mere snippet of time compared to the nights, which dragged on interminably. This evening she had chosen to sit quietly by herself, neither sketching nor reading. Eliza and John sat at the opposite end of the veranda, chatting amiably as Eliza mended a pair of Jack's pants and John read to her from the newspaper.

There were howls of laughter as one of the youngest boys flipped spectacularly over a stave another was using to roll a hoop along. Jack and the others picked him up and dusted him off and Margaret smiled. Jack was very sweet, but he had a core of determination and wisdom, too, which made her optimistic about his future. He also had an aptitude for languages, readily learning French from Margaret and even picking up a smattering of Chinese from his playmates.

Margaret sighed. Nothing had the power to occupy her mind to the exclusion of the thing which worried her most. Had she handled the business with Richard right or had she completely miscalculated? She was afraid she had botched it horribly. He hadn't seemed terribly interested but he hadn't rejected her proposal outright. On the whole, though, he had acted most peculiarly.

Perhaps she would have been better to let things stand as they were. He knew her door was open to him, and he was not a man who would take kindly to being maneuvered, no matter how gentle or well-intended the strategy. And that was what it had been—strategy. Margaret felt faintly sick to her stomach as she recalled Richard's expression when she had proposed marriage. He had been decidedly neutral about all her propositions to that point, and then he had gone a sickly shade of white and left hurriedly.

411

It was true enough that Jack needed a father but as for marrying anyone else, the suggestion had been the sheerest bluff. And she *did* need Richard's help to make wise decisions regarding business. Private ledgers in Charles's office had revealed that the state of affairs at Townsend and Townsend was even worse than she and Coggins had suspected.

But it was all as nothing compared to her need to see Richard, to be with Richard, to hold him and to love him, and to hear his huge, indecently hearty laugh again. To be cool and detached that morning had taken every ounce of self-control she possessed. She wanted the touch of his calloused hands, and the feel of his heavy, masculine presence in the night. She wanted to lay in the moonlight and watch his face as he slept, and curl next to him and feel his arms pulling her snugly into the curve of his body.

Margaret clenched her hands and felt her lip tremble as an instant hot ache sprang up behind her eyes. She had botched it, botched it horribly. Come a cropper and gone straight into a prickly hedge. Oh, if it weren't so awful, it might be funny. It would be easier to shinny up one of the *Java*'s greased spars in a running sea than undo the damage she had done. Margaret stood up swiftly. She would go and weed the garden in the back, and endure Hoc Sing's patent disapproval tomorrow, but she couldn't bear to be still with her thoughts another minute.

All the boys went whooping down the lawn where it bordered Cluny Road and swept around the corner in a tight bunch, with the girls in hot pursuit. She liked having them here, loved having them here. It had occurred to her that she might ask Reverend Childers to come out to see her, and bring a few of the children from the orphanage with him. Perhaps she could fill her life with children, teach them a trade, and spend some of her pent-up love for Richard on them. That way some good could come of it all. Another month like the last one, with too much time for contemplation, and she would need much more than Jack and the trading firm to keep herself sufficiently distracted.

412

Suddenly, the boys stopped and several of the girls plowed into them, getting tangled up in their own newly made, Western-style dresses. Margaret held her breath to see if any of them were hurt, and then she followed their astonished stares as a man leading a pony came around the corner into her drive.

He wasn't tall, not more than an inch above average height, but he moved with an aggressive muscularity that suggested power to spare. The dying sun cast a golden patina over skin so bronzed one might have wondered for a moment whether he was a European. He was hatless, his black hair tied back in a sailor's pigtail, and he wore a black frock coat open over a clean white shirt and gray pants. In one hand he held the pony's lead rope and in the other he carried an enormous bunch of yellow flowers.

Margaret curled her fingers into her palms and tried to still the shaking in her legs. She wanted to run to him and cry and laugh and tell him she loved him all at the same time, but she made herself stay where she was, at the top of the steps to the veranda. She had done the best she could, tried every way she knew how to bring them together. Now it was up to Richard to say what he wanted to say, to tell her how it would be.

He came to a stop in front of her and looked up at her without speaking, his jaw clamped tight with some unspoken emotion. His eyes were shaded by the thick lashes that always shuttered them at the most inconvenient moments. The children hung back, clustered in the corner and eyeing the pony with fascination. It was a frozen moment, a tableau in the Orient. *A Sea Captain Comes To Call.* The multitude of small birds that had returned to their nests and been chattering for the last hour fell silent without warning. It happened that way every evening, but tonight it lent an extra measure of tension to the moment.

Margaret searched Richard's face with eyes made anxious by absence. His bruises and cuts had healed, and the high proud cheekbones were marred by nothing more than the scar which had always been there, curving whitely along the prominent bone and ending at his left nostril. His cheeks were freshly shaven, blue-shadowed and taut. Margaret's hand shook as she thought of reaching out to touch them. At last he spoke, the voice clear and resonant but lacking its customary conviction.

"I've brought you something."

Margaret looked at him and saw uncertainty in the uneasy set of his shoulders and neck. There was only one way to make this easier.

"It's really lovely, but isn't it a bit small?"

Richard looked taken aback and then the faintest of smiles touched his mouth. He held out the flowers. "No, I meant these. The pony is for Jack."

"Oh, of course," Margaret said, allowing herself only a small answering smile even though her heart was filled with joy. "Will you teach him to ride it?"

Richard looked faintly rueful. "I don't know how to myself. Would you settle for me tying him on it? I do a pretty respectable half-hitch."

Margaret wanted to ask if that would involve staying for very long. "Well, that might be all right, I suppose," she said slowly. "Perhaps he'll take to it naturally. He told me last week that his mother always said his real father was a cowboy."

Richard went still. "That's an interesting piece of information," he finally said.

"I thought so, too," Margaret replied.

Richard turned and Margaret watched as the man and the boy eyed one another across the expanse of lawn. It was Jack who broke the stalemate, approaching hesitantly until he stood within a few feet.

"That's a fine pony, sir."

Margaret saw Richard's shoulders quiver ever so slightly. "I'm glad you like him," he said. "I brought him for you. He didn't much like the ship but he did well enough. I think he put up with it because he knew there was a boy named Jack waiting at the other end who would love him and take care of him."

Jack's small, thin face became nearly luminous with

414

happiness. "I would, too, sir."

"Maybe you could call *him* 'sir' and think of some other name for me," Richard said softly. "I'm not sure what just yet, but we'll think of something."

Jack looked faintly baffled but pleased. "Sure."

Richard handed him the lead rope. "Here, walk him around, let him stretch his legs a bit. He'd probably like to meet your friends, too, but just offhand, I'd say he's taken a particular shine to you already."

The pony wagged its head, making its stiff, short mane bob. Both Jack and Richard laughed and Margaret was grateful that no fly buzzed around the pony's head to give the lie away. Oh, she thought, if Richard doesn't mean to stay, then let this moment last forever. Her throat closed up and when Jack led the pony off, she had to clear it before she could speak again.

"Come and have a drink," she said.

Richard mounted the steps with careful reserve and they sat in the deepening shadows without speaking, tensely aware of one another. They watched as the children led Sir around the garden, gradually working their nerve up to let him trot. Darkness fell, and John took charge of the situation, sending An Wu's children home for the night and leading Jack and the pony back toward the rear of the bungalow. Now that they were all alone, Margaret wanted to see Richard's face. She leaned over to light the small lamp on the table between their two chairs, but there was a blur of white, and she felt Richard's hand take hers in the darkness.

A warm shock of memory went through her at the familiar feel of his roughened hands, and she returned the pressure of his fingers, unable to speak. A sharp sensation built in her chest as he rubbed his thumb across the backs of her knuckles.

"I've missed you," he said softly.

Margaret felt tears fill her eyes and knew that if she answered, the swell of emotion would overcome her. Instead, she squeezed his hand.

"I love you, Margaret, and I hope you still love me."

415

A tear slipped from the corners of Margaret's eye and ran down her cheek. She felt afraid and humble and very grateful. She sniffed noisily. "I do," she said, "with all my heart."

"Good," he said with quiet satisfaction. "Can you still arrange for us to use that Chinese temple?"

"Why?" she asked. She held her breath, hoping she already knew the answer.

Richard stopped stroking her hand but he kept his grip on it. At last, he said, "Well, I've decided not to let the past rule the future. You were right about that." He took a breath that seemed to come up from deep inside. "And although I'm a man of very few principles, as anyone will tell you, it seems to me that if I'm going to stay the night, we ought to get married."

"Are you?" she asked, swallowing the moisture in the back of her throat. "Going to stay the night?"

"Every chance I get, Maggie," he said. "Every chance I get."